HEALER IN THE MIST

D1707569

Healer in the Mist

This is a work of fiction. Names, characters, places, and incidents either are the product of the author's imagination or are used fictitiously. Any resemblance to actual persons, living or dead, events, or locales is entirely coincidental.

Cover designs and illustrations: Samantha Dearing

<u>Author Disclaimer</u>

This work of fiction contains adult themes and potentially triggering situations and subject material. All effort has been made to treat serious themes described below with respect, delicacy, and candor in a creative work of fiction.

For a specific description of potential triggering events in the book, notification is as follows set aside for those who do not want to potentially see into future events of the book. These themes include domestic violence, rape, trauma, and suicide.

Part 1

To Sleep, Perchance...

The dark of night was never the same, each night never like the last and never like the next. If it were, we would take comfort in preparation. Instead fear is ever-present in the never knowing, and nothing in this world embraces anymore.

Tonight was bright with silver light from the cream moon high in the night sky. Dangerous. No shadows to hide in, only light to expose everything. It was beautiful once, this silver light, but not anymore. They see better in the light, and what's to hide you while you sleep? They walk always, sometimes creep, sometimes run. Never sleeping, never resting, always driven like a ceaseless wind.

On nights like this Althea had to take precautions unlike those of a still, black night that naturally conceals. Every brightness in her would shine in this light, even the shine of her dark hair would shimmer as a beacon to those who hunt. And these nights were never restful. None of them were anymore. Not for her.

Althea decided that tonight in the Woods the best place to sleep would be high in the Ash. The Immortuos had tracked her to the stream at the edge of the woods, caught her scent, and drove her all day relentlessly. But in water, she had an advantage and lost them for a time. But they were clever, Immortuos were not mindless, and they knew as they could not sense her on the Plain side of the river, she must be in the woods. And while the woods had their disadvantages at night, so did everywhere else. In the Ash would be best. High in the leaves hidden in the only shadows that night. But sleep in a tree, even one as wide and thick as this Ash, was not restful for you cannot move once precariously balanced.

Althea secured her bow to her back and began to climb. Though the years of constant open living far from comforts and shelter had their toll, her hands remained soft and nimble. She always was in awe of this as she watched how well they grasped every hold of the tree and pulled her up. That was her mother,

her grandmother, and their mothers, all Healers with graceful hands. Nothing in life could change that.

This tree was old, not quite ancient, but it had endured. Within a three-fold fork, Althea secured herself within an acceptable balance well hidden in the trees. As she tried to fall asleep, she watched the woods beneath her. She saw small packs of Immortuos here and there moving without grace through the columns of trees. It was the right choice to be high above them tonight, for nothing could hide on the floor in this light. Had it been fall or winter, things would have been different. The leaves wouldn't hide her, and the Immortuos could pile upon each other high up the tree.

Althea knew that strategizing further her situation tonight would not get her to sleep, not get her the rest she needed. So she let her mind go into that precious place that held the pictures and sounds of the time before. When the land's Magic was beautiful and full of sweet surprises and wonder. A life of plenty, of color, when others sang in joy, not the mournings of loss. Enchantments not lost, spells not forgotten, the rites commonplace. She recalled with bitter sweetness a time when a home cradled and protected -- when it wrapped a family with security and living memory.

Now a home was a confinement and a trap. Four walls meant nowhere to escape, no way out when the Immortuos came. Or worse, the Purple Mist.

She was teetering precariously in the realm between asleep and awake. A place where the head swims and all life seems to exist magically as in the days before and frighteningly as the days at hand. Her eyes closed, and she could feel the hand on her cheek. Soft like hers, but stronger. It traced her face from top to bottom slowly, lovingly. She almost smiled. As the hand reached her chin and found its way to her throat, it suddenly clamped hard.

Mine!

Present Fears Are Less Than Horrible Imaginings

Pain came first from her back as she looked upwards to the three-fold fork in the tree above her. While the sound of her fall was somewhat muffled by the damp leaves on the ground, it seemed deafening. If the Immortuos didn't hear her fall, they would have felt the ground vibrate enough to come. They always came. No time for fear, no time for pain, just *run*.

Only checking for a moment which direction was uphill and that her bow was unbroken, she ran with urgency, she ran to survive. As she ran her Healer instincts worked in tandem with her strategic mind. Each step she assessed her pain. "Ankle isn't broken though hurts like Hell, I can move all my toes, that tree is too small and no good, my arm is swelling just slightly, assess later. Wait, that tree...it's perfect!"

On the top of a steep incline was an Oak, and this one was Ancient. It had seen ages in this land, weathered it all, bore through it strongly. And the incline meant safety, as the Immortuos hardly went against an incline, too difficult to manage. The climb up was difficult and not nearly as graceful as before. Her right arm and ankle were swelling more and more with each movement. "Nothing's broken, keep going. Not much further." As she reached sufficient height, only then did she look back behind her down the hill.

He wasn't there. He never was, and yet he always is. It was a dream, but she could still feel his hand on her face.

Unwanted.

She could still feel the pressure of a hold on her neck.

Familiar.

If she were to close her eyes, she would see his eyes. She would see their passion, their desire, their seductive beauty, and the darkness surrounding it all. So that night she would not sleep, not close her eyes, not invite him in. Though he wasn't there, he never was, he somehow always is.

Instead, she would focus on repairs. First, her ankle -- which was not nearly as bad as her arm. The small and tightly packaged bundle that was strapped to her back in thick, brown cloth was loosened to obtain wraps. Pressure and warmth, and rest. The fall was foolish, the frightful night terrors of a simple child, and she cursed herself for allowing it. Not she had to use her supplies that were difficult to restock to heal. As she rubbed the salve and wrapped her ankle. The glow from her hands was faint as she softly sang old words, nearly forgotten in time and hardship. Healer's words, Healer's songs, the kind that still held magic.

Normally she wouldn't dare in the night, the glow would give her away. But this tree was perfect with thick branches and giant leaves that hid her almost completely. And even if she was spotted, there would be no way the Immortuos could get up this hill. Her soft singing made a soft wind blow and the leaves sway. It was as if the very earth were awakened in joy at the sound of music too far forgotten. She pressed a hand to her arm where she was swelling. As she rubbed a reserved amount of salve on it, she sang louder. The wind became stronger and danced about her, it was almost beautiful. But it was cold, and as she shivered her concentration broke and the song was lost.

It was enough for now, she would heal the rest on her own. What her mother could have done with those words, or better still her Grandmother! The line of Healers was thinning, not many left now. When the Immortuos came, those who stayed behind to heal those who could not run were taken easily. Now there are so few Healers left, and even fewer with the heart and strength to endure.

Whether she knew it or not, she was needed, and no one else will do. She felt the pull to go back and help, and deep down she knew she had to. With every step she ran away with her feet, her heart resisted.

But there was always fear. Fear beyond the Immortuous, fear beyond the Purple Mist, fear that took her to Base Village, her Majesty's court, and the love that consumed her and violently devoured her.

Pluck from a Memory a Rooted Sorrow

Althea's skin glowed with the warmth of late morning sun coming into her home with a large woven basket full of the plants and roots of the earth in her arm and a pitcher of water from Blessed Stream on her head. As the sun rose higher, the outside work would be too tiresome in the heat, so she did her outside chores early leaving the inside work for the heat of the day. She took off her shoes to feel the cool, soft earth of her home's floor at her feet. As she removed her shoes one could see the mark of Healer just above her ankles, the mark of her Heritage. Naturally bending and turning with the bones and contours of her feet, it reminded one of the flowers on the vine, a mark to signal a Healer.

Then she let down her hair as it was bundled high on her head. In the heat of the day, her dark hair made her so hot, but now she was cool in her home, and her mother had always said her long hair was so beautiful, even longer and more luxurious than her great grandmother's. Even if her days were long, even if the need for her was great and she work tirelessly into the night to see the first light of dawn, even if she had worked until the dust and soil covered her completely, she had her hair that dazzled and amazed.

As she took out each bundle of a variety of plants from her basket and organized them on her work table in the front room, she felt a change in the earth beneath her. The air seemed to change. She closed her eyes to see all she could not see, extending all she was into the room to search before seeing. Too subtle, too complicated, and she still had much to learn. She lifted her eyes, not even fully expecting something to be there.

But there was.

This man was tall, built like a statue painstakingly sculpted. He had long hair, so he had to live a life out of the fields, and it was like sunshine. Most of the men and boys of Base Village were darker-haired. Even if they were born with fair hair, their life out of doors darkened it. And even if they wanted to have the luxurious and coveted longer hair, they couldn't bear it in the sun or could not grow it with a life of labor. But this man's hair -- it was beautiful. It was unlike anything she saw before in life, but instead the stuff of dreams.

She tried to concentrate on seeing beyond sight, assessing more than the present as she had been trained. His hands were slender, soft, and fair like hers, but he couldn't be a Healer. Though his boots concealed his ankles, she could tell this. His hair was too fair to have gone out and gathered plants and he walked high in stature instead of rooted low into the earth as she did. He had to be nobility, maybe even a member of her Majesty's court. His eyes were green; she'd never seen green eyes before. Her eyes were brown, deep as the earth as were most people's in Base Village. Sometimes she'd see a painter or artisan from Courtside with blue eyes, but never green and never this vibrant.

Enchanter

Yes, he had to be. Master of incantations and spells, Enchanters could pluck the very Magic from the air and dance at their command. It was even said that they could reach up and grasp the stars themselves! And one was in her home...and coming this way.

If it were ever possible to feel all emotions at once, Althea did now. He was beautiful, and the mere thought of what his skills must be was nothing short of wonderous. Though she knew she should say something, anything, she found she had no breath to give to words. The most she could do was muster concentration to keep her mouth from gaping open like some fool.

Before she could fully conceive the grace of his walk, he was stopped before her merely a few feet away. He said nothing either, and though at first, she thought it was from pride and status, she could see deep in his eyes he wasn't able to speak either. His eyes seemed to struggle with composure just as her heart was.

Almost as though drawn together by an invisible rope, they both leaned toward each other just slightly. Both stunned by the other, both thinking the other to be unlike anything they had seen. How absurd this moment, how unimaginable, how fateful. It was as if the cosmos wrote at its creation a meeting like this, and that was all the reason to burst forth into being in violent splendor.

Then a sweet smell, that overripe smell of fruit. And in the door behind him came a shimmering glittered with tiny starlight in a mist. A Purple Mist. It consumed him, covered him whole. And the claws encircled the door and entrance to her home.

Then it came for her.

By Medicine Life May Be Prolonged

Her eyes bolted awake; she didn't even realize she drifted to sleep high in the tree. Instinctively, with muscle memory, she clamped both hands tight around her mouth as she screamed from her night terror. The screams gave way to tears. The tree held her stiff in security, not in comfort, but security. For the first time she felt that the ability to be strong was beyond her reach, and in the stability of her hiding spot she fully let go of her pain into her clamped hands. The pain of her loss, her fear, her inexplicably unbearable guilt.

In her mind, this was all her fault. Wasn't it?

Though the theories on the why and the how regarding the Purple Mist were as varied and vast as the Plains themselves, the truth was gnarled and tangled...leaving only tears and anger behind as fact.

Those who spoke after said they saw it first coming from high on the Hill in the castle. More truly, they smelled it first. It was sweet, almost too sweet -- like overripe fruit almost fermenting into wine. It filled the air warmly, it was intoxicating and enticing, like something terribly forbidden and wicked. Those in the homes of nobility residing in Courtside, the city just within the courtyard and vast gardens of the castle on the Hill, were the first. They followed the warmth and smell coming from the castle and saw the Purple Mist. It moved as if alive, entrancing in its way. Flecks shimmered in it like starlight, and the people found that they stood still in awe, shock, wonder, and terror. People moved away as best they could until the Mist seemed to lunge at one noble. He dropped to his knees and struggled to resist the pull towards the earth with all he had. There was not a sharp pain, but an inexplicable weight. And care left, all will to do more than breath -- it vanished from the heart, and bodies buckled under the pressure.

Screams of terror.

Screams of panic.

• • • • • • •

The Mist passed beyond the Hill, beyond the villages and towns into the Plains, into the Woods, passed into the places unseen. It moved like a predator seemingly both mindless and calculating at the same time. It was living yet not alive, hungry but not devouring in anything physical. Its needs were unknown, and where it came from was a mystery. What was its purpose? Was it born from the earth to punish, was it the life in the air angry for something, was it a purposeful summons from an Enchanter, a request from her Majesty after her loss? Was it a mistake?

The people felt that the worst was over as the Mist moved onward -- that they could learn to live with the shadow of a memory of that empty feeling -- the weight of utter despair it laid. It wasn't until the days that followed that the land truly knew what the Mist truly did. What it raised...

The people thought certainly they must be dreaming, that their sights were borne out of the emptiness the Mist left in their hearts. But in a terrifying moment of clarity, everyone realized that those that walked were those that they had laid to rest in the earth and sent to Coelum. They were no longer at rest, and they were no longer of the earth. Those they loved in life, sent with precious songs to rewarding rest, came from the place of Goodbye and returned where a return was impossible. The same, but not the same; living but not alive.

Plucked from Coelum and the rewards of their lives beyond, the Mist passed over their sites of rest and brought them back to the air and sun. No longer in peace, no longer in joy, but back to what assuredly was Hellfire when compared. And their bodies no longer had the spark of true life. The bodies held pools of stale blood, cold and untouched with no hope of warmth. The spirits of ones cherished in life were stolen from painless and utterly joyful plenty and violently thrust into bodies that no longer lived. It was the most grotesque violation imaginable, the birth of Immortuos.

And they were angry.

I Do Desire We Should Be Better Strangers

Althea carefully gathered the items she had used in the night knowing she'd have to make her way down from the tree. Though she felt her strength returning and her pain at bay, her ankle surely needed to be used, or it would go stiff and make her vulnerable. Her arm was more complicated, but she would make it through. If a cold stream was nearby, she could soak it to reduce the swelling further.

She made her way down the same side of the tree she climbed up as she knew those footholds would hold. The last thing she needed was some break in a limb and undo the healing she had done.

Once upon the ground, she stopped for a moment and listened to the earth with her ears, her skin, and the bare foot exposed through the wrapping. She could not sense the constant and uneven strides of Immortuos. Her muscles relaxed only slightly to the thought of being secure on the hill and near the tree.

She walked slowly to the edge of the hill to look out over where she found herself. The Woods was a dense, thick maze, and where you could emerge was anyone's guess. She had surely reached the end of it, a Plain stretched out from the other side of the hill. And beyond, barely even visible in the distance, she could see its outline and undeniably distinct shape. The Hill and the Castle on top.

Dammit. Had she truly made it so close? Dammit!

"This must be Shimmer Plain then," Althea thought to herself. It truly upheld the name and shimmered in the sun like a pool of gold. Though she didn't want to be any nearer to Base Village or the Hill than this, she knew that Shimmer Plain had some plants for salves unique only to that area, and she could use it. "Just one stop."

She turned to go and immediately tensed. Before she registered consciously, her body reacted with muscle memory and poised in a ground-based stance. And so had he. How could she not notice someone on the other side of the tree? How did she not sense him?

Both Althea and this stranger found themselves still as posts despite the breeze and movement of the earth. Both in a stance could bear against attack or bolt in an instant. Both were clearly startled, even somewhat frightened behind their guarded eyes. Neither willing to make the first move even to breathe. They both silently assessed the other without making a single motion, both obviously trained to do so.

The stranger relaxed first after his assessment. This girl's eyes were clear and unclouded, her hair was recently put up in a thoughtful and calculated manner, and her stillness was not the driven impulse for violence like the Immortuos. His things were behind him, so he was safely guarded in his position.

But her things were on the other side of him too, on the side of the tree she had descended from. Stupid! Althea remained on guard.

"If I swear no harm, will I get the same?" His voice was not of music, but it was calming in a way that can't be taught. Despite her strong guard, Althea felt her muscles relax at his voice. His stance was confident without arrogance, short hair and dark, and in no way did he show any signs of nobility. But he was clearly trained, and the natural lilt of compelling calm in his voice was not common.

"Yes."

Both bodies relaxed a little. In times where fear and suspicion had made the world bitter, even the small chance of a moment of peace was too rare to pass up.

She looked at him closer, and he did the same. Something about him was still and soothing, nothing in him seemed startling. His eyes, the brown of the earth, dark like his hair. His skin was darkened beyond its natural tone from the sun almost as much as hers was, so he was not of a large and fortified village...the only places left with homes. But there were no scars or signs of a clumsy existence of hiding in nature as most had, at least those who were left.

15

He was adapted to living away from shelters. He was unmistakably handsome and not just in features and symmetry but in the aura around him. Even those without the Healer's eye for such things would be able to feel an aura as warm and gentle as his.

She hadn't even noticed his scan of her lingered on her wrapped and injured ankle. His continence suddenly changed and livened. He even developed something of an attempt to conceal a smile he couldn't help that came to him.

"You're who they're looking for. You have to be!"

What's Gone, and What's Past Grief

"I wish Althea were here," Mireya said behind the delicate lace of her black veil. Her voice was distant and weak. She was exhausted and heavy with grief.

"Yes, your Majesty. We all do, I know. But even a Healer can only do so much."

"I don't want a Healer, Durai! I want my friend!" Mireya had almost shocked herself with her outburst; she had barely spoken above a whisper for days.

Durai almost smiled to see the spirit in his ruler, but it was true, he wanted Althea back. Ever since she disappeared, the court had felt empty. He would do anything to get her back.

Anything.

Mireya was in a place beyond grief, and though she had attendants to see to her, feed her, bathe and dress her, she did not know it. The needs of her physical body did not reach her heart which was in a place beyond grief. Her brother had left her, left them all, left all of the world. And he chose to do it.

"The ceremony was beautiful, Majesty. All of your people for miles came to share in your grief. We are all with you." Durai's words seemed to come from a place far away, a place that didn't seem real to Mireya anymore; a place she didn't want to be real. The world was new, ugly, and empty now, without her brother. How can the sun continue to rise and fall without him?

Durai turned to leave Mireya sensing perhaps her desire to be alone with the freedom to grieve in her way far from propriety and perception of royalty. "Durai, how could he leave me like this? Was it something I did? Something I didn't do?" Her guard was down, and her mind could see the sight of what her brother had done. What she saw that morning could never be unseen. What he did to himself would scar her very soul for as long as she walked the earth and even after.

Durai immediately turned to be by his Ruler's side. He had been waiting for her to fully face what any person might feel. This might be the sign that she was coming back from the numbness she had been under for days. Things could begin moving again. "My Lady, I cannot begin to guess at what took your brother's heart. But I am certain, because I know you, that it was not because he did not know your love."

Mireya didn't move or show signs that this even registered. All she wanted was a second chance to make things right and say the things to her brother that she wanted to keep saying over and over-that she loved him deeply and without end. Saying it to a memory would never be enough.

Durai kneeled and tried to reach past her pain, "The unseen evil that speaks pain and whispers lies is full of malice. The heart is poisoned, and there is no turning back once fully consumed. I cannot even begin to imagine the full depth of your sorrow, Mireya." No one had said her name in a long time, not since her brother was still alive. Durai is the only one who would, the only one who ever did besides Althea. It was enough to jolt Mireya into the present, into more clear thinking. She lifted her head. She didn't see an unfocused figure as so many people had become since her brother's passing; she saw her friend and Counsel. She saw Durai.

He saw that he was reaching her, and he had to keep going. Anything to bring her back to the strength she had always had and the figure she had always been. "We are here for you, Mireya. All of us, all your people. We would move mountains for you."

"Would you really?" she said just barely above a whisper. "You, Durai, would you do anything? Would you shake the foundations of the earth?"

"My Lady, I would call forth the wind to carry away your pain."

"No." Suddenly her voice was her own, her mind in the now, her heart in unfamiliar urgency. "Would you, Durai, Enchanter of the court, shake the very earth for me." Each word she spoke was pushed with careful strength and the resolve of her stature. "Would you bring him back to me?"

Enchanters were powerful and practiced with the highest mastery over the Land's Magic. Other bloodlines could reach in here or pull from there within the living conjured wonders of the world, but Enchanters had the most power, the most mastery. If anything could be done within the physical world, they were the ones who could do it. And Durai was one of the most powerful which is why he was the Queen's Court Enchanter. He was her only hope.

Durai hardly smiled, even more so after Althea disappeared, but he smiled now. Durai's features were always beautiful, but there was something even more alive in his face with that smile. His green eyes were vividly alive, almost glowing. Or were they actually glowing? A slight wind in the closed room circled them both.

"Yes, Mireya. I think believe I can."

O Mistress Mine, Where Are You Roaming?

"Looking for?" Althea felt the blood drain from her face despite all her efforts to remain composed. She didn't want to be found by anyone; she had resolved long ago that the safest place for her to be was in memory.

"You have to be. You're a Healer. I can see the marks above your wrapping. You have to be the one they're still looking for."

Althea made a move to cover her ankle before realizing how foolish that would be; he'd already seen the twisting, floral mark above her wrappings.

Seeing her frightened expression, the man opened his arms to show he wasn't making any movements against her and that he had nothing to harm her with. "Please," he said with that calming tone, "I promise I'm not here to hurt you. I wasn't tracking you; I was just resting by this tree. Please don't run away. Please."

Althea didn't move to run, and she struggled to keep her muscles tensed to run, but his gentle voice and demeanor fought to relax her. What was that about him? Something old, something from long ago she just couldn't put her finger on.

"My God, you really are! I can take you there, they need you. We need you! I can't believe it, but you are here. And we're so close to ... I mean I could get you there safely." Galen went on with hope and excitement growing in his eyes. But then he saw that the more he spoke, the more she looked like she was going to be sick or scream.

"Look," he said as he lowered himself to sitting slowly and gracefully in a sign of peace, "my name is Galen. And I promise I mean peace." Galen fully relaxed again against the tree. He knew this hill was safe from Immortuos, and he knew the nature of a Healer. He was confident he was in no danger.

Althea took note of his goodwill gesture and relaxed muscles. She relaxed her own upper body in good faith. Though if he made a move, her legs were still grounded in the earth ready to dodge and run. "I'm Althea."

Now that Galen was relaxed on the ground, he heard the music in her words. Healers were noted singers to call forth magic from the air and earth with their songs, and Galen could hear it now. He closed his eyes very briefly to savor it; he'd never heard something so simple that could brighten the soul so much. He gestured for her to sit, "Please relax. I'm sure that ankle is still needing rest, and I come to this tree often and can assure you it's safe. Please, Althea." It was not in the nature of Healers to distrust, Althea was different. What was her story? Galen couldn't help but be curious.

Something in his eyes, or was it the aura she sensed around him, she decided that she could trust him enough to sit down where she stood. She was curious too. He had command of some kind of Magic; he had to. She just couldn't pull from her knowledge of long ago well enough to remember. That was a frequent problem, and it was troubling. She'd find out somehow.

"You said someone is looking for me?" Althea was still worried about this. "I'm really nothing out of the ordinary, nothing special, just a Healer."

"Nothing out of...?!" Galen checked the urgent shock and confusion in his voice. He resumed being calm and composed and began again, "Nothing out of the ordinary? Nothing special? Althea, you're the first Healer I think anyone has seen in a year, since just after the Mist. You may very well be the last one left."

The last one left.

Althea felt all emotions at once: shock, sadness, fear, memory, all at once to be a terrifying jumble that hit her like a falling tree. She was physically taken aback and had to catch herself with her good arm on the ground beside her. She didn't know anything specifically, not for many years, but they were all still of her blood, of her art. And she just couldn't fathom within her heart or deepest nightmares that she would ever be the last.

"I'm sorry. I should have been kinder than that. I really am. Were you close with them?" Galen's eyes were turned down. He was truly saddened and ashamed because of the hurt he could feel from her and the pain she couldn't hide in her eyes. Of course, she couldn't know, and he chided himself for pouring those words out like a child who didn't know any better.

21

"No, I...I haven't...I..." Althea had a hard time putting form to her thoughts. Her heart and her head were hidden in fear and sadness. "I mean, I've been...away...since before the mist." She felt there was more she should say, but the harder she searched for the words, the more elusive her thoughts became.

Galen was curious about this. Healers usually were based with people in a village or town, some group that needed caring for in sickness from time to time. And usually, there was more than one, and yet she had no one? But he could still see the sorrow on her face that ran deep. "I'm still sorry." But it was more than sorrow from his words; he could see the year of isolation and wandering in her face. Healers were often sheltered and very much treasured. Not as soft and sheltered as Enchanters who were guarded like delicate gold, but Healers worked in their huts mostly out of the sun, coming out only to forage for the needs of their trade. But her skin was darkened from a life outside of a home or village and under the sun, and not just from the time of Immortuos. She had been wandering for longer than that.

The words registered from far away, and she responded, "Thank you," more out of habit than of conscious thought. The logic of it sank in; it was a very real possibility that she was the last. She had often thought about how a Healer could survive a world like this. The Immortuos were clever and tireless driven strong in their anger and vengeful hatred. The Healers were with the sick and injured, helping at all costs...even if they were the cost. The truth of Galen's words began to sting. What would be of her blood and Magic now? And how long, in good conscience, could she hope to dwell in hidden secrecy? She had a duty now -- more urgent than ever -- if she were the last. But how could she ever hope to combat any of the growing sufferings on her own?

She was quickly overwhelmed by every thought and terrible imaginings that came without end. She tried to keep control, but her terrors and sorrows were coming without mercy, as steady and as assuredly as the coming of night. Before she registered her despair, the tears were already beyond her face and onto her neck and into the earth. There was no crying at first, just the tears that flowed as freely from her eyes as breath from her lungs.

She could not see through the tears to register Galen moving to her. He couldn't help but be drawn to the suffering in her soul that radiated outward. He was not afraid of it, not hesitant at all, but moved as he always had towards the suffering to comfort. In slow and graceful movements he was close enough to touch her, though he didn't. He just lowered her head to watch the ground as she did. Just to be in the same space so she did not suffer alone.

He began to speak words -- so old and ancient -- she couldn't quite distinguish them from the breathing of the earth. Before she heard words, she felt him speaking. She felt the embrace of her mother, smelled her grandmother's cooking, saw the glow of her father's eyes, felt the silk coverings in the room at Court that she would wrap herself in, and dream the sweetest dreams. Her negative energy that had been held back in her sorrow broke forth like an avalanche. She was surprised at her body shaking with sobs, but not ashamed and oddly comforted.

And she still heard and felt his words. Not songs -- there was no melody -- but it was still something as beautiful as music. She looked up and saw him still looking down and speaking his ancient and calming words. She stopped her crying, her grief melting into comfort. It was not gone, but it was now a part of her in a way that she felt control over. It was unlike anything she had felt in over a year.

But then she did hear music. It was music from the very earth. And birds! She could hear birds! Birds were seldom around, and when they were they never sang anymore to hide from Immortuos. But they were there in the trees and signing. She felt out with her legs and arms into the earth and felt its calm. She hadn't even noticed a rabbit burrow on the side of the hill as she ran up it last night, but there was a huddle of rabbits at the hill's edge now.

Leporem!

"You're a Leporem, aren't you?" Althea said having finally realized what he was and why he was able to soothe and charm with just his words and presence.

"I am, yes," Galen said without raising his head.

23

Leporems were not easy to detect. They were not of a specific bloodline like the Healers, Enchanters, or Eros. Instead, they were rarities within all bloodlines. Leporems could charm animals, earn their trust and endear them to the Leporems dearly. There wasn't much use for Leporems, at least not in the same way as say a Healer. Domesticated animals were easy enough to work within their labor requirements in a village, and those not domesticated were for hunting, and charming an animal to their death was considered taboo. They had many friends as they were naturally charming, and no one ever bore resentment or animosity towards all Leporems, it just wasn't something to demand status.

Althea had never known one before. She thought maybe she may have known one in the past and never knew it; Leporems didn't go around boasting of their skills. But now having sat across from one and felt the indescribable effects of their skills, she knew now she certainly had never met one before. He was even more beautiful now than the mere surface features (which were quite handsome), but he had a purity of soul that was almost intoxicating and irresistible.

Despite how guarded she had forced herself to become, she imagined what his touch would feel like. Would she feel this calmingly assured in an embrace with him? Would it even be possible to feel safe in an embrace again?

She was amazed that she could even contemplate such thought, even for the briefest moment, in a time like this. Knowing in her heart who would be looking for her, how could she imagine softness from anyone ever again? But as Galen looked up at her at last with his eyes brown and truly peaceful in intent, she thought of the good in another human being for the first time since she had made herself disappear.

And Therefore is Winged Cupid Painted Blind

Before she could fully conceive the grace of his walk, he was stopped before her merely a few feet away. He said nothing either, and though at first, she thought it was from pride and status, she could see deep in his eyes he wasn't able to speak either. His eyes seemed to struggle with composure just as her head was.

This day was five years before the arrival of the Purple Mist Althea was in her hut entranced and held captive by those vivid, green eyes. She would always remember the first time she met him; this day in her hut was where the course of her life turned away from all it knew before to another destination she never could have dreamed of. Unlike her nightmares, no Mist came in after him, no claws at the door. Just his eyes looking into her eyes.

Durai finally came out of the near trance he was held under when he stood before Althea and took in fully how beautiful she truly was. "Healer, I have a man … I mean..." Even Durai was surprised at how like a rambling fool he sounded, so unlike his noble stature and impeccable nature he prided himself in all his life. Surprised, but he was also charmingly amused. "Apologies, Healer. One of my men is badly injured. I was able to get him to the edge of the village, but I can't chance to move him further. I ask please that you come with me to him. Please see what you can do for him."

Althea found still no breath for words and simply nodded and gathered an emergency bag of supplies she kept on a shelf near the door to the hut. Bad injuries seldom happened; most people are able to bring themselves to a Healer's hut for treatment. On the rare occasions that this could not happen, a Healer always had an emergency bag to rush out instantly to help in extreme cases. Durai watched her movements as she left the hut ahead of him. She was also graceful like him but not in a way that was high in the air but more rooted to the earth. He was in awe of her more and more.

25

Althea paused as she walked out of the hut. She was in such a rush to help that she didn't realize she needed him to go first to know where she was going. Durai came out of the hut and remembered his urgency and changed his fast walk into a graceful run. Althea followed keeping up admirably despite being notably smaller than he was.

After they crossed the barricades of the city, small though they were, Althea could see a man on his back lying on the ground barely lifting his head. She immediately passed her escort to be by this man's side. He had the uniform of a guard at court, but the front was torn in many places, and she found the injury fast. He had a deep gash in his abdomen, very deep. She could see broken sinew of muscle and even the softness further deep of precious organs exposed from the gash. There was blood beginning to pool around him, and she was terrified.

There are times that people are injured or ill beyond the skills of a Healer. There were some things even the Magic of the earth could not fix and courses that could not be altered. This man, Althea thought, could be past the point of help. She looked from the wound to Durai and saw the worry for her guard. Perhaps they were even friends. She didn't need to say that he was very badly hurt, this was obvious. She didn't say that she may not even be able to help him, for if this man felt confident that he could, there wouldn't be a sign of worry and dread.

Althea put her soft and nimble hands comfortingly against the guard's cheek and gave him a soft smile. She pulled the man's arms away from holding his wounds and parted the pieces of cloth that remained of his uniform. She closed her eyes to concentrate. She would try with all that was within her to do what seemed impossible. No matter what the circumstances, she always helped, even if it was hopeless; even if she were sure to fail. Everyone deserved the chance.

She reached for the song deep within the earth and pulled it straight from her soul. The ground turned warmer and the breeze carried floral scents Durai hadn't noticed before. Althea laid her hands on the wound and sang. She radiated in otherworldly melody, and her hands glowed. The guard's eyes went from the terror of his painful gash to stunned awe at what he was hearing. Durai was held captive by the scene as well. Both men couldn't believe in dreams or all Magic that such a song could ever exist. The guard even began to have tears roll down his face; it was just so utterly beautiful.

The strength of her song changed as she pushed even harder for her powers to do the impossible. The song swelled with hope and determination, different but still breathtakingly beautiful. The guard felt relief like a drug radiating from his abdomen to reach every part of his body. He lowered his upper half still leaning on his elbow to rest fully horizontal on the ground. He felt at peace.

Althea couldn't believe it herself, but the wound started slowly to heal. Her skills may even be enough to save this man. She continued to sing, rocking as she did to pull as much Magic from the earth into her song as she possibly could. The glowing moved even beyond her hands up her arms. Durai couldn't mask how shocked and impressed he felt. He began to smile. He began to plan.

The healing grew faster and faster as her song became more and more intense and indistinguishable from the very breath of the earth. It was Ancient and new, indescribably complex and yet basic and simple. The ground beneath the guard welcomed it, and the blood spilled forth and returned flowers as if by a miracle. The breeze about the small group danced with what seemed like joy and pride at the music and purity of purpose.

Finally, the singing slowed and quieted until the last traces of it were carried away on the slowing breeze. Althea was just as much in shock over her showing of skill as Durai and his guard. She had no idea that she had within her such a powerful, Ancient song. The man was healed almost completely leaving only what seemed a scratch. But she had saved him when she thought for sure she was beyond healing.

"How did this happen? This was quite a terrible wound." Althea had seen severe wounds before from the men in the village that would go out and hunt or the builders of grand structures involved in accidents. But this gash seemed different and frightening.

The two men looked at each other with severity. Durai spoke for his man, "It was an accident in the woods. His horse – it got spooked. He was thrown from the horse and landed on his sword." The guard lowered his head almost as if in shame though it was a completely understandable accident. He must have a high sense of duty, Althea thought to herself.

The guard slowly got to his feet and was joyfully surprised he was able to stand without pain. He truly was safely mended. He looked into her eyes with tears in them and said, "My lady, you have my sincerest gratitude, and I am truly in your debt. May you be blessed." He took one last look at her to save her face within his mind and walked confidently away from her towards horses she never noticed before waiting patiently and loyally not too far off.

Leaving behind only Althea and Durai together.

"What is your name, Healer?" Durai asked. The trace of his smile was still on his face making him even more handsome and beguiling. Althea felt the blood warm her cheeks in what was surely the most embarrassing blush as the sight of his approving smile and request. In reality, the new color in her cheeks made her glow radiantly, and Durai completely surrender within himself to the spell she was casting over him.

"My name is Althea, sir."

"Althea, I am Durai, and I have never seen a Healer do something like that. I'm truly astonished. I thought for sure my man would die. You are," he paused as if any words he could find would be woefully inadequate, "an angel."

Althea flushed even more and smiled herself. She couldn't believe that this was happening. Even if he walked away now, got on his horse, and rode away into memory, she would be warmed from this meeting for the rest of her life she thought.

Perhaps she dreamed and fantasized so hard that she could truly feel his hands take hers as if the wanting made it so. No, it was real. She looked down in shock and excitement despite every attempt to reflect his calm, noble composure. "Just don't faint!" she thought.

"Come back with me," she heard him say. Durai tried to search for words to convince her with all his charm, all his persuasion. But he still found himself like a bumbling fool just staring at her.

As it turns out, he didn't have to.

"I will."

Broke from Company Abruptly, as My Passion Now Makes Me

She didn't remember walking to the horses waiting there. Did she ask the guard to get off the horse, or did he get off by himself? Was he even on the horse yet? It was like walking through the haze of a dream. She wasn't even fully conscious of her habitual motions of putting up her hair for travel, bunching her skirt away from the stirrups, or fastening the pack to her back.

Durai never broke from her hand since asking her to follow him. He didn't want to ever let go, he thought, for the rest of time. He had seen ages of time and all the wonders of Magic, so he knew deep down when he found something rare and precious.

And he didn't want to let go.

Althea was on the horse before she realized it, and she was blissfully numb to the whole ride. She was just taking in the excitement and strange anticipation full of sensations she never felt before. She was only aware when they crossed the other edge of Base Village after having gone through it. She hadn't even noticed when they passed her hut, the meeting hall, the pavilion where the village celebrated together and mourned together. Only when she passed to the end where the houses stopped and the climb of the Hill began did she realize where she was and what she was doing.

She was leaving

She hadn't fully thought of anything beyond the village, not in all her life. These were her people, and all her duty from her grandmother to her mother lived and breathed with these souls she had protected and treasured. When the full weight of what she was doing woke her from her trance, she looked away to see one or two villagers, people she knew, looking after her. Would she actually leave? Would she be gone long? Why would she not say goodbye?

Althea almost felt like stopping and running back to everything and everyone she had known. Before she could hesitate, Durai made some noise to turn her head to him. "My Lady Althea, I know that what I ask of you is a lot.

Those people - they need you very much. I would not ask this of you if I didn't see some need for it. Please, trust me. And know that I'm grateful for what you are leaving behind."

So this was for more than just a short visit. She could hear in his words that her life was changing and that she was no longer of this Village. She wished she had asked for at least a farewell. But then she saw his comforting eyes, and she felt that excitement and almost drunken giddiness return to some small extent. Sometimes the rise and fall of the sun and the dance of stars bring you on a journey you did not expect, but sometimes those are the journeys worth having.

She was thinking and mulling over every thought and none at the same time that she didn't realize that they had stopped. They had reached the gate of Courtside. She had never been to the grounds of the palace before, and she was now very much looking forward to seeing the gardens and homes of nobility. She was not the least bit surprised that this Durai lived here; she had sensed he was nobility from the first moment. She wondered if his home was where they were going, if it was close to the palace at all in the city, and what she would be asked to do.

As they rode by the elegantly grafted homes and beautiful displays of trees and flora, the people of the village stopped to stare at Durai. Althea could see that he was held in high regard; people almost stopped breathing out of some kind of awe or respect at his passing. He must be very important indeed. But what she realized even more as she rode past the people of Courtside and their elegant clothes and bodily adornments was that they were staring at her just as much as Durai.

She lowered her head slightly. In Base Village, she was comfortable in her necessary position. She wasn't the Village Chief or a member of the Elder Circle, but she was needed and important as the only Healer in that Village. Some settlements had more than one, but she was the only one in Base Village. And she liked the respect that came with it humbly. But that wasn't the case here. Courtside had many Healers, which she knew. Some noble families even had their own personal Healer. So they couldn't be staring at her out of that same simple village respect, and she felt dreadfully exposed. She didn't have fine clothes and certainly nothing decorative or what she would consider beautiful in this area. The only thing beautiful she had was her hair, and she had that bundled for travel.

But these people weren't looking at her in humor or malice. They were just as much in awe of her as Durai. Durai they knew and understood his stature and importance, and here was a woman he rode beside, not in front of like a master to a servant, and he was proud. He might even have a small amount of upturned curvature at the corner of his mouth. Durai was often much too reserved to smile, but here he was in the closest thing they had ever seen to one. And rightly so! This woman was radiant. Even though her clothes were clearly from a common source and her skin slightly darker from days in the fields and earth than theirs, she was nonetheless striking. And even if Healers were more common place in Courtside, they still garnered much respect. And the mark on this woman was more vibrant than they had ever seen. Her Magic must be something special.

Durai put out his hand to the reigns of Althea's horse to stop, brushing her hand in the process, which made him smile deeper. He looked at her to catch her expression, but she didn't look at where she was when she looked up. Just from their touch and then to his face. And the familiar flush returned. She even imagined what it would be like…

Embarrassed by her thoughts, she quickly looked forward and away from him as if he could somehow read her improper thoughts. Of course, he couldn't read her thoughts, but instead, he shared them. But he did not turn from them as she did, he swam in them. Soon, he thought, he might even surrender to them and be devoured in the warmth of fantasy that he would yearn to be reality.

But at Althea's forward gaze she suddenly was shocked into the present to see the grandest thing she never dreamed she would ever behold in all her life.

They were at the gates of the Palace itself.

This Above All; to Thine Own Self Be True

"I am very sorry I brought you distress," Galen said finally looking up to Althea very much dreading the sight of tears in her eyes. But to his surprise, he saw her curiosity. Maybe he was the first Leoporem she had ever met, he thought. He was at least glad he could coax her beyond her barriers to release the energy inside her that clearly needed to be faced and accepted if she were ever to move past the oppressive weight it brings. He had seen too often the slow decay of inner torment and the blackened beast inside that feeds on the pain and grows in the heart's agony.

"Thank you," Althea whispered, "but it's not your fault. And in a way, I guess I should have known."

"Still, I understand that this could not be an easy thing to hear. Out loud, I mean." Galen was still looking at Althea, and she at him. They were both too curious about the other to have any time for distrust. And they were surprised to find that once they took the faith to lower their guard, they could see much more clearly. Althea saw more of the attractive features in his face, and he saw the beauty in hers.

"So," Althea said with obvious apprehension in her voice, "who is looking for me?" Cold sweat began to make itself apparent on her head and the palms of her hands. She had an answer she feared, but she had to know.

"Well, everyone really," Galen said rather simply. Seeing that she didn't quite understand, he continued. "What do you know about the Purple Mist? If you've been away for as long as you imply..." He didn't want to insinuate that she was completely ignorant, but he couldn't be sure what she knew or even how far the reach of the Mist had become.

"I know it came about a year ago. I know that it descended from somewhere Ancient, moves with malice, and raises the dead. It's what brought the Immortuos. It is the blanket of sorrow." Her mind seemed to trail off mixed in the now and the scenes of the last year. "I know that it moves like a beast, prowls and hunts, feeding but not consuming. It doesn't seem to have a purpose to fill, and nothing stops it."

"That's what we are hoping is wrong," Galen said also seemingly from far away. "No one knows for sure how or why it came. And it's true that we don't know how to stop it, but that doesn't mean there is absolutely no way to stop it. The Queen on the Hill has called for a powerful Healer and the magic she may have. It is said that one Ancient Song of a Healer may bring an end to this. And that's good enough for everyone to look everywhere for a Healer to try. But as the days went by and the number of Immortuos grew, Healers started disappearing. They stayed behind with the sick and wounded, and when we came around to find that we should have been protecting those who protected others…"

Galen's words trailed off. He was filled with a pang of guilt he owned but not entirely his own. When the Immortuos came, he ran too. Just like everyone else he ran all for himself and left everything behind. He knew his gifts would keep him safe in the Woods and even places unseen. But the Healers - they all stayed behind because their hearts and sense of duty wouldn't let them leave the defenseless behind.

"By the time those in barricaded towns and those on the run still in touch with the civilization and the castle from time to time heard the words of the Queen, that a Healer could be the answer, we finally found the courage to venture out in some numbers to bring them all back. But there were none left that we could find. None…"

This time the tears that came were from Galen, not Althea. He was so horribly ashamed of himself, of all of them. And now he found himself in front of a real-life Healer, and his shame was overwhelming. He suddenly felt not worthy to be in the presence of the Blood of the first to fall to the horrors of Immortuos. And Althea, seeing the bare purity of his heart, suddenly had no trace of doubt even after swearing long ago to never fully drop defenses again.

Althea reached out her hand to Galen's shoulders and suddenly saw a glow at the touch. Not gold in the way she was used to, but blue and soft.

Shame upon shame baring forth seeking help. Forgiveness seeking behind the oppressive chains of guilt and remorse.

Innocent Heart meets Innocent Heart.

"Please come back with me," Galen said carefully s the glow died away. "I don't know what it is you're running from, but I could escort you, keep you safe. For all our sakes, please."

Had she any right to deny the frightened cries of all the world? She was a Healer, and the entire earth may need healing. But to go back…

Althea's head started to hurt at all of her fears coming together where she couldn't run from them anymore. She had been running from them every moment since the day she escaped. Though she told herself that day she was stronger for fleeing and disappearing away from all the pain and terror she lived, she realized now that her cowardly hiding only made her weaker. There was no denying that now. And now she was being given the chance to show true courage, to fully realize the strength that she was hoping for in herself a year ago. As much as she wanted to, and as much as the thought of turning to fight truly frightened her to her core, she knew she couldn't hide anymore. There was no one else in her bloodline left. She knew deep down this day would come – where all her sins she had in running would come back to possess her soul, and the only way to free herself was to do all she could that was right.

"I will go," Althea said, her voice wavering as she tried to swallow her obvious distress. She looked up suddenly at Galen. She knew what she was walking into, and she knew that it was no place for a gentle soul. "You do not have to come with me."

Galen rose from the ground with a determined look. He extended his hand and said, "Healer, you are not going alone. I'm not going to run anymore either. I have a second chance now, and this time I won't let a Healer down."

Althea took his hand which wasn't soft but strong and hardened like leather. She liked it. Honest hands.

• • • • • • •

"You've studied so long, Althea. Don't you want to play outside just a bit before the light leaves? You can't study all day; you'll hurt yourself."

"But Momma, what if I forget? What if I forget these songs and let you and grandma down?"

"Althea, baby, never in all the ages of all the world would you ever disappoint us. We love you so much."

"Still...I have a job to do, Momma. Playing isn't important. Remembering the songs is what matters."

"Althea, as long as your heart is gentle and good and your love is deep, you will always be able to reach into yourself for the songs. Your bond with the Healer magic is very special. You are uncommonly strong, sweetness."

"Do you really really think so Momma? Truly?"

"I know so."

She's Beautiful, and Therefore to be Wooed

Durai knew that Althea must surely be incredibly anxious at being in the palace. He hadn't prepared her for his intention of introducing her to the Queen. But he loved the innocent wonder in her eyes as she saw all the fineries in the palace halls leading to the throne room. And he relished leading her arm in arm protecting her, as it were. She was like an innocent bird plucked from a cage away from the sun, and he was going to carry her in his gentle grasp to the light.

Althea was too entranced with the intricate sculptures, the beautiful smell through the hall, the moving paintings along the walls, and the immense grandeur of the palace to be self-conscious about her modest clothing and the dirt still left on her from the fields earlier that day. She didn't even have time to realize it was mid-day and she hadn't eaten a thing since before she went out to gather. Who could have time to focus on such trivial things? This was all more than she could have ever spun in her most reckless daydreams. Even if she were to turn away at this moment without ever meeting the Queen, this small moment within high-cultured artistry was enough to fuel her soul for a lifetime.

Through the slit in the doors to the throne room itself, Durai and Althea could hear the faint and muffled sounds of the Herald announcing them. As the doors opened, Durai led Althea up the carpeted walkway before the elevated throne not breaking her from his arm for an instant. Althea blushed, but she certainly wasn't complaining. Though the thought of showing a flushed face in front of the Queen…

"Your Majesty," Durai stated as he bowed his head slightly. Althea bowed much deeper but dared not speak unless spoken to. Durai may be a member of this court (this was quite clear now), but she was not. She decided to wait in silence and take in the scene completely.

"Durai, always so nice to see you. And you have brought someone with you." Althea was quite surprised. The Queen's voice was not domineering or imposing. It was kindly and not what she imagined at all. It threw Althea off her concentration slightly. She looked up in her surprise to see her Ruler. The Queen was her age, maybe a little older, but couldn't be by much. She had the long, fair hair of royalty. No surprise. And her eyes were of course blue as her mother's and father's were before her, or so she had been told. Althea read her aura and found it proud and yet innocent. She had a purity of heart, but there was strength also. This Queen ruled with compassion and empathy, not terror. She then smiled at Althea as one smiled at a friend. Althea was instantly at ease and smiled back feeling instantly like a village dolt.

"Your Majesty, this is Althea, a Healer from Base Village. My guard today was thrown from his horse and suffered injuries. I thought for sure he was going to die. This Healer saved him despite the severity. I believe she truly has a gift. I think her powers may be what we could be looking for." Durai beamed with pride, but it was not the pride of someone glad to take credit for finding a lost treasure. His pride was genuinely for Althea and this chance to be all her gifts would earn for her.

Althea didn't blush. In fact, she felt all the blood drain from her face, and she felt faint. Looking for? Was there another impossible feat for her to do? She was lucky the last time; what if she failed next? Just the thought of failing for this Queen made her want to shrink into nothing. She wasn't afraid of punishment or retribution. Healers were never blamed if a case was beyond their Magic, even by royalty and nobility. She was afraid to let her Queen down. She had been instantly endeared to this woman, and failing her might break her heart.

Mireya's eyes became truly alive and danced with innocent hope. She stood from her throne instantly and walked down to Althea. She looked Althea right in her eyes, and Althea could bring herself to look away. Were there tears? The Queen was undoubtedly carrying a weighty burden, and even if she were to fail, Althea would give anything now to try and help her. Mireya then reached out her hands, and Durai released his escort of Althea. Mireya then took both of Althea's hands in hers. Althea should have been shocked, but she wasn't.

"Althea," Mireya said, "I do have a problem, and I know that asking any Healer to attempt to heal a case sure to fail is a terrible thing. Your compassionate hearts are often broken after connecting with someone's suffering and you cannot help; your kind's sense of duty is so great. But I am asking you to help me now."

Althea nodded her head as if to agree while not breaking her eye contact. She was intrigued as to what distress could be so great. What Mireya said was true, the connection the Healers make to those who are suffering is a well-known fact. This is why Healers were never blamed for cases they could not cure; people instead wept for them as they did their loved ones.

Mireya continued, "My brother is suffering. He doesn't complain much, but I see him day by day in silent pain. Some days are better than others, but on other days his pain is so great he stays in his room in his bed. His eyes sometimes are dark with despair." Mireya faltered then, realizing she had trailed off in a way. She reconnected respectful eye contact with Althea. "Many Healers have tried here in the castle and Courtside. He has mostly given up hope and resolved to silent suffering. But if what Durai said is true, you could be the most powerful Healer we have. Please, would you at least try?"

Althea reassuringly, sympathetically squeezed Mireya's hands. She could see the Queen's suffering, and said with her voice full of compassion, "Your Majesty, I will do all I can. However long it takes."

Mireya was proud of this young woman. "You haven't even heard what is wrong with him, and you agreed without hesitation. I like you. I like you very much, Althea." Althea was stunned that the Queen remembered her name. She was often quite bad at forgetting names the first time she heard them. She was honored. "Durai, will you show her to the Healer's quarters?" Durai nodded without smiling seeming very proper, but he was so happy he barely kept back his smile and light in his eyes. Mireya turned to Althea, "We have had a room ready for a long time. We've been waiting for you, Althea."

• • • • • • •

39

Althea was concentrating very hard on each turn and corner of the palace she passed as she was being led to her room. The last thing she would like was to get lost. But it was no good; her mind kept drifting to what she may be asked to do, what could the Queen's brother have been going through? What would she need to treat him?

Dammit! She didn't have anything! She barely had a day's supplies of herbs and salves in the pack still attached to her back, but that was emergency patchwork stuff, nothing like what she had in her hut to treat serious or long-term conditions. And her things! Her treasures at home were left behind without a thought until now. Things that belonged to her mother and grandmother, the heirlooms of her people, were all left behind. She suddenly felt cold and somewhat empty. She was very far away from the people she cared for all her life and the things that had defined her. But she would mourn later; still have to focus on her bearings here. She did give her word to stay, after all.

Durai finally stopped at a large door in the Eastern wing. "This is your room, Althea. I do hope you find it comfortable. It isn't anything like your hut, and I do know that it can take some getting used to. I've seen people come to Courtside from the smaller villages not adapt well to higher grade amenities. If you need a change in anything, the attendants are at your constant disposal." He seemed so kind to Althea, and she would have to find some way to adapt to his voice. If she were to constantly be put under a spell at the sound of it, she'd never get proper work done. Durai continued, "The Queen's personal attendants will come before long to take your measurements for a replacement wardrobe. If you have preferences, please let them know. We are in your debt, after all. And if you need anything else," he turned and pointed to the end of the hall directly opposite Althea's door, "that is my room. Please don't hesitate to let me help you."

Althea smiled what she hoped to God wasn't drunkenly. There was a long pause where nothing was said and the conversation seemed to be at an end, so Althea turned to the doors to explore her rooms.

"My Lady?"

Althea stopped dead in her tracks both frightened that she violated some noble taboo and seduced by the slight change in his tone. It almost seemed as if he had stepped out of his nobility persona and was speaking to her outside of it. She turned to him hoping that she hadn't made a fool of herself. He seemed unsure at first and then put on some kind of contrived confidence. It was adorable.

"My Lady. I mean to court you." Oh, that came out stupid, he thought. Althea was shocked and her face suddenly became completely on fire. "I mean, um, excuse me. That came out rather ridiculous. What I mean to say is, I would like to court you…if you'll consent."

Althea was a bit too stunned to speak and was embarrassingly wondering if her fantasies she'd spun on the ride up the hill suddenly broke free from her mind and into life. Or had she fainted? Was she unconscious? Dammit!

Durai took her hand now, finally finding the composure he wished he'd had at the beginning. "I know this might be somewhat sudden, but I have known Magic and beauty beyond those of normal men. I command wonders in this world and can bring forth enchantments beyond those of most Enchanters. But, Lady, never once have I been so entranced as I am in your presence. If you will permit me, I would love the chance to sweep you off your feet."

Don't pass out, don't pass out, don't pass out!

Althea knew her face was redder than it could have ever been and felt warmer in places she never had before. And while the new sensation was frightening in its foreign nature, she liked it.

"You have my permission," Althea said barely able to suppress what was almost a giggle. Durai lifted the hand he was holding to his lips and kissed it. His lips felt like the magic of some ethereal butterfly or the faeries of ages past, and it was not enough for Durai. He lowered her hand and was forced to turn and leave to his room forgetting entirely to take leave of her. He knew if he stayed a moment longer, he would lose all control and devour her.

Althea stood in silence watching him walk down the long hall to the opposite door and forgot everything else in the world but this moment and these new sensations. She was enveloped by all the possibilities and every happy future meeting she dreamed she could have now. New fantasies washed over her like gusts of wind before a wild storm. She had never before lusted after a man.

And she wanted more.

Whether 'tis Nobler in the Mind...

Despite her worries that she would have a fitful night in a foreign bed, Althea slept deeply on her first night in her new suite of rooms. It was no denying that the fine mattress and soft sheets were nothing like she had ever experienced before, she embrace her new, fine things instead of fretting over them. And she was so overwhelmed by her state of rooms that she was too exhausted to do anything but sleep that night.

Her rooms were so grand and large that she didn't know what she would do with so much space. The same amount of space in the village was enough for five or six families, and she was just her! But her balcony was so lovely, and she had a personal greenhouse of precious plants she used in her work often that thrived in the Eastern morning light. She certainly didn't need to worry again about supplies. The greenhouse had her plants and one of her rooms was a study and work room that had vials, jars, and familiar books that most Healer families had. And the attendants were going the next day to her hut at Base Village to bring the rest of her things up to her, news which made her very happy.

When she woke up that morning and went from her bed-chamber to the living area of her suite, she noticed the attendants that had come to take her measurements for new clothes already had a set waiting for her. She put on the new clothes that felt so smooth and soft, she thought she must have transformed into delicate, living gold. At first, her modesty felt uneasy about the low neckline and form-hugging design of her dress, but then thinking of the kiss on her hand from yesterday made her think that this dress might not be so bad. She also liked the color deep red which complimented her dark hair. Accents and embellishments of black danced about the dress pleasingly, and it was incredibly comfortable despite the fabric being heavier than she was used to; the weight was comforting and attractive in the way it made the fabric behave as she moved. She liked it very much.

She wanted very much to get started with her task, and then realized she was very hungry. There were fruits and such in her room last night, but she had been far too overwhelmed with all that had happened to her for her to remember to eat. And now she didn't know what to do.

She stepped out her door rather meekly and saw no one. She couldn't decide if that was good or bad. No one would see how utterly befuddled and lost she was, but then they weren't there to be able to help either. She tried very hard to remember how she got to this wing yesterday, but then she giggled to herself at how utterly pointless that would be. Even if by some miracle she could remember, that just leaves her knowledge of this room and the throne room. Doubt they ate there.

Suddenly she felt a hand take hers, and she let out a small scream in her shock. She could have sworn she was alone. "My Lady," she heard Durai's melodic voice and turned around so happy that a familiar face was there to help her.

As she turned around, Durai could see the full sight of her and her new clothes. He let his eyes linger far too long and the lowered neckline and the fullness beneath it. He finally broke away and couldn't help but look her up and down just one more time in pleasant shock at how alluring and natural she seemed in these complimentary clothes. He raised her hand to his lips again and kissed them, somewhat harder this time than last night. He couldn't help it.

"May I escort you to breakfast?" he asked. Althea let out an audible sigh of relief as she locked her hands into his extended arm. "You are going to love the food here. Our cook is gifted, and he is rather excited to show off to someone new, I must say." Althea let out another giggle hoping to hide the hungry sounds of her stomach. "And" Durai continued, "you'll get to meet your patient, her Majesty's brother."

After a thankfully straightforward route, they reached the massive Dining Hall. They were the first to arrive, and Durai led her down to the right hand of the head of the table. She looked at him frightened, for that was a place of honor in any dining area. He nodded at her that this was her seat, and pulled out the chair for her. After she sat, he seated himself next to her, which she was grateful for.

"Her Majesty is anxious for you to meet her brother and start your work right away. But I'm hoping after you would consent to walk with me?" Durai asked with a mixture of timid hope and confidence.

"I would like that very much," Althea said not ready to look into his eyes again and feel those warm feelings she had felt last night. Now was not the time, she would be meeting royalty soon and didn't need to look like an idiot child.

The doors to the hall were opened by attendants, and Durai took Althea's hand to rise at the arrival of the Queen and her brother. "Althea!" Mireya started walking faster in excitement. She burst forth with rapid questions wanting eagerly to know about the rooms, how she slept, did the clothes fit, and so forth. She then turned to the handsome young man at her side, not much younger than she and Althea were. "Althea, this is my brother Baldrik. He is the light in my life."

Althea reached out with her body and engaged her trained eye to see beyond seeing. She could see the kindness in his aura, his pride mixed beautifully with humor and a lightness of heart. She could see some slight looseness in the skin of his exposed arm that was very pleasingly filled with muscle. So while he looked very strong and toned, it wasn't what it once was. She saw laugh lines around his eyes that indicated someone who smiled and laughed often, but not right now. These eyes were somewhat clouded, though he was battling inward. This was probably the silent fight with pain that the Queen spoke of yesterday. Baldrik made an effort to reflect a fraction of his joyous nature, but he couldn't muster it this morning.

"Forgive me," he said with a light voice, not nearly as deep as she would have thought for a man of such stature. He truly was a boy in so many ways. "I'm not quite feeling myself today." He moved to his seat and sat before his sister had the chance to seat herself first. Durai went and pulled the seat out for Mireya instead, and Althea was already taking on the suffering of this young man into herself wanting and praying so much to be strong enough to help him.

· · · · · · ·

45

Breakfast was utterly delicious, and the cook was such a sweet, round man full of a desire to please. He ate up Althea's compliments and assured her that he was at her disposal night or day. She feared she ate too much to walk back with Baldrik to get started on her work with him, but she managed somehow to make it down the opposite wing to his room.

He immediately went back to his bed and lay there. He plainly was having a day worse than usual. Her heart bled for him as she saw his eyes darken more and more with a pain he tried so hard to hide away. Althea went beside his bed pulling up a chair to sit beside him. "I'm sorry," Baldrik started from his bed, turning to lay on his side with his back to her. "I'm really not in the mood for this today. I don't have it in me to get up and entertain your rites and try your drinks and salves today."

"I don't want you to do anything but lie down. I won't ask you to do anything; I just want to listen. I'll stay here as long as you'd like just listening. Your eyes are hiding something you both do and do not want to say. How terrible that must be." Althea's voice was low, calming. She sat back in her chair comfortably and was quite willing to wait all day for him to be ready on his time.

Baldrik turned to her with a surprised look on his face. "What?" He knew that his sister ordered her to get started right away, and all the other Healers that had come and tried and gone before her jumped right into treatments and songs. But she was asking him to just talk? He was intrigued. "I'm not sure what you mean, Healer."

"Well first, my name is Althea. You may call me that because I want you to trust me. Don't see me as the same tool who has tried and failed before. I want you to trust me. We won't get very far together if you don't." She was different. "Secondly, I want to hear you speak of this pain that makes you suffer. If you don't face it…if you don't speak about it and give it light, it'll be this elusive shadow that neither of us will know how to battle."

Baldrik had never thought about it that way. It was true; he hadn't looked at his condition honestly and directly. He'd pass it off with some excuse here and there and never truly admit that something was wrong.

"You have my permission to be vulnerable, your Highness. And it will only ever be between you and me if you want." Althea's eyes warmed his heart and silenced his doubt. He thought maybe it was ok, just once more, to hope again.

"Call me Baldrik."

Althea smiled so much that she thought her mouth touched her ears. "Ok, Baldrik. Let's talk."

And he did talk, he talked well past midday and even let loose the tears that he had swallowed for years and eaten his spirit. Althea was worried; she had never known something like his suffering before. He seemed to always be in pain in some form or another in a varying range that was never consistent. Some blessed days his pain was mild, others his body swelled with redness and hot aching. When he got sick, which seemed far too often, he didn't get over his ailments for far longer than other people did. Some days he itched, some days he had a strange rash, and some days he felt as though a bone had been broken in the night. "I even sent the guards to look for a prowler in the castle one night because I thought an intruder broke my leg. Turns out it was just me." Althea was more determined to do all she could for Baldrik for the sake of this tortured boy more than she was scared to fail.

Althea put her hand on his shoulder as he was propped up in his bed. He looked at her with hope. "We will work on this every day, you and I. Your suffering is my suffering now." Baldrik was overjoyed by her words and placed his hand on top of hers. And they connected in a kindred way. "We'll fight this together, Baldrik."

A Friend Should Bear His Friend's Infirmities

Mireya put on a warm robe over her nightdress and walked quietly through the connecting door and hall she had put in to secretly commute from her state of rooms to her brothers. The light was barely even a glow shaking the veil of the night off to the rise of the morning. She quietly opened the room to her brother's bed-chambers and made her way to his bed. He was not asleep, he had heard her coming. He could always hear her coming.

She lifted the heavy covers and crawled into bed next to him. They both just lay there quietly for a time listening to the other breathe in contentment. Mireya whispered, "What dreams did you have?"

Baldrik whispered back to her, "I dreamed that I was a great big bear and broke into the kitchen. I gathered up so much food I couldn't hold it all. But then I woke up."

"Did you get to actually eat any this time?"

"Do I ever? Stupid dreams," Baldrik and Mireya laughed as quietly as they could, but the joy was full and deep. They were like two small children creeping in the dark to the others room while their parent's slept. Mireya and Baldrik had done this for years, always Miraya coming in to check on him. Some days she was earlier than even the hint of dawn because her worry for him kept her awake. If he were still asleep, sometimes she slept next to him. And she would then finally sleep the deep and contented sleep of knowing the one she loved most in this world was safe.

"I like Althea; I'm glad you found her," Baldrik said, changing the subject from dreams. It had been almost a week since Althea arrived, and though she hadn't tried anything much quite yet but listen, just the act of letting him release did wonders for his mind. He finally found the courage again to battle the forces that fought against him in his own body.

"I didn't find her, Durai did. But I'm glad you like her. I like her very much, too." When Althea wasn't working with Baldrik, one of her pastimes was listening to Mireya unload her burdens as well. Mireya felt incredibly selfish. She certainly didn't mean to burden the Healer, and she had far less to trouble her than her brother did. She would love to see Althea take on the many facilities within the Palace or Courtside to divert her and entertain her, but she stayed with Mireya. It was as if Althea knew Mireya had her distress to face before even Mireya realized it. And Mireya was feeling much healthier as a result. Who would have thought the mind and heart were such an important part of physical healing? Obviously, Althea did, and the pair were grateful for her help.

"You know what she said to me, Mireya? She said, 'Your suffering is my suffering now."

"That does make sense," Mireya replied. "Healers have been known to take into themselves the pain of those they try to help; especially the more difficult cases."

"None of the others did that."

Mireya was saddened by this. She was always very disappointed that the others she brought to her brother were not willing to put forth this effort for him. Though she knew that this was asking a lot, especially since their songs and salves were more than likely not to work, she had a hard time forgiving those who didn't do all they could for her brother. All she could say in response was, "I know," in quiet shame.

"And I believe her, Mireya. I mean, sometimes after our talks, I'll notice her walk away with a limp. She may not notice it much, but I sure as Hell did. I don't ask that of people!" He suddenly felt very unworthy of this kind of devotion. And he sunk deeper into his pillow.

Mireya raised herself onto her elbow. She brought her hand to his chin and turned his face to hers. "You don't have to ask. You never should. You are a very wonderful person. She does this because she wants to! She sees love and light and beauty in your aura. She told me so. She wants to keep this light burning." She felt the knot growing in her throat and her tears were about to escape. "You big dolt!"

And they both fell back laughing.

Baldrik and Mireya spent the entire morning like this, just lying next to each other, talking about everything and nothing like new people discovering life all over again. Their eyes suddenly seeing with new hope a world full of beauty once again.

•••••••

"You've done very well here in such a short time. And I must say that you fit in quite well in these lavishly beautiful surroundings. You're like an early spring wind cutting through winter." Durai was walking with Althea in a semi-private garden next to their rooms no longer arm in arm but hand in hand. To most people, such rapid progression in courtship would be embarrassingly hasty. But they didn't care. The people of Magic danced with the living mystical breath of the earth, and they were not ashamed of being swept up by passion. To Durai, the amount he had slowed for the sake of propriety was painfully exasperating.

"You say such lovely things, Durai," Althea said as she breathed deep the morning air of honeysuckle and dew. She was very happy. Happier than she ever imagined. Not that she was unhappy in her home, but the connections she made here in the palace with Durai, the Queen, and Baldrik were precious to her in a unique way. Sometimes the winds of change blow to places unseen, but once discovered the sight is breathtaking.

"Will you have dinner with me tonight?" Durai asked.

"I have dinner with you every night," Althea replied. Althea, Durai, the Queen, and Baldrik had dinner together every night since she arrived, sometimes with more if a person of importance visited, but not often. But Althea wasn't a simpleton; she knew what Durai meant. How could she be so bold as to be a tease? The thought amused her and shocked her.

Durai stopped their walk while his hand still held hers and reached to hold the other as well. He knew she was teasing, and it pleased him. If she felt comfortable enough to coyly play this game, then their trust was sturdier and their bond more secure. "I mean," he started deeply in a way that sent electricity through Althea's blood, "will you, My Lady, have dinner with *just* me tonight? In my room."

Gulp!

Althea was all fine and good with toyfull playing, but she didn't think he meant to dine in his actual room. She thought there might have been some smaller dining hall for ... whoever! She tried to hide that she was breathing heavily. Was her heart beating so fast with fear, apprehension, or was this anticipation?

"Yes."

Thinking there would be no finer moment than this here in the garden with the light and air almost as radiant as she was, Durai couldn't help himself any longer and lowered himself to her lips. The kiss was out of legends, the kind songs were made from and stories were told of. It was gentle at first but quickly became hungry and full of need. Althea and Durai left the world they knew to trespass into the place of their dreams and fantastic imaginings. If others were present to look on, they would see the breeze wrap around them and roll their hair as intending to set the scene for a painting. There was no sight for her but colors and artistry of pure sensation of his lips on hers, and there was no sensation for him to ground him to reality than the touch of her skin. If they were not careful, they would be swept into the clouds.

••••••

"What is it you're running from?"

"I don't really want to talk about it now. The sun is almost set, and we need to focus on a safe place to sleep."

"Was it that you lost someone? Althea?"

"I...."

51

Nor Wit nor Reason Can My Passion Hide

An attendant left a new dress at the door as the sun was starting to lower. She hadn't an idea what to wear to her dinner, but his dress was sent with a note from Durai. The note read: "Waiting not too patiently for tonight. I hope you like the dress."

She unfurled the folded dress and the beauty of the designs and softness of the silken fabric took her breath away. It was sleek and black with gold embroidered floral designs very much like her Healer's mark. The gesture made with this detail was incredibly romantic, and she smiled widely. The fabric had the same alluring heaviness that she had come to adore, and every detail of the gown made the meticulous attention to detail apparent.

She put the gown on right away; she couldn't contain her excitement. The neckline was considerably lower than even the low neckline she was slowly getting used to in the palace. Her face turned white because she knew this was dangerous...for both of them. And there were very loose, short bell sleeves on this dress, and she wasn't used to having her arms so exposed. Her skin got goosebumps as a breeze blew in. The cut of this dress was even more form-hugging than her previous outfits. She knew that this was an insanely seductive dress designed very intentionally. She stopped at her reflection in the mirror as if making some kind of decision.

She knew what was proper, but she knew what she wanted. She knew that people would talk, and she tried very hard to care about that. But she didn't; not enough to stop. Not enough to keep her from going to the small vanity in her washroom to put extra detail into decorating her hair to fall in loose waves around her exposed arms and add the paint of vivid plants to enhance her facial features. Not enough to keep her from walking through the doors of her room and walking the hall to temptation and almost certain wickedness.

• • • • • • •

Before she even came to the front of the intricately decorated doors to Durai's room, the doors seemingly on their own opened before her. The sun outside had just barely started to disappear beyond the horizon in the west, but the front living quarters were completely dark. She tried to be brave and show confidence, but she stepped inside slowly and timidly. The doors closed gently behind her.

She realized that the darkness of the front living quarters wasn't complete, but candles were giving off beautiful glows. Many candles all over, and she was able to see quite well with only a moment's adjustments. She saw no one amongst the furnishings and flickering candlelight, but she did see a brighter glow towards another set of rooms and moved towards it.

It wasn't a room, but it was an outside foyer filled with many creeping, flowering vines along the walls, other bushes of vivid flora in pots were placed along the patio, and the furnishings. Her eyes widened with delighted surprise at the view. His view was not like hers of the rising sun, but his outer door faced the sun's setting. The dying light that flirted with the night was so incredibly beautiful painting the clouds with pink and orange and deep gold. A more beautiful sight couldn't possibly be dreamed of.

Althea felt Durai come up behind her before he spoke a word. "I don't believe I've ever had my view this beautiful," he whispered in a deep voice that penetrated deep within her. She closed her eyes and tried to compensate for her heart in her stomach making her legs weak. Was this what swooning was? She felt his hands slide down the length of her long hair and run his fingers through the full waves of it. He too closed his eyes to relish the sensation.

He had watched her intently for this past week. The way she walked was almost like a glide; people could even mistake her for an Enchanter with her weightless grace if it weren't for her dazzling mark wrapping about her ankles. He was always fascinated by the Healer's mark. No other people Magically gifted had a physical manifestation to brand them as the Healers did. And of all the marks he had noticed and marveled at over the years, hers was the most vivid, the most stunning, and the most intricately alluring. He watched as she worked with the Queen's brother, how she innocently wandered the castle to slowly learn each room and hall, how seductively she ate her food (though she wasn't doing so intentionally), and how she seemed to exist in music. Every time she spoke, every time she breathed, he heard music and was under her spell. In every action she was sublime, and he longed to discover more of her. Even more than knowing, he was tremulant over the promise of the journey of discovering.

And deep in her being, she yearned to be discovered.

· · · · · · ·

Of course, the food was delicious and the setting sun painted light of sublime poetry over the scene of their meal in the foyer. They hardly even remembered the automated act of eating. There had been no awkward small talk to cover the moment in pretense. In the past week, they had done nothing but talk. They talked at meals, talked on their walks, and talked before parting to their separate rooms. The more they had talked and swam in each other's words and thoughts and intellect, the more they knew now that this moment together and finally alone was not a time for more of the same.

Instead, they read each other silently, something that would appear awkward or utterly foolish to those outside the world of their trades. If they had done such an act in the presence of the court's nobility or even the Queen or her brother, they would be utterly confused while feeling inexplicably exposed and embarrassed. They spoke without speaking and heard without words. They reached out with their bodies unmoving to read the world deep in the other's eyes. They extended their aura to mingle in the air with the aura of the other. He discarded his veneer of nobility to let her enticing intensity come into him and fill every part of him. She let go of her doubts, her hesitation, and her social propriety to let in the sensations of his palpable and earnest hunger.

They didn't even remember getting up from their meal and coming inside into the darkness and candlelight, but they were there still reading each other sitting within the reach of an outstretched arm together.

Durai extended his hand with his palm facing upward. A stream of softly glowing light seemed to be born of it and dance and bend in streams of blue and green. And from the light's bending, beautiful ballet an object appeared. Durai took the object in both hands and the light blew away into the air leaving behind the scent of rain. It was a thin, glimmering necklace made of a delicate golden chain and a pale not quite blue but not quite white stone intricately shaped like the flower of her Healer's mark.

"Angeltite," Althea whispered in breathless delight.

"The rare, resplendent gemstone of Healing." Durai stretched the chain wide and leaned into her to fasten the necklace behind her neck. She breathed deep his scent and felt his heat, and he breathed deep all of her in the act as well. She was like the earth alive in the awakening blossom of spring, and he bowed his head in agony.

"Althea," Durai began. He rarely called her by name; he usually said "My Lady" in his noble propriety. Hearing her name in his voice was like a drug, and she didn't know how much more she could take. "Althea, I want very much to kiss you. Not any small kiss either. I'm not asking for a gentle flutter before speaking goodnight. I want to *kiss* you, Althea. I want to kiss you deeply. But," He stopped for a moment as if in a battle of some great torment, "I'm surely afraid." Althea looked at him both confused and exasperated; she too was in great torment. He brought his face inches from hers as his hands slowly left behind her neck and made their way down her bare, exposed arms slowly.

"I'm afraid, Althea, that if I kiss you now. I'll never stop. Not tonight, not ever. What would you think of me then? And if I did dare, could I even bear the scorch of your light without burning?"

He didn't wait for an answer or reaction from Althea. He barely waited for the completion of his sentence. He took her deep in his arms and didn't merely kiss her, he was consuming her. His arms embraced her completely and explored every inch of her back. She smelled of flowers even so far as tasting them on her lips. Each second within their embrace with their lips together was like sparks from fireworks at a festival. The more Durai had her, the more he wanted more, the more he desperately needed more.

And his fervor was matched in her. Her surprise at his speed lasted less than a moment as she participated fully in their dance. Durai's hands behind Althea clenched fistfuls of her dress, and he moved closer pressing his chest into her. He could feel her shallow, excited breathing which only spurred on his passions more.

His parted hungrily inviting hers to do the same. They were no longer two mouths kissing and two bodies caressing, they were merging their very souls in a heated, lustful surrender.

Durai broke away as if in great pain. His chest was heaving in breathlessness, and he watched the rise and fall of the revealing contours of her chest do the same. "I want you," he nearly panted, "so much."

"But..."Althea said gratefully in a way that he broke off the lustful swelling of their passion before she was forced to. "But we can't. Not now. Not yet."

Durai clenched his eyes shut happy that she understood so he didn't have to explain, but also in agony over the sudden cessation of coming so close to every fantasy he had since laying eyes on her in that modest hut.

"I know," she said. "Me too. Before I can't control myself anymore, I better leave for my bed." Oh, God! The mere mention of the words shot fire into her deeply and sensually, and Durai let out a moan that surprised him. She didn't rise to go, and he didn't rise to escort her. They sat there suffering together wondering if being wicked would be so bad.

After what seemed like an eternity, they rose together. They walked automatically to the door and exchanged parting words in place of a farewell kiss they knew would be the end of them.

Though neither would hardly sleep that night, they both dreamed of promising tomorrows and fantasized about what they both decided they had to have. The night was cooling unseasonably and wrapped their bodies in a welcomed cold. What had they unleashed?

Where Love is Great, the Littlest Doubts are Fear

Althea regained her strength steadily with another day of rest. Durai was by her side constantly tending to her even after she had well surpassed the effects of her Healer's sickness. Althea couldn't even get a moment's privacy as he followed her like a lost lamb. But she did adore him, so she was glad of the time he was spending with her while he could. Surely he had some duties that would require his attention eventually.

Baldrik and Althea's reconciliation after that night was heartfelt and in no way drawn out or left a trace of resentful doubt. They were indeed kindred spirits and very much a part of each other now. They worked together each day towards building his strength or soothing his ailments during episodes of worsening pain. They would go for walks or even ride their horses if Baldrik was well enough, which was often lately, and exercise to make sure his body retained its vigor.

And Durai would be there when they returned to sweep her away with intensifying attention. Their courtship had not stalled in the least, but they dared not tempt each other more with a night like before. Not for a while at least. Instead, they shared more of their Magic together. Durai had seen much of what Althea could do, and he was now adamant to show her the same. His conjuring and summons of the Mystic were intimidatingly powerful. She couldn't believe some of the things he could do. It was no question to her now how he became the appointed court Enchanter. She had never seen a mastery of the earth's Magic like he had.

What small moments she had apart from Baldrik and Durai Althea happily spent with Mireya. Althea didn't much care for alone time; as a Healer, her needs were best filled in the company of others. And Mireya and she quickly became sisters. They often found the only time they could reliably be alone together was during dressing and bathing rituals, so they found themselves indulging in this time longer and longer. They shared stories of their childhood while brushing each other's hair, they exchanged their hopes and passions while bathing in a large, communal hot spring that was in the queen's courtyard, at night they sometimes snuck into each other's rooms and exchanged stories of ghosts, witches, and the old faeries by the light of a single candle. Neither woman could remember laughing so much in their life before.

Althea felt as if she had a new blood family filled with so much love. In her village, she had respect and admiration, but never love and affection as she felt here. She was happy deep into her soul, fulfilled in work and warm in devotion.

·······

"Aaahhh!" Althea yelped with a jump as she left Baldrik's room after some morning stretches. "You startled me," she panted out to Durai who was waiting for her just outside the door. Durai slipped his hand around her waist and escorted her down the hallway toward the garden for their walk without much of a word to her, his eyes somewhat darkened.

"Is there something wrong?" Althea asked as they reached the garden still in silence. Durai attempted to lighten his continence, but Althea could still feel something off. He tightened his hold of her waist as they continued to walk. What she felt coming off of him made her feel uncomfortable. She stopped and pushed away from him. "Durai," she pressed stronger, "what is wrong?"

Durai moved to close the distance and took her hand. "I'm so sorry. I can't stop seeing in my mind what he did to you."

"Baldrik?" Althea asked confused; she had all but forgotten the incident as it was forgiven, and honestly, she had been treated worse before. She had no idea he was so troubled by it.

"Yes, Baldrik."

"Durai, I'm so sorry. I didn't know you were so troubled."

Durai looked at her strangely. "Of course, I would be troubled," he said lovingly yet sternly. He put his arms around her and embraced her protectively. "You mean everything to me, Althea, and he struck you down. He hurt you!"

Althea raised her arms to embrace him back. She felt the passionate feelings behind his words, and she tried to see his concern despite her understanding of the effects of Baldrik's pain, of all pain. She was at a loss for the right words to try and effectively reason with him and try to turn his emotions from resentment to understanding. It hurt her heart deeply to know he had been harboring this venom against Baldrik this whole time. "Durai," she started to say before she knew where her words would end up, "please try -"

"Yes! I have tried!" Durai nearly shouted with as much frustration at her words as his failings. "I've tried understanding, I've tried empathizing, I've even tried pity, but it all comes out as anger! He knew what he was doing; he felt the relief knowing exactly the miracle you brought to him, and then he made a choice. He consciously decided to strike you to the ground!"

Althea didn't know what to think. She had never in her life had someone react this way out of a sense of protection or injustice for her. She was lost and didn't know what to do. And his aura had changed. Where usually the air about him was of enlightened and almost superior calmness and grace it was now a burning, hot redness. She almost made physical moves to guard herself against it as if she were afraid she would be singed.

"I..."

"What if he had really harmed you? What if you were broken somehow?" He paused and had desperation in his words. "What if you ran..." he couldn't bring himself to give the thought full words.

Althea thought about what he was trying so hard to say and not say at the same time. "Duari," she started shakily, "I'm not a bird afraid of the world that will fly away."

"But you are a bird," he started softly. "You're my peaceful Dove. You've brought peace to my heart and renewed my life spirit. And he..." she saw the anger in him start to rise again, "he just didn't care! Did he even know how much you suffered for him?!"

"Durai, I don't see it as suffering-"

"Is that what you like?!" Durai continued. He was like a man possessed. His anger and passion overtook him in a way he had never felt before. He almost seemed to grow in size and the very air trembled around them in the garden. "Is that why you go to him every single day? Do you hope you'll be beaten down again? Is that how you are?!"

Althea was absolutely frozen, too stunned to even contemplate her physicality in the world. She didn't even feel the tears leave her eyes betraying her or register her body's tense shaking. What was this? What was happening around her?

Durai took a step back as if he were the one who had been struck then. He saw the tears roll down her frightened face, and he wanted to disappear. He was unleashed in a way he had seldom let happen, and it was towards the most precious part of his world. Like a frightened child, he turned his back to her and almost ran from her and vanished into the castle.

Althea stood there for a long time confused, hurt, and abandoned. She couldn't even feel the midday sun's warmth on her skin. Even the trembling breeze didn't touch her as if even it were afraid.

• • • • • • •

Durai hadn't been at dinner that night; Mireya and Baldrik thought nothing of it until they sensed Althea's unnaturally reserved nature. Most of the meal was spent in silence save for short anecdotes here and there from the siblings until they realized it was barely received by their friend. Mireya wanted desperately to know about her sister's troubles. She almost shooed away her brother to be alone with Althea to find out what was troubling her. Neither of them even considered it was Durai. They had only seen admiration and devotion in him towards her, and he sometimes was overtaken in study to realize meal times, so they didn't think much of his absence. But here in front of their eyes, she was like a flower curling into the night.

After dinner, Althea sat alone in her room neglecting to even light a candle for the night. She held herself and was still mostly numb with confusion more than she could register her hurt or sadness. She didn't even notice the first knock on her door.

It wasn't until the second knock which was only slightly louder and even slower that she came out of her melancholy and realized the calling. She smoothed back her hair and wiped away any remnants of sadness on her face. She went quickly to the door to welcome Mireya who was surely coming to check on her.

She opened the door to Durai.

She took a step back to see his face and was both wanting to see him and not wanting to at the same time, and she was frustrated and uncomfortable with the complexity. She reached out with her body to feel his aura and read him. He was no longer red and burning but a deep blue contrite sadness filled with remorse and shame. Whatever had possessed him in the garden was gone.

"May I..." he asked looking at her and the span between them.

Althea backed up to let him in. She didn't respond with words because she couldn't trust the strength in her voice. They both stood in silence when he entered, both as timid as two strangers meeting. Durai felt this change in them and it brought him to his knees.

"Althea, I am so …. so incredibly sorry. I was stupid, beyond stupid, and I'm begging to fix what I've wounded. The words I said...I didn't mean those hurtful things. I was so wrong." Though he was on his knees, he still seemed so strong in his stature. How could he be so weak and so powerful all at the same time? He looked up at her with eyes full of remorse and earnestness. She walked towards him and closed the gap as he quickly embraced her legs and waist from still on his knees. "Althea, I'm so sorry," he kept saying.

Althea lowered herself to embrace him back forgiving him completely. After all, he had spoken from his caring so deeply for her and not malicious. They embraced from the floor on their knees for a long time before she felt his hand stroke the back of her head down the length of her hair.

"I love you, Althea."

Althea heard the words for the very first time and felt Durai's breathing stop as though her response held his still-beating heart. She pulled back and saw his eyes full of anticipation, and her heart raced with giddiness at the terrifying unknown territory she found herself in. But through all the tumultuous rush of her feelings, her heart pushed forth with a voice of confidence. She had known long her feelings long ago and was safe to lay them bare now.

"And I love you, my Durai."

She almost wasn't given leave to finish her confession before his kiss was upon her with relief and passion. He hadn't lost her as he had dreadfully feared but found her anew. Durai had one arm wrapped around her small waist while the other hand clutched the hair on the back of her head. Althea threw her arms around his neck and returned his kiss fervently. The sudden rush of rekindled passion was too much for them this time, and they both knew it.

Durai slowly rose from the floor still wrapped around Althea and brought her up with him. The moment she felt her feet leave the floor in his embrace, she bent her knees to press hard against his waist. They were the East wind and the West wind meeting and creating a whirlwind between them; even their entangled limbs reflected the tempest made in their passion.

Durai's hand slowly relaxed his hold of her waist and moved lower, feeling her curves beneath her robe and feeling his passion rising. Althea began to feel excited and stimulated in ways she had never felt in her waking life, and between the grips of her legs against her lover, she could feel that he felt the same. She began panting and threw her head back in ecstasy as his kiss moved from her lips to her neck. Neither of them even realized it when they bumped against the side of the bed, their balance lost, and they fell upon the mattress.

Althea's robe had already loosened in their dance and exposed the curves beneath. Durai rested his face against the half-exposed breast of his lady as his hands moved to undo the rest of her waistband. While Althea was terrified of the end of this path knowing where it was leading, she knew she desired nothing else. He kissed the rise of her chest from her sternum to the rise on both sides, and his hands slipped into her robe feeling the bare skin of her waist. He moaned as he had before – like a tortured animal – but this time his passions could not be bound or tamed, and he smiled knowing he wasn't even going to try. He wasn't even meeting protests or a hint of resistance.

His nose parted the top of her robe to finally fully expose her full breast, and he was suddenly so consumed by the storm that he lost himself to its rage just as much as she was. Like flags against the wind, they were tossed about each other with similar reckless motions. Their movements were not clumsy or fumbling in their haste but synchronized and harmonious, almost as if their bodies were made for only each other – to be tossed into abandon forever. They were the fire raging across the Plains ignited by lightning and driven ever further by passionate wind. Their motions were like the breathing of the earth rising and falling, rocking back and forth like the bending of trees against the thrust of each warm gust in summer. And the swell would rise and fall over and again. Over and over again.

The sound of their muffled ecstasy penetrated the night, and finally the last breathe of the tempest heaved it last and rested against the earth utterly spent.

Stars, Hide Your Fires

"I do love that color on you, Dove."

"I know, that's why I wore it." Althea glided down the halls with her lover at her side wearing a trailing, green gown. Althea preferred red on herself as she always loved the way the color within the sunset and sunrise alike complimented her hair. But she was so blissfully full of love this day that she wore the color Durai admired her in most.

The days passed and seasons turned from the heated skies to the painted earth and rested at last to the days of chill. The castle had grown delightfully accustomed to the closeness and warmth Althea and Durai brought to the halls. Even their dread of the colder seasons disappeared. With the coming of the cold, Baldrik's condition usually worsened, and the castle seemed in perpetual mourning. However, with Althea's help, he was barreling through the days much stronger than before and was filled with the spirit of the good-humored soul they remembered from childhood.

Durai was hardly from Althea's side; he even took to bringing his studies in the room with her and Baldrik as she worked with him on some days. He was never presumptuous enough to participate or get in their way, but he often quietly watched. Baldrik hadn't remembered a time he had seen Durai before so much. The only time Durai was apart from her was her personal time with Mireya or on the rare chance he was sent away to work on a troubled field, investigate rumors of troublesome spirits in the Woods, or renew protection spells of a village. He made sure never to be gone long and always returned to sweep his Dove up in an embrace and twirl her around. Their lives had turned into the tales in the times of fairies told to children to guide them to dreams of love and hope.

"Shall I have dinner tonight brought to your room? Just the two of us?" Durai asked as he prepared to part from her one day, her to work with Baldrik and him to study in his room.

Althea blushed at his seductive tone and delightful proposition. "I would like that very much, yes."

"Dinner at sunset, and don't be late. And keep the green dress."

Althea went through the rest of her day in the smooth routine she came to delight in. After she worked with Baldrik she went to spend some time with Mireya as Durai was still studying his texts. Mireya was overflowing with delight in spending extra time with her spirit sister. They decided to take a long bath in the hot spring next to Mireya's rooms.

"You and Durai seem to be…getting along," Mireya said coyly. She beamed from ear to ear seeing the attractive blush on Althea's face, and she loved to tease her about her smitten antics. "Is he all you dreamed of when you were young?" Mireya shifted from her teasing to earnest curiosity. While she had had suitors and had periods of infatuation with this boy or the next, she never really felt the full possession of heart-filled love. Not that she felt empty in its absence, in fact, she felt incredibly satisfied with where she was in life. But she was curious to hear how Althea described it. She loved to hear Althea's musical voice and her way with words.

"I never really dreamed much of love and the tales of romance when I was young. I usually studied hard to live up to my mother and my grandmother. They were the light that guided the village, and I wanted to be that light too."

"You always speak so highly of them," Mireya said as she gently rested her head upon her folded arms enjoying the warmth of the water. "You always seem to go to another place when you speak of them."

Althea sighed. Mireya was right. Her mother and grandmother always shined brighter than other parts of her life, and they were the true measures of greatness to her. "The first love I knew was theirs, and always was the greatest. Even when I didn't believe in myself, they did. Whenever I wanted to give up, they didn't. They didn't force me because they said so; they embraced me and reached deep into my heart and always helped me discover faith and love in myself."

"You mean you didn't always have that?"

65

"I guess not always. But whenever I had any doubt, whenever I would find fault in myself and hate it, they would bring the lantern to my darkness and drive it out. In a way, they would heal me in ways I didn't realize until I think back on it now." Althea did seem to go then to a place far away in memory. Mireya just stared at her and felt the warmth of her thoughts and was happy about it.

"Lady Althea!"

Both women heard the servant's voice coming upon them fast and instinctually ducked lower in the water to cover themselves.

"Lady Althea, please come right away. Baldrik is calling for you, he's in some kind of trouble." Without asking for details, just as she always had, just as her mother and grandmother before her had done, she set right away to go towards suffering. She didn't even fully dry off or clothe herself. She simply put on a robe and ran barefoot towards Baldrik's rooms.

As Althea walked through the door, she saw Baldrik curled and bent inward muffling sounds of stifled pain. She quickly went to him to assess what was wrong. She wasn't sure how he came to be this way, but what she saw upon that bed brought tears to her eyes. Every part of this man she cherished had bent itself inward. His hands were fists clenched against their will and silent tears went down his face as he tried to mask his pain. "Oh, Baldrik," she whispered sympathetically.

"It's not that bad," he nearly spat out in false bravado. He looked up into her eyes to see if she was buying it, which of course she wasn't. But they let out an honest laugh at his attempt. "Listen," he said in seriousness, "don't you do what you did before. This isn't that bad. Just get me to limping, and I'll do the rest."

"You're not the boss of me," Althea said as she sent an attendant for supplies and began massaging the more bent parts of his hand.

Baldrik pulled his hand away from her or at least tried to. "I mean it," he said deepening his look into her eyes, "you will not give away yourself like that again. Not to me, not to anyone. This world needs more of what you have, and you're not going to be reckless with yourself on me." Althea made a move to protest before he stopped her. "You've made me strong, Althea. And not just the work with my body. I mean you've made all of me stronger, Althea. I have the will to fight because of you. So I mean it when I say get me to limping, and I'll manage the rest."

Althea felt overwhelmed with pride in her kindred brother, and even more remarkable still, she felt pride for herself. She had never heard thanks and unwavering trust like she had just heard. While she couldn't believe the words completely, she was still proud as much as she knew how.

Althea worked on Baldrik's muscles until they released their stiffness and spasms that kept him curled. The chorus of the night creatures began to hum through the window signaling the deep of the night and ringing out louder as the song Althea tried had died down and she covered Baldrik with blankets for sleep. It was then that she realized the time and felt her heart sink at missing her dinner.

Baldrik noticed her change in mood and asked what was wrong sleepily. His pain had subsided enough to allow him to sleep, and the fight he was putting up against the pain had rendered him exhausted. As much as he wanted to shrug off the veil of sleep to be there for Althea in her clear distress, her skills had been far too effective. He was asleep before she could respond. She brushed back his hair and doused the room's candles before she ran to her rooms.

The doors opened slowly and timidly as Althea peered from behind them like a guilty child. She wanted so much to find an empty room; she knew it would break her heart if Durai was still waiting for her. But there he was behind two candle stubs and cold, untouched food. She said from the door, "Oh, Durai. I am so so sorry. An emergency came up -"

"With Baldrik. I know. I gathered from the way the servants dashed in and out of here grabbing this and that." His hurt tone stung Althea and she felt herself flinch. She knew Durai had negative feelings toward Baldrik before, and she despised the thought they could get worse.

"You should have seen him, Durai," she began in a pleading tone. "Every joint in his body had stiffened into a curl. It was frightening. But we worked

67

through it, and he thanked me so very much." Althea tried to turn the situation to a lighter tone. She knew that Durai was protective, so she wanted to assure him that this situation was not like the last. She was hoping he would be relieved.

Instead, Durai rose from his seat and started to walk towards the door in a manner that made Althea's stomach drop to her feet. "Durai?"

He stopped with his back to her with his body held tall and stiff. "You left me here. You broke your word to me."

Althea had hardly seen it that way at all. Someone needed her, and she answered. She supposed she should have sent word to Durai, and suddenly she felt embarrassed. Durai turned around to face her. "Look at you," he said with his face downturned and sour. "You didn't keep your green dress as you promised." And then he looked at her in her robe and nothing more. "Were you with him barely dressed?!"

Althea had forgotten her state and pulled her robe in tighter. "I was with Mireya at the spring when they called -"

"And you couldn't be bothered to at least be decent. You went before another man nearly naked while I was here like a fool waiting for you to keep your promise?"

Althea dropped her head. She had not meant to hurt Durai at all, but she could see he was wounded by her. She had never hurt someone like this, and she wanted more than anything to not feel this way. When she raised her head to beg for forgiveness, he was gone.

....

The next morning there was a note on her door that Durai would be gone for an urgent errand by the Queen beyond Shimmer Plains to the other side of the Woods. She was quite sad that he had gone before she could clear things between them. Her soul was in torment, and she wanted to cry. She pushed the tears back until after breakfast.

Baldrik stood when she entered the dining hall and pulled a chair out for her. Though his movements were still stiff, they were much better. His grateful smile made her feel slightly better.

"Will Durai join us this morning, or did he get wrapped up in another book?" Mireya asked. Althea's head shot up in panic and confusion. Mireya's words echoed from a place far away, or so it felt.

"Wasn't he sent…I mean, didn't you send him to the Woods for some errand?" she nearly squeaked out like a mouse.

"No," Mireya said not seeing the color leave Althea's face and putting a bite of food into her mouth, "I haven't seen him for a few days actually. Why?"

Althea's sight faded to gray and sounds came through her ears like they were blocked with cotton. She rose from her chair clumsily, almost knocking it over.

"Excuse me, please. I left something in my room."

• • • • • • •

"What is it you're running from?"

"I don't really want to talk about it now. The sun is almost set, and we need to focus on a safe place to sleep."

"I want to know. Why did you run? Was it that you lost someone? Althea?"

"I…."

"Listen I know it's not easy, but it might help if you talked about it. Are you running because you lost someone you loved?"

"Yes."

To You, Your Father Should Be as a God

A young boy in the village looked upon the empty bed in an empty room where his mother used to sleep. His young face, no older than eleven or twelve years, was stoic as he took in the full bareness of the room that no longer held his mother's warm presence. He stood like a marble sculpture like those made by his father whose immense strength was carved often for the village and even for nobility at Courtside.

"She's gone, boy," the intimidating and almost frightening voice of his father spat from behind him. His father often had the ability to make people cower when he was in this mood, but the boy was unflinching in his vigil. He knew his father was a passionate man. "Selfish pig," his father added as he went back to his work outside the home. "Stupid bitch."

The father was a man of intensity that was often feared by others. The boy followed him often even as an infant and saw his many deeds. His father's strength was never questioned, and he never feared for safety because no one dared cross the man that towered like a mountain all his life. And the boy knew his father was a passionate man.

The boy still stood there in thought through the passing of the day in the empty room without his mother. He remembered her last embrace and kiss goodnight amidst his studies of spells. She was the one to embrace his early signs of aptitude in the art of Magic and nurture it like a young flame. And the next morning, she was gone.

However, she had not departed in death but ran into the night without warning leaving all her life behind. The boy kept thinking he would rather she had died. Leaving him behind with conscious purpose broke him far greater.

"My baby boy," the boy heard his mother's voice behind him. He hadn't even noticed the passage of day into night, but there he was in the light of the moon seeing his mother's face. She held him tightly and desperately as tears poured through her blackened eyes. "I found a place for us. So come with me now, but be very quiet."

The boy came back to himself from the far away he had been since she left. He saw her broken face and the mix of old scars among new cuts over her exposed arms. His father was a passionate man, the boy always knew that, and he registered then that his mother had come back to him and what she had done.

But he was not relieved. He was burned deeply by the betrayal he felt deep in his spirit knowing how easily she left him, how easily she took her love away from him. Instead, his face hardened further in his pain against this woman he trusted, loved so entirely, and who wounded him so easily.

"You left me, mom. You just…left me behind. Didn't even say a word."

"Shhh, baby. I am so sorry, but you know I had to. I was just finding a place to hide, a place that would take us in safety. And I found it now. I knew he wouldn't…not to you." She grabbed her precious son's hand and pulled for him to follow. "Please, baby, we don't have a lot of time. I don't know where he is."

The boy was unmoving against her pleas. His body stood rooted in place and paid no mind to the hurt and panic that spread across his mother's face. "You know I love you, and you still left. Do you even really love me at all, or are you taking me away to hurt him?"

Sweat poured down his mother's face as she was filled with panic over so much time wasted and the pangs of her child's words. "You know I love you!" she whispered quietly but fiercely. "With all my heart I love you."

"I don't believe you. You certainly aren't acting like you do, like you ever did. You want to take me away from my books, my things, my security, and my father who loves me! And he loves you too." The boy could see all the color leave his mother's face.

He knew his father was a passionate man.

"Your father…"

"My father, who is part of me, loves me, and he loves you so very much. He loves you even when you speak to other men in the village, he loves you even when you're late with dinner, and he loves you even when you don't understand him. He loves you because you are a part of me, too. If you don't love him,"

71

tears pushed from the boy's eyes if not from his heart, "do you even really love me?"

The woman fell to her knees before her son who she could see was suffering. Her child's every word cut like death into her heart.

"You ran away from us, and you didn't even try to be better for father and me who love you so much."

The woman was broken completely then, and she felt such shame and guilt overhearing what she had done to her baby boy. "I'm so sorry, my baby boy. I was so wrong. Please believe I didn't want to make you feel this way."

"Then you'll stay here with me?"

"I will stay," the woman said through painful sobs. To ease her son's doubting face, she kissed him and went into her bed as proof. She watched in torment as her hardened boy accepted her gesture and walked out of the room into the darkened hall.

The boy sensed his father's imposing aura even before he spoke from the darkness outside the door. "I'm impressed, boy." He said quietly but with genuine pride. "You did with words what I haven't been able to do with all I've done." His father stepped from the darkness toward his boy with his usual intense expression. "You really are something, far smarter than I gave you credit for."

His son just looked up at his father. He knew his father was a passionate man. "Just try not to screw it up." He had never been much afraid of his father, but now he had no trace of it. And his father knew it. He looked at his boy proud of the man in strength he had sculpted and knew that this was his greatest creation.

"You know, I think you're going to be far more powerful than we thought, Durai."

Oh, That Way Madness Lies

The herald signaled the return of Durai into the borders of Courtside, and Althea's mind and heart didn't quite know what to feel. She missed him too terribly this week he had been away with no letters or word from him, and she was relieved as well that he was returning safely from wherever he had been to. Over and over in the dark at night she heard Mireya's words echo even deep into her dreams: "I swear, Althea, I sent him nowhere."

Whatever drove him to leave and lie about it haunted her and caused the blood within her veins to run cold with panic. Was love so fragile as to break so easily? Maybe it was in the life away from fairy tales. What would she know, she was just a simple village girl.

When the herald's words reached the hall where the three of them sat, both Baldrik and Mireya tried secretly to look at Althea and gauge her state of mind; their tactics failed miserably. Althea could feel herself on the stage before them. They had both guessed that something must have happened, but Althea wouldn't talk about it. She just continued with her work diligently and even secluded herself amongst her suite of rooms and took some meals there alone. She was far too emotionally exhausted to put up a brave face for every moment of the day. To that extent, she went against her normal, social nature and was very distant.

The doors to the hall opened, and the three souls within found themselves holding their breath to see what had happened to Durai. Althea even closed her eyes somewhat as if her eyelids would hide or her make the tenseness disappear from the moment.

But Durai didn't come in the door. It was his guard, the one Althea had saved so long ago it seemed. He passed Althea trying hard to avoid a glance and went straight to the Queen and bowed. "Your Majesty, Durai reports his return but regrets his fatigue will keep him confined to his rooms tonight."

"Very well," Mireya said looking more at Althea than the guard. She dismissed him absently with a gesture. Mireya wanted so much to go to her sister, but just looking at Althea made her worry that this fragile, porcelain doll would break at a touch.

The guard walked past Althea as he departed and couldn't keep from looking at her. Althea tried to have a neutral face, but the expression she saw in the man took her by surprise. What was that look? It wasn't quite disdain, it wasn't quite disgust, it wasn't quite pity…whatever was she seeing in his eyes that he couldn't lock away?

The room was silent and still upon the guard's departure and the door to the hall closing. Finally, Althea looked up with the weight of indescribable despair in her eyes to her friends… her family. She didn't need to say out loud what was compelling her feet to walk out of the room in silence; Baldrik and Mireya understood without explanation her need to leave and be alone and free to feel the impact of the scene she was just a part of.

········

Althea lay asleep in her bed as the glow of the moon danced across her face between passing clouds. Each passing of the silver light showed the stain of tears dried upon her cheeks and her face swollen from hours of crying. Durai watched her sleep for a long time, still so awestruck by how beautiful she was, even now in neutral sleep.

But she would have to learn.

Althea felt the presence of Durai in the room after some time and slowly opened her eyes that strained against the movements. She saw him and froze not knowing what she should do. What action was right here? How could she know what to do when her own heart didn't know what to think?

Durai finally broke the silence with the neutral declaration, "I'm back." Althea braced herself hard against the tone of his voice. It had no music, no affection, and she felt like she had been slapped.

Finally, Althea pulled enough strength to speak. "Where were you? Mireya didn't send you on any mission." She fully expected then to see the remorse on his face for his deception, but he was as unchanging as the face of the mountain. And this hurt her even more. "You lied to me, Durai."

"Does that distress you?" he asked still aggravatingly even and calm.

"You're good and damn right it distressed me!" She wanted to strike him then, and she had never wanted to strike anyone in all her life. "How could you do that? How could you make me worry so much? Why would you do such a thing?!" She was breathless as she asked these things terrified not so much of the answer but more dismayed at her anger. It made her feel so far away from all that she was. The very nature of a Healer and who she was - her mother's daughter - kept her closer to love and farther from negative anger. It was how she had existed her whole life.

Up until now.

Durai saw everything he had done to her play before his eyes, and he began to sink slightly at her words. Then he looked at her with pain and hurt. "You know then. You know how I had felt that night. Waiting here without a word, without a sign that you cared about me. You know now how I felt as you lied."

Althea shook her head in disgusted confusion as if she tasted something putrid in her mouth. "I lied?"

"You broke your word to me that you would come to me. Is not breaking your word not the same as a lie?"

Althea's boiling blood stopped dead within her remembering his words that night and remembering the pain in his eyes. It was the same pain he was feeling now. "But this is not the same…" she tried to explain as much to herself as to him.

"No," he said not in question but fact, "yours was worse. You were the first to break the trust between us. I was ready to hand over my very soul to you, and I found out that night I didn't even warrant an afterthought from you. Am I just a play-thing to you? Are my feelings so paltry?" Durai started to bring the tears from his eyes if not from his heart.

Althea heard his words and saw his hurt. And like the sun pushing through thick clouds, all her loving heart came to her and whispered all his words back to her. She had sworn not to harm, and to the man she loved, she had done the most dreadful harm of all. She was overcome with the grief of knowing how she had broken the heart who held her own.

She got out of bed and dropped to her knees before his feet, just as he had done before. "I am so sorry," she whimpered through her sorrow and remorse.

"You know now, then?" His voice was deep and daunting, with no music in it at all, and she feared no forgiveness either.

"Yes," she squeaked like a small child before her disapproving parent.

"And?" He asked.

Did he want more? What more could she give him? But as she looked up into the face of the man she adored more than she loved herself, she realized that there was always something more she could give him, more she would give him.

"I will do anything to make it up to you." She didn't know how she had any tears left, but they managed to find themselves flowing from her eyes. Durai caressed her face from his tall stance. This small gesture of affection so relieved Althea that she breathed out a small sob she had been holding back. Durai still stood before her and caressed the top of her head. "I love you," she said in gratitude that he had made some show of forgiveness.

"Of course you do."

With Devotion's Visage and Pious Action We Do Sugar O'er the Devil Himself

In the following weeks, Althea was like a pet with its tail between its legs. She was lovingly devoted to Durai in his return and did everything she could to prove her humble affection to him and that she did deeply care for his feelings. And with each loving demonstration, she received half-hearted returns. He would smile with her from a place of superiority and a distance she felt very keenly.

It slowly started to drain her spirit. Even Baldrik and Mireya noticed that she had lost some of her natural glow. Her heart was only half in her work with Baldrik. He didn't complain. In fact, he was feeling very well as the spring started to approach, but he was increasingly concerned for his Althea who he treasured very much. Mireya sometimes would brush Althea's hair in a deafening silence not saying a word and realized that what concerned her the most was that Althea didn't even notice that they were not talking. She just sat looking forward in a place far away.

One night Althea forgot to go to the dining hall for dinner. She had just sat near her greenhouse looking at the setting sun and not fully feeling the cold. Her hands had turned slightly purple as the sun set, and still, she sat watching the sun disappear.

"I brought you some dinner."

Althea hardly registered Durai's voice behind her. He walked in front of her and saw her pale face and discolored fingers. He quickly grasped her hands in his to warm them up. "What are you doing out here? Do you want to fall ill?" She looked up at him and his questions, but she couldn't see him. He picked her up and quickly brought her inside to the bed. He covered her with thick blankets and rubbed warmth into her.

Once she had regained some color back in her face, he decided to try and reach her from the far place she hid herself, "Listen, Althea. We both know that you are sorry for what you did, but getting yourself sick will not prove anything." Althea barely felt the warmth of a tear run down her face. "I forgive you, Althea, if it will stop you from doing this to yourself. No matter how hurt I am, seeing you do this hurts me even more."

As Durai finally stated forgiveness even after all this time, Althea started to come around. She wanted so much to feel his embrace and his loving kiss again, though even at these words she dare not assume the first move to him. She simply looked at him with understanding and obedience. "I'm so sorry. I won't break my word ever again."

"I know you won't."

That night they embraced each other and kissed as they once had. He held her with the devotion and ardent passion as he had before, and she succumbed to his possession with such grateful pleasure that she felt tears of relief spring from her eyes after their lovemaking. As he rolled onto his back after the throws of their passionate reconciliation, she lay on her side and clutched at him needing him terribly. She passed out despite her desperate struggle to stay awake; she was physically and emotionally exhausted – spent in every way.

As her breathing slowed and Durai knew that she was asleep against him, he shifted to face her and watch her sleeping face. "Mine," he whispered. "You will always be mine, my lovely dove."

· · · · · · ·

The light of the sun the next morning woke Althea slowly from her deep sleep. As the fog of dreams lifted from her, she remembered the night before. She turned frantically half expecting to find herself alone in her bed. Her heart was elated to see that Durai had remained with her throughout the night.

"I'm so glad you're still here," she admitted.

"I felt that you earned a good night's sleep." She was relieved at his kindness and brought her bare chest to lay with his. He slowly caressed her back as she embraced him and savored her smooth, naked skin. His desire for her increased with every inch he felt of her until they both could see the evidence of his lustful intent. Althea smiled at this thankful that she could still elicit this kind of emotion from him despite all she felt she had done to him. Perhaps he truly had forgiven her.

They lovingly caressed each other long into the morning forgetting about breakfast until a knock at the door roused them from their fervor. "My lady?" a lady's voice from behind the door beckoned.

Althea looked at Durai who teasingly kissed down her neck as she tried to respond. "I am not decent," she replied trying not to give herself away. "I'm dressing. What is it?"

Muffled giggling came from behind the door. Obviously, Durai and Althea were fooling no one. "My lady, My Lord Baldrik inquires about you. He is ready for his daily regiment with you."

"I'll be there as fast as I can!" Althea called back to dismiss the girls at the door who will no doubt be rushing to gossip to the rest of the castle.

Althea kissed Durai and moved to get dressed and start with her responsibilities. "Where are you going?" Durai asked with his expression instantly changed.

Althea looked back at him and was confused. "I'm getting dressed?" she more asked than exclaimed. "It's time for my work with Baldrik."

His darkened expression stopped her from going any further. "So he calls, and you would leave me just like that? He says jump…"

"No?" she answered still confused and a new type of scared that came without her realizing it had arrived. "It's not like that. He needs my help…"

"What about I need you?" he asked as he rolled onto his back and exposed more of his bare chest reminding her very much of what she was walking away from. "We were busy, and I was needing you. I AM needing you. Doesn't that matter?"

Althea discarded her robe she hadn't had a chance to slip into and went to his side as though he were a wounded animal. "Of course that matters. You matter a great deal to me. I love you."

"Then I think you should start acting like it." Althea searched his face for signs of a joke or deception and found only seriousness as hard as stone. "I am the man you love. You may go when I am finished. Don' you owe me at least that?"

Althea felt aggrieved from his biting words and the look in his eyes. How could she just leave him like this after she had just started to gain his trust? She did love him, and she decided she should stop simply saying the words. The man she loved deserved to feel that devotion completely and without a doubt. And he was doubting her love, and that was a fault with her – or so she felt. It was up to her to change it. Besides, Baldrik had been doing so well for about a month; it wouldn't hurt him to wait.

She slipped into bed beside him. "That's right, Dove. Don't fly away from me." His hungry arms held her tightly and possessively.

But Never Doubt I Love

"Althea, sis, are you ok?"

Althea hadn't even noticed that she had stopped massaging Baldrik's slightly swollen leg as she looked worriedly at the door. She had wondered if Durai would be coming in that morning to watch or if he would stay away. She wasn't sure which she preferred.

"Huh? Oh, I'm sorry. Is it feeling any better?" she asked as she resumed her pressure and motion.

Baldrik bent over and took her hands in his. "Never mind that," he said with genuine concern in his eyes. "I want to know if you're ok." Althea looked at him confused. "You've been late all week, you haven't been eating much, and you don't look like you've been sleeping."

It was true that she had not been sleeping well. Her sleep had been haunted with dreams of disappointing Durai again, experiencing his hurt all over again. But more than that, she had dreams of the fast-running river and mysterious fog for the last two nights. This vision troubled her most of all, and she found that she could not return to sleep for fear of its return.

"Just some troubled sleep is all; bad dreams. It's nothing. I'm sure it will pass. I'm sorry I've been late. It's probably something I ate."

"I doubt that; you've barely eaten at all."

Baldrik's words didn't seem to register again.

"What have you been dreaming about?"

Althea looked nervously towards the door. "Oh, just the occasional bump in the night stuff. The kind you don't go back to sleep easily from," she said nervously presenting her half-truth.

Baldrik seemed to battle within him over a response. "Althea," he started determined to speak his heart truthfully, "I'm really worried. I don't mean to put my business where it doesn't belong, but you've seemed ... I don't know, off? I don't mean to pry at all in your private relationship, but since Durai went away, you know... lying to you, you ..." Baldrik was suffering; he didn't have faith in

81

his words to fully convey his caring intent. Seeing her eyes darken at the mention of what transpired between her and Durai only made him fumble more.

"I'm not sure what you mean," Althea admitted genuinely. She believed to be much better now that they had reconciled, besides the dreams. She was spending more time with the man she loved, he seemed much happier now and more satisfied with their relationship which made her happy, and she was making more time for things away from working so hard after following his suggestion. Of course, those things away from work she loved doing most were being with him and seeing him smile. She was very perplexed at Baldrik's concern.

Baldrik led her to the mirror against the wall in his room. He placed her in front of it while standing behind her. "Look at you," he said painfully. "Your eyes have lost their shimmer. You've lost your color. When was the last time you went outside? You're always here with me or hidden away with Durai." Althea's brow furrowed at the suggestion that this was wrong. Baldrik tried to redirect, "I'm not saying don't spend time with him. But maybe get some fresh air. And maybe just spend some time with you for yourself. Your hair has even started to thin a bit."

Althea wanted to ignore his words as ignorant and maybe jealous, but her guard against his truth was penetrated by the intense concern in his eyes. He did love her as family, and she was reminded that she did love him too. She had forgotten that it was ok to love someone as a brother and not a lover. When she woke to the fact that his words were not in malice, she did take a look at herself. She saw through his eyes and became even more confused. Was she becoming ill? She certainly looked like it.

Baldrik gently turned her around to face him. The warmth of his affection almost burned her in her fatigue, and she involuntarily looked down in shame. Baldrik lifted her chin, "Please don't think I'm scolding you. I have no right even if I was. I just..." he faltered as his voice broke. "Please be careful. I just want you to be well and happy. Your soul deserves only the best of things."

Althea said, "I am happy." The words trailed off at the end as if carried away to wither in the sun.

Baldrik simply replied, "I just want you to be happy."

• • • • • • •

Durai was held up with a meeting of the Courtside nobles, so for the first time in a long time, Althea had time to herself. She wasn't entirely sure what she could or should do with herself. Before she realized it, she found herself slowly walking the halls of the castle without purpose or direction. Her mind was swirling like a whirlpool in a rushing river tossing between Baldrik's words, the sight of her tired face, and the nightmares she was being plagued with.

In her wanderings, she came to a common area for the palace guards and attendants and encountered Durai's guard that she had healed. She was jolted out of her absentminded haze by his stare. Again, he looked at her with that indescribable expression. While the whole area was a continuous motion of interaction, laughter, and conversation, he alone stood still and intent.

She wasn't sure if it was her fatigue or exactly what possessed her to confront him, but the words spilled forth even before she herself knew they were inside her. "Have I done something to wrong you? I can't understand these looks I'm getting." She didn't even recognize her own voice. She really must be tired, she thought to herself. But she spoke from her heart, and she wouldn't apologize for it.

The guard looked down briefly as if realizing she really wouldn't understand his reactions to her. He had been watching her for a very long time. He saw this once vibrant flower wither and dry as if plucked from the earth. He came to her and pulled her away from the crowd into the hall. He was taller than she remembered and much stronger. He was built like the very hill on which the castle stood. His aura was proud but also sensitive she sensed. Though he appeared domineering, something radiating from him was far from malignant.

"Look at you," he said with a voice he didn't expect. She had braced herself for a voice that boomed like thunder, but instead, she heard something much lighter. "I mean, just look at you. This is not what you were when you arrived here - when I first met you... when you healed me." His face turned and contorted at the memory of that day, and she was surprised at it. She didn't understand where this feeling was coming from.

"I don't understand what you mean," she lied.

"Yeah, I'm sure you don't," he replied sarcastically as he looked over his shoulder to make sure no one had followed them. He grasped her by the shoulders, and she looked down at his hands in shock at his boldness. She fought the fear she had at his sudden grasp on her and tried to remain controlled; she was just so tired. "You used to shine like the sun; everything about you glowed. It's all gone now, hasn't it? You look like you could fall over in a second." Even as he spoke, she could feel her weakness.

The guard continued to look past her into the hall and behind his shoulders. "You know what I'm talking about, don't you?" he whispered to her.

"I really don't," Althea replied not matching his quiet volume, which prompted another scan from the guard.

"Your spirit is being sucked dry, isn't it?"

Althea opened her mouth to protest, but she found she couldn't. All she could do is stand there with her mouth open as if silenced by the force of God himself.

He took a deep breath as if he made a decision. "You saved my life. When it all comes down to it, the rest doesn't matter. I'm sorry for what I've harbored against you. It wasn't your fault."

Now Althea was really confused as to what he was talking about. He didn't have the patience or energy to try and solve riddles. "What are you trying very hard not to say?" she asked trying not to sound as annoyed as she felt. "I'm sorry, I'm usually more patient," she added as she realized how unlike herself she had become with this man.

"Please, for both our sakes, keep my words between us." He stopped until she responded. His eyes practically begged for her to understand, so she nodded. "You saved my life, now let me try to save yours."

"Save...?"

"Shhhh," he said as he looked around again. "That day that you met me and Durai, that was not the first time he saw you. He came to Base Village some weeks before to collect a child for training to be an Enchanter. He saw you walking across the way from him. He noticed your hair, he noticed your glow, he seemed like a man possessed.

"I've known Durai for many years. I've seen his charm, his craftiness. Never once in my life have I seen him *not* get what he wants. And that day that he saw you, he had decided that he would have you."

The man paused hoping that he wouldn't have to continue, that she would have the wits to figure out what he was trying to tell her without him having to say it. But she was too spent and too in shock over his desperate tone to think clearly.

"He set up a trap for you. He was the hunter; you were his prey. I don't know why; I never try to fully understand him. I'm sure if he just asked..."

"What do you mean 'trap?'" she asked still registering what he was saying.

He took another labored breath, "I'm sorry." He tried again slowly and with more control. "Durai wanted you from the moment he saw you. He could think or speak of little else for a week. All his world revolved around having you. You had put a spell on him. And when he gets this way, he finds any way to get what he wants.

"He wanted to see all you could do, to get close to you. I didn't fall from my horse that day. That gash was no accident. He had to find any way to get you close and to see what you were capable of."

Althea felt as if she wasn't truly there, that she was still in a nightmare. She willed herself with all she could to try and wake up. She couldn't possibly be hearing what she was hearing. Wasn't she also hearing the fast-flowing river now?

85

Before she could come to herself, he looked past her and down the hall and left her side quickly. She was alone with too many questions and too many thoughts. She thought back to every detail she could possibly recall of that day.

Hadn't Durai worried over his man? She couldn't recall his concern, only his eyes on her and her work. Hadn't he hurried into her hut with urgency? To be honest, she couldn't rely on her memories of that day; it all seemed to happen slowly like the fluid nature of a dream. Well didn't they both confirm this was a terrible accident? They did, but she did remember the look between them when she asked about what happened. Like there was something wrong...

Then all that was wrong with the meeting came to her very clearly. The man wasn't on his horse to ride away as she followed Durai; he was off the horse waiting for her as if he knew she would be coming - as if it were planned. My God had the man she loved sacrificed this man's life just to …

She flinched at the hand on her shoulder that came from behind her.

"Sorry to keep you waiting, Dove."

Devils Soonest Tempt, Resembling Spirits of Light

Upon hearing his voice from behind her, given all she had heard and all she was battling in her mind, her heart broke. She was dying inside attacked by fear, doubt, love, desperation, and pain. She readied her face to hide the secrets of her tortured soul as she looked into the eyes of her lover. He looked at her with a look that was equally seductive and equally terrifying. Before her stood the man she loved, and she couldn't understand how she could be so passionately devoted and overwhelmingly petrified.

"Who was that you were speaking to, Dove?"

Althea swallowed the growing bulge in her throat as she forced a smile to her lips. "I was taking a walk. I ran into your guard. I…I haven't seen him since that day. He looks well…I mean no lingering problems from his injury." Her voice trembled despite her every effort to appear normal. She could even feel the blood fleeing from her face in her distress. She prayed he would not see the cold sweat she found herself in.

But he kept looking at her with his eyes still piercing straight into her heart and soul. He still held power over her, and his handsome face and devoted gaze weakened her knees as they always had. Whatever she had thought before had to be the result of fatigue, madness, even sickness. Maybe she just needed rest. This was her most precious heart, the very completion of her soul. Suspicion of him would damn herself. Before her stood the man she loved. Although, something in his eyes and his face kept shaking her deeply.

He took her hand and placed it on his arm as he led her away from the common area not saying a word. His silence was comforting. Or was it frightening? Althea decided to just keep close to him either way. How could she not be safe in love?

Durai passed Althea's room and continued with her to his own room. Althea didn't even realize she had unintentionally slowed down in apprehension until she felt his forceful tugging of her resistant arm. She muttered some small apology as she continued with him through the doors of his room growing darker with the setting sun.

"Shall I get us something to eat?" Durai asked. Had his voice become deeper? Althea hadn't even realized she had missed a meal. How late was it? Perhaps she truly was losing her mind or becoming ill.

Before her stood the man she loved.

"Not unless you're hungry."

Durai didn't answer this. He had closed the doors to his suite behind him, and he now moved her to the bedroom. Althea was hoping that she could find some way to gracefully excuse herself. She certainly had no energy to reciprocate advances tonight. She looked and studied the room as best she could, but she was too unfocused, too tired. She was so drained that even her eyes began to darken in fatigue. No, not her eyes, the other doors were being shut along with the window coverings. She could barely see a thing now.

"I see more than you think, my love." She could hear his deep voice dancing through the room with the most ominous melody. She widened her eyes to try and see further into the black. She felt his hands first behind her pulling her long hair back away from her shoulders. His hands brushed past the skin of her neck. "I saw the way he looked at you, my flighty dove. Not that I blame him, my beautiful girl. What man could help but look on you with such lust?"

She felt his hands travel from her neck down her back and move around her waist. It wasn't a gentle caress as his touch had been before. There was a powerful pressure that sent a shiver through her body. "I'm afraid," she stammered, "I don't quite know…"

He turned her around quickly. She could barely make out the details of his face but knew full well the intensity behind it. "I'm sure you don't. You are my simple girl, so innocent." She couldn't tell if he was toying with her, and she wanted to buckle and collapse. It would be easier to just feign fainting and run from it all. But something in her would not let her.

Before her stood the man…

She reached deep within her for strength. She raised her hand to his face and caressed it with gentle strokes, tender and soft. She sought to calm his fire, use every last power she had left to her to push back his passions wherever they might dangerously lead. But the mere touch of her skin to his made his appetites boil out of control. "Durai, I didn't sleep well last night. Could we perhaps discuss this tomorrow?"

He grabbed her hand, and his very eyes glowed with unnatural light. She stepped back thinking she had hallucinated in her exhaustion. Indeed it was no hallucination. He had called forth Magic she could not understand. In the stillness of a sealed room, she could feel the movement of air like the heated wind before a storm. His eyes seemed to devour her and dimly light the room in their vivid glow. And though she tried to step further away, he held firmly to her hand.

Then came his voice, but it was not his voice. It was the breath of darkness and deep, untouched mysticism that rose from the core of the earth that came from his lips. "You are mine. You belong to only me." He pulled her hand behind him to draw her closer. She wanted to let out a scream in her shock and fright, but his lips were hard upon hers before she could let out a sound. "You are mine!"

Before her stood...

Her lover was gone. Instead, she was held by the Devil himself. She could not recognize the man in front of her. "Durai, please. You're scaring me." All she could make out of his eyes were slits of pure, brilliant green. She wanted to turn and run, but she dared not turn her back on him. And if she ran, where would she go? But how could she stay? "Durai, please," she felt tears behind her eyes, but even they were too afraid to fall. "Please don't."

Durai seemed not to hear, or if he did, her fear excited him more. He took her still bound hand and drew it to his ravenous lips. This gave her just enough room to take a further step back, but she was close to the wall with nowhere to go. She could hear a low growl in the room like that of a feral beast in the woods, primal and voracious.

Before she knew what had happened, she was against the wall with the pressure of his body against hers. Her hand was still bound in his and raised above her and pinned to the wall just as her body was. He grabbed her other hand to do the same. Still, all she could see were the glowing green of his eyes. His lips kissed her neck in desire. She could feel his intentions harden against her hips, and the air left her lungs in distress.

"No…please…"

"Mine!"

As he pushed himself onto her, against her, into her, she desperately searched every limb she had to fight back. She felt her head knock against the wall with every ardent thrust, and the pain began to overtake all conscious thought. Soon she forgot all about fighting or escaping and merely focused on surviving. She felt him overtake every inch of her feverishly and violently. And his lips remained on her leaving passionate signatures with every motion, punctuating every crash against her soul. He had truly become the fire that devoured the field in the heated summers that destroyed all in its appetite.

She wasn't sure when she had been moved to the bed or how long he continued there. She was far away now locked deep within herself. She only came back from her hiding place when she felt the motion stop and the weight lift off of her broken body. Her heart that loved him and her mind that protected her could not reconcile with themselves. She was his, and he was hers, but how could this feel so very wrong?

Durai's familiar voice reached her ears then, the voice that she had heard before was gone, and she flinched at the sound. "You see what you do to me?"

…………..

"What is it you're running from?"

"I don't really want to talk about it now. The sun is almost set, and we need to focus on a safe place to sleep."

"I want to know. Why did you run? Was it that you lost someone? Althea?"

"I…."

"Listen I know it's not easy, but it might help if you talked about it. Are you running because you lost someone you loved?"

"Yes."

"Who?"

"I lost myself."

A Wretched Soul, Bruised with Adversity

Althea walked towards the sound of the raging river knowing for the first time that she was in her nightmare. And she was glad of it. She looked deep into the river's rushing waters to watch the pieces of bank break away. Instead, submerged in the river, she saw her own body lying deep beneath the current. Her eyes were open under the water fully conscious and aware, but she lay perfectly still, unmoving and wretched. Althea watched her body in the water begin to break apart piece by piece as the river bank had before and was carried off in the uncaring rush of water.

In the distance, she heard the deep voice of the earth crying out to her. "Mine!"

She raised her head to the opposite bank towards the shadows of the woods. Her eyes were met with a pair of green eyes piercing through the blackness. And from these eyes came the fog slowly crawling towards her. She could even make out hands outstretched to her. As much as she willed her limbs to run, as too often in dreams, she could not move.

"No!"

Her cry pushed like a wind, and all before her had been blown away in its force. She looked around at only darkness, only pitch before her. She could feel herself drowning in it, and she was ready to be consumed by it.

"We are here."

She felt hands on her shoulders and heard the words flow into her ears as sweet as honey. She didn't need to turn to face the voices, she knew them all too well. She simply sat in the darkness on her knees in guilt and despair. The hands became arms encircling her, embracing her.

Her mother.

Her grandmother.

"We are here. Oh, my precious girl, we are here."

"Momma..."

"It's time to get up now."

"But, grandma, my body is broken."

"Will you simply let the river take you away? Will you let the darkness win?" Althea finally willed herself to face her matriarchs. They were beings of pure white light, their features barely distinguishable in the rays. She wanted to run to them, to hold them tight and not let go. She wanted to be taken away with them. More than anything. Instead, their light extended into her. She felt embraced by them deeper than any physical touch.

"Althea, we are the protector of the lights in all hearts. We are Healers." She saw her mother and grandmother speak as one, and as their voices ended, they gestured behind her.

Althea turned as she was instructed to see herself. She was with Mireya. She saw her with her chosen sister as she told her, "I am the protector of the lights in all hearts. I am the soldier against the extinguishing darkness and the suffering that snuffs out the light. If I were to stop, it would defile the very blood in me. I turn my back on my mother, my grandmother, and those who battle with me. This is who I am; this is who you cannot stop me to be." She remembered this time when she spoke with Mireya. Seeing her image from before, she could see clearly now the glow she had lost.

"Do not let the darkness win."

●●●●●●●

Althea opened her eyes to the soft glow just before the dawn in her room, her sheets damp with sweat as they had for the past two weeks since the night of her encounter with Durai. Since that night he had her constantly at his side with superiority in his affectionate possession towards her. He had dominated most of her time, and her strength had dried up even more than before. She hadn't even tried to put on a façade of bravery or happiness with Baldrik and Mireya, and they didn't know what to do or say. It was as if their sister was dying before their eyes, and they didn't know why.

The morning was unseasonably warm, and Althea rose from her bed still weak but now determined. She stepped onto her patio and faced the rising sun.

When the rays burst forth from the top of the horizon giving birth to the day, she recoiled in its brilliance but steeled herself to face it. The light of the sun that morning resembled the light of her dreams that came from her mother and grandmother.

"Don't let the darkness win."

"I won't."

Althea turned with as much strength as she had left. She felt somewhat renewed and strengthened by her mother and grandmother in a way she couldn't explain. She went about her room taking stock of what she had, what she could use, and assessed what she needed. Her movements were lethargic still, but she continued steadily as the sun rose.

Footsteps were audible outside her door, and she knew that it was Durai coming to escort her to the dining hall. She hid her morning's labors and adjusted herself to present a normal guise and demeanor. He opened the door and walked to her in his accustomed grace and confidence. He looked her up and down in her green gown which pleased him greatly. Before him stood the woman he loved, and she belonged to him.

"You look radiant this morning," his musical voice floated into her ears making her heart break even more. She could never again hear the sound of his voice without hearing what she heard from him that night. She could never again look in his loving eyes without seeing its dangerous glow and passionate possession. She could never again feel the embrace of his arms or his skin caressing hers without feeling the pain he had inflicted throughout her body in his ardent violation of her. Even now, the bruises he inflicted upon her hadn't even fully healed.

He bent down to kiss her lips and moved to her neck. Althea tried not to be as stiff as stone, but she knew no other way to respond. Durai didn't seem to notice or rather didn't care for her discomfort at all. He took her waist and led her out towards the dining hall.

Throughout the meal, she tried to eat more than she had been previously to regain her strength. But these long months of reduced appetite shriveled her stomach to only hold so much. Baldrik and Mireya were elated to see her eating as much as she was and to see her smiling again not even realizing the mask she was wearing.

Althea took long looks at the people she loved as she sat beside the man she now hated.

God Knows When We Shall Meet Again

Althea waited for the cover of darkness on a night without a moon to leave. She had effectively sealed herself away in her room alone that night dodging Durai's advances more skillfully than she had thought she could. She glided through her room collecting the packs she had hidden away. She had very carefully gathered many supplies, packed away salves and medical necessities, and chose food and tools to give her the best chance of surviving in the wild away from anyone and everyone.

The week that passed from her dream to her departure had been one of silent resolve. Althea slowly regained her strength by eating more, resting more, and using her time with Baldrik and away from Durai for her own healing as well. When she was with Durai, she retreated into herself back into a place she made for her soul where she couldn't feel all of his caresses, his lips against her body, and every opportunity he had to possess her. She became a shell of herself hidden in a place all her own deep inside her mind. And the worst part was that he didn't seem to notice.

She had special clothes made with her own hands in neutral colors of the earth. No loose-flowing skirts or decorative embellishments, only breathable cloth for lightweight, skin-hugging pants and shirts. She knew she would have to be on her own far from any village or town, away from anyone who could see her face and know her and bring her back. She had to be sure to make herself as hardened and prepared for the challenges of her solitude away from the comforts of society as possible. She had to become more a child of the earth than she had ever been before even at her simple hut. But anything was better than this.

She opened the door that night for the last time quietly and carefully. Her movements were as stealthy and noiseless as a cat's. Her packs and supplies were fastened tightly against her and didn't make a sound with her hurried steps. And as she had studied every small path in the castle, she avoided the detection of even the tenured guards.

The first place she stopped was Mireya's room while Mireya was fast asleep. She felt the regret hardened in her heart upon seeing the woman she loved so very much asleep. She knew Mireya would be terribly hurt to find her gone without a goodbye. But she couldn't risk Mireya trying to stop her. She was the Queen, after all. Althea stood for some time and watched her sleep. She smiled as Mireya snored daintily every other inhale, and she forced herself not to cry at the thought of how desperately she would miss her.

As Althea turned to leave, she stopped at Mireya's bedside table and placed a small, hand-held hairbrush that belonged to her down on it. Althea remembered how they would trade with each other back and forth sessions of brushing hair and grooming each other affectionately. Althea could even hear their laughter in the walls and felt Mireya's hands stroking her hair saying, "You do have such heavenly hair! Cast a spell for me, and make mine like yours!"

"I'm sorry, Mireya."

She opened the passage and walked without a sound to Baldrik's room. She didn't know what she would do for him, she had no trinket and she had already stocked his rooms with all the salves and ointments she knew for him. But she had to see him, even this one last time. She had to take one last look at the brother that birth hadn't given her, but love had.

His eyes were closed as he was stretched out on his bed. She wrestled hard with the thoughts of staying if only just for him and Mireya. But she would be destroyed if she stayed. The darkness would win. And she made a promise.

"Can't sleep?" she heard a voice say in the darkness from the soul in the bed. Althea jumped and wanted to duck or run or hide, but stood frozen in indecision instead. Baldrik hadn't even opened his eyes, but he knew she was there. "Yeah, it's too warm tonight for -" Baldrik stopped mid-sentence as he opened his eyes and saw Althea the way she was. He saw it all: the pack, the clothes, the supplies, and the resolution in her eyes. And she could see in him the moment it all registered and his heart broke.

"So where will you go?"

"As far away as I can to disappear. Baldrik, I -"

He held up his hand and lifted his face to her more as he sat up in the bed. She saw the tears threatening to fall, and she could no longer hold back her own. "I know you cannot stay. I see more than you know,"

At the sound of those words, her mind was thrown into a panicked trauma response thrusting her back into that night and all that had happened. Baldrik saw her freeze up and knew instantly how much she had to get out. No one could live like this.

"I've been watching you slowly wither like a plucked flower. I can only assume it was something with him." Althea winced visibly. "See? I knew it. If I had the power, if I were only stronger, I'd send him away myself. But even Mireya isn't that powerful, not really. Not against him."

"That's why I have to disappear. And that's why you can't tell Mireya. You know how she is; she'd act against him and fail."

"I know."

Althea sat on the bed, and they both took each other's hands. For the longest time, they sat together in silence. They didn't need to say a word, their love was passed between them, and they would know each other forever. They knew without saying that they would be a part of each other no matter the time and no matter the distance.

If only they could part tonight.

Althea grasped his hands more tightly as she spoke through her tears. "I thought I would be here forever - until we all grew old together and died happily. My family. I thought for sure we'd be together for all the many years of our lives."

"I didn't."

Althea looked on in surprise.

"I knew this wasn't going to last. At first, I thought I would be going soon. I was so sure that I would meet death before I became an old man. Hell, even before I saw another five years. And then you came. You gave me hope; you gave me my life back. But as time went on, I knew it was you who wouldn't live for long. Not if you stayed.

"I saw you shrink; I saw you thin into the earth as if you were the rain swallowed in the heat. I noticed every possessive and dominating glance he gave you and every wincing recoil you had in return. I still don't know for sure what he had done, and I don't need to. Knowing you and knowing how he changed you, that's enough for me. I saw in every way how he swallowed you up and sucked you dry. You lost yourself in him. In a way, I lost you too when that happened."

"Why didn't you tell me?"

"I tried. So many times I tried. But you were so far gone, first in love, then denial, and then in misery. I'm surprised you had the strength to stand to come every day as you did. I'm surprised you hadn't already died. But now -"

Baldrik faltered as he lost control and his chest wracked with silent sobs. He was so torn with joy and pain and pride and despair that he couldn't remain the stalwart picture he wanted so much to be.

"I sometimes would lay awake at night and thought about life without you, sis. I imagined you dying and how all would cry when we should have protected you, I imagined how he would look so destroyed in the wake of his destruction, and I wondered if my heart could take it. And I dreamed over and over of you leaving and taking all of my hope with you. I fantasized about how I would stop you, how I could hold you here with just a look, or how you would cry at leaving me behind and think that you should stay. I was so ashamed of those thoughts, but I don't want you to go.

"But now I know that you're keeping alive in yourself that hope within me when you go. You'll be safe, Althea, you'll be alive. More than anything for myself, I want that. Only that."

"Please…please don't say that. You have strength for yourself, too. Remember all the work we've done, and you'll make –"

The more she thought of how he couldn't possibly survive without her here the more she lost the will to go. Even if she had drilled exercises into his mind and supplied him with all she ever had, he would need more than that someday. Maybe not today or tomorrow, but soon and desperately. And she will have abandoned him who she loved even as she loved her family in blood. His pain would be on her. She was condemning him to such suffering.

"No. I can't…"

Baldrik gripped her hand and became as resolute as a force of nature. "Don't you do that. Don't you dare back down now. Whether you run away and go from here or you stay and slowly die, you're gone from me. I'd much rather you be alive and gone from sight than watch you die. You and Mireya are all that I have, and losing even one of you to death would end me. If I'm wrong about everything I ever thought I knew, the way I feel for you is a fact without question. Althea, I love you. I love you as any brother ever loved a sister."

In the same instant, with the same motion, they pulled each other close into an embrace and bonded so complete they were as one person, one light in the dark. Baldrik felt himself die and be born over and over again while he begged his heart to stop shattering inside his chest. Althea pulled back and placed her hands upon his face for what she knew was the last time. He held her hand to his lips and kissed it gently and lovingly.

"No matter what happens, you take a part of me with you always. Whatever you may hear, no matter what the world may bring, you stay away and keep me with you here." He reached out and held his palm against her heart. He held it there, felt its beating, felt her alive. If he had nothing left to give in this world, he'd sacrifice anything to keep her heart going.

"Don't you give up. You have a part of me in there too."

As the West swallows the light of day in the end, they slowly released each other into the night with a pain that would scar forever. Baldrik watched as she skillfully disappeared into the night into safety and into memory. He held onto the feel of her embrace and held tight to the last sound he heard of her voice with the beautiful pain it was bringing.

"No promises."

Part 2

Hell is Empty and All the Devils are Here

One Year Before the Present Day
Two Months After Althea Disappeared

•••••••

The doors to the throne room opened. Mireya sat on her throne utterly spent. She had been exhausted in the grief of loss, the pain of broken hope, and the anger over what had become of everything she loved. She had lost her color and energy as she had been up many nights with the nobles and delegates of many towns and villages since the coming of the Mist just a week ago. Even her three Healers that had been brought to replace Althea could do little against the abuse her body and spirit had so recently suffered.

Durai walked up the carpeted path towards his sovereign in his same accustomed grace and confidence. Mireya hardly let him fully arrive before her before she spoke with seething anger and disappointment, "What happened, Durai?"

Durai took a knee before her and bowed his head in a show of contrition. "My Lady, I do not know. I have reviewed the spells over and over. Some miscalculation -"

"Obviously!" She raised her voice to a near shout. "But you don't make miscalculations, Durai. You're the most careful, calculating man I know." Mireya barely let slip some of the hostility she had held against her trusted court Enchanter. Since Althea's disappearance, she had looked upon him for answers and received none where before he had them all, and she didn't know how well she could trust that.

"My Lady," Durai began feigning deep remorse flawlessly, "even the wisest and most vigilant soul can make a mistake. That is the nature of life itself. Don't we all have regrets?"

Mireya could hardly rebuke or argue with him about what was truth no matter how much she wanted to. Too well did she know, especially now, mistakes and regret.

"Maybe some things are never meant to be and should never be tried," Durai continued.

Mireya sighed in frustration and defeat. Most of all she felt guilt. Her deepest wish and request to this Enchanter did this, so this was her fault. "What do we know, at least?"

"The spell I tried to bring your brother back is an Ancient Magic long forgotten outside the crumbling pages of archaic books. Something went wrong, some interpretation maybe. Regardless, it didn't bring your brother back -"

"No kidding!" Mireya interrupted. "He was just about the ONLY thing it didn't bring back." She sighed long and loud in her contempt. "Go on."

"From the altar of the palace temple, a mist was born from the spell. This Mist seems to be...well, alive. It moves with will and purpose. As it moved from the temple to the land beyond the castle, it appears to have brought forth the souls of ones long buried. They have escaped their rest in the earth, and they are...Immortuos."

"The undead..." Mireya whispered to herself. "So, it is true?"

"Precisely. And the Mist has not dissipated. It keeps moving and, I don't know, feeding on the land somehow."

Mireya stood and began to pace. "Meanwhile the Immortuos are terrorizing everything. They are angry, they are destructive, and they are unstoppable. I mean, how do you kill that which doesn't truly live?!" Mireya sat again at her throne. Even the small pacing drained her. "How do we stop this."

Durai dropped his head feigning his false shame even more. "I have tried all I know since this began. Nothing I do seems to stop this. It's like a wound spreading sickness and death. I began studying books long buried in the archives intently, books even I hadn't looked upon before. I have been desperate to fix this. From all I could find, I cannot."

Mireya buried her head in her hands feeling utterly defeated at Durai's pause. That was it then, the word was doomed to this. If the most powerful master of the world's Magic couldn't find a solution, then what hope was there for anyone else?

"But," Durai began again, "maybe a Healer can."

Mireya raised her head at this news dumbfounded. "A Healer?" She found this news hard to believe. Her own three Healers at court couldn't even give her the strength to sleep through the night anymore. She had little faith they could do anything to make this right.

"This Mist is like pestilence spreading from a wound in nature brought forth at the palace alter. It's a spreading sickness, and only the nature of a Healer's mastery of their special Magic can have hope to mend this. But," Durai paused to make sure Mireya certainly understood, "it would have to be an exceedingly powerful Healer."

"Althea?"

"If only we could find her - if she is even alive. Whoever it is, they would have to be as powerful in their knowledge as she was."

Mireya's eyes became distant in memory. She recalled the morning waking up with Althea gone. They searched the castle all morning and into the late afternoon. It wasn't until she found Althea's hairbrush left at her bedside that they extended the search beyond the palace. They searched for a full month. That's when Baldrik started to get worse.

And then she lost them both.

"Where could she have gone? What could have happened to her?" Mireya thought out loud to herself.

"Yes, I miss her too." At least in this, he wasn't putting on a show. He had been truly destroyed at losing her. He'd do anything to get her back. Anything. "Maybe if she hadn't left, Baldrik wouldn't have chosen to leave us; he may have been more willing to stay with help."

"Don't you say that!" Mireya spat at him.

"Which part? The part where he decided to end his own life, or the part where it's Althea's fault?"

Mireya slumped in her chair. "Either."

"I'm so sorry, Mireya. My heart is broken from her leaving, and I can't help but be bitter."

"Maybe she didn't leave," Mireya quietly suggested in almost a whisper. She hated to hope that Althea had met a terrible fate, but she hated more to think that she would be so cold as to leave.

Mireya called an attendant to her and made the proclamation that all Healers be brought to the castle to try everything they could to undo what had been done.

· · · · · · ·

Durai closed the doors to his rooms after he left Mireya. He smiled to himself at things going better than he could have hoped. Usually, in complicated plans, there was always one thing or another that doesn't go as predicted. However, everything had for him. His endeavors must surely be justified if fate had smiled so highly on them.

He went out of his doors onto his open patio. He looked out upon all he could see and all he could not see spread vastly before him. When he closed his eyes, all he could see was her. His memories of her enveloped him completely, tantalizing him in exquisite agony. Though his Dove had flown away, he may have found the way to bring her back. And this time...

"You'll be back now," he said out to the horizon, "I'll be waiting."

But Screw Your Courage to the Sticking-Place

After agreeing to trust one another, Althea and Galen spent the rest of the morning into midday on the small hill with the large oak tree assessing their combined supplies. Althea remained off her ankle and continued to massage it and reapply pressure wrappings. Galen climbed the large tree to survey the base of the hill and paths around the area for Immortuos. There were some of them wandering in scattered places below them, no doubt having been drawn out by Althea. Not that they were searching for her consciously or with intent. They didn't have enough consciousness to do so. They were compelled towards a chase that faded in time, but the compulsion remained even if it was unfocused. Their bodies lurched and jerked forward in a grotesque, horrifying way. It was enough to fuel the nightmares of the living a hundred times over.

He also watched Althea from his vantage point and tried to read her in his limited way. Galen didn't have the training to read a person in the same way that those gifted in learned Magic were, in the way a Healer or Enchanter was. But he had limited and natural skills to read people more than most others. He caught her becoming lost in herself multiple times. It was like she was there in body only, but her spirit was somewhere far away. The hardened parts of her were learned, not natural; her rigid movements, her timid and guarded glances in suspicion weren't something that fit well with her and the aura she exuded. The grace, the caring, and the gentleness – those were natural. And they were stunning and even alluring. Those parts of her have been with her all along and probably would be a part of her forever.

Galen descended after midday and had gotten a better feel for the Immortuos and their movements. He walked over slowly towards where Althea sat as he could see her watching him still cautious of her new partner. He didn't blame her. Innocent souls like the one he could sense in her had their reasons to go against their nature. He'd like to know what those reasons were, though.

He sat down next to her and was glad of the coolness of the grass and shade of the tree. "Immortuos are circling the hill in small packs here and there, nothing dense, and nothing we can't avoid. They aren't attempting to tread the incline, so we're safe for now, and I think we should be ok when we decide to venture out."

"And when should that be?" Althea asked. It had been most of the day since he heard her talk; he had almost forgotten the kind of spell the music of her voice could cast. He stopped himself from a small laugh at his childish reaction to it - just barely. What a joy it would be to know here carefree.

"Well, that all depends on you. How's the ankle?"

Althea rubbed her ankle to test the pain, and it was bearable. It still wasn't the best, but she didn't want to waste any more resources on it. "It'll do. I could run if I have to."

"I hope we don't need to." He looked at her worried. Everything about her made you want to protect her. But he reminded himself that she was a Healer, and she had made it a year alone in the Wild intact. She was far from a breakable glass ornament.

"After looking at our supplies further, I don't think we have enough water to cross the Shimmer Plain. We'll have to go an indirect route to find a river. Did you see one from up there?"

"I saw one, and it's some miles that way. We might get there before dark. But we certainly won't get back here before we have to sleep."

Althea thought for a moment, "Well, do you feel like we could find a good place to sleep in safety? It'll still be a fuller moon tonight, but I can sleep in trees."

"I can't quite do that. I've never found a way to balance with my center of gravity."

"Then we'll have to be careful to leave plenty of time to find somewhere or something that works for both of us."

Galen smiled inwardly as she proved her good nature. No matter what may have happened to this woman, she wasn't going to only think about herself. She would do all she could to make sure he would be taken care of, probably everyone she met as well.

"We should get started then," Galen said as he rose from the ground and extended his hand to help her up. Althea couldn't help but hesitate slightly. It had been so very long since she trusted someone, so very long. But the hesitation was only for an instant as she remembered the inherent good she felt from him and took his hand. They were like two small children venturing out from home for the first time without the natural distrust found in adults; they may not know each other, but the trust, whether by nature or necessity, was certainly there.

They moved slowly and stealthily for a good portion of the day towards the direction of the river in silence listening to the air and feeling the earth for Immortuos and other dangers. Althea's ankle wasn't causing her anxiety half as much as when she could feel Galen watching her. His curiosity couldn't help him from watching her now and then trying to figure her out. She was very good at hiding the fact that she knew he was watching her, so he kept on more and more as the day went on. Her movements were confident despite her small injury, and she was very skilled at navigating the Wild which wasn't much like other Healers who never ventured far from a village.

The more he looked, the more the mystery of this woman he traveled with grew and gnawed away at his brain. She became a delicious enigma that weighed on him heavier and heavier. She became a force that piqued his interest that pulled and destroyed his focus against everything else but her. He was lucky that she was focused enough on their destination and movements for the both of them, and he followed his newfound figure of inexplicable vulnerability and seduction.

Though he knew he would be straining the strength of their very new relationship and the trust they held, he found that the unknown about her nagged at him to the point of consuming his entire consciousness. The only way to move past it was to know. And as fortune favors the bold…

"What is it you're running from?" Galen's words came out almost on their own. He even made himself cringe hearing his impertinent question, but what was done was done; what was said was out there.

"I don't really want to talk about it now. The sun is almost set, and we need to focus on a safe place to sleep." Althea didn't even look at him when she answered. She truly didn't want to live through the memories again. How would she be able to travel with this man after her story was told?

"I want to know. Why did you run? Was it that you lost someone? Althea?" He was so anxious that she would continue to ignore him and not answer. Then as he felt the fear coming off of her in the silence, he felt more anxious that she would.

"I…." How could she put herself back there? How could she face what she had been spending a year running away from and burying deep within herself?

"Listen I know it's not easy, but it might help if you talked about it. Are you running because you lost someone you loved?"

"Yes."

She was answering; she was truly answering. Perhaps the only way to move forward in strength was to turn to the pain and face it. Perhaps the only way to defeat the demons was to fight.

"Who?" Galen was concerned at the tone of her voice. And he was sorry for the misery he heard in it.

Althea turned around. He looked at her beautiful face that looked like something precious, something that had no business around misery. But he saw even deeper that knew this soul knew misery all too well. She had lived in the heart of darkness and bathed deep in sorrow. What had he done?

"I lost myself."

They came across a place where they could rest for the night. There was a hollowed hill that could shield and hide them from the light with a large tree blocking the entrance. It wasn't the most ideal place to spend the night, certainly a far cry less secure than the large hill they had left with the sturdier oak, but

109

they could make it work in shifts. Once they were situated in safety and spent some time assuring their security, Althea let out a sigh and faced her companion.

She was ready to tell him everything. It was true that though she had agreed to physically go back to do what she could to heal the hurt in the earth, she hadn't been willing to go back within her spirit. In all honesty, she hadn't thought about what going back truly entailed. How ridiculous was she to think that she could honestly go back and avoid confronting her past?

She was about to fight her first battle in a war that was far greater than she could fear. Whatever came next, at least she knew this fight she could win. She would face all that had happened to her, all she had suffered, and in this way, she donned her armor. What didn't kill her...

He Will Make the Face of Heaven So Fine

Galen sat overwhelmed in silence at the ending of the tale that was just told to him. The light of the day was falling fast beyond a horizon they could not see. Now he understood so much of everything he saw in her. Everything that seemed unnatural was because she had developed a scar over her damaged parts. Of course, she ran away, and no one could or would blame her for what she did given the indescribable abuse. However, Althea did.

She blamed herself at this moment now thinking back on all that had been done as she said it all out loud. It was now, as she was removed from her past in relative safety, that she fully realized the remorse and shame in herself for leaving. She knew the truth of it now, after so long, that she was still letting the darkness win. Choosing to run from it was not fighting it. Turning her back to it was not conquering it; instead, she had let it conquer her.

"Maybe you were right, Galen. Maybe I have let that be buried down for too long. Maybe I should have faced these demons long ago. Maybe then the world wouldn't have suffered for so very long…just because I suffered."

"That is a drastic understatement," Galen said finally adding input. "You were mentally abused, you were manipulated cruelly, and you literally gave away parts of your life energy because of the sheer purity of your love… and were raped besides…" The words seemed to choke within his throat, they were so ugly to speak. His head and his heart started to hurt in full lament of the malice in the world that would seek to tear down the good and virtuous. "'Suffered' doesn't nearly do it justice."

Althea never really thought of the labels of what had happened to her. And yet here they were put forth in front of her in glaring clarity. She wanted to argue with them, downplay them if she could, but it didn't make it any less true. She knew that.

Galen began to reach for her hand but stopped himself within an instant. He wanted to comfort her with the instinct any human would have towards someone completely broken and vulnerable, but he dared not touch her. He could tell from the way she was holding herself, the way she seemed to still be physically hiding behind a wall of protection she had erected these long months in solitude, that physical contact would be the last thing she would want. In that moment, he was nearly consumed by his pity for her. Not in any kind of condescension or superiority; far from it. He admired her strength and resolve so much more now. How many people could say they endured so much and even willed to continue on? And what he felt wasn't sympathy, for that would imply that he felt some form of shared experience with her position. How could he? How could anyone? No, his pity came from a place of compassion with full sorrow for what she had been through.

"At least now," Althea started to say with a desperate need to continue with progress and not fall back into her darkness, "at least now I will have a chance to make things right. I will do better for those in the world suffering now and those I left behind - those I love. I can do right by Mireya...er, the Queen, and Baldrik. I can go back and take care of them."

Baldrik...

The sting of her words and the realization of her innocent ignorance given her time in self-banishment entered his ears and coursed into him like poison. Galen dared not move a muscle. Her hope was so pure and so tragic that he was frozen where he sat. He couldn't be the one to break her again. How would she be able to hear the truth and bear another defeat? Oh, God.

She sensed the change in him and his retreating presence. She knew something was wrong. In a way, she knew something had been wrong for a very long time. Not like with the Mist and the Immortuos, but something else deeper and more intimately dreadful. Deep down there was a shapeless, terrible burden that had descended and weighed on her soul that she actively ignored over and over. Now it seemed she couldn't ignore it any longer. The specter of some distant calamity that had been haunting her from some unknown place must be known.

"Althea…oh God…" How could Galen even find the words to say it? He knew all too well that he held her still-beating heart in his hands, and by his hands would it break. Again.

Althea reached out with her kind words as she sensed his struggle. "I know there is something you have to say that I won't want to hear. But I promise…I mean, I guess I have to know whatever it might be."

He tried with all his gifted soul to be as comforting as he could while he spoke words like daggers even to himself. He must take this woman as vulnerable as she had made herself to him, like a small, trusting bird, and thoroughly destroyed her. He had seen and heard the love she spoke of for the family she left behind, Baldrik probably most of all. But he did have ways of soothing and calming, and there was at least that small amount of comfort he could give to her. If she had to hear it, the alleviating Magic in a Leporem might be the best way to do so.

"A year ago, just before the Mist, we were all…" no use drawing out the truth, he realized. He stopped, recalibrated, and did his very best for better or for worse. "Baldrik has died. It happened just before the Mist. I cannot tell you how utterly sorry I am for your loss. Your loss far more deeply than anyone else besides the Queen." He wanted to cry for her. He watched in awe as she had told the whole story of herself without a tear, and it was a story that would have crumbled the foundation of the most stalwart person alive. But now she was not reliving something she survived but was being struck with another blow that could be the blow one too many.

Althea sat there somewhere between relief in the certainty of truth and the sorrow of it all. "In a way, I know. In a way, long ago, I had felt an emptiness in this world - in my soul - that I couldn't quite explain. I know it sounds crazy and fanciful, but I felt it. It makes sense to me now. It wasn't the isolation, and it wasn't the running away; it was the breaking of the other part of me, of the heart I left behind in him. I should have known that he wouldn't survive long without care. If he had another attack like I had seen in him before, of course, it would claim him in the end. He even said so to me. I shouldn't have left."

"Althea, it wasn't that…" he whispered barely loud enough for even himself to hear. Maybe if she didn't hear it, he wouldn't have to say it. Maybe he didn't have to say it at all.

"It wasn't what?"

Damn.

This time he had to reach out and take her hand. If not for her comfort, then for his own. "Althea, he was not taken in sickness. He died by his own hands." He registered the hands within his harden in a deep terror, and he knew that no gifts of his would be able to make anything he had left to say any less monstrous. "Word spread quickly from the palace down the hill and onwards until everyone knew despite the Queen's wishes that it be kept secret. Something so shocking could not be borne in silence, and the servants who had to bear witness to the sight could only find relief in their misery by spreading their grief. Or so I guess. In the end, perhaps the fight was just too much for him to keep at it." The look in her eyes at what he had to say made him wish he were dead. He saw her crack as if she were made of glass.

"Then it *was* my fault."

• • • • • • •

Althea found herself beside the river again. The same unnatural speed carried the waters down in an unsettling way. The sight of her body was not found at the bottom of the river as it had been before; she had escaped it a year ago when she left, after all. But now more than ever she wanted to jump in with conscious purpose. Even if this was only a dream, as she knew it was, maybe somehow this river would take her away in her sleep. She didn't want the burden of her life anymore.

"Can't go that way," she heard a voice behind her say.

She turned around with tears in her eyes at the sound of his voice. "Baldrik?"

He appeared before her as she had known him during the best of his life. He was not in pain, he was not in doubt or grief; he was whole and perhaps better than she had ever known him to be. He stood beside a tree facing her and seeing deep into her heart. She felt the warmth of him there. And he smiled at her.

She was carried toward him in a whirlwind of tears and sorrow, or so it felt. The swirling feelings of love mixed with pain drowned her as she rushed to hold him. There is something inexplicably tragic in a dream where one sees those loved in life while still being conscious of the fact that holding them, embracing them - seeing and feeling them - were unnatural and unreal. That though they were there, they are not. And while the moment is so beautiful and so precious, it is doomed to fail and fall into nothingness upon waking.

But at this moment, this dearest, treasured moment, they were together.

"I'm sorry. It's all my fault, and I'm so sorry!" Althea sobbed as they both fell to their knees still in embrace until the sorrow and weeping became deeper than any true emotion.

"There is absolutely nothing for you to be sorry about – not then, not now, and not ever."

"But you're dead because I left you to your pain. I killed you!" The world became dark in Althea's guilt, and the air became thick in her sobbing. The fog moved around them, and she saw now that the fog in her dreams was actually the Purple Mist. They were one and the same. They always had been. Perhaps that, too, was her fault.

"Don't you do that!" Baldrik chastised firmly as he took her shoulders and looked into her destroyed face. In that moment, the Mist disappeared. The darkness was held at bay. "What I've done, I own the weight of it alone. Just me, and no one else. Least of all you."

Althea heard his words but still couldn't believe in her heart. She had the sorrow and misplaced guilt and remorse of those left behind in the wake of such acts.

"I came here because of how proud I am of you. I don't blame you for a single thing in life. Not now, not then. You are finally free of the hold the past had on you, and you were strong enough to face it and turn around to fight it. With that the door was opened for me to find you here and now. And I love you, sis, just as much now as I did back then." Even as he spoke the light of love spilled forth from his eyes, and it was a heavenly light.

She poured herself into his arms and embrace again. If she could help it, this moment would last until the stars went cold. She would live forever in a dream to hear his voice again. If this was the only world left that held him, then it was the only world she wanted to have.

"You know there is more to do, and that I can't stay with you. What's left to be done isn't over."

Althea shook her head violently as she felt the veil of sleep slip away from her. She held onto him even more desperately. "No, no, no! Not yet, just a moment more. Please!"

"It's time. But I'm always with you here," and he laid his palm on her heart just as he had before. The ache inside her grew more and more with every second. "I'm proud that you are turning to fight. Just like I always knew you would."

"Baldrik, no yet!"

"But you know this isn't real, and it's time to wake up."

"It's real enough for me!"

The light of the moon was reflected in her eyes as the dream was ripped away from her. Galen had tried so hard to keep a lookout, but he had fallen asleep beside her tucked into the hollow of the hill. She didn't move upon waking, and though she knew that she should stay up and keep watch while Galen slept, she shut her eyes hard willing the sleep to return and bring the dream back.

But the dream was gone, and sleep would not lay upon her while she had a duty to protect the sleeping man beside her. In her ears she still heard Baldrik's voice as he disappeared in her waking:

"I believe in you."

They Say Miracles are Past

Galen had watched her as she slept and was grateful that she was able to. He had worried her tortured soul would not find sleep, but she succumbed to exhaustion in her emotional tempest. She had taken one bad news blow after another. He felt horrible for being the messenger. So he watched on over her as she slipped into peace in her sleep. He watched again as her face contorted in sadness and he listened as she cried deep from her dreams, unwaking and piteous.

He turned his back on the scene no longer able to endure what he blamed himself for. Her body shook against him in her soft and rhythmic cries. His attempts to shut it all out proved effective, and between her movements and the warmth of her body, he was lulled into sleep despite his efforts to keep watch.

When the sky became brighter with the approaching dawn, he opened his eyes first with the haze of sleep and then with sudden panic as he realized he had fallen asleep and left them both helpless. As he turned, he noticed she was sitting up beside him keeping watch and hugging her knees. She still looked so wounded circling her arms about her as if she were trying to keep her broken heart from spilling forth onto the ground. When she felt him move, she turned from her vigil and looked down on him.

"I'm so sorry. I didn't mean to fall asleep," he admitted sheepishly.

"Don't be. It was my turn anyway."

Galen sat up too and looked in the direction that she had been looking. The air was silent; no movement of any kind. Not even the air moved this morning. As if anticipating his questions, she volunteered, "No sign of anything all night."

They sat in the deafening silence then with Galen still remorseful at his part in her pain and Althea was still deep in the memories of her dream. The world felt like such a strange place to them on this morning, even more so than when the Mist and Immortuos had arrived.

"How are you..." Galen started his question and trailed off as he had felt foolish and insensitive to ask. Even as he spoke, he felt his words being sucked into a void of blackness from her; he felt as though she were far away, deep in an unreachable darkness. No words of his would reach someone in that much sadness.

"I'm better."

Galen raised his head in surprise at how much he could have misjudged her state. He thought, if this had been him, he would have fallen silent as if dead for at least a week. But here she was responsive and even cared enough for him to keep watch over him the rest of the night. He smiled to hear her respond and at the continuous proof of her resilient soul.

Galen looked around then and then said, "I'm a little embarrassed to say, but I'm a little turned around. Last night was, uh, intense. My directions are all messed up. Which way is the river?"

Althea had relied on him for directions yesterday mostly and had not been paying attention either. She lowered herself to the ground with her palms spread flat against the dirt and fallen leaves. She closed her eyes to fully feel the earth beneath her. Althea then felt the movement of the river, and she could smell the water in the air. She stood up and pointed in its direction, and they gathered their things and made their way towards the water.

Despite the terrible night they had just had, their company together seemed much more harmonious. It was as though the weight that they had been carrying was somewhat shed. Even though they had only just met, and even though their new relationship had been tested greatly, they traveled with a newer, stronger sense of trust and unity even if they weren't consciously aware of it.

The gentle sound of the river became clearer with each step. Althea realized that the sound was not what she was preparing to hear. She half expected to hear the sound of the river of dreams, and laughed at herself at how foolish that was. This river was not that river, and it was of this world and not of her nightmares.

When they arrived at the river, they saw that it was very wide and, though fast-flowing, very calming. Althea was the first to bend down to the water to drink straight from the current and felt invigorated by the cold water. She splashed some on her face and smiled at the rejuvenating sensation. Galen watched her and saw her smile. It was like sunshine that fought and pushed its way through storm clouds. Though she was beautiful to him before, and a source of continuous inspiration at every turn, now she was purely stunning. He could certainly see how that man became entranced by her.

"Galen, behind you!"

Galen heard her words and was snapped into the present instantly. He saw her dash up to her knees in the cold waters of the river as she gestured both for him to look behind him and join her in the river. He turned swiftly around to see a single Immortuo behind him. She was a woman who had died maybe in her late twenties and relatively recently. Her body had not deteriorated much before the Mist brought her spirit back into it. She had spotted the two from several meters away and started to run towards them. Galen had been so wrapped up in his own head to notice the signs of her approach. But Althea had noticed the change in the air and the subtle sounds of the labored strides they had and been quick to respond.

Now the threat was charging at them with the anger and hate that the Immortuos were now known for. Galen was so caught off guard by the sudden onset of danger that his turn to run was less than graceful. He fell over his feet but was up almost instantly and making a dash towards the water. As his body hit the water, he took a sharp breath in from the shock of the cold.

Once Althea had made sure that he was hip-deep in the water, she turned to swim against the current and better assure her safety. Immortuos had limited control over a body that was in fact dead, and swimming was one thing they could not do well at all. But as she got deeper and further, she realized that the flow of the river was stronger than it had seemed nearer the bank. She was a very strong swimmer, but she was worried about her companion who she knew very little about. She tried turning to face him in the water, but even the slightest break in focus from fighting the current started to take her downstream against her will.

"Galen! Wait!" She tried calling out to him, but the roar of the river from being in the middle of it was far too loud. Galen soon realized the strength of the current and started to struggle against it. But turning back was not an option as the Immortuo had reached the bank and began to rush into the water after them, and this one had more skill at it than they had hoped. The plodding into the water was strong and consistent, and Galen had no choice but to get further into the river.

Though he was by no means a bad swimmer, he was losing his battle with the current and slipping further and further downstream. Althea turned to see him drift further from her, and she let herself be taken down the current to reach him. They were getting much further from where they had entered the river and where they had left all of their supplies, and they were both starting to panic as the water beat them mercilessly. Galen's lips started to turn blue as the river's chill penetrated his blood. He could no longer feel his arms and legs with surety that they were doing as he willed them.

Althea looked around her surroundings desperately as they slowly got pulled further and further away despite their desperate struggles. She saw the changes in Galen's face and knew that he wouldn't be able to keep this up. A few meters downstream on their side of the river she noticed a tree whose large roots reached out into the water. At least they would be able to gain a hold against the pull of the current there. Althea was so close to him now, and she shouted at Galen to grab a hold of the jutted-out roots and limbs.

As she reached the tree herself, she pushed off as best she could from the bottom of the river to launch as much of her body onto the tree as she could manage. She then turned towards Galen almost in the same motion to make sure he had a grip. Though he managed to get a small grasp of the wood, its wet surface quickly proved too much for his grip. Althea grabbed his wrist and hand before he was taken away by the river. Her grasp of the tree was strained as she tried to pull him towards her. Galen's eyes were starting to blur as the world seemed to be in a kind of haze in his mind; he was only vaguely aware anymore that she was holding onto him. He fought to clear his head of the unnatural confusion and took one final step against the bottom of the river to help her.

With that final push, they were both securely on the tree watching the river rage past them in the swifter, downstream current.

Althea held onto Galen with one arm and the tree in the other. She could feel the heat that came off of Galen, and it wasn't nearly what it should be. She could tell he was going into shock as she felt his strength to hold onto her lessen more and more. However, the real trouble came from behind them as she could still hear the Immortuo's labored breaths and water splashing as she walked knee-deep in the water along the bank towards them. They had jumped into the river for nothing, for they had not lost their pursuer. She had stayed safely along the shallower waters and saw still that they were within her ability to reach.

Althea did her best to keep her heart from racing in panic as she held Galen in one arm and their lives in the other, for sure if she let go, they would both be pulled under the water. But if she didn't let go, the Immortuo would be on them in minutes and descend upon them with such venom and aberration for existence that they would not survive.

Suddenly an instinct came over Althea from a place deep inside of her that she could not place. She closed her eyes and held tightly to Galen. She pushed away fear and panic in her mind and focused on the life within the earth around her. She felt the river, she felt the air, and she pushed out her consciousness into them. She could no longer tell where her body ended and the earth began. Her body became the river, her mind became the wind, and her heart beat with the life of the shore. The river was now the blood in her veins, the wind was now the breath in her lungs, and the earth moved with the motions of her legs and arms.

Galen thought for sure he was hallucinating, but light and warmth came from her then. Streams of curving light danced from her body and flowed outward as if they were alive. To his surprise, he was pulled into momentary focus to see that he was being held in safety by the arms of an angel. And he could then see behind her the devil that persisted in its pursuit and felt the panic rise within him. He held onto her as tight as he possibly could, but he knew that his strength was draining from him as fast as the river flowed around him. The cold was biting and overwhelming.

Althea felt his grip tighten but kept her focus. The increased pressure she felt in his arms brought the slightest smile to her face. She didn't know how she did it, or even what exactly she did do, but she pushed out her life force beyond her body and joined with the earth. She could feel the power of her beating heart rise as the roar of the river became louder. As if she had become the very river itself, an unnatural swell from the current reached wide towards the bank and caught up the Immortuo like the hand of a living body plucking away thorn.

The sound the Immortuo made as she was carried away was so full of malice and loathing that Althea felt such pity towards every one of them and their curse. Althea watched as the helpless creature was swept away with the force of the river at her bidding. The Immortuo watched her with hateful eyes before disappearing below the water and out of sight. She knew then with a broken heart that she had a responsibility not just to the people left in fear of the Mist, but also to those who were condemned to misery after death because of it. It all had to end.

Althea struggled to get herself and Galen to the shore when the danger passed. He had become so heavy that she strained beyond what she thought possible to get him to the bank. He dragged his whole body out of the water as he tried his best to help, but his limps were uncontrollable as he shivered.

"Galen? Can you hear me?" She scanned him over with her hands to check for breaks or bleeding from being tossed in the current. "Thank goodness you're shivering. That means your body hasn't lost the ability to react to the cold and is doing its part to warm you up. That's good." She kept scanning him as she talked through her own body trembling and shaking. She noticed some bruising, but nothing major. His lips were still discolored and he seemed disoriented, but he wasn't passed help.

She got up to run for their supplies several meters up the river; she had some fresh clothing in there to keep him relatively dry and one small, thin blanket in her pack. But as she rose, she felt his hand hold tight to her wrist. His eyes were wide in terror at the thought of being left behind. He looked so helpless, and she knew she had to move fast to minimize the damage. But she took her time to kneel back down beside him gently and put his worried hand in hers with patience and caring. "Galen, I won't leave you. I swear I'm coming back. But we need our supplies, and you need to trust me." She felt his grip on her hand relax, and she ran as fast as she could- determined to return before he could panic into hurting himself.

When she returned, she found that his shivering had stopped. "No, no, no!" she muttered to herself as she hurriedly unpacked her bag to get at the blanket. The fact he wasn't shivering meant that his body was too cold and was no longer trying to heat itself. His blood would start to slow in his veins soon, so she had to hurry. "Galen, please, you've got to help me." She said as she pulled him to sitting as best she could. He was barely able to keep himself up to sitting as she undid his shirt and peeled it off of his chest. Even the skin on his chest was turning purple. He didn't have enough heat within himself to trap in the blanket; she would have to give it to him.

She draped the blanket around his bare shoulders as she undid her top to get rid of her chill and wetness in order to add her heat to his. All she had left was the wrappings around her breasts as she pushed her skin up against his and enclosed their bodies in the thin blanket. Her arms encircled his body as she rubbed his back and arms frantically to push his blood back to circulating properly.

Through the rays of heaven, Galen had heard the angel speak and soothe him in his state. He had never believed in them before, or if they had been real, they had long since left this world like the faeries. But perhaps now he had died and was held in the arms of a creature sent from the sun and clouds. Surely this light and this feeling couldn't be real. This angelic vision was a dream.

And as his mind cleared and his blood passed warmer into his heart giving life back to his body, he saw that his vision was Althea. But even with his restored clarity, he was convinced he was being held by an angel.

"You're going to be ok, Galen. I've got you."

Healer in the Mist

More Things in Heaven and Earth

Althea and Galen had moved their huddled bodies against the tree that had saved them from the river for protection while they both recovered. It wasn't much cover if they needed to hide, but at least it provided security behind them given the tree and the river at their backs. Galen's body went limp against hers as he regained warmth and passed out from the physical exertion. His breathing was strong and steady; he would be alright, she thought. She let him lay his body on top of hers as they reclined against the tree so she could keep a lookout for any more Immortuos as well as more easily pass her heat onto him.

The trees were thick where they sat, and the sun barely penetrated the canopy in patches. The air around them was very cool still without the sun, so they continued to share their combined warmth as the sun could not reach them. Althea held him tight against her, and as time went by and she felt more assured that he was regaining strength, her mind started to try and unravel what she had done in the river. What exactly was that? How did she do what she did? How did she know what to do without consciously knowing?

Galen started to rouse slowly back into consciousness against her chest. Althea relaxed her hold around his body to let him sit back if he felt strong enough. She realized instantly that she missed the warmth as he started to pull away, and not just the heat of his body.

Galen wasn't fully aware yet of where he was, and it was purely instinctual movements that moved him to sit up away from where he lay. He became more cognizant by the time he was fully upright that he had taken the blanket around his shoulders with him. As he sat up, he realized he had left her exposed beneath him. He looked down on her with her upper body bare save for the wrapping around her breasts, and he found he was unable to react. For a moment he couldn't remember what had happened or how they got there in this position, and he just looked with a million sensations, thoughts, and feelings further muddling his brain. Most of all, there was a strong regret that he had not stayed laying down longer.

Althea had forgotten that she was mostly undressed when he moved back until he saw him looking strangely at her. Inside she was shocked for a moment, but then she reminded herself that she was covered (if just barely) and that she had done this to save his life. Embarrassment from her wouldn't do either of them any favors. She calmly rose to her feet and walked over to her pack and her dry clothes. After she donned a top, she walked over to him and looked him over asking, "How are you feeling?"

Galen's sluggish reflexes delayed a response. He didn't know if it was from the residual cold or what he had just seen. He had never seen a woman so exposed before, not even his mother. He'd never had a lover before. At least not one serious enough to have their relationship progress that much. He wanted to punch himself for his delayed reaction feeling like a base, mindless creature easily distracted and made foolish by her stunning physical beauty. "I think I'm ok. I'm not sure."

Althea used her hands to probe his limbs, checked for a fever, and felt for breaks and bruises. He saw that his legs had born most of the river's beating, and they were going to show some remarkable discoloration for a while. But nothing that he wouldn't recover from or even be badly hindered with, and there was certainly nothing much she could do to help it. He didn't have a fever, so she was glad of that.

"What happened to me?" Galen asked.

"I would say this was mild cold sickness; not a severe case. Your body's temperature dropped too low. It causes your blood to stall and your heart to slow making you confused. In more prolonged cases, you could seriously damage your body. But you're fine now."

Galen thought back to all he could remember. "That makes sense. The confusion, I mean. I thought I saw the strangest things," Galen paused embarrassed at his thoughts that she was a heaven-sent angel figure. Though, in many ways, he knew that she was.

"Like what?" Althea wanted to know.

Galen thought it best not to further look like an ass, so he decided not to mention his vision of her. "I know it sounds a little deranged, but I thought I saw the river defend us. It reached out with – I don't know, sounds crazy– like a hand reaching out of the river. Wait, more like the hand figure I saw WAS the river, and it grabbed that Immortuo and carried her away."

Althea sat back against the tree at his words with the strangest smile mixed with fear and confusion spread across her face. "Then I didn't imagine that. I thought I had been seeing things too. But that's what happened."

Galen finished spreading his clothes out against a patch of the sun near them and sat in front of her wrapped in the blanket. He sat in silence for a time thinking more about what he could remember. More details started to come back to him with more clarity. He looked at her when the sudden, clear recollection of all of it flooded in. "There was light. There was light coming off of you like ribbons in wind. I know that sounds crazy, but I could swear that's what I saw." He leaned into her then, "Did you do that? Did you call the river somehow and make that happen?"

"I don't know." She honestly couldn't say. She couldn't logically justify it, and she didn't think she could do it again if she even had done it in the first place. But the fact remains that she did something, that there was a force that came from her. Something deep inside of her pushed forward through something like instinct took over. She could remember that now. "I think I did."

Galen looked on at this woman with even more respect and awe. He had never in his life heard of a Healer being able to do what he had seen her do. Even most Enchanters couldn't pull off a feat of that magnitude. "I don't understand," he admitted. "I didn't know a Healer could do that."

Althea had been giving this some thought, for she didn't realize this was a possibility either. It was certainly uncommon. "I guess, in a way, it makes sense. A Healer's power is drawn from the earth and from the light. We take from our world the plants and herbs to make our medicines, and our songs come from deep within the life force of the earth. I wonder if that's what happened. I was able to connect with that life force and manipulate the elements."

The two of them thought about what she had just said and couldn't fully believe it was possible. But the proof was there; she had done this feat, and the world seemed more complex and wonderous now because of it. Maybe this world could be saved. Maybe it was possible. And maybe she was the one to do it.

"Oh," Galen began to add, "thank you very much for saving my life back there." Althea felt her face blush as she remembered what she had done for him. She blushed even harder when she remembers HOW she had done it. "I know that it might not have been easy to...do what you did for me given what you've been through."

Althea looked at him surprised at his empathy. She was even more surprised at how easily she had held onto him, both of them nearly naked and vulnerable, without the natural traumatic responses she would have expected. Maybe she was stronger than she had thought or gave herself credit for. Maybe he was just so filled with honor and purity that could be felt coming from him at all times that she was able to trust him and care for him easier. Maybe it was both.

Regardless, fate had brought these two together. And together there was hope.

· · · · · · ·

"You've studied so long, Althea. Don't you want to play outside just a bit before the light leaves? You can't study all day; you'll hurt yourself."

"But Momma, what if I forget? What if I forget these songs and let you and grandma down?"

"Althea, baby, never in all the ages of all the world would you ever disappoint us. We love you so much."

"Still...I have a job to do, Momma. Playing isn't important. Remembering the songs is what matters."

"Althea, as long as your heart is gentle and good and your love is deep, you will always be able to reach into yourself for the songs. Your bond with the Healer magic is very special. You are uncommonly strong, sweetness."

"Do you really really think so Momma? Truly?"

"I know so."

In a Better World Than This, I Shall Desire More Love

By the time Galen and Althea had regained enough of their strength to start moving, they had decided to go back to the safety of the large hill with the oak. At least there they knew they were secure and could get a full night's sleep safely. That way tomorrow they could set out from a place of strength. Althea walked comfortably behind Galen as she had not been injured from the river at all, and this way he could set the pace, and she could follow.

When he caught her looking at him and realizing that she was still watching him for further signs of physical injury, he turned to her and said, "Really, I'm all right now. You did a very good job." To even show off a bit, he walked backward as he talked, hoping to amuse her.

"Well," she started, "those bruises are no joke. I'm just … being considerate. I know if those were on my legs, I'd be limping a bit."

Galen started to walk forward again and faster not realizing it. The last thing he needed was to be a further burden on the woman he had made up his mind to protect.

"I'm not saying you're weak or anything," Althea added as she noticed his walk quicken. But he didn't slow down, he even sped up a bit more. "Wait!" Althea called out to him as she noticed him almost at a jog. She even had to jump herself into a trot to keep up. She wondered for a moment if she had wounded his pride, and that same fear returned to her stomach. She almost froze up feeling those same, distant feelings.

But then Galen turned his head around, stuck his tongue out, and blew a raspberry at her like a small child. Then he bolted.

Althea first was taken aback at this sudden, utterly confusing turn. But then she let out a hearty, melodic laugh and began to chase after him keeping with his same playful spirit. Galen heard the sound of her laugh behind him and smiled wide. The sound of her laugh was the most beautiful sound he had ever heard. He had heard the songs of the rarest birds in every wood, heard the singing of his mother, and the melody of harp and flute. But this…this was truly the sound that put them all to shame and could bend the will of the heavens.

Obviously, Galen was faster with his longer legs, and he had the benefit of the head start, so he purposefully slowed down slightly so she wouldn't get discouraged and give up. Besides, he thought, the faster they got to the hill, the sooner they would be safe and rest. Never mind that this was probably the most fun he'd had in longer than he could remember.

Both of them had completely forgotten her injured ankle in their sport, and suddenly Althea took one misstep on the uneven ground that sent her falling forward. Once she realized the fall was inevitable, she tucked into her body and tried to minimize the damage. She let out a small, helpless sound despite herself from the pain of once again hurting her ankle that shot white light up her leg and blinded her.

Galen quickly stopped. The sound of her distress took an instant grip around his heart and crushed it tightly. By the time he turned, she was already on the ground holding onto her ankle and rubbing desperately to keep the blood moving in and keep the swelling at bay. But it was too late; he could see the redness and swelling from where he was a few meters ahead of her. He ran to her; not in a casual run, but a desperate dash with urgency and purpose.

"Oh, God! Oh, no, Althea." He bent over to her when he reached her side and put his hand on her ankle too. It was hot. He wasn't a Healer, but he knew that wasn't great. "Can you move it? Oh, God! Althea, I am so sorry."

Althea let out a kind, reassuring laugh and pushed against his chest so light it was hardly a push. "This was not your fault. My mother should have named me Grace." Under other circumstances, Galen would have laughed, but he was far too worried. Althea straightened her knee to extend her leg and ankle. She moved it slowly and stiffly in a circular motion. He could see the pain behind the mask she put on for him. "Yes, I can move it. Not broken."

He looked at her good-natured face that cared more for his feelings than her hurt ankle. And that face was so close to his now. He wanted so badly to extend his hand and stroke her cheek in affection. He realized the moment he heard her distress that he would innately jump into a fire if she ever needed it without hesitation. His realization seemed absurd, but that didn't change the fact that the feeling was there, it was natural, and it was from the heart of him. He couldn't explain it, and it didn't make sense knowing her for a little over a day. But he had always trusted his instincts, and everything he read in her and felt from her was of the highest merit. Maybe it made more sense than he thought.

Still, better to not make such a brash move as to caress her face just yet, so Galen lowered his hands onto the ground to resist any urge. Althea was sorry that he removed his hand from her ankle as his touch was very pleasant and comforting to her just like the sound of his gifted voice. She tried not to let the disappointment show on her face. Why should she be disappointed? But then she realized that the fact remained that she was. She couldn't rationalize it, and it didn't make sense knowing him for a little over a day. But everything she read in him was good and pure. Maybe it made more sense than she thought.

Maybe the halves in them were always meant to meet.

Just as they had touched at their meeting – innocent heart meets innocent heart.

Fear no more the heat o' th' sun,
Nor the furious winter's rages;
Thou thy worldly task hast done,
Home art gone and ta'en thy wages:
Golden lads and girls all must,
As chimney-sweepers, come to dust.

They felt the strange vibrations of the earth at the same time and knew that they would not be alone soon. Galen looked up trying to find the direction in which the Immortuos were coming and spotted them in the distance. "Well, time to go," Galen said to her.

He bent over and picked her up without thinking and held her in his arms. He realized immediately that this could easily make her uncomfortable, but as he looked down at her ready to apologize, she wrapped both of her arms around his neck and gave him a trusting nod. With her touch, he felt like he could do anything, even take on the world if he needed to.

"Hold on," he said as he began to run up toward the hill and soon start the path up the steep incline with Althea in his arms. The Immortuos had spotted them and began running towards them in their clumsy, determined way. But they were soon outdistanced and quickly forgot what they had pursued and resumed wandering without purpose.

When the hill got too steep, Galen slowed down slightly. Normally he would be using his arms to balance against the incline, but they were now unavailable to him. But he was determined to get her up the hill and safe. "I can walk a little. Really. Just let me lean on you a bit," Althea said assuredly.

"No." Galen was not about to consider it.

"Listen, it won't be good for either of us if we end up falling."

Galen looked at her apologetically. She was so radiant, and her voice so dulcet even now in pain. "It's my responsibility. I got you hurt; I'm carrying you."

Althea brought down one arm from behind his neck and placed it on his chest, signaling him to stop. "I think," she started calmly, "that you and I will do a lot better together if we don't blame ourselves for silly, innocent things." She then smiled at him in an attempt to release his guilt and lighten his heart.

Letting go of his guilt was hard, and the move to release her from his arms was harder. But she was right, she was logical, and he would do much more for their partnership if he trusted her judgment. He carefully lowered her to the ground and felt her bear her weight on her good foot and the rest leaning on him. "Ok, let's go," she said.

Step by step they steadily moved forward showing extraordinary teamwork. They made better progress than either of them would have thought, and they smiled at each other. In another time or another place, they might have even laughed. But the smile was enough. It was worth more than riches to them at that moment. And with each harmonious step, they felt themselves connecting more and more. His aura reached out and intertwined with hers, and together they were a powerful pair.

The final steep step of the hill was reached. Althea balanced on her good ankle while Galen jumped up and reached down to help pull her up, and they were both still smiling. When Galen's hand closed around Althea's, a light glowed between them faintly. It was incredibly pure light, not gold or silver or colorful, but pure white and innocent. It wasn't blinding and overwhelming, but soft and subtle. Behind the light of the sun, one would hardly notice it was there. But the heat within it swept down their arms like the wind in summer. They locked eyes in surprise and stood still for just a moment. Then Galen snapped back into what he had been doing and pulled her up the rest of the way.

He had never seen something like this before, but he had heard stories of love, Magic, and valor in the long-ago time back when there were still faeries in the world of a light borne out of purity and devotion. And in his childhood imaginings, he had always dreamed of what something like that would look like. And even in his most spectacularly stunning daydreams, it was not early as breathtaking as the light he saw between them then.

But when Galen turned to look at her, he found only her back. She was busy working on her ankle, unwrapping it to tend to it more. She was slumped forward and exaggerated her motions to appear more engaged than she truly was. When he looked at her closer, he could tell she was trembling. The elation he had felt before crashed down almost as if his heart was being broken in half. Was she crying?

He moved to sit opposite her. He would give her assistance in wrapping, talk to her, and do anything. Something in this silence seemed to wound him deeply. They just shared a moment out of a storybook, and she was actively turning her back on it.

Finally, he reached out his hand to hers. They were busy rubbing something out of a jar on her swelling. When he touched her hand, she flinched and almost whimpered. "Althea?"

"I'm sorry. I mean it – I am. Please…"

"If I did something wrong," he floundered, "I'm sorry. I take back whatever it was I did that was wrong."

Althea let out a breath that was a mixture of a cry and a laugh. He saw a single tear fall down her face and hit the ground beneath her. That single tear cut him like a dagger, and he thought he didn't know why. But then he realized that yes, he did know why. He cared for her. It may not be the legends and songs of love at first sight, not anything so incredibly naive and imaginary. But in his heart, he carried respect, admiration, and a sense of compassion towards her. Yes, he cared for her very much.

"You have nothing to be sorry for, and nothing that you did was wrong." She wiped the trail left behind in her tear away. "How stupid. How like a damn child."

Galen still sat there not knowing what to do next or what to say next. So instead, he was just there, and he just listened when she again spoke.

"A long time ago, I saw that light before. I felt that warmth with another human being, a man I loved desperately. And that love would turn and destroy everything in me. And now here I am afraid of my own damn shadow. Even smells I come across make me think of him when I want nothing less. Oh God," she paused and more tears went effortlessly down her face without ceremony, without strain. "How can I keep on like this? How can anyone?"

Galen saw the parts of her that were broken now, the parts that she had hidden behind a wall of strength even last night when she faced the telling of it all to him. He saw the deep scars, the bleeding, and the loss. He saw the things taken that she would never regain, and the burdens she would probably never shed. He may have seen her today without clothes, but truly now she was naked before him. And her eyes begged for compassion, forgiveness, or any understanding. She was faced with her own destroyed shell and wished that it held beauty in it again. He knew then that she may not necessarily need a lover, but she needed someone who loved her.

Galen didn't reach out for her, he didn't pressure her to acknowledge his affection or share in its displays; he simply looked at her and spoke. His voice was calm, and she felt comfort in the melody of a Leporem. But this was not the gifts of the Leporem that he spoke from, but the sound of genuine, tender devotion. "You keep on by being you. Your strength is unlike anything I've ever seen. If I don't know anything else about you, I know your resilient strength. Even if you don't feel it, I see it."

Althea heard him, heard the words that he was saying and those he wasn't. He wasn't desperate, he wasn't intrusive, and he wasn't insistent that his praises and admiration be returned. Maybe perhaps because he hadn't fully grasped the full understanding of these feelings yet, she thought. But she was starting to feel them too.

"And if it helps, you don't have to keep on alone. If you'll let me, I'll be here to help you."

And for the first time in a very long time, almost another life ago, she believed that.

Love is the Greatest of Dreams, and Yet the Worst of Nightmares

Althea turned from the sound of the unnatural river and walked away from it towards the ending of the Woods. She would have no part in that nightmare tonight, she thought. "This river in sleep cannot harm me," was all she told herself as she walked toward the sunlight and out of the wood.

However, as she passed the final tree at the edge of this unnatural forest, she found herself surrounded by stone walls and fine tapestries. The place was dimly lit and seemed beautiful for a moment. She could see tall candles inlaid in gold and satin coverings around the furniture. Then she recognized the pieces of elements that made up the room, she could even recognize the feel of the air and the smell on the satin and realized with a blood-chilling fear where she now found herself.

"I found you."

The voice was deep again, without melody, without compassion. It was predatory coming from somewhere behind her in the black to hunt her.

Every muscle in her body cried to run, she was desperate to get herself far away, but she was frozen in place unable to move a single muscle, as is often in dreams. But this dream felt so vivid and real, she could smell him behind her, feel the air of his breath on her neck, and she was aware of sensations sharp and lucid. How could she not wake being this aware?

"Durai."

His hands pushed back her flowing hair from her neck, and she could feel his lips on the skin of her neck. They were like ice, and his touch pierced like needle pricks. Her hair stood up in the sensation she could feel as clear and solid as life. He stroked the top of her head like a master to his pet. His long, slender fingers reveled in the sensation of every inch he felt of her. Why couldn't she move?

"I've missed you so very much," he whispered into her ear. She felt his hands from behind her still travel now further down her back and encircled her waist. His fingers spread wide to cover as much of her as he could grasp.

"This is a dream. This is only a dream." Her voice seemed more desperately pleading than in confidence.

"You know better than that," he replied behind a faint laugh. Then he squeezed into her even tighter and she could hear his pleasured moan in her ears. "I've been searching for you in sleep for a long time, Dove. You forget how much Magic I have at my command. Though somehow, you've been hard to track. But your mind was so brightly clear tonight. Why is that?" She felt him continue to press himself tightly against her as she closed her eyes, desperate to wake up. "Is it that you've decided to come back? Are you on your way back to me?"

Althea tried so hard to move away or disappear, but her muscles refused to obey. And she knew that it wasn't the dream, it was him. He had done this somehow. Something he had done to her in sleep was holding her in place unable to move. She was helpless to do anything but stand there and accept every invading touch.

"I'm coming back, but not for you. I feel nothing for you," she lied. "I'm coming back to stop all this."

"Ah," he said with sinister delight in his tone. "So, you did get my invitation."

Even in sleep, she could feel the blood drain from her body in the most mortified terror she had yet felt. "Then it is true. You did this. The Mist, the Immortuos, it was you. And it was no mistake."

Durai's hands started to travel upwards from her waist making Althea sick with disgust at the touch that once set her on fire. "How else was I going to get you back?" He released her and turned her to face him. For the first time in over a year, she saw his face distinct and clear. The face she had been running from had pulled her back and was unavoidably close now. "You ran away from me. Very naughty, Dove." He raised a single finger to her in reprimand. How she wished she could wake! "There are dark and buried books that I had studied for a long time. I guess I somehow knew I would need the knowledge someday. And I knew just the right curse that your noble heart couldn't help but try to fix. And why shouldn't you try? You made me do it, after all."

"No," Althea stuttered and faltered in her feeble protest. Try as she might, her lungs seemed insufficient to keep giving her enough air. She started breathing harder and shallower in panic.

"You can't fool me. You've known it since it came. You heard where it started, you heard what it did; deep down, you always knew this was because of you."

Althea broke with tears that choked in her throat. Yes, she had felt this. Yes, she had known this was because of her. What use was there now in denial? It wouldn't stop her from doing what she could to set it right, no matter how heavy her guilt weighed on her.

"If this is how you show affection, you are deranged."

"Oh, Dove, we are well past that. I've already given you all of my heart. This I did to punish you for running away. Very naughty indeed."

Durai stopped his speech and ran his fingers down her cheek and neck before brushing past her breasts. He took in a sharp breath in his ache to touch her further. But he would wait. Soon he would be satisfied. "And so you'll come back because that's what you do. My noble little Healer, my peaceful Dove. You'll be mine again."

Althea couldn't even raise her hands to push herself back from him. He moved in so close that she could feel his lips brush hers as he spoke.

"Never yours. Not ever again."

"How will you stop me?" he laughed as his eyes began to glow again. There was darkness like smoke now. It was surrounding them both. She felt the darkness start to make her heavy and pull her down. "You will be here, and you will be mine. Because this time..."

At his pause, flames of brilliant green seemed to come from the glow in his eyes. The entire room was light from the fire in his eyes. And always the piercing green that sent the very breath from her chest. The darkness closed in tightly around her like bonds holding her down. She couldn't breathe; she was choking!

"No!"

·······

Althea's eyes opened to the site of the stars in the night sky and felt the cool, outdoor air. But she still felt arms circling her, holding her. Had her waking pulled him back with her? Was she still in danger?

In a reaction of panic and terror, she cried out and pulled away, crawling along the ground beneath her. Her fingers dug into the earth as she scrambled to break away from the arms around her. She felt the cold air chilling her already cold sweat from all over her body as she finally came to her senses and realized that she was no longer in her dream, no longer in that room, and no longer in his spell.

She looked behind her to see it was Galen that had held her, not Durai. She was safe on the hill with him. She had only been in a nightmare. It seemed now she was always in a nightmare.

Galen looked at her with worry, confusion, and fright. He had heard her whimpering in her sleep, and then she started to cry. This time, though, he wouldn't let her be alone with the demons in her sleep. He turned to lay against her and held onto her in some attempt to protect her as she trembled. Seeing how she woke, he could only imagine the monsters she had been fighting.

With the realization that she was safe, that she had not truly been there, that she was still so far away, she felt relieved. But her relief was instantly crushed when she realized that she HAD been there. Her spirit or mind had somehow been taken there, and could probably do so at any time. No matter where she was, he could now find her. Somehow, he had made that possible. She would never be safe, not even in sleep.

She covered her mouth and screamed with all she had within her. Though the sound was muffled into her hands, Galen could tell that it was a damned scream of a tortured soul that had been broken. And she screamed again, and again.

She screamed so long and so hard that she finally passed out.

She was in total darkness now. In this darkness, she was alone. Nothing was reaching her here. No light, no sound, no sensation. She thought that at last, now, she could be free. Just like she always wanted.

Right?

As the darkness surrounded her longer, she realized that this wasn't what she wanted. Deep down in her heart she may be afraid, she may always have the instinct to run from the terrors of her past, but more than anything else, she wanted to fight. It became more than a promise to her mother, it became more than her duty as a Healer; she wanted to fight for herself. She wanted to fight because she knew she deserved better. Someone recently had helped to remind her of that.

"Althea, please wake up."

Althea opened her eyes finally laying in Galen's arms. He looked pale and frightened, and she felt his hold of her tight and trembling. As soon as he saw her eyes open, he pulled her into his chest in a relieved and grateful embrace. "Oh God," he said into her hair, "I thought...you weren't waking up."

Althea tried to lift her arms to return his embrace but found her arms heavy and stiff. She fought through it anyway to hold him back. "I'm ok. I'm sorry I scared you. I'm ok now."

> *Fear no more the frown o' th' great;*
> *Thou art past the tyrant's stroke;*
> *Care no more to clothe and eat;*
> *To thee the reed is as the oak:*
> *The scepter, learning, physic, must*
> *All follow this and come to dust.*

Make Not Your Thoughts Your Prisons

Althea felt Galen's breathing slow and deepen beside her and knew he was asleep – just as she had pretended to be. She knew that she could not fall back into dreams, for she was no longer safe even there. She didn't know how in the name of heaven she was going to be able to manage this. How could she ever sleep again? How will she survive without it? How would she protect herself? How could she stop a force she didn't have the faintest concept or understanding of?

When she felt Galen start to rouse, she closed her eyes hard to keep up the illusion that she had gone quietly back to sleep. He turned to her to see her lying on her side. He knew, though, that she was fully awake. The rise and fall of her chest were not the kinds of sleeping. He decided not to call her out on it. Instead, he started to make enough motion and noise that she could justify her show of waking.

When Althea felt that she could turn to him, she began to do so and realized her body had completely stiffened. She let out a small whimper in pain that immediately drew Galen back to her. "What's wrong? Are you hurt?" Galen reached out to touch her, then drew back his hands thinking better of it.

"I don't know," she said in a concerned voice. "I can hardly move. I can't...I can't even turn my neck."

"Ok, I'm going to help you to sit. Is that ok?"

Althea was confused by the question at first. Then she thought how she must appear in his eyes. His confusion and timid apprehension towards her were completely understandable given the story she told and whatever last night must have seemed to him. The thought of it weighed on her heart with heaviness as her mind flashed to the two of them walking as one up the hill - even more when she remembered him holding her. While she accepted and appreciated his considerate soul, she still found an ache in herself.

Althea replied with an affirming noise as she tried her best to do as much on her own as she could. Galen reached behind her and brought her upright to sitting as his arms circled behind her to support her neck and her back. As she was brought to barely sitting, the pain she was feeling from the toxicity in her muscles brought tears to her eyes. She didn't know what had happened, and they were supposed to set out soon. She felt incredibly defeated and sorrowful, and even more so when Galen started to pull away from her once she had become securely upright.

Almost as though they moved on their own, her arms reached around him and clung to him tightly, bringing him back into her. She no longer wanted to bear the burden of her sorrows alone. She now truly realized that he had wanted to help, she wanted him to help, and she didn't want to be the solitary sentry against the darkness anymore.

Galen returned her embrace as he felt her stiff body start to tremble, which seemed to cause her more pain as she could feel and hear her start to softly cry. He closed his eyes. He wanted to savor every part of this moment despite how awful doing so would seem. He wanted to focus on the feel of her arms and the smell of her hair. He was so proud of her strength, for it takes a strong person to accept help and show vulnerability.

"I don't know what's wrong. I can't travel like this. I honestly cannot move my neck, and my back..."

Galen brought his hand up to the top of her head still in their embrace. He ran his hand down the length of her hair to stroke her reassuringly and comfortingly. But to his surprise, she stiffened at the affectionate motion and began to breathe fast and shallow. He pulled back still holding onto her shoulders to see her and what was wrong. Her eyes were distant and glazed over, and her trembling started to increase. He thought maybe she might be having some kind of fit.

"Althea?"

The sound of his caring voice reached deep into her distress and pulled her into focus. Her eyes cleared as she saw him before her. She looked at him like she was seeing him for the first time. She let out a deep and controlled breath, almost as if the devil himself was leaving her body at her command. She wanted to apologize for frightening him yet again, but she couldn't find words in her to speak.

But Galen could see clearly in her eyes the remorse she was feeling. He leaned into her slowly, or at least it seemed slow to Althea. His face became closer to hers, and she could almost sense the sensation of his aura against her cheeks. His eyes were soft and alluring, and he looked deep into hers as well. She wasn't sure if she wanted his lips on hers, but she wasn't sure that she didn't either. His face was so close to hers that she almost couldn't bear the thought they wouldn't kiss.

But instead, Galen was moving in to use his strong arms to support her back and neck again to lower her back to lie flat. "I think," he said quietly faltering. He was surprised in himself that he had been so close, had smelled the floral scent on her skin and the warmth near her lips, and hadn't kissed her. "I think that maybe lying down is better now. Don't strain yourself to sit."

She couldn't see it in his eyes, but the restraint with which he had held himself at bay was agonizing. He had twice held his angel in his arms, and every time he had to let her go had been like giving away part of himself. But he would not harm a flower by selfish plucking it just because he desired it lest it wither and die. Even if all he could do is admire it from afar, that at least would be better than life without it.

She lay flat on the ground beneath him obediently. This was no time for false shows of strength. Right now, the only way to get better was to not rush her body's healing whatever this affliction was.

"Wait here," Galen said to her, and she laughed slightly. He hadn't meant it to be funny, but when he paused and thought about it, he laughed too. He slowly walked towards the large Oak tree at the edge of their plateaued hill. She admired his slow, graceful walk. It was different now than it usually had been. Wasn't it?

Galen sat for a while against the tree and started to hum quietly. What she could hear from her position was the same kind of relaxing melody that reminded one of light rain against the leaves on trees. The kind of sound that lulls all securely and peacefully when heard. She could feel herself relax more at the sound, not even fully aware that she wasn't already relaxed on the ground. As she released the tension she had unwittingly carried, her muscles sent spasms throughout her body, and she muffled a tortured sound.

After a few moments of his stillness and song, Althea saw a black crow descend from the upper branches of the tree down to his hand that rested against his raised knee. This was the first time that she saw the powers of a Leporem with her own eyes. She had heard stories, but it was exhilarating to see. How she wished she could have such power too. She was always fond of birds and the children's stories of princesses and their creature friends. She started to giggle to herself at the thought but stopped so she wouldn't spook the crow.

She watched for some time as he seemed to "talk" to his new companion. Then the crow flew up into the tree as Galen stood and walked over to Althea. He knelt beside her and put his hand on her shoulder reassuringly. "I've got an idea that might help, but we don't have the means by which to do it. I need to go down the hill to get some things, and maybe even find some more food so we don't deplete what's in our packs. The crow there is going to watch out for me; he can fly high and spot the things we need and danger if it's near."

"What's his name?" Althea asked playfully.

Galen smiled at himself trying to remain serious and focused, but failing. "His name is 'Wait here, and don't hurt yourself,'" he joked back. "I promise I won't be gone long, and you'll be safe here."

"Yes, sir," Althea replied keeping in the lightened mood she tried to give off. And as Galen turned to walk away on his mission, he couldn't help but look back at her warmly. He knew she was suffering, he knew that she was in pain, and he knew she was being haunted in her sleep. Yet, through it all, she wanted to do her best to put him at ease and make him smile. He had never experienced that kind of selflessness and consideration given to him. She had truly become his angel.

And nothing would convince him otherwise.

Althea lay on the ground beneath her feeling the patches of grass until the sun rose almost directly above her. She was bathed in the subtle rays of the sun that was warming the still cool air of the morning. With the comfort it brought, she succumbed to light sleep.

When she opened her eyes, she saw Galen had returned. She was relieved to see him safe, and she was grateful for her uneventful sleep without dreams. When she saw the position in the sun, she realized she hadn't slept long at all. Her body started to shake dully in protest at waking too soon and began to feel miserable again.

Galen was building a fire in the center of the hill. It wasn't a huge fire, and he was able to procure enough dried wood that it didn't smoke too much. Even if it did attract the attention of the Immortuos, they wouldn't be able to will their yet dead bodies up the steepness of this hill. However, even the fact that they would notice this fire was unlikely at this time of day. Althea also noticed other supplies. He had laid in a pile beside the tree and medium-sized, flat river stones he was placing onto the tiny fire.

When he was finished with his work, he walked over to her. "I've put some stones in the fire to heat them. I'm going to take them out and put them on your back. The heat should help relieve the stiffness in your muscles."

Althea looked at him impressed. She usually used heat for muscle aches as well, but she usually used her Magic released through her hands or towels warmed in hot water. This seemed much for efficient as stones held heat longer. "I think that's a great idea. Thank you!"

Galen turned from her towards the smile with the cheesiest smile on his face so proud of himself and giddy over her approval. He felt like a child being given candy, and he didn't care how silly that seemed. He began to remove the stone from the fire with wide, flat pieces of wood and placed them on half of a hollowed-out log he found. He walked over to Althea to put the stones on once they had cooled slightly and started to panic and flush at what he realized he would need to ask next.

"Um, Althea," he faltered feeling like a bumbling moron. "Uh..."

She looked up at him seeing the blood in his face and tried not to smile at how adorable he looked to her. The focus to keep from showing that she noticed and potentially hurt his feelings or embarrass him more was incredibly difficult. "What do you need?" she offered to help him along.

"This will probably be most effective if, uh..." he looked at the ground beside her not daring to look in her eyes as he asked, "if the stones were on your skin. The heat will not be as effective through clothes...on you...I mean cloth. The cloth on your clothes."

Dammit!

"Oh, yes," she said as she struggled to get herself upright. "That makes sense." She somehow managed to get herself upright on her own as Galen just watched in dumb shock that she was so willing to do as he had requested. Althea tried gingerly to remove her top to do as she was asked, but she started to cry out in pain that shot from her neck to all parts of her body.

Galen immediately put down the log with the stones and put his hands on her shoulders to steady her. The sound of her pain hurt him deeply - as if her pain were his. Perhaps it was even worse as it injured his heart. He looked at her, their faces close again until Althea asked quietly, "Do you think you could help me with this?" Galen's face felt on fire as he would like nothing more. With all his heart, he wanted …

"Ok," he started with the fastenings of her top to loosen the ties, "you tell me if anything hurts or if this is too fast."

His voice gave Althea goosebumps. "I will. I'm sure it will be fine." She felt her heart beat harder at the touch of his fingers loosening her clothing. She felt more ignited as she felt him lift away her top. The breeze was cool and tickled her bare skin making Althea fully realize her exposure to this man. Only a small part of her felt vulnerable and defenseless, but the larger part of her didn't care.

"Go ahead and lie on your stomach. Do you need me to bring a pack to rest your head on?" His voice was like the warming air dancing inside of her. She felt relaxed. She felt safe. She almost forgot that his voice was asking a question and not simply a delightful sound in her ears. She nodded her head in affirmation, and he rose to grab her piles of clothing and the blanket from her pack to rest her head upon.

She lowered herself slowly and carefully onto her stomach and rested her head on the softer pile he brought. She was completely bare on her back except for the cloth wrapping around her breasts as before. This time, Galen took a longer look at her as he had been frustrated that he hadn't earlier. Her skin was so smooth and fair that he thought it shamed satin. He could only imagine how soft it must be.

He laid his hands on her skin as tenderly as he could. He expected her to flinch at his touch, but she didn't. This even surprised her, but the touch of another caring human was so incredibly comforting, that she even relaxed more.

"May I?" he asked after putting his hands on her shoulders. "I promise I'll be gentle."

"Ok," she barely whispered.

Galen started to apply pressure to her back. Her muscles felt strung as tightly as a bowstring. He wished he knew exactly why, though he had theories. More than that, he hoped that he was able to help with his ideas.

The touch of his hands and the slow, methodical massaging made Althea happy. And she realized then that she hadn't felt happy for too long of a time. She was happy to not be alone, and she was happy that she was with him specifically. He was a virtuous soul filled with pure and natural good. Fate sent them together, and she fully felt the blessing.

Galen slowly increased the pressure against her resistant muscles until she started to let out noises in pain. "Ok, that's enough. I'm sorry. I'll put the stones on now. They should be cool enough." He picked one up with his hands and held it there for a while to make sure. The heat was strong, but it didn't burn after prolonged touch, so it should be ok. "Just let me know if this is too hot or gets too hot."

"Of course."

He laid the stones on the larger muscle clusters along her back and the parts of her that felt most tensed and knotted. The heat felt so good that Althea let out a large, audible sigh that made Galen beam.

When he completed placing all of the heated stones, he lay down flat on his stomach beside her and looked at her. She smiled to see him do this. He looked so ridiculous purposefully pressing his face into the dirt to look funny that she laughed. "Just let those sit a while. I borrowed your bow when I went out. I got us a couple of rabbits. I'll cook those up while I still have a fire."

Althea smiled in response and said, "Thank you, Galen. Thank you for taking care of me."

Galen responded as he started to stand, "My Lady, it is my genuine pleasure."

Time passed as Galen took care of the food and Althea soaked in the heat and focused her energy on healing herself. When the rabbits were cooked, he came over and checked the stones. "These aren't warm anymore. Should I put them back on?"

"Thank you, but no," she responded as she started to sit up. "I think it's best if I start to move around. Then we'll see." Althea moved her arms underneath her and pushed off slowly. She was glad to note that her stiffness had diminished and that she was able to move her neck. "Oh yes," she exclaimed as she reached for her top, "this already feels so much better. You have Healer instincts, Galen."

"Well," he laughed at himself, "I'm no Healer, but I have a few good ideas." He was both glad and sad that she was able to put her top back on without assistance. He liked doing things for her, and he was ready to fully admit to himself that he liked it best when he had the chance to be close to her and touch her. Part of his mind chastised his impulses for being rash and impetuous as he had only known her for a few days, but another part of his mind felt like he would be a fool not to feel this way towards the most wondrous person he had yet known in his life. It only made sense.

As she went to sit beside him near the fire. Galen stoked it absently as he watched her movements. "You know," he started, "I've been thinking. I think I know why you woke up this way."

Althea looked at him intrigued.

"I had a friend back in *my* village years ago. His father - he used to berate him awfully. Made him feel like a continuous disappointment. I always hated to hear when his dad would go off on him. Well, after some time, his dad passed. But even though his dad was gone, he still felt like a disappointment. He could only hear those words and thoughts so often and for so long before that outlook became a part of how even saw himself. Sometimes, he would come up to me before our work in the field rubbing his neck or his shoulders. When I'd ask what was wrong, he would just say he didn't sleep well. Then it became more and more frequent, and he admitted to me that he was thinking about his dad. He'd have nightmares of him. And we both thought it out, and he was carrying the weight so heavily in his mind that his body followed."

Althea looked down to the ground not wanting to face the thought of her nightmares. Even the site of the fire before her pushed the memories to the front of her mind. But before she could tense herself in her memories of it, Galen reached out his hand and placed it on hers.

"I've found that the weight of oppression is felt in more than just your head. I know you had nightmares last night, and I know you're suffering."

Althea looked down again pathetically, "I guess you're going to say don't let it get to me? Don't let the bad stuff win? Don't you think I've tried? It's not as simple as casting away a stone from your shoe."

Galen edged closer to her as he sensed her growing agitation, "No, I wasn't going to say that at all. I was only hoping that, with this thought, you might find some comfort in the fact that you aren't...I don't know." He stopped. He wanted to find the perfect words, words that would truly express what he was thinking. He was coming up short, and he was frustrated that here - when it mattered most - he couldn't find the natural comfort in his speech. But he kept trying.

"This...this is a part of who you are now. Maybe only for now, or maybe for the rest of your life. No, it *will* be for the rest of your life. It's the worst thing, I think, that you can continue to be harmed by someone who never deserved you and your goodness."

Althea saw him flounder like there was some great revelation he just couldn't quite grasp but that he was desperately trying to find. And he was. He wanted to pull the answers from heaven and hand them to her as a gift, but it was elusive.

"Althea, I don't have the answers. But if it were up to me, I'd tear the world apart to find it."

Althea blushed as these were the most passionate and affectionate words he had ever spoken towards her. She blushed not so much at his show of affection, intentional or not, but at the fact that she enjoyed it so much. How was she not shying away? Given everything that had happened, wasn't she just asking for more trouble? Maybe not, she thought; maybe not with him.

Galen gave up trying to find the right words and settled on his words. "I guess all I'm saying is that it makes sense. It's not because you're weak. You're the strongest person I've known. I guess...just don't blame yourself. This isn't you. This isn't because you're not strong enough."

Althea still looked down at the ground in shame. How could she not think that? How, given all she experienced in that dream, if it was even a dream, and all that she heard that it ALL wasn't her fault.

"Do you want to talk about it?"

"Yes."

Who Art Black as Hell, as Dark as Night

"My God."

"Yeah."

"Do you think any of it was real?"

"Galen, I have no doubt in my heart that it was all real."

Althea told Galen all about her dream, or whatever it was, and all that had been revealed to her with it. They now both knew the depth of Durai's power, the extent of his malicious will to use that power, and the truth that he had indeed conjured this curse.

"So he perverted nature itself, pulled our loved ones from their peace to become the damned of the earth, so he could…?" Galen stopped. He saw the pain that was riddled all over her face. There were no tears, though. She felt she had no more tears left to cry; no more heart left to break.

"Yeah. He's found some way to bring me back, or punish me, or both."

"That damned devil. I never thought…I mean you hear about evil when you're a child. It's in the old, ancient stories. And you know bad people, but real evil? It doesn't exist, right? I guess now I know." Galen was angry deep in his blood, deep in him where he dared not lose control and seldom did. "He can't win," he added resolutely.

"Huh?" Althea was confused as to what he meant. "I don't think there's a way he can fail at this point. I'm coming back, and I feel thoroughly punished."

Galen rose from his spot on the ground and began to pace in enmity and rage. "Like Hell! We'll stay right here. Your power is strong enough to beat this. I know, I just feel it. So do it now. Try right here and now. Show him he's not won!"

Althea tried to offer her explanation with compassion. She was so touched by his caring but also pained by his vexation and distress. "Oh, Galen. It doesn't work that way. I have to be there. I have to be at the site where the curse began. This sickness on the land is like the sight of infection. You don't put medicine on a shoulder for a wound to the knee. I have to be at the site where the earth was attacked and this poison was allowed to spread from. Only there can I be of any help."

"Any help?" Galen sensed that her confidence faltered as she said these words. He saw that a sudden realization struck her with anxiety and the pallor of death washed over her. "Althea?"

"Galen…" she whispered almost as though she were miles away, "Galen I don't know what to do. I don't know how to fix this. I don't even know where I would begin."

Galen saw her torment and went to sit beside her. Whatever was building the anger inside of him could wait. "I'm not sure what you're talking about. What's wrong?"

"Galen, I'm walking in blindness. I'm going to try and save everyone, to stop this curse, but I don't know how. I'm just a Healer, and I know they're saying and he's saying that only a Healer can fix this. But, Galen, I have no idea what to do. I don't know what Magic I have that will be the cure for…" she trailed away as she went into her own mid, sought any answer, any possibilities, and came back with only defeat.

"So, this isn't something you studied before or been taught, not something you know how to fight?" Galen looked at her as she stared at the ground in front of her. She seemed as low as the dirt and ashes at the base of the spent fire. The only color on her face was the color the sun cast against her skin as it was setting fast beyond them.

"I'm so sorry," Althea confessed as she looked up at him. Her eyes were nothing but overflowing grief and guilt. "I'm going, but I don't know what to do when I get there."

"When you get there?" Galen was washed over, blown back like an autumn gale, at her words. He moved in front of her and knelt before her and held her hands in his. "My God. Listen to you. You don't know what to do, you're lost in the darkness that is hunting you and consuming you. Even before we met, you were fighting a destructive battle that was ravaging your sanity and crushing your spirit."

Althea looked down in shame. Healers were supposed to be the guardians of the living light and the sentries against the darkness. And she was such a disappointment now.

But then she felt Galen's hand move to her chin and tilt it to look him in the eyes. His eyes were filled with brilliant and overwhelming admiration. "And yet," he said softly, "you still go. You didn't know what you would do, but you still decided to turn and fight. You were confronted with the fear that torments you the most, and still, you turn and fight. You even realize now that you could very well fail and be met with nightmares, and you still decide to turn and fight. The world is giving you every chance to give up. But you aren't."

His words both terrified and inspired her. And for even just a moment, she felt pride in herself. And when the moment felt like passing, she allowed her pride to stay. If what he said was true, maybe she deserved to love herself.

As her tension seemed to leave her with a sigh, she bent her head forward slightly and rested against his. They were so close that their noses were touching. Their auras turned to one another and intertwined like the supporting, strengthening vines around an ancient tree. Both of them slowly realized how close they were, and neither would be the first to break away.

"And as for the other thing," Galen began still holding his head touching hers, "you should not feel punished. His only strength over you was his willful violation and abuse of a caring, loving heart that felt she should take on the troubles of the world as her responsibility."

He then raised his hand and placed it beside her cheek still with their heads against one another. His move may have been a gamble, but he didn't care. His heart would be betrayed if he didn't. When he pulled away, his hand still against her face, he saw that she was not annoyed, offended, or even alarmed. "You...none of this is your fault. This was all him. His reasons are not your responsibility."

Althea placed her hand on top of his hand against her face. "Thank you."

•••••••

Fear no more the lightning flash,

Nor the all-dreaded thunder stone;
Fear not slander, censure rash;
Thou hast finished joy and moan:
All lovers young, all lovers must
Consign to thee, and come to dust.

•••••••

"I'm not sure who we're looking for. She used to be here in the castle?"

"Yeah, about a year ago. Well, maybe a little longer. Before the Mist for sure. She used to live here and took care of Baldrik; she was his Healer."

"May he rest in peace."

"Yeah, this was before you came here. Back when you were still at your mother's skirts."

"Ass! I think you mean YOUR mother's skirts."

"Hey, you two, we can't afford a scuffle tonight. The queen is sending us out passed the Plains tomorrow to look for this Healer. And you know some crazy shit lives out there, not to mention the Immortuos. You gotta be at your best. You're the elite palace guards, at least try to act like it."

"Yes, sir."

"So, since I don't know this girl, what does she look like? I mean, what am I looking for?"

"Oh, she was absolutely *gorgeous*. About this tall, with the most attractive head of dark hair you could ever see, deep brown eyes that would break your heart..."

"Yeah, she came from Base, but you couldn't tell. She was real classy."

"Too bad Mason isn't still around, he would tell you all about her."

"Mason?"

"Oh, yeah, still before your time here. He was Durai's old guard."

"May he rest in peace?"

"Holy shit, he's dead?"

"Yeah, some terrible accident just after the Healer vanished."

"Yeah, sure, 'accident.'"

"Man, shut your mouth! You know the Queen shut that shit down right away."

"More like Durai did. The guy is straight out of Hell sometimes."

"Yeah, so don't piss him off!"

"How about you all shut up, and let's all get some sleep. With any luck, the search will be short now that Duarai got that vision that she's actually alive and out there somewhere. I don't want us out there any longer than we have to be."

"Yes, sir."

By Day My Limbs, by Night My Mind, for Thee, and for Myself No Quiet Find

"Are you sure you've given yourself enough time? The crossing won't be easy."

"I'm sure, Galen. Thank you."

After two solid days of rest on the safety of their hill, Althea's muscles and hurt ankle had recovered enough to make the swift crossing across Shimmer Plain. They started to pack away all the supplies they had and began to mentally prepare themselves for the arduous road ahead.

In the plains, there was nowhere to hide, and every moving, living thing became a target.

The plains had been mostly abandoned after a few short months following the first coming of the Mist. The openness of the plains presented unique problems that made them exceptionally treacherous. Most villages within plain regions were abandoned. The people found themselves without a natural barrier to use as a shield like a river, hill, or mountain. They quickly discovered the Immortuos were able to come to landmarks like their homes from all sides, and they met their ends with nowhere to run. Most villages within Shimmer Plain or Golden Wheat to the North were nothing but empty shells of abandoned homes and dismembered, unburied bodies.

"You about ready?" Althea asked Galen. "We need to start as early as possible; I don't think we should be in the plains when the sun sets."

"I agree. Just a few more things, and we're good."

The way they spoke to each other now, the way that they regarded each other, was no longer the way a charge regarded an escort, or strangers spoke even in forced politeness. In these few days, their relationship had changed from two strangers setting out with a common goal to a man and a woman who made a bond between themselves and set out with each other and for each other. Their trust in one another was set in a deep and natural place within their very souls. It was no longer a link borne out of necessity, but an alliance of the truest kind.

However, Galen had to hide from his eyes just how deep his ties with her had become. The nature of his caring and concern for her was something he couldn't understand fully or even rationally explain. He never once believed in the myth of "love at first sight." Such thoughts are for children and naïve fools. Love takes time, love takes patience, and love takes understanding. But the more he thought about it, the more he knew that while his attraction for her stunning physical features was unquestionable and most certainly caught his attention at the beginning, he found that was not what drew his eyes to her so often now. The feelings grew the more he knew her and the more he understood her; the depth of her character that fought and persevered despite the most monstrous of haunting challenges dazzled beyond physical beauty. Perhaps he was falling in love even in such a short time. Well, at least he had acknowledged devotion and admiration towards her. But, no, this felt like something much more.

When Galen finished his final preparations, they started slowly down the steep hill. Once at the bottom, they stood at the borders of the Shimmer Plain. It stretched out for miles and seemed much more daunting as they stood at the foot of it versus what they had assessed from the top of their hill. They looked at each other worryingly both acknowledging the possibility that they would not be able to cross the entire span of it before dark. The Hill of the Castle was very distant and barely held a grey outline in the distance.

"How are we going to make this across in a day?" Galen sighed to himself. His mind was racing with each potential danger and pitfall while still being worried about Althea's ankle and whether or not it was up for this.

Althea put a hand on his shoulder and replied, "One step at a time. Starting with this one." She then took the lead and began a light jog to set the pace. Galen, hopeful but still apprehensive, followed alongside her.

Their bodies were well in shape having been trained to be fit for survival in the wild. Though they hadn't taken on a task of this size recently, they were both able to keep up a paced jog for a long duration. Their journey was in silence, as much silence as they could manage, and they kept constant vigilance against any potential Immortuos groups that could be found in their vicinity.

When their bodies could no longer keep up the pace of the jog, they slowed to a fast-paced walk. They paused only for a moment as they reached for water and food from their packs which they consumed while still walking. They couldn't afford to stop any more than absolutely necessary. The very air seemed to hold its breath with them as they kept up their guard and heightened their senses to spot any other presence beside theirs. But with the stillness in the air came a more oppressive heat from the sun. Remarkable what tree cover and a breeze could do to lessen its intensity. In the woods, and especially in the river, the world was almost like winter. But here away from cover and devoid of the air moving, it seemed more like summer.

They hadn't accounted for this heat and its effects when evaluating their water needs, and their bodies ached for more than they allowed themselves to keep up supplies. There were wells in the towns of Shimmer Plain, but no rivers to resupply. But that was an option they were hesitant to take given the dangers in town.

The sun was moving across the sky much faster than they had been able to cross the plain. While their destination became more in focus, they soon began to realize that they would not reach the borders of Shimmer Plain before nightfall.

"What are we going to do?" Althea asked short of breath after another jogging spurt. They dared not stop, but they could no longer keep such an unrealistic pace.

"I don't know. None of the options are good," Galen replied also short of breath.

"Agreed. We can't just keep going through the night. Our bodies are too dehydrated from rationing our water and exhausted from running all day. We'd collapse before we reached the end. And being helplessly spent anywhere is not something I'm happy with."

"Yeah, but the only other option is stopping for the night in a village filled with hiding places for the Immortuos and no defense in a house and no cover in the streets."

They both finally stopped their fast-paced walking and bent over to catch their breath. They looked at each other with a distressed and nearly defeated look. The more they caught their breath, the more they realized just how thoroughly exhausted they were. Their muscles started to cramp painfully with their mind becoming fuzzy and dizzy with just how badly they needed water. It seems the choice was being made for them.

"Lesser of two evils, I guess," Galen said still trying to catch his breath. "We can either go back to the last village those miles back or hope to find another one soon further ahead."

"Damn," Althea responded. "I do not want to go back. We gained so much ground since that last little village. I say let's try a little further."

"Ok, I'm with you."

They gave themselves a few more moments to gather their last reserves. With a mutual nod to each other, they set out again at a jogging pace to try and race against the setting of the sun. Their chests ached more in desperation and sinking hope than the burning in their lungs from their pace. They had no idea what they would do if they couldn't find a village soon. And once they did, what condition that village would be in, or how safe they would find themselves.

Their feet started to stumble and lose stability as their remaining strength was spent. Galen's feet found a small unevenness in the earth and sent him falling to the ground. Althea stopped, turned to see him on the ground, and ran back to him to help him up. "God, Galen. I'm so sorry. We should have turned back."

"No, I still think it was a good call," Galen replied struggling to get up even with her help. Both of their voices seemed so far away from each other as they became more lightheaded. Their muscles were screaming, and the light was quickly fading. Soon they wouldn't be able to see well except for the light of the moon. Given their fatigue and their nearly unresponsive limbs, they would be incredibly vulnerable in the open. All they could do was keep going no matter what. They couldn't afford to give up now.

"I'm ok," Galen informed her as he finally got steady on his feet. "Can't be much farther."

They both held onto each other as they walked at a slow and steady new pace. They felt as though they were trudging through deep sand, and their spirits were reaching desperation and panic. The darkness spread not only on the plains but on their frames of mind. How can one search for the light when the spread of the darkness is ever so pervasive?

But just as all those who battle for the light meet some hope, in the end, the outline of a rather large village appeared before them just as night fell upon them. It seemed a mirage, too good and too convenient to be true. They had finally come to what they were searching for so desperately. However, their elation was only fleeting as they remembered that this option was only the lesser of two incredibly dangerous evils.

Before entering the village, they drank their fill of the water they had saving only a little for the morning. They would find a well in town and restock before setting out again.

They walked the streets of a village long abandoned, and this one seemed larger than most they had passed before. It was still too defenseless to fortify, and therefore all the people left alive fled to anywhere else that they could find better. Without realizing it, they clasped their hands together and kept close as they passed houses and small merchant stalls and shops. They were almost holding their breath they were trying to be so quiet. Their eyes strained against the shadows created in the light of the moon against the deserted structures.

Every so often, they found the decaying parts of bodies ruthlessly torn apart by Immortuos. Althea unintentionally slowed her pace and looked in horror at the site. The ground before these bodies still held the red stain of their blood. The site was savage, the mutilation ferocious. It was the kind of vision that would haunt any sane person for the rest of their lives. And Althea knew in an instant that she would carry the weight of what she was witnessing until she died.

Galen wasn't sure why she had slowed down. Sites like these he had seen before and didn't care to linger over. He had seen his village done this way, the ones who couldn't retreat in time. He may not have held any long endearment to those lost by the time it came, but he still felt the burden of their gruesome end. But it was different for Althea. Each one of these souls that were lost as a result of this Mist weighed on her conscience. These people were gone now, painfully, because she held the heart of a psychopath.

After getting the feel of the village, they decided to camp out the rest of the night in the most defensible structure they could find. There was a small kitchen building resting with a shared wall against a communal dining structure. These buildings were usually for grand gatherings, celebrations, and town meetings. This building seemed to hold the kitchen to facilitate these occasions. But with one wall protected against the other building, it was one less access to fortify. The building itself wasn't large at all; it could probably hold maybe ten people at maximum. There were so many large cabinets and places to hide, and they checked each space thoroughly for Immortuos. Every cabinet and door opened came with overwhelming anxiety and muscles tensed to run.

Much to their relief, the building was empty besides their presence. They let out a sigh of relief. "Hey," Althea called out to Galen, "take a look at this." Galen looked over to find Althea inside one of the larger storage pantry units. She had her foot on something.

"What is that?"

"It's an underground storage area for foods that are best kept in a dark place to make them last longer." She opened an almost invisible door on the floor to reveal stairs and what resembled something between a room and a nook. It looked just big enough to hold two or maybe three people. "If we closed this door to the main pantry and then closed this hatch to the basement room, we would be not only well hidden but well-fortified. We'd both be able to sleep and get a full night's rest."

"That's genius! How did you think to look here?!"

Althea gave out an embarrassed laugh, "When I was a very young girl, I always liked little pastries. And in my village, they used to keep cream-filled pastries in a cellar like this. I was a bit of a thief." Galen looked at her little sheepish smile and felt warm inside. He thought about how beautiful a child she must have been. She must have filled the room with such innocent delight. It had to be true, for the woman she was today gave him the same feeling.

She descended the stairs first making slow progress in the dim light. "Ok," she called out, "I've reached the bottom. Not more than a few meters down. Be sure to close the door before you come down."

Galen turned around and closed the large door to the main pantry behind him and braced it with a few shelves as best he could in the darkness. "Ok! It's done!" Then he turned in the darkness he found himself in. He let out a chuckle though when he found he couldn't see his hands in front of his face.

"What are you laughing at?" Althea called up to him.

"I just realized that I'm going to probably tumble on my way down. I can't tell if my eyes are opened or closed."

"Oh, that is a problem. Hold on." Althea then thought about how she could help. She thought of an idea that may work as she held out her hands, her palms facing each other. She closed her eyes and concentrated very hard on the light within her. She softly began to hum, and a beautiful golden light danced between her hands from the music she made and the light she guarded within her.

Galen felt like his breath was seized from his body at the sight that appeared before him. His angel was bathed in a radiant, golden glow. It was like seeing every good feeling he sensed from her being manifested in dancing rays coming from her body. Every passing thought he had about her being an angel...it was real. He would never doubt her goodness. Nothing as beautiful as her could ever be anything but pure grace and virtue. Even if he hadn't fully had faith that such things truly ever existed in a world that had decayed so thoroughly, he knew now that some benevolence was left.

"Can you see well enough?"

Galen shut his mouth feeling like the biggest idiot in the world for having stared at her so dumbfoundedly. "Yes, sorry." He started to descend the stairs and reached the bottom. He felt warmth from the glow that was a welcome change from the coldness in the cellar they found themselves in. Both of their faces were softly lit by the glow that was now shared between them.

"May I?" Galen finally asked. Althea nodded and offered her hands still held facing each other. He slowly and hesitantly reached out to hold her hands that produced the light. He didn't care if his request seemed absurd or idiotic, he had to know. He had to hold this in his hands if only once and only for a little while. As his hands touched hers, the light wrapped around his hands as well and changed from a golden color to one of pure white. The brilliance dazzled like the sun in their eyes, and they both smiled in delight. To Galen, touching the light was like reaching into the deep memories that held one's heart in bliss and contentment. He was suddenly a boy playing with his friends, he was in his mother's arms hearing her sing, he was with his friends laughing in the fields, he was seeing her for the very first time. The light even changed for Althea then. For the first time in over a year, she felt worthy of it. For the first time in over a year, she felt like someone beyond the victim, beyond the pain, and more than the sum of her tragic past. She was once again a gifted guardian of light.

Galen hadn't meant to do it, and he hadn't realized he had done it, but he pulled her hands towards his chest and rested them there. The distance between them was almost nothing at all. In so doing, the light spread and wrapped around both of them entirely covering every inch of their bodies. And the spectacle was lost on them as all they could see was the caring in their companion's eyes. Galen couldn't be sure if Althea's affections were the same as his, but at this moment holding her hands and sharing this bond, he didn't care. This moment he had, if it was all he would ever get, he'd hold it as enough.

Althea sensed them both moving into each other. Not just him, but she had closed her distance between them. She painfully brought herself out of this spell knowing now was not the place nor the time. "I think," she said whispering and trying her best not to struggle with the words, "I think it would be best if we started to rest now. We're both exhausted."

Galen did well hiding the pain and disappointment. He knew she was right, and he was exhausted. Besides, romance was the last thing he should be pushing. "You're right. I can barely stand up." They looked at the cellar around them as best they could still be holding the light fading from her hands.

"Not much room, huh?" Althea said innocently with a smile.

"We'll have to get kind of...cozy."

Idiot!

"Haha," she lightheartedly laughed. "Not much else we can do. I'll be glad for it, honestly. It's so cold down here."

Galen squeezed her hand with affectionate pressure, and he felt the light that had faded still warm in his heart. But he then obediently released her hands and they both found their way to the floor. Althea felt around her pack and took out her small blanket that was barely enough to cover one of them. She thought for a moment and then handed the blanket to Galen. When he felt the cloth being passed to him, he protested not wanting to take it away from her.

"No, it's ok," Althea started to explain. "Listen, since you're bigger than me, you can hold me and keep me warm better than a blanket, but since no body heat is at your back, you should take the blanket. Unless," she hesitated suddenly feeling awkward, "you'd rather not."

Galen didn't speak to answer. Instead, he took the blanket and wrapped his arms around her waist, and help lay her to the ground pressed against his chest. In the darkness, she could not see his contented smile and he could not see hers. But they soon fell fast asleep together in warmth and physical safety.

If only the peace of this moment could last in dreams.

'Tis Now The Very Witching Time of Night

Althea could hear fire crackling, and she opened her eyes at the strangeness of the sound. She felt no arm encircling her in warmth and comfort. As she turned around in the dim light, she saw that she was alone. She was no longer in the cellar. As she looked around the room, she realized she was no longer safe.

The fire she heard was in the bed-chambers of the room, and her body was compelled to the side of the fireplace at the far end of the room. She could hear the sound of the door shut ominously behind her. She could feel the fear and panic rise within her chest and hold tight against her lungs and quicken her heart. She closed her eyes to focus all her concentration to wake. She silently begged and prayed to be the master of this nightmare and escape it. But the dark and powerful Magic that had pulled her to this place, having her both there and not there, would not allow any will of hers to pull herself back from it.

"I can feel you're closer now." Althea heard his voice from within the shadows of his grand, curtained bed slithering through the air like a serpent.

"Durai, let me go." Althea had no power behind her plea and only went to show just how terrified she truly was. She despaired to know that, just like that, she was his prisoner again. But the veil of his treachery was lifted, and she could see clearly where before she was blinded.

"No, Dove. I don't think I will yet. I have waited so very long. I find that my patience is gone now." His figure emerged from the bed dressed in fine bed robes that flowed with the graceful heaviness of fine silk. "I'm glad to see you've dressed for the occasion," he replied gesturing to her.

Althea looked down at herself and found that her appearance in the place had been manipulated into false clothing. Another trick inside this spell. She saw that she was now in a deep green negligee also of heavy silk. The length of the soft dressing gown reached the floor and barely covered her feet in the front and trailed just slightly in the back. There were no sleeves to show the smooth skin of her bare arms. In the coolness of the room, she saw and felt the goosebumps on her arms appear. How could this be in a dream? These sensations were painfully real. The neckline was lower than she had ever had on before in all her life reaching almost to her waist. The curves of her breast made subtle shows into the exposed neckline and were teasingly alluring. She closed her eyes in torment and self-conscious shame at being put into something so obscene and revealing.

"Durai, this is disdainful. Give me back my own clothes." Althea could feel more strength behind her words as she started to allow herself to be angry. She realized then that before she had not allowed herself to feel anger at him. She had felt so much because of him such as shame, humiliation, and betrayal, but she never allowed the anger that she had towards him to have its moment in her mind. In a moment of clarity, she realized that the anger was not a weakness, for it was the part of her that loved herself and wouldn't stand for this treatment anymore.

"You don't like my gift? I'm hurt. I think it becomes you most...beguilingly. But if you insist on being without it, I could have it removed." He had closed the distance between the two of them by now and looked down at her revealed chest and repressed every screaming urge to caress the parts of her that he had dreamed of for over a year.

"You know very well that I did not mean that, Durai! Don't be any cruder." She could feel herself tremble with the tempest of emotions raging inside of her heart like a wind out of control blowing about the leaves in autumn. Durai could see in her eyes her instability and the weakness she was desperate not to show.

"Oh my dear darling Dove, crude is what I simply cannot wait to be with you finally here." He lowered his face to rest on top of her head and he inhaled her scent deeply. He had so long missed her natural, sweet smell.

"Why have you brought me here?"

"I told you already," Durai said forcefully as he turned from her then to pick up a glass of wine he had on the small table next to the fireplace. "I have waited far too long to have you back, and you have yet to arrive. So you come when I call you. And I've called you."

"You do know that this is not what you will get when I come back to stop everything you have set in motion," Althea said still unable to will her limbs to move. "I will do all that I can, I will bring an end to all of this if I possibly can, and then I'm as good as gone again. I've learned so much stealth while I was away, you may not even know I've come until I've gone."

Durai took a drink of his wine and savored the sweet heat of it. He then walked over to her gliding like a predatory animal standing once again in front of her. "You truly believe it will be as easy for you as that? What has all this time out in the wild done to your mind?" He let out a low and taunting laugh that made her blood boil. "Althea," the sound of her name in his voice made her wretch, "it really won't be long now. I have felt just how close you've come to me now, and they are looking for you. Oh yes," he continued seeing her panicked confusion, "men have been sent to fetch you to me. How long do you think you could evade the palace's trained guards? I don't suspect long. And then…"

He lifted a hand suddenly, and Althea found herself flinching. Durai smiled at her, and indeed it was loving. If it could be believed that the devil was capable of it, he truly did love her. His raised hand then moved to her face and brushed aside a stray wisp of hair back into place behind her ear. His hand then moved slowly down her neck and rested at the small of her back just resting where her alluring, curving swell began.

The lucid feel of his hands on her body brought a single tear rolling down Althea's cheek. Memories invaded her mind then. She could feel every time he had ever touched her, every inch of her that had been possessed by him and invaded by all of him. She felt the lasting burn of every pierce and the painful piercing of every caress in their long history of lovemaking. "Please, Durai, please let me go."

"No," he said with a domineering and commanding tone of finality. "I told you. I let you go once, and that will NOT happen again." She saw his eyes glow brighter, and she knew better than to think it was an illusion.

"Please," she pleaded still unable to move, still unable to wake herself away from where she wished she could escape.

Durai saw the tear as it made its way down her face. He lifted his hand to it and wiped it away with the tenderest touch of a single finger. "Now, now," he whispered so close to her face that she could feel the movement of his lips. "You'll be with me again. I'm going to give you the entire world, and you will give me all of you in return. We'll be happy again." With that, he placed his lips gently upon hers. She could feel his pain and desperation in that kiss. If he were any other person, she might pity the ache she felt from him. He was a man begging again for the woman he loved – if it truly were love.

But soon she felt the familiar, ardent passion return, and with it the power of dominance in his kiss. He parted her lips forcefully with his and demanded her love in return. His gentleness faded, and he was again the monster of her nightmares who would stop at nothing to consume every part of her over and over again. He would never be sated; he would always hunger for her.

Durai could feel her chest rise and fall with her heavy, frightened breathing. The alluring sensation of her breasts brushing against his chest sent exquisite shivers down into every sensual part of him. He could smell her floral smell stronger now even in this illusion. To him as well, each touch was solid and lifelike and he relished the agony of the anticipation of having her fully in his arms soon. Though his kiss had been solid, it was not truly her. Though the heart against his chest gave solid pressure against his robes, it wasn't truly her. But it would be all of her soon. Very soon.

"Durai, I wasn't happy. I left because I was very unhappy. I was dying inside, and you were the one killing me."

"No," he said again. "There were too many other things that were drawing the life out of you. Too many eyes following you hungrily, too much expectation drowning you in responsibility. It's different now. Baldrik's gone, so you'll only be mine now. You'll see how this time will be better."

Althea felt herself choke in her disbelief and the repugnancy of his words. "Better?" she gasped and nearly spat at him. "Baldrik's tormented end is in no way better!"

Durai's wicked smile returned to his face as he looked down at her face flushed delightfully red in her anger. "Oh, you mean this isn't what you wanted when you left him to face his misery alone? This isn't what you envisioned when you abandoned him to a life of unassisted suffering?"

"No, Durai!" Althea said as she raised her voice. "Don't you do that. You don't know anything, and you cannot make me feel guilt over him!"

"You're right," Durai deeply whispered. She could feel the vibrations of his voice deep in her bones as they shook her from the inside. "I don't need to. You already have that guilt, don't you? I know you're smart enough to know what is yours to bear. And if you don't blame yourself, you'll still have to face someone else who does."

Althea suddenly felt the terror and dismay that she had done so well fighting against suddenly breaking through the guards she had mounted. She was suddenly at the mercy of fear that seized her soul. Durai could see the sudden loss of her control, and his smile deepened along with his embrace of her. He pressed her body into his stronger than before and looked down at her terrified eyes.

"Oh yes, Dove. Her Majesty is most angry with you."

· · · · · · ·

Althea screamed without knowing she was back inside of her real, living body, back where she was hiding in the abandoned village where quiet was essential. When she realized what she had done, she curled up into herself and clasped both hands around her mouth. And all she was left with was an all-consuming loss. The feeling of indescribable loss snuffed out all of her will, all of her hope, and she withered within herself in renewed despair.

Then she felt the arms around her again from behind. This time she wasn't afraid, she wasn't mistaken. His hold on her was strong and stalwart. He didn't say a word, neither of them did. They stayed silent for a long time listening for signs that they had been discovered. They waited in the darkness for an hour, but no sign came. Luck had at least been generous in this.

"Were you gone again?" she heard him whisper finally. She nodded to affirm his response, and he held her tighter. She wished more than ever that it wasn't true. It couldn't possibly be true, could it? Please let it all be false, and let his words be vicious lies spun with the shadows bread forth from the evil he conjured from. She begged silently into the darkness, but only silent darkness responded.

And in the darkness all around her, Galen held her body that wracked itself in silent sobbing.

"Mireya. Please no."

✳✳✳

No exorciser harm thee!
Nor no witchcraft charm thee!
Ghost unlaid forbear thee!
Nothing ill come near thee!
Quiet consummation have;
And renownèd be thy grave!

When Churchyards Yawn and Hell Itself Breathes Out Contagion to This World

They both stirred in the darkness from their sleep. Althea turned into Galen's chest half asleep searching only for the safety of his embrace pressing against the strength of his toned chest and wanting to sleep further. The two layers of barricaded doors between them and possible daylight made it impossible to tell if they were still left with the night to sleep or if it had passed to midday. They had no way to know. But Galen could still feel her tremble from the horrors in the night that still apparently haunted her. He felt no need to rush their waking.

Even if part of his reasoning to let her sleep was purely selfish, he let her sleep and he dozed in and out of consciousness with her. He would hold her for as long as she would let him. An ever-growing part of him wanted to keep her here, in safety, and away from the monsters clamoring for her flesh. His heart suddenly cared less and less for the suffering of the world and cared more only to keep her from further agony.

Hours passed or perhaps only minutes – time was an elusive shadow that they had no grasp on - and Althea stirred with more strength. The darkness was no longer complete and total, but still overwhelming. Only the dimmest shades and outlines could be distinguished in this light. Althea reached out her hand towards the outline of Galen and held his face. Galen held out his hand and held her face as well. He found her cheeks still wet with tears.

"What time is it?" she asked him. Her voice was horse, almost weak sounding. But he could still hear strength in it. No matter what had happened to her last night, no matter what she had faced, he knew she hadn't been beaten.

"Hard to tell. I'll go out and see."

"No, we'll go out together," she affirmed as she started to get up to leave as well. She refused to wait alone in the darkness. She longed to see the light she was hoping was there.

They both ascended the stairs carefully and quietly and opened the hatch to their cellar hiding place. The pantry itself held a dim glow as the light showed from under the door. It was indeed day now and not night, though how late was hard to tell. They both felt rather rested physically, all things considered, but they were hungry and thirsty. Althea was the first to reach for the door, and she opened it slowly. The light in the room poured quickly onto her and her eyes painfully adjusted. She held her breath to listen intently for any signs of movement. She could hear none.

As they both emerged from the pantry, they felt the warmth of the day indicating it was no longer morning. The air held no dampness of morning dew; the sun had taken it all. Galen held out an arm to signal Althea to wait behind as he stepped out the door to assess the sun. It was well past midday. He looked around, made sure they were alone, and then turned to her and said, "We've slept most of the day. It's getting on towards late afternoon."

Althea seemed discouraged, but not surprised. "We'll have to stay another night. We can't set out this late. The hill is still a day's journey from us."

Galen dropped his head feeling some guilt at how much pleasure he found in holding her until they were both so far into the day. But that guilt was slightly overshadowed by how much he looked forward to more rest and another night holding her.

"We should find this village's well. I don't know about you, but my head hurts from dehydration. Maybe we can look for other supplies too. Carefully," Althea added at the end. The villages even outside of the Plains were pitfalls for danger, but villages within the Plains were even more so.

"I think I remember seeing one in that direction."

"Ok, then let's start."

Their search didn't take long before they found the well at the village center. Galen started to pull the rope to bring up the water and realized the gears were in bad need of lubrication and made a lot of sounds. They looked at each other frustrated at this, but Galen soon continued slower this time. Althea took her bow from across her chest and stood ready if their presence attracted any attention. Galen's arms started to burn with the effort it took to pull the weight of the water-filled bucket slowly, but he didn't want to show any signs of strain to Althea.

The first bucket full of water reached the top after what seemed like an eternity. Galen rested it on the wall of the well and immediately dipped his face to the water and drank until his belly was filled. The water was cold and quenched the burning in his lungs. The water seemed to soothe his insides which were strained and sore from the pace they kept the day before. He wanted so much to pour it out on his head and feel that same relief all over his body. Instead, he turned to Althea and silently offered to keep watch while she got her fill.

Althea drank and drank until she felt that her insides would burst. Between the two of them, they had managed to drain the large bucket. Althea slowly lowered the rope and bucket as quietly as possible to bring more up to refill their packs.

With their chore at the well completed, Althea took back her bow, slung it across her back, and they began to quietly search the town with the remaining light of the day. Most of the village was ransacked either by those alive when they were fleeing or the Immortuos that pursued them after and destroyed everything in their rage that they could get their hands on. They felt as if they were walking through the bones of a slain beast bleached white from the oppressive sun years passed after its demise. Nothing left resembled what had once been. It was devastating to think that once each home was filled with the lives of a family, each shop held the livelihood of a living soul, and a community cared and held pride for a place that was now held in ruin. It was no longer a place that nurtured lives; this was now a graveyard. Only death was found here.

Galen sensed the weight that burdened Althea at each step, and he silently slipped her hand into his own. She was so far into her thoughts, drowning in the signs of suffering around her, that the warm touch that she suddenly felt made her jump slightly in surprise. She gave Galen an apologetic look, and he just looked on at her with concern. She shied away from his eyes; she didn't want to be pitied even if he meant well. Nothing was going to get better for her or anyone else if she hid behind being a victim.

In an attempt to shift focus from her, she walked herself to a demolished merchant's stall and picked up some long pieces of broken wood. "Maybe," she said, "we could make some torches to bring into our cellar. If there is any food still good here, it would be there or in places like that. The light will help us look." Galen nodded and picked up a few pieces of wood himself that would be appropriate.

Althea suddenly reached a hand to his bent back to stop him and stood frozen. Galen stood still as well and listened intently. Somewhere in the distance, they heard signs of movement, shuffling of uneven feet. Althea passed the wood she held in her hands to Galen and once again removed the bow that rested across her chest and back and held it ready. The rustling became louder and was moving steadily towards them. Without a word between them. Galen placed his back against hers. His sight saw the way ahead, and her sight covered his back. He began to move forward towards their cellar, and Althea followed walking backward with her bow still held at ready with an arrow in place desperately praying she wouldn't have to use it.

Their progress was slow and methodical. Each corner of the town they passed was checked before moving onward, but still, the sounds came louder. When Galen caught sight of their kitchen building, he reached back behind him with his free hand and stroked her elbow in reassurance. They were so close, but they knew they had to keep their silent and slow movements until the last minute. Any careless sounds made in haste would reveal them. They couldn't afford to give away the one place of safety that they knew and give signs that there was something to hunt within those walls.

Galen held out his hand and placed his palm on her back signaling her to stop as he opened the door to the building. She could hear him shift the weight of the wood he was carrying even as quiet as he was trying to be. Both of them felt that even the sound of their rapid and frightened heartbeat echoed down the streets of this town calling loudly to danger. When he released her hand on her back, she started to once again move backward in his direction into the building.

As the door closed behind them, they could hear the movement quicken as if suddenly given direction and purpose. They immediately sat low on the ground pushing their backs and weights against the door to barricade it. The sound came closer. It was every bump in the night one feared as a child. It was every nightmare given form lurching closer and closer. It was no doubt an Immortuo, and it was getting ever nearer. There suddenly came a stench of death as the noises suggested their unwitting pursuer was right outside their building now. All they could do was desperately pray that it didn't detect them.

So little was known for certain about the Immortuos other than they were living souls within their previously dead bodies. But so much of the unknown began to fuel their anxiety and fear in Althea and Galen now. How alert and aware are they? How intelligent could they be? Their raw, base anger and rage were well known to all, but could they detect or distinguish like a sentient, living being? Were they clever enough to open doors to search, and what would drive them to do so if they could? All that Althea and Galen knew, was that they could not afford to assume any less. Their muscles tensed and ready, they braced themselves to run or defend themselves within an instant. Galen reached for Althea's hand and found it as frozen in sweat as his. But she took it nonetheless.

Althea detected it first. Galen noticed her body stiffen and tense beyond any fright he had yet seen in her. She took in deeper breaths as if she were smelling the air. He couldn't imagine why; the stinking stench from the death outside the door was nauseating. Althea turned and Galen saw sheer, white panic in her eyes. In everything he had seen her go through, he never saw fear in her like this.

Then the smell of death seemed to disappear as it was replaced by a new scent. It was sweet, detestably sweet. It pervaded the air like newly fermented fruit and was purely revolting. Galen knew now the shear dread Althea was feeling. They were now trapped despite how hard they tried to avoid it. They couldn't flee from their spot without being descended upon by a vicious Immortuo who wouldn't hesitate to destroy them, but staying meant bearing the effects of the approaching Purple Mist which would render them helpless if the Immortuo happened to feel compelled to enter their building.

"Oh God," Althea said almost inaudibly. She had felt hopeless before, but not like this. Nothing like this. She felt terror and despair before, but never like this. In all her life, whatever devastating evil she had faced, whatever the difficulty of the trials she overcame, she always had some measure of control. Even if she could not grasp it at the moment, she always had some way to do something to save herself, even if it took her time to realize it. But not now. Despite how far she had come, she was helpless against this.

Soon they both felt pricks against their skin like shards of ice and glass against their hands that lay on the floor. They looked down at the same instant to see the Mist in its shimmer of purple seep into the room through the slit in the door they braced themselves against. Suddenly a weight bore down on their bodies like the sky had descended with cruelty to crush them into the dust. The lights in their hearts were suddenly extinguished, and only darkness remained so pitch black that it seemed to consume all the light in the world around it. All goodness in the world faded away and was consumed by fire.

Galen turned to Althea. He was not concerned for her, but desperate for her to save him. He turned to her, the only light he knew could be left in the world, but the darkness was even closing in on his eyes weighing heavy in defeat. He reached out to her and pleaded with his eyes for her to make it stop and to save him, but the weakness became far too much to bear. He collapsed in a heap on the floor under him, and his eyes closed succumbing to defeat. In the darkness behind his eyes, he not only lost the light he held within himself then, but he seemed to lose any spark or trace that he had ever held the light before. Suddenly the world was not only devoid of the blessings of life at that moment but in all moments before it. He was consumed in an existence without any heavenly radiance. He felt the death of his parents, the death of his grandparents, and the loss of all of his friends before him, all at the same time and compounded over and over again.

Althea held herself up as long as she could endure holding onto the light with everything she had in great determination. But soon the Mist encircled her entirely as if knowing the strength and effort she was putting forth to fight it. It seemed then to create thick chains that wrapped around her neck and arms and pulled her violently down to the ground. She tried so fiercely, so desperately, to pull herself back up.

"Althea, do not let the darkness win."

"Mother..."

Her fingers dug into the earth to help her move away from the mist, but its grip on her was tight and unyielding. The Mist found a source of enduring hope, and it was determined to obliterate it.

Althea was completely pushed into the earth with the weight of her oppression felt through the bonds wrapped around her body in the Mist. She heard the cries of the earth through her connection to its Magic and lifeforce, the wailing of its pain and the moaning of its misery and sorrow. She heard the dying voices of a thousand souls and the mournful screams in the rage of those yet undying and unable to rest. The ceaseless persistence of unimaginable torture perverted the earth, the air, and the water of the world and reached through the ground into her fingers and through her whole body turning her blood and heart black with unimaginable pain and bearing the wounds of the earth.

And suddenly her struggles left her, strength and will left her, and her sight descended into dark obscurity.

Moderate Lamentation is the Right of the Dead, Excessive Grief the Enemy to the Living

"You can't stay down like this. You can't let it win. It's time to get up."

"I can't. It's too much."

"I know, Althea. That's the reason why you HAVE TO. You're the only one that can."

She was in a place of pure darkness devoid of sensation. Perhaps this was the rest that met the dead in the end. But in death, there should be no pain, and she could feel that clearly.

Then Althea felt a palm beneath her chin lifting her gaze to meet his kind, smiling face. She laid her cheek against the warmth of the hand as her heart ached unabatedly. She saw again her Baldrik full of life gazing down on her. A light seemed to shine from him, and her eyes were filled with its brilliance. She had always held him as a beautiful soul, but now she knew for sure that his special radiance was maybe too much for his body in life. He truly was of heavenly light now bathed in peace that evaded him on earth.

"I think that maybe this is too big for me. I couldn't even face the Mist. How can I be expected to stop it?"

Baldrik lowered himself to sit beside her in this place with no beginning, no end, no up, and no down that had shaped itself around them. He just sat in silence as she looked back at him still washed over in so much unhappiness. She opened her mouth to say something, but no sound came out. How could she say anything that mattered? How could any of it be enough? "I just want…"

"I know. And I wish I could let you. I'd give it all to you if I could."

"Really?"

Baldrik looked again at the eyes that he had held so precious in life misty with tears she dared not let loose. He took her in his arms and held her tightly with the affection she missed from him so very much. She raised her arm to hold him back. "Althea, I wish I could keep you in safety. I wish I could take away all of your sufferings as you did for me so many times. I'll never be able to repay you for that. And it pains me that you must agonize against many more perils, but your work isn't done yet. The whole world needs you, Althea. You. No one else will be enough."

"Please don't say that."

"I can't lie."

"Why?" she whimpered. The heartbreak in her voice caused the sadness to show on Baldrick's face. She immediately felt bad about it.

His voice came to her then deep from within her heart even though his mouth seemed not to move at all, only smile. "Because you are the defender of the light of this earth. Maybe the last one. And you are the only match for him."

Just thinking of Durai made her heart beat faster with anxiety. "I don't think that's true. I don't think I can."

"I can't wait for you to see that you're wrong." Baldrik smiled so warmly, so tenderly, she almost believed him then.

She held out her hand, and he took it gladly. Time is so cruel that in such moments it will never last forever. No matter how strongly they could will it, no matter how deep the bond between them might be even now, time would always be the knife that would cut the cruelest. It was the inescapable fire that would consume them all in whatever end.

"But, Baldrik, what about…I mean, Mireya…" Althea suddenly remembered what Durai had, said it left her with an all-consuming dread. "How can I even look at her? After what I did to her, how I failed you both, how…" but the shaking of her body increased to where she couldn't finish her thoughts.

Baldrik looked upon her pain and said, "Let me show you something." He reached a hand to her chest over her heart. With his thumb and forefinger, he seemed to pinch and pull at something. She saw a light being pulled from her chest, from her heart, in a long, slender string held between his fingers. It curved and danced like a ribbon, and it was stunningly beautiful. Then Baldrik held out his palm and the light danced up from it like a flame. Suddenly, the light gave out a burst of blinding light, and from that light, an image emerged. It twisted and curved, and after a moment the distinct form of a brilliant flower, much like the floral mark on her ankle, glimmered more breathtaking than anything she had seen in life.

Baldrik didn't look at the flower even as it continued to grow; he looked at Althea and saw the wonder in her eyes at what was in front of her. "There's a light that you protect," Baldrik explained to her. "That light in your heart is a source of life and growth. It is sacred. It is important. And you are its guardian. This is exactly what the world needs right now. It needs you."

Gently the light faded and was carried in the air like the petals blown gently in a spring breeze back into her heart, and she could feel it there. She realized then that it had always been there. Even in her darkest moments, the light had never left her.

"As for our sister," Baldrik continued, "her love is not fragile and her trust, once won, runs deep. She has a gift of far greater wisdom than maybe either of us realizes. Do not mistake her to be easily manipulated."

"Would she have to be?" Althea asked with her voice filled with the same guilt as before. "As natural as it was for me to blame myself for how life ended for you, I can't imagine she would feel differently."

Baldrik grasped both of her shoulders and looked her straight in the eyes in hopes that she would fully see his truth. "There is a piece of her that was always in me, and I know that there is a piece of me that she holds in her still. The light in you both is not so different, and the love you forged together is not so easily killed. The bond of sisters, whether by blood or love, is the most resilient of all. And I do not doubt that her love for you has weathered this storm. And neither should you."

Althea noticed that the darkness in the place she was in seemed to push in on her further, and Baldrik started to fade into far reaches that she could not follow. She reached out for him desperately, just to feel him once more. "Please, just a little longer."

"It's time to wake up."

181

· · · · · · ·

Althea felt something cold and wet being pressed to her forehead; she could only assume it was a damp cloth. She tried to open her eyes, but they were too heavy and she felt too weak. She felt unable to even move her head or give any sign that she was awake. Every single muscle and drop of her blood seemed to ache with heaviness and pain. She could feel the heat inside her like a fever, but it wasn't a fever. Luckily her mind was lucid, and she could hear voices.

"Are you sure it's her?"

"From everything I was told, I'd say so."

"Well, they weren't lying about her looks. She is very pretty."

"Yeah, but looking no touching. Better yet, no talking."

"Eat shit."

"Why don't we just take her to the castle now? Might be easier with her like this."

"Oh yeah, sure, great idea. Let's just deliver her to the Queen and Durai like this. It won't piss him off at all because he's always reasonable. I'm not going to run the risk that he thinks we've drugged or hurt her somehow. I'd rather not meet with an... accident."

"Shhhh! Don't even think like that. He can read your thoughts."

"You are so full of shit."

Althea realized that these men must be the guards Durai spoke of, and they were here to deliver her to the palace in grand display. She felt the urge to escape, get to where she had to go on her terms and in as much secrecy as possible. But she was trapped in a useless body that couldn't yet bring itself to move. She sensed more people come into the room, and upon their entrance, she could tell that the air tensed and the bodies of the two previous men beside her stiffened. They must be responding to a senior authority entering.

"How is she?"

"Hard to tell. She's breathing ok, so I mean, she's not dead. But we can't bring her out of it."

"Well, keep at it. I don't want to move her until we know she's better. The town has been swept and cleared of pests, so we have the time."

"Sir? What about the other one?"

"I don't care. Not my problem."

"You gonna just leave him here, sir?"

"Like I said, not my problem."

Althea suddenly thought of Galen and felt a surge of panic within her. Was he alive? Was he hurt? Where was he? The adrenalin that followed willed her muscles to stir slightly as she determined to go to him.

"Sir!" Althea heard the one voice call attention to her movement, and she could feel the air around her close as if all present had moved closer to her. She wasn't concerned about the attention or whatever potential threat they might be to her now or later; she just wanted to make sure Galen was alive.

Then she felt a warm hand on her head and a soft voice call to her, "Althea? Are you Althea?" She tried to respond somehow or even open her eyes in response, but her body still fought the lingering lethargy that she just couldn't shake. She felt the cloth on her forehead be taken away and replaced after a moment of being refreshed with cool water. "Maybe we should try to prop her up just a little."

She felt multiple sets of hands gently lift her from her back and lay her back down at an incline on supports. She could feel the difference in each set of hands. One was confident and strong, another wasn't quite as large and strong but still sure of its actions, and there was another that was smaller which trembled in uncertainty and hesitance. And again, the authoritative voice called out to her.

Finally, she was able to manage some kind of response. She was able to move her head ever so slightly and make an unintelligible sound that indicated she was trying to respond.

"Sir! I think she's coming around!"

Althea felt herself be held in muscular arms to a greater incline rather roughly. Not that the captain meant to be rough with her, he just was less graceful and very relieved that she was starting to regain consciousness. Althea finally was able to slowly open her eyes then and saw two large, blue eyes staring back even if they were blurred and out of focus.

"Althea?" The voice came from his mouth so close to her face, yet the sound seemed like it was coming from miles away. "Are you Althea?"

Althea blinked hard to try and clear the haze from her eyes. Her head suddenly started to throb and pound like a bad hangover, and she groaned ever so slightly from the pain. She struggled to respond to him and finally managed an affirmative nod as she was still too weak to speak.

"Thank God," he said quietly as he lowered her back to the soft support they had previously propped her on. "You just rest now. We'll get you out of here as soon as you're strong enough to move."

Althea wanted so badly to protest, to explain her situation, to do anything, but she found that all she could do was lie and wait for her strength to return. She could still feel the Mist inside of her, as impossible as it seemed. She felt the hopelessness that had seeped deep into her body still linger like the smoldering char left behind in the trail of fire.

Her vision slowly cleared and sharpened, and her body was able to move better, even if it was only a slight difference from before. She turned her neck to look around for Galen, to see where she was, and to see how many men were around her. But the sensations and sights that came flooding into her seemed to overwhelm her, and she closed her eyes to block it all out and give her brain a chance to catch up. She felt the world swimming around her, and she wished the feeling would stop.

After what felt like an eternity, she found herself with enough strength to speak. "Galen?" she weakly called out barely above a whisper.

"What?" she heard from the younger of all the voices she had heard before.

Althea turned her head towards the voice and saw a boy barely old enough to be a guard looking at her. When their eyes met, she saw his eyes widen in a combination of shock and panic. Almost as though he felt scared to look her in the eye, but was too stunned to look away very much like a moth drawn to light.

She saw a sweat start to form on his face even as she tried desperately to appear as harmless as possible.

"Where's Galen?" she asked again still very quiet.

"Sir!" the man called out and shouted towards the light of the open door. Instantly the same imposing man with the blue eyes came into the room and dropped to his knees before Althea. He then looked up at the young man with a questioning look. "She's asking for someone, sir."

The man that she could only assume from his authoritative presence was their captain looked again at Althea. He put a hand to her forehead to feel again for the fever, but it was breaking.

"Where's Galen?" Althea asked slightly louder this time, almost as loud as her normal speaking voice.

The captain looked at her puzzled at first, but then he figured out who she was speaking of. He looked back behind him to the man who still lay face down on the ground. Althea's eyes suddenly widened in disbelief and then turned to the men in the room with an angry look. Here she had been treated with tender care and left this other body on the floor. How could they be so cold?

The captain suddenly had a flash of embarrassed shame spread across his face as he gestured to his men to pick up the body on the floor. He saw Althea watch their handling of this man and her chest rise and fall rapidly. He could see that she was concerned, maybe even scared. He cleared his throat and adjusted his demeanor to be softer towards her. "He's alive. He's ok, just out like you were. But he's not injured." He turned again to inspect his associates' handling of the man. "Hey, gently!"

The guards laid Galen down flat on a table a few feet from where she lay, and she turned her head to assess his condition as best she could. His breathing seemed unlabored and steady; he just seemed fast asleep and not in pain from the calm look on his face. Satisfied, she relaxed slightly and looked back at the guard.

"What's...name?" Althea tried to speak although her throat was dry and cracking.

The man turned to the youngest guard again and barked, "Hey, get some water!" The young man ran out of the room without a word. He turned back to Althea, "My name is Hemele. I'm here to take you home."

She tried not to scoff at the idea of "going home." This man was just following the orders of his Queen, and goodness knows what stories he was told. She did not doubt that he felt he was doing a good and honest deed.

"As soon as you get a little stronger, we'll get you out of here."

Althea closed her eyes and turned her neck towards Galen. She managed to bend her elbow slightly to gesture to him.

Hemele looked at the Galen and was conflicted. His orders didn't include him, so he hadn't cared. But now that he saw her concern for this man, he was worried about friction and complications from her if he would be left behind. "Who is he? What is he to you?"

She sat up slightly more to show how determined she was on the subject. The young man burst into the room and handed her a ladle of water he had drawn from the well. It was cold, and her throat was so hot and dry it felt like it would sizzle at the touch of the water. She took a slow, deep drink. The water made her feel much better. "A friend," she responded sounding much stronger. "A friend I'm not leaving behind." Althea looked into Hemele's eyes and did not break for a moment. She wanted it clearly understood that she would not stand for any mistreatment of this man.

"I don't have orders to bring anyone but you," he responded resolutely. He saw that this answer was dissatisfying, and her look was even one of condescending disappointment.

Althea's strength was returning more and more rapidly as the lingering haze left behind with the Mist fell away. "Sorry, maybe I wasn't clear enough. He is my friend, and I will NOT be leaving him behind."

Hemele seemed to stiffen himself a little perhaps flexing his authority, "I cannot just bring anyone into the palace. Unless," he then looked around a bit before bringing himself in closer to her, "was he the one who took you?"

Althea simply dropped her head in exasperation. She had neither the strength nor inclination to explain the situation. She sighed as she tried to gather her patience with this man. "No, he did not. But where I go, he goes."

Hemele was both frustrated with her stubbornness and admiring it. He liked her spirit even at the moment it was making his job harder. He could see how so many admired her and found himself admiring her as well. In his experience, tenacity and strength were hard to come by, especially in women. He then simply conceded, "I'll see what I can do. Not the orders I was given."

"I know the Queen, and she'll respect my wishes." Hemele showed slight confusion at her words. She was curious at the reaction but stood firm in her determined stance. "As a member of the Queen's guard – a captain I can see from the insignia – you should do what she would honor. I know her enough to know what is acceptable."

"Miss Healer, I'm not under the direction of the Queen at all. I am a captain of the Court Enchanter's Royal Guard. I'm under orders from Durai to take you to him directly and only to him."

Uneasy Lies the Head that Wears the Crown

Mireya stared out the window to as far beyond the castle as she could strain to see. She never really knew why, but she stared as if searching out this window often. Maybe it was an involuntary manifestation of hope within her. Her people relied on her to show the strength of unwavering hope, and they couldn't afford her to be without it. But what exactly she expected to see even she didn't know. The Mist? Her sister? The unresting souls of the dead? All of these possibilities were highly unlikely as miles around her castle were heavily fortified, vigilantly guarded, and had been kept clear and safe; she hadn't seen the Mist herself since it first appeared.

Regardless of why - she still stared.

Even when the sun was high in a cloudless sky, her days were often dark. She couldn't find the brightness even in summer. Her garden and Courtside used to bring laughter and music to that window through the caress of spring breezes, and now all was silent. No one lingered in the streets anymore. The walls around the village stood higher, the doors were barred or boarded, and the doors were thicker and stronger. Along the borders of the town were barricades, traps, and other painful or even deadly manners of obstruction. Though Courtside was probably the safest and most fortified village in the entirety of all the land, no one rested easy within it. The sound of children's laughter, of mother's singing, and young boys practicing seemed to fade into forgotten memory.

But even with the desolation, even in the grey, she saw the shades of what used to be. She saw the visions behind her eyes of her people and their lives living at the foot of her castle long before they carried the fears and worries they did now. And if they hadn't been completely forgotten, maybe they had a chance to return.

"Hello, Durai," she said still staring ahead not turning to look at him. "What is it?" Her voice was monotone almost as though she couldn't be bothered with him today. She heard his clothes rustle as he bowed. Curious. He hardly ever bowed anymore. Something was different, so she turned to see him indeed with his knees on the floor in respectful genuflection.

"Your Majesty," he responded still towards the floor.

"Durai, get up. You look ridiculous. Bowing? You haven't bowed to me in forever." She stood from her chair annoyed. However, she dealt with her annoyance as it dimmed in comparison with her curiosity. And then there was concern. She braced herself, ready to react to whatever he was coming to her with.

"Mireya, my guards have returned."

Suddenly all of her attention was sharply focused, pulled from wherever her mind had been lingering before, and was filled with the adrenaline and anticipation of any news. Her eyes were filled with faith and promise and she failed in her attempts to hide a smile. "And?" she asked impatiently.

"They found Althea."

Within a second, Mireya had run down the small set of stairs that led to her thrown and threw her arms around Durai. Ever since he told her of his vision, that she was out there somewhere, she hoped and longed for her sister back. And now her faith was rewarded, and she felt overflowing with all within her that had been lost. No matter what was past, she would hold her tight in her arms again and never let go of the light she held left to her in the world.

But then she stopped. She couldn't help but notice her embrace was unreturned. The clouds rolled in to cover the sun. "No, Durai. No."

Mireya then felt Durai's arms weakly hold her in return. They were trembling and weak. "I'm sorry." She pulled away from him and turned to hide her face. "They found her body in a village not too far from the Hill. I'll spare you the details I'm burdened with."

In the silence that followed, Mireya moved back to the window and held onto herself as she stood out of it once again. How long had her sister been lying there abandoned, discarded? The tears that escaped her eyes were filled with shame and despair. The treachery of life! She should have tried harder to find her, looked longer and farther. Just the thought of her sister's body devoid of her living soul abandoned and alone...

"So," Mireya said swallowing her pain bitterly, "that's it, then? There is no hope now for this world?"

Durai walked up behind her. Mireya tried not to show how much she wanted him as far away from her as possible. As much as she wanted to be alone in her grief now, the truth was that she barely had the fortitude to be with Durai lately even before this. But she reached down deep and accessed her compassion. As much as this news broke her heart, she knew he must be even more distraught. He had kept the search for her for so long. Even the morning she was discovered missing or gone or whatever, he was like a man destroyed. She turned to him and saw the pain on his face as he was looking out of the window just as she had.

She sighed; she was not strong enough at this moment to comfort someone, but still, she needed to be a compassionate leader. She wanted more than ever to throw her responsibility, her title, and all of the expectations in a fire and blow the ashes as far as the wind would carry it. It was so unfair, and she felt so unable to keep going and going unending without rest carrying so much for so long. The burden and weight were crushing her so hard she had to be a diamond by now, but all she could see within her heart was the blackness of coal. How was she ever going to keep this up? And alone?

"So, what can we do now? Is there anything we can do?" Mireya spoke without even a trace of hope. In her mind, she felt that she would soon be creating plans for the new future with this unrelenting curse. "This would be the world now, and we must find a way to live in it," she thought silently to herself. What brought them all to this? She still blamed herself.

Durai said softly and with confidence, "There is always hope. There has to be. She wouldn't want us to give up hope in the end." This optimism was very unlike her Durai, and she looked at him impressed. Though she couldn't see the light in the darkness now - if he hadn't given up hope, neither would she.

"Do you really think so? I'm strong enough to shoulder the weight if there isn't. I'm not as fragile as that yet." Maybe his words reached her, maybe she had the courage in her heart all along and waited for her spirits to reach their lowest. Regardless of why or how Mireya found some small reserve of her leadership prowess and wore it proudly. She could still be who her people needed her to be. After all, these people were all she had left.

"As a matter of fact," Durai said as he turned to her, "I truly do think there might be ways left untried, secrets left undiscovered. I may not be a Healer and master of the life of the earth, but I do know Magic." He extended his palm to her and from it emerged dancing ribbons of light in all hues of green. Tricks like this had always delighted Mireya in a child-like way, and she couldn't help but smile at him if only simply for the attempt he had made to lift her spirits. Maybe her people weren't all she had left. Maybe she just hadn't been giving him a chance. All they had was each other now.

"I believe that there are texts hidden deep somewhere that may hold answers that I may be able to power through. It may take time, but I won't give up trying. The people are counting on us."

With his final inspirational words, he held Mireya's hands in his own. She felt a tear fall from his face onto her hands. She took one of her hands back and placed it tenderly at his heart. "She will always be with us both. We'll finish this for her."

"For her." He kissed her hand as he took leave of his Queen and walked the long hall to leave. And with his back to Mireya, she couldn't see the deceptive, sinister smile spread across his face.

And Yet I Know Him a Notorious Liar

"No, we'll wait for him to come back before moving out. He may bring news. Change, ya know?"

"I just don't like us all out here any longer than we have to be, sir."

"There are enough of us here keeping watch and armed, I'm not worried."

"Of course not, sir."

Althea feigned sleeping, reached out with all of her senses into her surroundings, and painted the picture of what was happening through the feel and sound behind her closed eyes. Galen had started to stir slightly, but not enough to be awake. She was left alone in the large kitchen room where she had been laid on the table; the rest of the guards were outside and speaking amongst themselves. She couldn't hear it all, but she could hear the captain quite clearly. He was the one she was most concerned about. All actions waited on his word and revolved at his command.

In moments of silence, which were often, she focused on some kind of plan. So many variables to consider, and she was never known to be a great tactician. She knew that it was imperative to be calculated about the next big moves as there was so much danger, so much at stake, that even the slightest miscalculation would end up dooming her or Galen or both.

But the one truth she knew, and it was an important truth, was how well she knew Durai and how she held no doubt in her heart about the extent to which he could manipulate, pervert, and control a situation and the people within it. In this, at least, she was defended against naiveté and the blindfold of love that had trapped her for so long. As long as she kept in her mind and remembered who Durai was and what he could do, she would be stronger and wiser.

Now she was sensing only the Captain and one other guard outside the door, and they weren't talkative. Perhaps the other men were patrolling around the building or the rest of the town. She decided to lay before her what she did know before trying to build the plan she did not yet have formed. These guards were not Mireya's; they worked directly for Durai. This didn't necessarily mean these were villains. That guard she knew from so long ago tried to open her eyes and save her, so perhaps these men just followed orders and not necessarily Durai's unique ethics.

However, even men marching steadily to the drumming of specific commands presents its issues. Hemele clearly held some strong resistance against taking Galen along. Althea may have convinced him to not leave Galen, but once they were on the move, there was no telling how defenseless she might become or what they would end up doing to him. What if they bound her? What if they left him here or some random place once they had her secured? How safe would he be?

No, she felt certain that they were very cautious about her from what she heard from the other men before. It might only be slight, but she held some leverage, some power, in the situation. She would have to find some way to use that hold to keep Galen safe.

The more she thought about it, though, the more she wasn't sure what she wanted for Galen. If she was being hand-delivered directly into the den of the devil, did she want to put him in such a perilous position? How would Durai see this man? In her experience, any man with her – innocent or not – was in danger from his possessive jealousy. Should I demand that he must be kept secret and hidden at some home in Courtside? Would Galen even stay put if she asked him?

The more Althea tried to move the pieces on the board the more she lost sight of it all. There were so many elements, so much unknown, that she started to feel overwhelmed by just how little she might be able to do. One thing she knew for certain, time kept steadily on, and her chance to make a move, if any, was quickly vanishing.

She opened her eyes then to the light. As she looked around, she saw only herself and Galen in the room. She turned her head to look at him and found that he had regained consciousness. He was blinking his eyes heavily and hadn't noticed her movements. She deduced he was still hazy with blurred senses just as she had been. She wanted to call out to him - make a move toward him - but she decided to keep waiting. Even the smallest movement on her part could set events in motion that she didn't have a confident enough grasp on.

Althea sensed the clouds roll in as the golden light shone through the door and was then stolen into the grey. The shadows from the sun became darker and deeper, and she began to smell the moisture in the air. A storm was coming.

"Althea?" She turned her head to the music of Galen's voice. She was so happy to hear him with some manner of strength and clarity. However, in the same instant, she held out her hand slightly and looked out towards the door. Galen caught her meaning instantly and quietly listened. He realized then that they were not alone and flashed her a questioning look.

They waited in silence for some small time to make sure that the guards weren't going to come in reaction to hearing Galen. Althea spoke very low, but it was clear enough for Galen. He felt that he could hear her through a thunderstorm. No matter what, he would find a way to hear her.

"These are guards from the castle. They are not the Queen's, though. They've come to bring me to Durai...directly to Durai." Althea could see the protective instinct flash in Galen's eyes and felt both happy for his caring for her and warry of the problems it could present.

"Ok then," he whispered back equally as quiet, "what's the plan?"

Althea laid her head back and closed her eyes in frustration. She let out a sigh and replied, "I don't know yet." Galen could tell then that she had been wrestling with this problem for some time. He wasn't sure how he could help. He wasn't sure even what he wanted. He wanted Althea, he wanted to be with her and protect her, and he wanted to see the other side of this after its ending together with her. But he also didn't want her to come to any harm, and he wasn't sure if he was going to be an added variable that could throw off a precarious balance. What is best? He wasn't sure if there was a difference here between what was right, what was easy, what he wanted, and what he needed.

In the darkness, those who were lost looked for a light to guide them home. And the brightest light he knew was her. He would look to her for what was right and trust in her strength and wisdom. If anyone could get them both safely to the journey's end, it was her.

"You lead, I'll follow."

She was grateful for his trust and also terrified of failing it.

At that moment, Althea and Galen could hear the sound of a horse and rider approaching their building. Althea gestured for Galen to be quiet and feign sleep as she concentrated on what she could feel out.

"You're back," she could hear Hemele responding to the rider. "Thank you."

Althea could hear parchment rustling as though he was handed a notice he was unraveling. He must have sent this messenger ahead and was brought back further instructions. More silence, but something else. There was a sound like gentle clankings like glass or tiny chimes. Althea strained to hear more, but all she could hear was the increasing wind rolling the darker clouds closer.

"Ok, understood. Let's start packing things up. You, bring some water before we move her out."

Althea knew she had suddenly run out of time. There was no more time to develop intricate plans. The best she could hope for was laying a few advantages as best she could in the little time she had left. She heard him say "move her out," which meant they had no intention of bringing Galen. She started to worry about what they *were* going to do with him. And what was in the message from who she could only assume was Durai?

"Hey."

"Yes, sir?"

Hemele started talking to another voice she had heard before. This man seemed to have Hemele's trust and slightly more reverence than the other men under his command. "I don't like it." She heard the parchment rustle again; he must have handed the order to this other man.

"God," the other voice replied after a time.

"Must be doing it to keep her safe."

"You think so?"

"Orders in the end."

Althea felt the coldness in her damp palms as her anxiety started to rise. What was on that order?! She felt Galen's gaze on her, and when she turned to look, he saw panicked concern in his eyes. She even saw the sweat start to form on his face. She realized then that whatever that order meant for her, whatever the cost, her first priority would be to keep him safe. But, Damn, what did that even look like?!

She heard the men enter the room, and she was too tense and frozen in place. Galen closed his eyes to give the appearance of sleep, but it was too late for Althea to try to do the same. She just decided to look over at Hemele and this other man he had been talking to as they entered and tried to appear to be as strong and confident as she possibly could. From what she heard, they were moving out regardless of if she had recovered or not, so feigning further weakness wasn't going to delay anything.

Hemele went to her side and sat beside her. He had a warm, caring smile on his face that she did not trust for a single moment. She had heard the concern in his voice before, and this was a stark contrast. Whatever he was doing, whatever he was going to say, it had to be a lie.

She had experience with lies.

"It looks as though we are getting ready to go. You'll be home soon and safe. I promise you." Hemele even put a comforting hand upon her hand as he said this last part. Something about his promise of safety did appear sincere. Perhaps he genuinely did mean to hold her safe to the best of his ability. Maybe he didn't truly know that there was nothing safe about where she was going and who she was being brought to. Who can truly tell the innocence of a soul?

"Both of us?" Althea asked as she looked over to Galen and then back at Hemele with a determined look.

Hemele steadied himself to try and be as persuasive as possible. He wasn't the most approachable person; he had no illusions about that. But so much hinged around her trusting him. He wanted to avoid struggling with her at all costs. "Let's be reasonable, I cannot deliver this man to Durai; I was ordered to only bring you." Althea knew that bringing Galen to the devil himself would be too dangerous, but she didn't give away any thoughts to see just how much she could win from all of this. "What I can do," Hemele continued, "is bring him as far as Courtside. I promise to take him somewhere where they will care for him. They have set up something like a hospital, and he can take it from there."

This might have been the best that she could hope for, but she decided to act disappointed just a little longer. Just one last gamble to win something, anything.

Unfortunately, Hemele was stubborn, too, and he had conceded all he would. He leaned in closer to her face. "It's the best I can do, or I can leave him here. Your choice."

Her gamble was lost, so she took what she could and dropped the matter.

"Besides," he added as he stood up and began to walk towards the door, "do you really want..." and he suddenly stopped himself. He barely glanced over his shoulders to see if she noticed what he said at all and then quickly walked out of the room.

Galen and Althea were once again alone, and he opened his eyes to look at her. "What are you thinking?" he asked her.

"I can't tell what he's hiding, but he is hiding something." She looked at him. She wasn't sure why, but she suddenly felt sad. "I think that maybe this is for the best. I don't know what would happen if Durai saw you. What he would think, you know? No, what would he *do*?"

Galen tried to fake ignorance as to what she was meaning. But he knew exactly the truth in his heart, and he wasn't sure he could keep his feelings secret in front of this threat. He was sure that, at the first sign of any danger, he would be jumping to her aid and his intentions and affections would be known. From the little he knew about this man, he wouldn't suffer any rivals.

That sound again. Glass? Chimes? What was that?

"How am I going to find you?" Althea heard his question and felt warm inside. And yet, at the same time, she felt some heaviness. She looked at him with all the complicated feelings written all over her face. Galen simply added,

"I know they're going to separate us. And I will find you. I just...I don't know how. All I know is I want to find a way to get to you."

"Galen," she said like a sad song, "they'll get me to where I need to go to do what I can to finish this. You don't need to carry me any farther. You did what you said you would. You've kept me safe, and I thank you for that. But you don't need to go along anymore."

He wanted so much to go to her then - say so many things. "Althea, this I ask because it is what I want to do, not what I feel I have to do."

Althea wasn't sure if she wanted him to stop or keep going.

"I guess," he decided to say, "my purpose has changed somewhat. How could it not?"

But so much would remain unsaid as Hemele and the other man came into the room at that moment carrying some packs and some water. "Oh, good. You're awake," Hemele said seeing Galen sitting up and conscious. "That'll make it easier. I guess we'll get you water too, then." He gave a silent order with a nod to this other man, and he left the room.

Hemele came again to sit at Althea's side. "My men are ready. Here are your things." He laid down her pack and her bow beside where she sat on the table. "It's a long ride. You should get some water here while we have it cold from the well. We won't stop until we're safe near the castle."

She took the water he offered to her while she kept her eyes on him. She was glad for the cooling and refreshing sensation of the water. It was almost sweet.

Then she felt Hemele's arms around her as she fell back. Everything fell away in darkness.

No Man Means Evil but the Devil

Althea felt something cold and wet being pressed to her forehead; she could only assume it was a damp cloth. She tried to open her eyes, but they were too heavy and she felt too weak. She felt unable to even move her head or give any sign that she was awake. Every single muscle and drop of her blood seemed to ache with heaviness and pain.

Wait?

Was all that came before a dream?

The wet cloth on her forehead was taken away and refreshed. She started to regain some sensations and was starting to get a feel for what was around her. Though reaching out at this moment was such a struggle, she sensed all she could in her limited, weakened way.

She could feel softness all around her. She couldn't detect a single hard corner, hard surface, or rough sensation. All around her were cushions, satin, and silk. She felt warmth from a fire. It was not so intense and close as a campfire but softly distributed in an even blanket of gentle comfort from something like a fireplace. She could smell any number of exotic flowers. Not the kind that found and endured the harshness of the sun, wind, and rain of the unsheltered wild. The floral smells that danced in her nose were delicate, fragile, and carefully tended rarities.

Though she couldn't be certain exactly where she was, she had a pretty good idea. And the prospect seemed more than she could endure. Not now, not after all she had done, not after how much she had fought.

Her insides felt dense and heavy; she felt she could barely move her chest to breathe! The more feeling she regained, the more misery she felt herself in. She tried to open her eyes, move her limbs, or shake it off in any way. How could her heart continue to beat against the strain, and how could blood that felt thick and slow be keeping her alive? She had known sickness before, but this was nothing like what she had battled before except maybe the effects of the Mist. But even with the Mist, once she was able to move slightly, her strength and spirit regained rather quickly. But with this, she felt like she had been killed and somehow had been asked to keep breathing. She moaned against the torture she felt coming from her body.

"Shhhhh, shhhhh, you're safe now. I've got you now."

The melodic voice seized her breath, and she felt the terror of the harsh certainty and the sharp, inescapable fact of who she lay helpless to. Where she knew she was now felt more real than her illusions, his voice was clearer than through the veil of his dream spells, and the truth of her being held defenseless here with the monster of her nightmares was an absolute certainty. The adrenaline from her fear shot electric energy through her veins and gave her the strength to push through her distorted mind and open her eyes wide with fear.

She saw his green eyes looking at her longingly and with immense satisfaction. His prize was returned, and he was pleased. Very pleased.

She tried to swing her legs off of the bed to run, fight, get away from him, anything! But she couldn't move them. She tried to move her arms to push him away, but she had the same struggle. She wiggled and fought, but she soon realized that her arms and legs were bound together. She was powerless and completely at his mercy. His mercy.

Durai laid his hands against her restraints at her wrists and gently subdued her thrashing with the weight of his body. "Please don't strain yourself," he gently said to her. Something about his tone came from long ago. If she were the woman she was even two years ago, she would be melting and swooning over the melody from his voice. In the glow of the fire before them against the darkness of the night, he even seemed angelic with his fair hair glowing almost like a halo. She saw the man she had fallen in love with, the man that had stolen and held her heart and swept her off of her feet, and she saw how easily she had been fooled long ago. With this beauty hiding the beast within, it seemed like such a piteous waste.

As he released his pressure on her, she felt his arms slide along her back and gently, carefully lift her to a reclined sitting position on the bed he had put her in. She was terrified to look down to find herself out of her clothes and to see what she had been put in. The thought of him changing her clothes made her feel ill. To her surprise, however, she was still in the same garments from her time in the wilds. It seemed so far she had not been touched outside of binding her in these satin ropes.

She looked up at him confused at this. He had turned his back away from her and was pouring cold water into a crystal glass. He turned back once it was filled to offer it to her. She simply looked from the tempting glass to his eyes with disgust and distrust.

He placed the glass in one hand and stroked her cheek warmly with the other. "This is just water; I promise. No tricks, no drugs – just water." He paused to see if she softened at this, but her continued distrust was abundantly clear. "I'm sorry I had to do that to you. Even if this particular drug was simple and sweet to the taste, it does indeed take a while to shake. I hated that it came to that, but you are a handful when you put your mind to it. And I wouldn't be able to live with my men if you hurt yourself fighting them."

The subtle threat implied in his words was not lost on her.

He pressed the glass against her lips very gently, and she held fast against it despite how desperately thirsty she was. "Don't be stubborn, Dove. This will help clear the drugs out of your body faster. Do be a good girl."

In no way on this earth did she want to be his "good girl," but she knew that he spoke the truth about flushing the toxins out, and she conceded to drink the water. The sensation of the cool water on her cracked lips and down her dry throat was pure ecstasy. She tried not to let him see just how much she enjoyed it or how grateful she was for it, but she drank the whole glass in a single go. Durai smiled in delight at her obedience and filled the glass again which she finished just as fast.

"Very good," he whispered to her as he put down the glass. He then took a moment to look at her up and down slowly. "I held you so fast in my dreams since you left. Every night I thought of you; every day I mourned you. And I see now my memories paled greatly and didn't do you justice." Althea listened intently to the hypnotic lilt of his voice, saw how easily she had been put under its spell before, and tried desperately to fend against it.

But in her memory of how that same voice sounded not so long ago, she began to have a burning lamentation in her heart for the love that had wasted and died when she gave it to him. As much as she had tried to deny it before, there would always be a piece of her that would be lost because she had given it to him. She would never be able to give the gift of her first kiss, her first passionate night, and her first dreams and fantasies of forever to any other man, for she had irrevocably given it to him. What was worse, she had all of that lost to herself as well. She had given so much of herself to this man she had been certain was forever, and now there was less to walk away into her future with. If she had one.

"What will you do with me?" Althea asked knowing whatever answer he put into words were going to pierce like swords. Nothing shy of letting her go was going to mean any good for her. And there was no chance of him saying that.

Durai wrapped his arms around her then and held her small frame against his broad chest. His hands spread wide against her back and grasped fists full of cloth and soft, thick hair in his fists. He remembered every passionate embrace before this one and was caught up in every feeling of fulfillment they had given him. "What will I do with you? Well, I'm going to keep you, make you happy. It will be better this time."

She could feel her heart bleeding. God, how she wanted those words to be true in a way. There was a huge part of her that remembered how she held him in love and respect. Surely the time had not been so long ago, and surely this love that she saw now, in this moment, in his eyes couldn't be false and couldn't be evil. Perhaps he did mean it. He had gone through such great lengths to find her, bring her safely to the defense of the palace, and now he behaved the angelic gentleman. She had not been violated, she remained clothed and tended to, he had not taken advantage of her while she was drugged….

Then she closed her eyes hard at the ridiculous thoughts that she was having. How twisted did she become, how foolishly susceptible had he made her for her to believe that for even a fleeting second that she would hold any of his actions in gratitude? She had not been found and saved. She had been hunted down, drugged, and kidnapped against her will.

This was not love; this was control.

Carrying her through danger, pain, and injury - *that* was love. Seeing her through her moments of weakness with as much admiration as moments of strength and courage - that was love. Listening to her pain and offering to share the burden of its emotions even if they were painful - that was love. Nursing her back to health - that was love. Holding her in the grip of the hellish nightmares that haunted her and stole her away from serenity, that was love.

Oh, Galen...

She looked up at her adversary then and knew that she could not fully despair. Through whatever deed the devil may do, she was gifted a glimmer of hope to give her strength to endure. She had a future explode and burst forward in her heart with brilliantly illuminating possibilities, and they paved the way in faith before her, and she would fight to reach that end with all she had.

And We Shall Know Him by His Horns

Much to her surprise, Althea spent the remainder of that night in the soft bed alone. Durai had kept himself in another room to sleep and left her in peace. She counted her blessings at least for that. As much as her mind was racing and her anxieties whirled around her, sleep came quite easily and deep as she still had the heaviness from the drugs in her blood. And despite the luxury of the bed, a luxury she had not felt in over a year, she awoke with stiffness and soreness everywhere. She felt as if she had been cruelly beaten. Even her eyes seemed to ache.

She awoke before Durai did, or at least before he entered the room. She could sense he was still asleep, though. He always had slept later than her, and the comfort of knowing she had been returned to him must have made him sleep well. The thought made Althea roll her eyes. She also found she was still bound at the wrists, ankles, and knees. The bindings were soft silk and not so tight as to cause immense discomfort. It was just an incredibly irritating nuisance that it had been done to her. She searched the bindings at her knees and ankles with her nimble fingers to find the knot to free herself, but there was no knot. She passed her fingers along the entire silk and found absolutely none as if it had been fused together. Magic. His Magic.

She sat back then in frustration. She had thought maybe she could be so clever as to free herself, and of course, it wouldn't be this easy; he would not be nearly so careless. However, she took the time then to stretch her muscles as best she could while still being clumsy in her restraints. She used her fingers to massage at least a small measure of stiffness away, and after a good amount of time, she started to feel much better.

Looking around the room then, things were so much like she had remembered them to be. The colors of the room adornments were of dark hues that encouraged the darkness. Curtains of dark green, blankets of deep purples and reds, all of them helped stop light from lingering. She guessed she had never really thought of it that way before even as obvious as it was. The fireplace only had an orange-red glow upon the last remnants of wood left smoldering, but the rich smell of the fire still lingered in the room. Candles left had been burnt down to the last bit of wax. She tried to remember other things about this room, specifically exit points she could use, if not now then sometime. However, she could only remember the one, and it was closed and more than likely locked.

As she continued to look around and stir some more, she realized that she was also incredibly weak. Her limbs started to shake and tremor, and she remembered it had been at least a day and a half since she had eaten anything. She hated being in the position where she needed something from him. Just being given the water last night was ignominy enough. But she knew that her body was now reaching dangerously low levels of energy, and she needed food desperately no matter where it came from. Until she got some, she reclined back on the cushions on the bed to reserve what she had left.

What little light could reach into the room grew brighter, and she kept her eyes on the door in anticipation of when he would enter. She hoped he would anticipate her needs; the thought of having to ask him for food was enough to make her wretch. Her mind also wandered beyond her plight and focused on Galen. She prayed that Hemele kept his word and delivered him somewhere safe. She was not sure how much she could trust a man who would willfully drug an already weakened woman.

She heard the wood of the door slightly crack and snap at the pressure of slight movement or pressure, and she knew that he was preparing to enter. Perhaps he was pressing into the wood to listen for signs of her waking, maybe he was carrying something clumsily and trying to open the door with it in balance, maybe it wasn't him at all but a servant, who knows? Regardless, she was about to have company, and she was ready for it.

The door opened then with Durai carrying a tray of some fruit. "Thank God," she thought silently to herself. It took all her restraint not to reach for it immediately. She kept herself as composed as possible. Durai had a huge grin on his face, which was so unlike how she often saw him. It provided her no comfort. It was frightening.

205

He set the tray of fruit down on the table beside the bed and then sat next to her upon it. He gracefully leaned in, placed a hand behind her head, and pressed his lips to hers as if he had been dreaming of doing so all night. At first, she was too shocked to react, but then she struggled against him. She expected to be held firmly in place with his considerably stronger force, but he let go immediately. "I'm sorry," he said still with the large, unapologetic smile. "I guess I just couldn't help myself." He paused then and took the sight of her in like it was the first time. "You know, I have loved you this whole time. Never once did it even diminish. I never stopped."

She had absolutely no doubt of that.

After she continued to simply look at him in silence, he turned to the fruit still wet from washing. Despite her best attempts to remain unresponsive to him, her body tightened with anticipation, and though he didn't show it, he sensed it. "Are peaches still your favorite?" he asked as he picked up a rather large one. Her mouth watered so much that she was worried she might drool out her mouth. She gave him a very small nod of approval. He began to offer the fruit to her as she extended her bound hands to the fruit hungrily.

He then retracted his offering and looked at the silken ties. He looked from the ties to her eyes. He gave her a look that was equal parts sternness and teasing. "If I take care of these," he gestured to her restraints, "do you promise to behave?"

The tone he had with her was a sickening mix of superiority, sensuality, condescension, and feigned vulnerability. She felt like an animal in the woods knowing that there was a trap somewhere, and every moment and every step were tensed with danger.

She had no choice but to nod in acknowledgment as she needed the food desperately. Durai reached out his free hand with his palm facing her ties. Red swirls of light extended outward and danced around the silk. She flinched slightly just from the idea of being touched by his Magic though she didn't feel any sensation from it at all. In an instant, the bonds loosened and fell away. She spread her wrists away from each other and realized how much they ached. She was not able to massage or tend to her upper body the way she had been able to with her lower body given her restraints. She couldn't keep the minor pains from showing on her face.

Durai frowned slightly at seeing her discomfort and decided not to tease her any further. She handed her the fruit gently. He rose and started to walk towards the door, "I'll leave you to eat on your own for now. I have some things I need to do this morning." He looked over his shoulder then and looked at her. Every part of him ached to just go to her and take everything he had been wanting. But he decided to wait. There were better ways, and he would get to all he wanted in the end.

Althea heard the door close and the subsequent bolting of the lock that followed it. Not that she would be able to get away anyway as she was still restrained at the knees and ankles. But at least her hands were finally free. She ate the peach hurriedly despite her better judgement to be slow and careful about it. It was still warm from the sun; it was probably picked this very morning. The juice that escaped her ravenous mouth ran down her chin, but she didn't care. She felt its sweet sugars enter her blood and soothe her shaking muscles. As there was another on the platter, she ate that peach just as fast.

She took a long, relieved breath after the second peach was devoured. She wiped her chin with her sleeve and sat back silently thanking the life-giving nutrients as she felt them pass through her body. She looked over at the rest of her offerings and picked through the pears, strawberries, and small mandarins, and ate the best of the selection slowly so as to not overwhelm her probably highly acidic stomach.

Then she found beneath the fruit offerings some assorted blocks of cheese and small amounts of cured meat. She held a small piece of bright orange cheddar in her fingers and felt joyful at the first chance in so long to have some. She held it to her nose and deeply inhaled the long-forgotten scent. She forgot how good cheese was, how much she loved the creaminess and sharpness and intricate differences in varieties. She slowly savored each and every small bite and prolonged her enjoyment of a delicacy that she had missed so much. The elation was almost overwhelming her.

The rest of the morning she spent both massaging seemingly stagnant blood back into her upper body and arms along with whatever limited planning she could do. She tried not to be discouraged by all she did not know and could not plan for; the best she could do was work with what she had. She thought perhaps the best place to start was to sort through what she did know and what she needed to learn. She knew that she had been drugged, but what drug and what the lasting effect could be were a mystery. However, some self-meditating seemed to indicate that she was shaking the effects fairly efficiently. She knew that she was here with Durai, she was bound, and she had no defenses or allies near her.

Unfortunately, that was the extent of what she knew for certain.

Everything that remained unknown flooded and overwhelmed her like the river breaking from its bank in a storm. She worried so much about Galen, where he was, whether he was safe, and whether or not he would do something rash and impulsive to get to her. She knew now that she did not want him to. She wanted him safe, she wanted him as far from the reach of demons as he could be, and she wanted him happy no matter what it meant for her or what he had to do to be so.

The day passed on in slow anxiety, and Althea found that she would perhaps rather Durai be here where she could see and know what he was doing. The list of how much she didn't know was growing more daunting in her mind. Whatever terrifying turn this had to take, she would rather it be over with quickly. To calm her mind, she went into further, deeper meditation and focused on all she could sense and feel. It didn't take long for her to feel the darkness oozing into the air around her. She recognized the feeling as the presence of the Mist that she had felt before, but this was different. It was almost as if she could feel the source of it or perhaps the power of it from the conjure site. The evil she could feel from it had fangs and claws, and she sensed an insatiable, persistently dire need from it. Though what that meant was entirely unknown.

While still deep in her meditation, Durai was able to quietly enter the room undetected. He stood by her on the bed and watched her in her trance. His inner self was a dangerous mixture of serene control that was happy to take in the sight of her peacefully and the violent, lustful urges that wanted only to consume her. However, he prided himself on patience and control, and he continued to just watch her as he took a seat on a chair beside her.

Althea then finally heard the rustling of his clothing and sensed his breathing beside her. She opened her eyes to find him so close that it was startling at first. However, she retained her composure. He was still smiling, and it still filled her with unease.

"Did you enjoy the food?"

"Yes." She responded shortly. Then she thought better of consistent abrasiveness since she was still needing things. She, therefore, added, "Thank you."

At the sound of her words, he closed his eyes and seemed to savor it like wine. She turned her head from the site as it put her at further unease. He leaned forward in his chair and looked her up and down once again before saying, "Just wait. Dinner will be much better. I promise."

Althea straightened her back and said, "I don't intend on staying here that long. All I came here to do is put an end to this curse if I possibly can, and then I will be more than happy to be on my way." No matter how much false confidence she tried, just hearing her own words made her cringe at just how futile they were. She knew that what she intended was not even a remote consideration at this point. "So, I would like to be taken to the site now and finish my job, please."

She expected to see disappointment register on his face, but it didn't. She expected a display of anger or dominance, but it never came. Instead, something like pride shined through his eyes. He was proud of her strength to make such a show to him; she had never been so forceful before. This change intrigued him and only fueled his infatuation with her further. She became a more difficult and therefore more worthwhile prize. He was now more determined to have her.

"That will come when you're stronger. I promise I will take you to the temple to try and be the hero as soon as your body is up to it. But you do understand that you are not leaving here. Not ever again. I will not allow it." Durai began to show the same forcefulness as Althea had remembered in the past. She had wondered when he would start to show his nature, and at least she had fortified her spirit against it. At least as much as she could.

"Durai, what you will allow and what will be happening are two completely different scenarios. You don't expect me to just stay again and be ok with it, do you?"

"No, of course not. At least not right away. But you know me," he said as the glow in his eyes flashed for just a brief second. She was determined to not let the triggered fear in her overpower her resolve, but she couldn't deny that she was afraid. Every impulse in her knew that he would make good on any threat, and there were no depths to which he would not sink. "I do have ways of making things happen. I always do. And I will. You'll see."

The mere thought that he had a calculated plan that she could only react to and not strategize against made her face pale with unease. He was cunning, and she was not. All she had to rely on was her kind heart and good intentions. How can one battle evil with that?

"Listen to me, Durai. I have absolutely no intention of staying here with you. I will do my duty, and then, if I have to, I will have Mireya make it so you stay as far away from me as is possible in this world. You mark my words. This time I will win."

At that, Durai moved from the chair beside her and onto the bed beside her. His movements were eerily like that of a snake, and she could feel pricks of apprehension tingle across her skin. Her shoulders pulled up around her neck as she leaned away from his advancement. But he closed the distance skillfully and pulled her back by the arms. He leaned in almost on top of her and brushed aside a strand of hair that had fallen across her face. He inhaled deeply savoring the smell of flowers that always managed to come from her. The warmth radiating from her skin in her restless unease penetrating his own body.

"You've changed, little Dove. I'm impressed."

"I didn't do it for you. I did it for me."

"Doesn't matter, the change is there," and he slowly lowered his face closer to hers, "and I like it."

Althea visibly shivered, and Durai laughed low and deep at it.

"As for Mireya, I wouldn't rely on her to come in and save you."

"Durai, you can't scare me. I know you are a liar, and your control over me has to do with manipulating my fears – always has been. I know what you had said before is nothing but lies. I do not believe that Mireya would cast me out in anger. I do not believe she holds me in contempt. We were bound as sisters, and you can't come between that no matter how powerful or influential you *think* you are."

Durai just continued to smile at her as he stroked the top of her head. "How well you know me. Look at you; just so clever. You are right. She's not angry at you. She never was. She loves you so much – er, *loved* you so much. It broke her heart to hear that you were found dead."

And all she saw then was the fire blazing green in his eyes.

In Thy Face I See the Map of Honor, Truth, and Loyalty

"I guess," he decided to say, "my purpose has changed somewhat. How could it not?"

Before Galen could say anymore, explain any further, confess all he wanted, the imposing leader of this group of men came in. Hemele he thought he heard was his name. He didn't have time to pretend to still be unconscious. I guess it didn't matter now.

"Oh, good. You're awake," Hemele said. "That'll make it easier. I guess we'll get you water too, then." Hemele gave a silent order with a nod to this other man, and his man left the room.

Hemele sat at Althea's side. "My men are ready. Here are your things." He laid down her pack and her bow beside where she sat on the table. "It's a long ride. You should get some water here while we have it cold from the well. We won't stop until we're safe near the castle."

Galen wasn't sure what the plan was, but he implicitly trusted that Althea would make sure that Galen was kept within the plans for moving forward if she hadn't already. He saw the ladle of water offered to her and was very much looking forward to one being brought to him. He felt parched from his lengthy time unconscious from the Mist.

Galen watched as Althea took the water he offered to her while she kept her eyes on Hemele. He saw how she was watching the man and took note of her suspicion. He'd be wary as well; he trusted her instincts and judgment.

Then in an instant, she saw him move into her with his arms circling her. Galen was stunned for less than a moment as he saw Althea's eyes close and her body collapse into the guard's arms. Galen jumped up only to realize that his muscles protested the sudden motions with stiffness and aching. He steadied himself on the table for only a moment, though it seemed like an agonizing eternity, pushed past the awkward motions of his body, and quickly darted to Althea's side.

Galen was prepared to fight Hemele's resistance and whatever authority he would try to assert in the situation, but to his surprise, the man's hesitation to allow Galen to take over holding this woman was only slight. He released Althea from his arms and into Galen's admiring the concern. Hemele couldn't quite ascertain before what their relationship was, and her part in it remained a mystery to Hemele, but he had no doubt that his man was in love with this woman. It was as clear to him as glass and still waters. Hemele then felt such sympathy for this man, for his orders were his orders.

While Galen held Althea in his arms and tried to find an explanation for her sudden state, he kept half an eye on Hemele out of the corner of his eye. When the guard backed away to give them some space, Galen's face dropped down slightly towards the ladle of water. Something about it smelled not quite right. Something different came to his nose when he bent his face down, a very faint trace of sweetness.

Then it suddenly came to him that this was the smell of the Somnum flower. Apothecaries carried it as a sleeping serum in whatever extreme cases needed subduing, though it was incredibly difficult to make and was not something widely known. His extensive time in the wild with his creatures of the woods, hills, and mountains had given him quite the knowledge of the natural world. Their wisdom had become his over time. This particular serum, though, he knew without his time spent in nature. He knew of this because of his mother…

He shook off the memory, and when his mind put the pieces together, he was filled with so many negative emotions that he clenched his fists. He laid Althea back down gently and tenderly and stroked the top of her head. "I'm sorry," he whispered to her. "You are going to have a Hell of a time when you wake up."

He looked behind him and noticed Hemele had stepped outside, probably gathering things up and speaking to his men. So then, when he turned back around to face his angel, he bent down and kissed her head. As badly as he wanted to kiss her lips, he would never do so without her consent. But with the uncertainty of what was to come next, he took the chance to impart even the smallest endearment. Though it would seem, it was more for him than for her. The sensation of his lips against her skin was enough to break his heart.

Before he could begin to gather his thoughts to try and formulate some kind of strategy, Hemele came in with another ladle of water for Galen. Galen took it without showing suspicion; he didn't want this man to know just how clever he could be or how much he held the guard in distrust. Before allowing the water to pass his lips, he inhaled deeply. But in this, there was no smell or trace of drug or even poison. Not any that he had known of anyway. He drank and savored the relief it gave to him.

But even with this gift, this charity, he didn't trust Hemele. How could he trust someone who would so willingly drug someone already so harmless and incapacitated?

The two men spent a very long time in silence each sizing up the other. They were both too engrossed in their evaluations to notice the awkward amount of time pass. It wasn't until the other guard, the one Hemele had talked to before, came in the room and cleared his throat to make himself known. The two men simply looked at him not in embarrassment or surprise, but actually with a slight trace at the annoyance of being interrupted. Both of them couldn't quite figure the other one out. No simple label was coming to either of them about the man they were facing.

The other guard didn't seem to care that they were annoyed or that he had interrupted anything. He simply continued to address his captain, "We're ready. How do you want to move her?"

"Thank you, Jian. I'll carry her on my horse. She doesn't weigh much, and we aren't that far."

The man Jian looked slightly concerned, but the just shrugged it off and replied, "Just be careful. You know there will be Hell to pay otherwise."

At that Hemele looked straight at Galen to register a reaction to this mystery element. Hemele merely responded to Jian with, "I know," while still looking at Galen. But Galen managed to keep his face completely blank and unreadable. The patience of Leporems was exemplary, and they could sit as still as a windless night without showing a trace on the outside any feelings on the inside. As hard as the captain of the guard would try, he wouldn't get anything out of Galen that he didn't want him to know.

Hemele seemed to struggle with what was best to say next. He couldn't decide how much of a difficulty this man was going to be or how to prevent that if at all possible. He finally decided to just go with what came to mind first. He turned to Galen as he began to gather Althea's things. "My men and I thank you very much for guiding her this far from wherever she had been taken."

Hemele's choice of words intrigued Galen, but he kept staring at him in feigned innocent ignorance to encourage him to continue. He'd contemplate that later.

"As you may know, those in the castle have been looking for a Healer for some time. As a matter of fact, we've been looking for her specifically. She may be the only hope left. The only hope left for all of us," he said as his eyes went somewhere a little distant then, but only for a moment. "So we do thank you, but we'll be taking her the rest of the way."

Galen stood up then, his body slightly stronger, and squared his shoulders against this man. "Of course. I understand. I will go with you."

Hemele sighed as he had hoped he could avoid this. "Listen, it's really not necessary. You've done your part, and we're grateful for it, but you are free now to go back to your home and your family."

Galen stood unmoving as a mountain. He may not have much ground to stand on, and he was completely outnumbered, but he wasn't going to budge on following. "Listen, you seem like a man of honor. I could read it all over you. I respect that, I do. And I know that you must have your orders, and those orders certainly don't include me. But I made a promise to her, and she and I have been through a lot. If you don't mind, I would like to make sure for myself that she gets to where she is going. Not because I don't trust you or your men and the duty and honor you bear, but because I would like to satisfy my own."

As Galen finished, Hemele looked at the man impressed. He knew that he was not an approachable man. He was told numerous times that he made people

215

intimidated and uncomfortable just by standing in a room. Jian had even said he had the airs of an asshole once. So a man standing strong in opposition to him, even respectful as it was, had to count for something. He walked over to Galen and put his hand on Galen's shoulder. He expected the man to flinch, and he didn't; again, impressive. "Listen, out of respect for the lady who was concerned about you too, I will allow you to come as far as Courtside. You're right, I do have my orders. But I did promise her that I would take you as far as the hospital that has been built in the town that's run by the closest things to Healers that we have left. Let them check you out; I'm sure you have both been through a lot and could benefit from a medical looking after. Then I'll…come back after a while and make sure you're taken care of."

The last uncertain pause from Hemele spoke volumes to Galen. He suspected exactly how we would be taken care of. But he knew it was the best offer he would be getting and decided to go along with it at least at the start. He'd find some way to reach the other side of all of this with Althea.

After everything was packed and the group of men including Galen on a spare horse began to move out. They came very soon to Base Village and began the climb of the hill towards the castle. Galen knew then that he was running out of time to make a plan. He didn't trust Hemele, but the more he thought about what he could read in the man the more he realized that a simple label of villain just didn't quite fit. But he couldn't be certain.

Every step onward became one less step to act, decide, or plan. He knew that he was running out of time. His head began to hurt. He was still suffering from residual effects of the Mist, but more than that, he kept thinking of all he didn't know. How much could he trust Hemele or any of his men? Could he trust the people of Courtside? They were nobility, and nobility and his kind often did not mix well. What was going to happen to Althea? How was he going to keep her safe? What was Durai going to do to her after she had run away from him?

Every small thing that was unknown at that point became like particles of dust in the wind. At first, they seemed few and harmless, hardly noticeable. But then each new thing that couldn't be held in certainty joined in the space. The particles kept growing and compounding until they suddenly became like a dust storm. Clarity of sight was stolen away as the tempest violently blew and swirled its worst.

The very air felt hot and dense. It was like trying to breathe through thick cloth while inside of a fire. Soon the heat permeated into his lungs and caused his blood to race and painfully prick with every fear he had ever felt. The darkness creeping into his heart now had teeth and claws. He felt the world become larger and bigger like a dragon emerging from a cave revealing his immense stature while his body kept being crushed smaller and smaller beneath its weight. Expectations began to stack up on his struggling body until the rocks became boulders and the boulders became peaks. And it didn't stop. Each defeat crushed harder than the last until the mountain on top of him became ever mightier and more unscalable. Hope had long blown away from the same wind that brought this pain. He even felt that prayer screamed to heaven would fall dead to the merciless storm.

His mind focused more and more on what he wanted to do, what he needed to do, and watched them twist and contort turning into the things that he just couldn't do or shouldn't do. All of his power and control shrank and sizzled into nonexistence like a drop of water on a heated summer rock under an unforgiving sun. No matter what he tried to do to make his desires fit into the pattern of what would be best, he could not make it match or make it work.

Before he realized it, the company of men stopped in front of a long building in Courtside; he hadn't even noticed that they entered the town. This building was new and heavily defended and strong. This had to be the hospital that Hemele spoke of.

He had run out of time.

The Devil Shall Have His Bargain

Althea was roused from the sleep she fell into that afternoon by Durai gently scooping her up into his arms. He took her out of the bed-chambers, through the main room, and into the bathing room. He set Althea down on a marble countertop near a washbasin. Althea seldom had visited this area in his suit of rooms before, electing often to use her own washroom instead. She looked around and gathered as much as she could in her sight in the short time she had.

His washroom was a stark contrast to all of his other rooms. Whereas his bedroom, living room, private dining chamber, and study were all decorated and adorned with dark and opaque colors, this washroom was incredibly bright. There were no windows of any kind for much natural light save one clear glass skylight on the roof to let the sunshine in at one place. All of the surfaces were sharply clean and smooth, and all were dazzling white.

She saw that a spacious and very deep tub was directly under the skylight, and it rested above a sunken pit where she could see barely illuminated embers of wood. There was already water waiting in the tub and it was warmed by the embers beneath. Resting on the gentle surface of the water were many red rose petals. On a shelf next to the tub she saw many bottles and scented soaps. The air was warm with perfumes. The whole room was immensely luxurious.

Althea had deduced that all of this had been made in preparation for her to wash, and she dared not look at Durai out of fear that he would expect to stand and watch her or, even worse, wash with her. She simply stared forward and kept her guard up. Her heart beat so strongly in her chest that she felt for sure he could hear it. The thump of each beat boomed in her ears, and she felt that all of the strength she could muster wasn't going to count for much.

Durai stroked her hair and sent the same ribbons of light from his hands to the bonds at her ankles and knees, and they gently fell away and landed in a pile on the ground. He ran his fingers along the site where the restraints had been on her skin and inspected them for any signs of bruising. When he was satisfied that she was relatively unharmed, he stood up and looked at her. She could see a conflict, a struggle, in his eyes. Then he blinked long, and the struggle seemed resolved as he sighed. "Everything is ready for you. Take as long as you need. Your body deserves a little luxurious pampering after all it's been through with the Mist."

Althea jumped on the opportunity to take a jab at him. "Not just the Mist," she stated annoyingly, pointing out that she hadn't forgotten his treatment of her as well.

Durai hardly seemed embarrassed, but looked down in show anyway. "Take as long as you need. I brought all of these over from your rooms after you left." His tone seemed to suggest that he wanted her to feel some semblance of guilt at leaving. She was surprised he even tried to do so. It seemed beneath him. "And when you're finished," he continued, "I've left a gown for you."

Althea's stomach turned at the thought that he had picked out a dress he expected her to wear. She felt like a doll he was dressing. She was not a puppet and refused to be made to feel like one. "My own clothes –"

"Will be disposed of," Durai interrupted forcefully as his eyes flashed a stern look at her. Of all the battles that were ahead of her, she felt that this one was hardly one to lose energy over. She just hoped that what had been selected for her wasn't too vulgar. She sighed in resignation.

Durai took her hand in his and bent it to his lips. It reminded her of the very first time he had done so. He was so marvelous back then. She recalled sorrowfully how much of a gentleman he had been to her then, how much she admired and revered him. Just thinking of how far they had come since then, how far they fell from how high they had flown, made her heartsick.

He then turned and took his leave of her. She heard the heavy door close behind her and bolt shut. She wondered how she would let him know when she was done, but something in her felt as though he would have some way of knowing. The thought made her shiver. Even if she thought she was alone, she would try to be as discreet as possible.

First, she familiarized herself with where everything was in the washroom. She didn't need to be walking around after undressing searching for this thing or that. She found a stack of thick towels, the bottles from her old washroom were the ones along the shelves near the tub for washing and indulging herself with, and she found the various drawers and cabinets with combs, brushes, and other necessities.

She was disappointed to find that there was no screen that she could dress or undress behind. She couldn't be certain that he was watching her except for her strong instincts and feeling of disgust. She ended up grabbing a towel and sat on the opposite side of the tub away from the door as she carefully disrobed. She wrapped her body in the towel before standing. She swung her legs over the side of the large tub and stepped into the very warm water.

She slowly lowered herself into the nearly steaming water and discarded the wet towel over the side after her whole body was submerged. Though she felt some guilt at it, she closed her eyes and leaned against the wall of the tub, and sighed deeply in relief. It had been so long since she had a warm bath that was not in a cold lake or river. Even in the summer, the water was always too cold for her. Now her muscles melted with the soothing heat. The scent of the water filled her head with the sweetening, musky perfume of the rose petals. She ran her hand along the length of her opposite arm and felt the oils in the water soften her skin.

While she washed her body and hair with the multiple shampoos and mixtures of delicate pampering, she started to notice the changes within her body in the last year. Her once cream-colored skin had deepened in color from exposure to the sun. Her skin was no longer delicately thin and fragile. She felt that the nights of rain and the days of dust and wind, not to mention the winter through the snow, and without a shelter, her skin had become tougher and more resilient. The one thing that hadn't changed was the softness of her glamorous hair. It was her greatest source of pride filled with personal connections and memories of her mother and Mireya; she had kept diligent care of her hair.

She felt as though she were a new person. Instead of mourning those fair features in her that had been lost, she smiled at who she had become. She had been a shrinking violet in comparison to the force she was now. And perhaps her changes in strength would be enough. Perhaps now she would be a match for him.

Long moments passed in that tub while she enjoyed the safety and quiet of the solitude. Soon the water became tepid, and she felt that she had to face the future before long. She took a towel she had set close to the tub and quickly wrapped her body in it as she stood. Any prying eyes would not have gotten the chance to see much if anything at all.

Once she had brushed and put up her hair, she walked over to the gown laid out for her. Though she expected it to be green like he always liked, it was actually deep red. That was her favorite color to wear, and she hadn't worn it in a long time. She stepped into it and looked at the cut of it in the mirror as it flowed down her body. It was modest and decent with a scooped neckline that didn't reveal much. The sleeves were long and contoured around her skin much like the rest of the dress. The fabric was heavy but clung to her like a lover's embrace and showed every bend and curve of her waistline and backside before finally flaring out elegantly. There were no embellishments, no intricate designs. Just the deep color and smooth fabric.

The dress felt like a compromise. He was getting her as he wanted, but he was giving her a comfortable and modest dress that seemed something she would choose as opposed to something he would choose.

It felt like a trap.

The moment she seemed all finished, the door opened. Durai walked toward her and stopped a few meters short. He slowly looked her up and down more than once. She could swear she could even see the slightest trace of a tear in his eyes. She had to concede that in his perverse, despicable way, he did love her and had missed her. And now she appeared before him much the same way as he had known her when they were together. It must have felt like the long year's patience finally reached reward.

He reached out his hands and took both of hers. "You look…just so beautiful," he said as he could not catch his breath from the mere sight of her. Even if her look back at him was contempt, he found all the ways to admire her. This new fire he sensed in her was going to be delicious, he thought.

"Dinner is waiting for us," he said as he started to lead her away by the hands. But Althea held her ground and resisted going anywhere with Durai.

"I told you before," Althea began, "that I had no intention of dining with you. I have a job to do, and that's what I intend to do."

He then turned back to her, smiled his wicked smile, and closed the distance to be very close to her. "Perhaps I hadn't made the situation clear before. For that, I apologize. Let me explain to you plainly. You will have dinner with me because it is what I wish. You will only do what I wish you to do. You have nowhere else to go but to me. The rooms have my guards posted, and *only* my guards who are loyal to only me. No one else in this world even knows you are still alive. If you want anything, anything at all, it will only be through my good graces."

With that, he brushed a hanging piece of hair behind her ears and brought his face closer to hers. His lips brushed her ears as he continued to speak. "So if you want a chance to be noble and stop the Mist, you gotta play nice. I will deny you nothing as long as you make me happy. So you better get very good at saying 'please…'"

And with that, the devil laid out his terms to the angel. The life of the world for her very soul.

Modest Doubt is Called the Beacon of the Wise

The brightness of the orange and yellow flames starkly contrasted with the darkness of the night. The blackness of this night seemed cold and absolute; even the stars seemed to hide away as the storm continued to threaten the skies but not quite hit. Two men stayed at the fire this night and kept their conversation when all of their comrades retreated to their bunks.

That night the common area for the royal guard was heavy with unease. There was always a noticeable separation and contrast between the Queen's guard and Durai's personal guard, but today the difference and divide between the two groups were undeniable. Though the two groups had separate barracks in separate buildings, they shared the same courtyard common area and dining hall. And the silence that Durai's men were consumed in after returning from the wilds was a tantalizing mystery to the other guards. Finally, the tension within that secrecy became too much for either set of men to sit comfortably with, and they all retired for an early night.

Only Hemele and his close friend and first lieutenant Jian remained behind into the quieted night. Jian had a long wooden pole that he kept poking the fire with. He was older than most of the men, though not an elderly or even middle-aged man by any means. He looked far younger than he was as he took such good care of himself physically. He was always an endearing combination of an older man's jaded sarcasm and a young man's mischievous playfulness. It gave him an undeniable charismatic brilliance. Perhaps this was why Hemele liked him so much.

And Jian's closeness with his captain was in no way because of his seniority over him and the company. Hemele was a man whose honor, duty, and truthfulness were sickeningly idealistic. It was enough to make most men violently aggravated, but he never compromised any of who he was to the point of stubbornness. And that's what Jian loved most about him. Too many times in the world when faced with the harshest pushback against one's ideals do men often bend against the hurricanes of judgement and ridicule. But with Hemele, one couldn't even tell that there was a breeze blowing against him. He stood like an unbending oak. In the end, this quality in Hemele made his men want to be better.

Jian looked up from his fire poking and saw his captain, his friend, deep in thought. Hemele's metal cup full of wine sat untouched as it warmed by the fire whereas Jian was already on his second refill. "What do you look so damn glum about?" Jian finally asked. "We had a job finally after all these months, the job was a success, and best yet, we didn't lose anybody in the process."

"Yeah," was all that Hemele said to that. His brow still knotted as he wrestled with the thoughts in his mind.

"But...?" Jian prodded.

Hemele relaxed his face a bit as he began to verbally unravel to his friend what was on his mind. "Anything about the job sit wrong with you?"

"Uh, no? Well, what do you mean? Like did we miss something?"

Hemele went back to his wrinkled brow and just muddled through his troubled thoughts. "No, not like we...I don't know. I mean, the orders. Did the orders feel off? At any time did they hit you wrong?"

Jian gave an uncomfortable chuckle, "Hey, orders are orders. Right? That's what you say? They lead, we follow. Not our place to question?" Jian said the words his friend had touted over and over again but knew that if the end of the world were near, he'd follow Hemele's instincts over any orders in a second.

But Hemele was so lost then in his inner thoughts that he seemed far away. Jian decided to try another approach. "You know, I'm just so damned glad to have gotten a job at all. They could have had me go looking for a unicorn, and I would have jumped at it like a dog. Since they pulled us to this stupid new division to serve Durai specifically, we've been sitting on our asses waiting for something. And now we're finally doing something, and I don't give a shit what it is. I'm just glad to not be wasting away, ya know?"

Hemele looked at Jian then not having thought of what this assignment had been doing to his men. Shortly after the Royal guard was called off from searching for the Healer Althea when Baldrik became even weaker, a decree was made that the Court Enchanter would have his own personal guard. If some outside harm came into the castle to take one court-appointed person away, they could come after another, so this decision stood to reason. But then Hemele was made a captain and given this group of men, and they had nothing to do. The Queen's guard patrolled the palace, protected it, and the Queen and Baldrik, and Hemele's men just sat and trained amongst themselves with nothing more to do. No wonder they all jumped eagerly at the opportunity, and no wonder they didn't question it.

So then why was he? What was bothering him about it?

Now Jian looked concerned at his captain's silence. Hemele tried to continue, "You're right. We've been sitting here with barely a sign of life from our appointed man, and then all of a sudden, just like that, we're moved on the double to go and fetch a girl that had just disappeared into nothing before. I mean, you remember us looking for her before. She was nowhere."

Jian responded quickly as though he had indeed been giving this thought. "What if she got away from whoever took her and was making her way back to the castle? Maybe before she was taken so far away that we hadn't looked out that far before being called back. And once she escaped Durai was able to sense her closer and called us to get her." Jian wasn't fully convinced of his theory, but it was the best he could come up with, it was the best of the rumors that had been passed around, and was comfortable with that.

"What if she wasn't taken? There were no signs of struggle, and even her stuff had been carefully packed away."

"Oh, you know Healers, they always have packs of supplies ready to go at a moment's notice. Maybe..." but seeing Hemele's unconvinced look, he didn't finish his thought.

"I mean," Hemele continued as if picking up from a thought in his head not yet spoken out loud, and even as he did so he looked over his shoulder out of habit, "here is a guy that we're working for that seemed as steady and quietly unmoving as a statue up until the second he gets the slightest notion that she might be close, and he suddenly comes alive. And then to be so secretive?"

"Oh, yeah, that," Jian recalled the first moment they were given the orders from Durai in person. He swore them to secrecy about their mission both before the mission and upon returning. It was unusual. Durai's Guard and the Queen's Guard were in such close quarters that everyone knew everyone else's business. Then at their first real assignment, they had to shut up tight about it. Jian just tried to pass it off, "Like I said, I would be happy being sent after a unicorn."

Hemele smiled a bit at Jian as he knew that his friend was just trying to lighten the mood. But he was still troubled, and Jian knew it. "I guess maybe it's something about this woman. Because of her, Durai suddenly turns out of character. I mean, have you ever seen him that animated?" Jian simply shook his head to confirm that he had not. "I mean, don't get me wrong, she seems nice, and she really is gorgeous."

Jian interjected, "Yeah, I'll just keep my mouth shut on that one. It's been so long since I've seen a really pretty face that I might make a jackass out of myself."

"Might?"

And the two men took the moment to laugh and relieved some of the tension.

Hemele paused for just a moment more, but then continued as the little tickle of doubt in his mind would not let him rest. "Then there's this other guy who is willing to stand up to my protests that he stay out of it, but he insists on following her, caring for her, no matter what I say. And then we get the order from Durai to keep the fact that we found her alive a secret from the Queen. I mean, what's going on? Is she some kind of witch? Is there a spell on these guys? What exactly is the story with her?"

Jian started to understand what was bothering him. "You mean, is there some kind of spell this woman put on these men to make them protect her? What would she need protection from?"

"Is that why we have to keep quiet? We're protecting her? Protecting her from what?" Hemele kept being more and more perplexed.

"What I thought," Jian offered, "was that the Queen blamed her for Baldrik's death. So wouldn't Durai want to keep her a secret then...?" Then Jian seemed to realize the hole that their logic had been put in. He had just been spouting the rumors that were never officially denied, and only then just realized the contradictions in them. It seemed so obvious now their contradictions, why hadn't it been clear before?

"You see?" Hemele asked as he registered Jian's realization. "If she was snatched from the castle, why would the Queen blame her? It doesn't make sense that we're keeping her a secret for her protection if she was taken from here and not, say, a runaway."

"Runaway?"

"Yeah, and if she did run away, why is Durai trying to protect her?"

Jian just looked at him like his world had exploded.

Hemele then said what was really on his mind, "And is that what he is doing, protecting her? I mean, I used to work near the Queen, I've been in the same room a ton of times. She seems level-headed and even compassionate. She doesn't strike me as an impulsive dictator. So, what are we doing? What's going on?"

The only sound that remained was the crackling of the roaring fire between the two men. It was done; all the evidence that they had been deceived at some point was clear and unmistakable. But which part was a lie? Who could they trust? What did all of this mean? Was the Queen a tyrant that had to have secrets kept from her, was this Healer some kind of manipulative witch, was she a victim, or was Durai the center of all of this conspiracy? And whatever turned out to be true, what did that mean for them?

Jian went back to poking the fire. He tried to look up to the stars, but there were no stars. The only light was from the fire eating at the stack of wood placed in the pit and breaking it down slowly. The world seemed different to him now.

At the same time, both men reached for their mugs warmed by the fire and drank long from them. As they finished their wine, they looked at each other. Now that this feeling was given form and their words were said, what was next? What should they do? What could they do?

Jian said the only thing he could think to say to break the tension, "Well, orders are orders. None of our business, right?"

Hemele didn't answer as he heard his own words said back to him then. He wasn't so sure of them now.

Part 3

Some Sins to Bear Their Privilege on Earth

The scene was set no less than she expected. The room glowed in only candlelight, and the warm smells of scented wax filled the room. A wide selection of meats, loaves of bread, and roasted vegetables filled the space of the table, and the two chairs were not at opposite ends, but alongside each other. Rose petals filled the spaces on the tables that did not have food or dishes. The forced romanticism of this display made her irritated and resentful. She wanted to turn and strike him with whatever she could get her hands on. She could feel his fingers towards the puppet strings she had long since cut, but she feared the lengths he would go to try and reattach them.

She walked past the table slowly to the glass double doors of the room that led out to his courtyard. She looked out to the darkened night that was before her and watched as distant flashes of light sporadically light the sky. The storm that had been threatening for two days had sat heavy over the earth as far as she could see; it was coming closer to exploding. She could tell that it was going to be truly terrible.

Galen...

As she looked out into the black and the oncoming storm, she hoped and prayed within her heart that Galen was safe and secure wherever he was. She thought back to their last moment together and what was left unsaid. She resented the most that she couldn't have more time to ensure that he would be safe beyond what little she had already done. She kept thinking she could have done more, been just a little stronger, and protected him longer. She didn't know what would become of her, how she would find him again, or if she even could find him again. But she did know that no matter what happened, she would do her best to do right by him. Whatever the cost may be, she would …

She felt his cold hands on her shoulders then as she was lost in her thoughts. She marveled how his hands could be so cold in a room so warm. He was like a snake. She endured his touch, and he ushered her to sit down for their meal together. Her heart had no appetite and pushed back at the thought of his offering, but her body was in desperate need of food. Pride and company aside, she began to take the food he had placed before her.

The meat was so warm and perfectly seasoned that the sensations sparked and danced in her mouth. She tried her best not to show how much she thoroughly enjoyed the food. She thought that an elegant display such as this had to take a cook a whole day of diligent preparation. She felt grateful to the faceless person who blessed her with it.

She ate steadily at everything, and Durai smiled genuinely at the sight of her contentment at the meal that she could not hide from him. At that moment, seeing her enjoyment and her guard down, he forgot all wicked intent, all motives of manipulation, any strategic moves he was making to place the pawns for his end goal. For that moment, he was just a man staring at the woman he loved enjoying what he provided for her. He was twelve years old seeing the bright eyes of his mother before she left; he was innocent of the world and the methods of men like his father. He was staring at the light again.

Althea enjoyed the silence in which she was allowed to simply enjoy her meal. When her stomach began to fill and could take in no more, she started to anxiously fear the beginning of a conversation or whatever else he had planned for her that night. Low rumbles could now be heard of the thunder steadily approaching. Little by little, she picked at small pieces of food to prolong any interaction and slowly placed them delicately into her mouth.

Lights started to flicker as the wind began to build up outside and come into their room from the fireplace. The shadows that grew and shrank, as a result, looked like miniature black beasts dancing around the room. Althea couldn't help but be uneasy at the sight. The most sinister of shadows were the ones that moved across Durai's face. When his face was cast in shadow, even for just a moment, the sinister nature of his eyes was evident. Even in darkness, his eyes glowed and watched her. She kept finding it harder and harder to be brave and defiant. How easy it would be to just shrink away and not fight. Then he might have mercy. Then it could all be over.

"Don't let the darkness win, Althea..."

She closed her eyes only briefly to gather up all of her courage. She held tight to the image of her mother and her grandmother before her, put down her utensils, and began whatever it was that would begin. Durai noticed her signal, and the smile once again turned villainous in the promise of all he could do – all he *would* do. The pieces on his board were meticulously set, and the game began as lightning lit the room.

"Did you enjoy your dinner?" Durai asked her.

The deep and sensual voice that once made her quiver now simply made her heated and bitter. She had thought long and hard this past year that she was away on the snares he set that had trapped her before. She was more cunning now to fall for the same spells again. Instead of answering, she just looked at him with annoyance. She would not gift him any softness in her expressions or kindness in her eyes. Durai smiled some more as he had expected her not to be the woman he once molded so easily to fit his whims. Now she was a far stronger challenge and all the more desirable and valuable to win.

He looked out the glass doors that were behind her. The flashes of light that could be seen behind Althea became more frequent and splintered out intricately across the sky and resembled a dangerous and deadly web more and more. How appropriate, he thought. Still, he decided to ask again and assert himself. "I asked you how dinner was, Dove."

"I would have enjoyed it more with better company. I want to see Mireya." Althea kept pushing him on this subject for more explanation. She was determined to get one now.

Durai sat back and interlocked his fingers and laced them across his chest. "My darling, I told you before. Your sister believes that you are dead. I had to do it to protect you, you see. And her, really. If you were to, say, try and run away again, I would have to do something very drastic. And if you had tried to elicit her help against me? I would promise you her death would be a painful one. Just for you." Something seemed to snap slightly in him, and Althea registered it.

"So," Althea clearly stated, "you lied to her that I was dead. Just as easily as that?"

"Just for you."

Althea bent her head slightly at the thought of what her sister must have felt having heard she was dead. She hoped that the love held between them was still the same, that she thought fondly of her in mourning, and she knew that there was another wrong to right in the end.

He spoke again feeling the need to add more. "You see, I stayed behind. I didn't run away. So in the end, what I said was the only story she was able to hear. If you wanted your truth, you should have stayed. Because you ran, I won."

She felt like fire would come out of her own eyes her venom towards him felt so strong. Before him, before now, true hate and loathing seemed so disgusting and unthinkable. Now it was all she could feel at this moment.

"The storm is getting closer. Whatever shall we do?" he whispered to her as he leaned in closer.

To his surprise, she leaned into him as well. He had expected her to pull back at his advancement. She matched his whispering tone and volume and said, "I think, I should bash your head into this table and run as far from you as I can."

He lightly laughed in a teasing way, "I wouldn't let you get very far."

"Then maybe I should scream."

"If you do, I will have to gag you. Wait," he said, his eyes lighting up, "maybe I'd like that anyway."

Althea felt the disgust swell in her throat at the mere thought of his perverse tastes and backed up from him then. From where she sat, he was between her and the door out to the castle. The only place she could run to was the courtyard that sat before a cliff – so a dead end – or the bedroom which was even worse.

She tried another approach; maybe just keeping him talking might give her more time to plan. "But if I get out even one good scream, people will come to investigate. People will know I'm here. And even if you manage to hide me away before one of those gossiping biddies finds me, the rumors will spread so quickly that your life will be a hell putting out the fires."

Durai simply leaned in further and stroked her hand left on the table. "When did you get so deliciously sneaky?" She tried to take her hand away, but he grabbed her wrist and held it painfully tight. Her face couldn't help but reveal the ache she felt in his tightening grip. "I can't wait to find out what else about you is new."

The pressure he held her with flashed her back to that night so long ago. She would fight with all she had before going through that again.

He finally let go of her wrist, and she was up and out of her seat in an instant to get as much distance from him as she could get. She looked down behind her to make sure she wasn't blocked or about to fall, and when she looked back to the table, he was no longer in his seat. The room was dark; somehow the candles had all blown out the instant she rose. The room was lit only by sporadic lightning, and in the darkness, only slight outlines of the furniture could be distinguished from the rest of the black. She was breathing heavily as she lowered her gravity and strengthened her stance. She heard the loud and pounding beating of her own heart as if they were drums.

She slowed and quieted her breathing to listen out for any movement in the dark. As brave as she had tried to be, she was fully terrified then having been suddenly thrust into a dangerous cat and mouse game. She could feel the draft coming in from the fireplace. All she could hear was the relentless wind against the glass of the door and the walls of the castle. No matter what she tried to do, she couldn't help but feel afraid.

Suddenly she felt pain in the back of her head as her head thudded loudly against the wall behind her. She was pinned there by familiar hands and found that she couldn't move. More than just being held in place by his body and his embrace, she couldn't move anything about her. Even as she realized it, she felt her body being flung from the wall, leave the floor, and come crashing down to the floor. Loud crashes of the dishes were heard falling to the ground despite her not being anywhere near the table. She quieted her instinct to pant and moan in the pain she felt from her fall. Still, she could hear nothing and could sense nothing of where he was in the room.

A flash of lightning raged across the sky and lit the room in pure, white light, and the embodiment of her nightmares was right before her face. She opened her mouth to scream at the sight of him suddenly before her eyes, but he silenced her as his hand struck across her face with immense force. A different white light showed in her eyes then, hot white light of pain. She closed her eyes to it and felt her body being dragged slightly along the floor as his hands tightened around her ankles.

She felt her body being heaved into the air again and she braced herself to be hurled once again to the ground. Instead, she felt pressure on her abdomen as she was slung across his shoulders. Her body bounced with the few steps that he took before she felt the hard landing from him dropping her body on the table now cleared of any food or dishes.

She then felt him clawing at her body and turned her face down onto the table. She tried to push up with her hands, but another flash of light seared into her head. She couldn't tell then if it was lightning or pain because all she could feel was shock and unrelenting terror. She tried to wiggle herself free or at least squirm enough to be a handful and buy herself time if she couldn't manage to escape.

She felt Durai place his knee on her back at that moment and press against her spine. She let out a pitiful sound of sharp distress then. In reaction to her cry, he pushed down harder and sharper into her back, and she put her hands up in a sign of surrender. She ceased movement and showed utter compliance, anything to get him to let up and show some mercy. Her pain was sharp and hot; she felt she couldn't even take a proper breath without it slicing into her. Silent tears rolled down her face as the lightning flashed again and deep, foreboding thunder rumbled shortly after. And for a moment she couldn't tell which booming shook her body more - the thunder or her heart.

As the last lightning flash darkened the room, a new light appeared and flickered its light in the room with a deep green hue. Althea turned her head only

235

slightly as it was still pressed against the table and saw flames out of her periphery coming from Durai's left hand. He bent down closer to her still keeping his knee on her back. His movement put more pressure on her nerves and she couldn't help but let out a small, pathetic whimper.

"Don't let the darkness win, Althea..."

Though she could hear her mother's words, she couldn't find a way to see her face. All she could register before her eyes was her pain and the villain at her back. She felt his hand stroke her cheek already wet with painful tears. His hand traveled down her face, down her neck, traveled the length of her arm, and pinned it down at the wrist. Althea was afraid, so horribly afraid.

She felt his lips at her ear and the heat from the fire in his hand as he softly whispered, "Shhhh, shhhh..." and reached for something he had secured under the table. She couldn't tell what it was. The only quick glimpse she had was of a long, metallic rod of some kind. He straightened his body, and the pressure on her back was relieved slightly. She took deeper breaths at that moment to try and calm her racing heart, but it wasn't working. She noticed the flame grow brighter and cast their shadows on the wall in front of them. She saw her shadow helpless and trapped, and she saw his slender, graceful form move and bend above her like a snake gliding across the sand. She saw from his shadow the metal rod held in his hand be bent into the green-flamed fire he made.

"Hold still," he whispered in that same demonic voice she had heard before as if he had been taken over by the Devil himself. The sound was pure, embodied evil and malevolence. It entered her ears and spread like poison in her blood paralyzing her. She dared not move or disobey in her terror.

His shadow moved again as he took the metal rod from the fire in his hand. He then moved faster than she could register, doused the fire in his hand with a flick of his wrist, and ripped away a part of her dress.

She heard the sizzling of her flesh before she felt the pain on her exposed right shoulder. She felt his hand still warm from his Magic against her mouth as she screamed violently. She screamed in pain muffled against his hand over and over again.

When she collapsed utterly spent, she felt his lips at her ear one last time before blacking into unconsciousness.

"Mine!"

That Not Your Trespass but My Madness Speaks

"Oh, my head." Galen opened his eyes to the light of a strange room. He was lying flat on a strange bed, and the back of his head pounded with pain.

The last thing he remembered was arriving at Courtside and being on his horse looking at what he had assumed was the makeshift hospital building that Hemele had spoken of before they set off. The next thing he knew, he was lying on this bed in his pain. He concluded that he had been hit on the head to unconsciousness and dropped off here. He could only imagine what false pretenses that he was admitted under. He was entering this situation at a strong disadvantage, so he would have to be quick to utilize everything he could in himself to turn that around.

There were no other beds in this room, just his. The room itself was very small and could only accommodate one person living comfortably. The only light came from a single window too high to reach or even see out of except the sky. Nothing else adorned the simple room. There were no chairs, no tables, no furnishings or ornaments. There was only the bed and a single pot. Galen was not thrilled about what was clearly resembling a prison the more he studied it, and it was familiar to him.

He sat in silence for over an hour. He could tell by the heat of the sun that it was coming onto mid-morning, so he had been unconscious for some time. He tried not to dwell on the anger he felt towards these men who had done this to him and, even worse, had done what they had done to Althea. Instead, he focused on her. He meditated and drew from her strength, her bravery, and her resilience in the face of adversity. He knew that, with her help even so far away and her inspiration, he would find the right way out of this.

When the door did start to open, a small-framed girl who looked barely the age of a woman came in with a pitcher and a loaf of bread. She was at least a full head, if not more, shorter than he was with large, innocent-looking eyes and straight black hair. She entered the room timidly. Galen noticed her shoulders arched into her neck with high tension and her steps small and the objects in her hand held close to her body. She was afraid, yet she was brave. What was she afraid of?

In an attempt to per her at ease, Galen spoke out to her in his soft, naturally comforting voice. "Good morning." His dulcet tones reached her ears, and her eyes lit in what seemed like surprise. She relaxed her tension only a small amount, but nodded to him at his words and smiled somewhat.

They simply looked at each other not knowing what to do or say next for what seemed like an eternity, though in reality, it was only a minute or so. Galen felt the pressure to continue to put her at ease as she just stood there looking at him almost as if she were inspecting him. He reached out his hand to her very slowly, "Are those for me? I could use some water if that's alright."

At that, she seemed to realize again her purpose in coming and blushed a bit in embarrassment as if she had lingered too long. She set down the pitcher of water and the loaf of bread on the floor before him and quickly retreated backward with her back to the door and facing Galen. Her movements reminded Galen of a rabbit or timid fawn so reluctant to trust and inherently cautious. But he knew how to deal with traits like that.

He bent down to the water and drank deeply from the pitcher. The water felt so good, and he drank about half of the pitcher. He put it down afterward and worried that he wasn't going to be getting more than that pitcher for the day; perhaps he should have rationed. He wasn't sure if he was being held as a prisoner here for some crime or something else. He looked at her again then, and she still held an innocently inquisitive look. Galen smiled as warmly as he could to her in an attempt to ease her mind. "Thank you very much. That water was very much needed."

Still, she said nothing, but at least then she smiled brighter. The sound of his voice began to both put her at ease and seemingly confused her. But with the smile she gave, he felt that at least he was getting through to her.

A shadow crossed into the room from the high window and made her jump for just a second. They both looked up and saw a crow sitting on the ledge in the room. Before Galen could move towards the bird at all, he noticed her smile a warm and familiar smile. She placed her hand into a pocket of her skirt and pull out a handful of something. She took one step towards the window and knelt on the ground depositing what appeared to be breadcrumbs from her hand onto the floor. Then she backed away again.

The bird simply looked at the gift from his perch, tilted his head towards the sky, reangled himself with a jump, and then flew away with a cry. Galen looked at his companion thinking her innocent eyes might show terrible disappointment, but she just seemed to shrug then and smiled a half-smile as if she knew her offering only worked now and then.

"My name is Galen, and I appreciate your kindness here. May I ask your name?" The melody of his voice at first made her smile as she closed her eyes to listen to it. However, her face darkened when she heard his question. She gave no response, just a frightened look. "I'm sorry," he replied at her reaction. "Did I say something wrong? I don't mean to be rude or intrusive. I just want to know your name to thank you for your help."

He saw her hands feel the door at her back and move toward the handle as she smiled at him with an obviously forced smile. Galen could tell she was moving to leave then, and he had so much he wanted to ask and find out. He reached out his hand and used as much of his comforting charm as he possibly could to try and keep her there. "Wait, please. I'm sorry. Please! I didn't mean to scare or offend you. I need help."

With his last words, she smiled and gave a knowing nod. She quickly opened the door and hurried out of the room. He could hear a latch being bolted, and he knew that he was trapped in that room.

At that moment, Galen fought hard against the crushing disappointment. He didn't have time for playful and infuriating mysteries. He had to get out of there and find some way to help Althea. The more he thought about the situation and what the guards had done, the more he knew that she was in danger. If he could find some way to help, he knew he had to do it no matter what it was. But here he was in a familiar barren room locked away without even an accessible window to escape out of. Even if he learned to climb the wall to reach it, it wasn't even larger than his head. He thought then that he could maybe try to break the door down, but what good would that do? He didn't even know where he was, where he would go, or what the people in this building would do to someone who showed such aggression escaping out of a room like this.

He sat on the floor then with his legs crossed. He stared at the bread and hadn't the heart to even pick it up off the floor, much less eat it. He bent his head down, closed his eyes, and thought again of Althea. The sight of her collapsing body into the arms of the man who drugged her played over and over again, and his fists clenched harder in his vexation.

Then a fluttering sound above him and then soon near him brought him out of his meditation. The crow had returned and was pecking at the offering left by the girl. After a few pecks, the crow looked around the room, saw only Galen, and seemed to take a hop closer. He reached out his hand to the bird and said, "Don't be afraid. It's just you and me." His voice wafted to the bird like a spell, his gift in action, and the bird flapped once to fly up and rested on his offered hand.

The two regarded each other for a long time. Seemingly having that inexplicable connection that only Leporems could have and understand. The warmth of the sun increased the heat in the room making it uncomfortable. But the connection was kept even as both of them became increasingly uncomfortable with the heat.

Finally, Galen's posture relaxed, and the crow flew away out of the room through the high window. Galen stood up and turned to the bed and paused. His thoughts were still wrestling with so much of the unknown, but at least now, with the help of the crow, he knew a little more about the woman who was caring for him in this place. He laid down then and stared at the ceiling deciding to sleep away the heat and pain in his head until the next move was made.

•••••••

Upon waking, Galen was surprised to see that the light in the room was changed to shades of deep orange and red. It had to be just before nightfall. He had slept most of the day away, and he was grateful for that. His head still hurt, though, with the rest, it wasn't as bad as before. And now the heat was starting to dissipate, so he wasn't conscious to try and suffer through it. Though he registered his hunger, he was more concerned about the feeling that he was not alone in the room anymore.

He looked around him and saw a figure standing in the corner of the room along the same wall as the door. He recognized Hemele right away with his arms crossed and one leg bent with his foot resting behind him on the wall. He made a good effort to appear superiorly nonchalant, almost as if he was inconvenienced having to take his time out to visit this man.

Galen didn't want to play the game with him of moves and countermoves. He wasn't going to draw out the silence dramatically. "The hit on the head wasn't necessary, you know."

Hemele's expression changed from holding in reserve his thoughts to an impressed smile and nod. He had to admit to himself that this man was brave and even had a sense of humor. But he didn't respond right away; he just put his foot down and squared his stance more.

"Where is she?" Galen asked in a more serious tone.

"I told you before where we were taking her."

"And you're ok with that?" Galen was holding back a flood of resentment and not too successfully.

Then Hemele took a step closer to him. "Why shouldn't I be?" This he asked not in jest or any trivial intent. Hemele's question was genuine.

Galen registered the change in his tone. He thought carefully about how best to approach this as he still didn't trust Hemele or any of his men in the least. They were the type to follow orders strictly and simply. No amount of his words was going to register to him much less change his mind about his charge. Galen finally decided that if this man hadn't snapped to what was wrong with this situation, he wasn't about to now no matter what manner of persuasion he used.

So, Galen decided to change the subject. "I appreciate you getting me to a hospital and providing me the need to be seen in one," he added harshly, "but I'd rather leave now. I can tell that is only going to happen with your permission given the nature of the locked door all day."

Hemele resumed his laid-back posture then as he recognized he once again held the upper hand. "That will depend a lot on you, I think."

"I kind of figured."

Hemele knew that this man wasn't an idiot. He was dealing with a highly perceptive individual. The way he was carrying himself, he seemed to be used to manipulation or at the very least expected it now. "What would you do," Hemele asked slowly, "if I were to let you out of here? I mean, I take it you are a long way from home. Can we be any assistance to you in getting you there?"

"Oh, I appreciate your offer," Galen lied as he matched Hemele's false tone. "Unfortunately, all of this business has left my hometown pretty much abandoned. I have no home to go back to." Galen continued to look into Hemele's eyes with a conviction that his determination wouldn't be diminished no matter how hard the man may push against hit.

Hemele decided not to try and be passive anymore. He found he respected this man, and he wasn't about to insult him with false niceties. "Let's not waste any more time then."

"Yes, and thank you."

"I have my orders, and you are about to complicate them."

"I can promise you that I don't willfully intend to be complicated," Galen responded genuinely. Hemele even believed his sincerity.

"Regardless of your intent, the fact is going to remain that your very presence and existence is going to complicate things." Hemele decided to sit on the bed opposite Galen. He wished he would have thought to bring in a chair, but this would work. He wanted to appeal to Galen and make this as easy as possible for both of them, but he could see where the complications could be as well.

"Complicate things for who, exactly? For Durai?" Galen took the risk of showing his knowledge, and he noticed Hemele register his words with surprise.

"Among other people. Not the least of which being your friend. I have my orders that, for Althea's protection, she is to be reported as found dead. As I understand, this is to protect her. But you know that her death isn't true. And thus, you see my problem."

Galen couldn't respond to the shock that he felt at the directive that had just been explained to him. What was he going to do?

"My God, man. Protect her from who?"

Hemele rested his elbows on his knees and leaned forward. "Wasn't my place to ask. Isn't my place to ask. But I imagine to protect her from any number of things. The Queen's anger, the people who took her in the first place, the people who might panic if her powers to stop this don't work. It could result in mass chaos, I should think if it was known that a Healer was found and she couldn't deliver in the end."

Galen looked intently at the man sitting next to him. Galen wasn't sure if Hemele himself was convinced of his own regurgitated reasoning or not. He kept himself reserved and was so hard to read. Galen was at a loss as to what to try. How can you fight against a believer?

But then Hemele looked at Galen, and the look was an incredibly subtle call for help. He wanted Galen to challenge it. It was like he needed to know the other argument. Galen returned the look confused and almost afraid. Hemele's eyes remained persistent.

Galen took a deep breath first, and then he said, "Have you spoken with her? How does she feel about being pronounced dead?"

Hemele looked down in resignation. Of course, he would ask that, and of course, he had to answer shamefully, "I have not had any contact with her outside of what you saw. My mission was to get her safely to Durai. Durai, by the way, was the one that kept pressing to continue the search for her long after it was called off by the Queen. I have no doubt he cares deeply for her and will keep her safe."

Galen then felt pity for this man and his unwavering faith in someone who was using him. "Did those orders include to drug her?"

Hemele dropped his aggressive tone as if he was a small child being reprimanded by a parent, "Yes," he admitted shamefully. "Yes, it did."

"I kind of figured, sir. You don't seem the type to have your own drugs on hand for poisoning young women into submission."

Hemele felt anger rise in him at this. How dare this man speak to him in such a manner about his orders, which he followed with the honor afforded those who follow through with their duties? He couldn't imagine what made this man so brave in his impertinence. Yet, at the same time, nothing he said was a lie. Nothing he said was wrong. But did that mean something about his orders was wrong? Was *he* wrong?

They couldn't both be right.

Hemele didn't like this feeling. He didn't like the thought of following orders and being in the wrong. He did his duty; he upheld his honor. Then why was he feeling this way? What was it about this man that made Hemele even engage in this dialogue? His frustration turned to anger, and as he felt his limits being reached, he stood to go.

He reached the door and looked back at Galen. "Obviously you see the problem. You pose a threat to this secret that I have been sworn to uphold. I'll leave you here another day. Let's just make sure that you understand the situation clearly. You know where you are, right? You know what this is?"

"Yeah, I know." Galen had long figured out that he was in a room all too familiar to him given his mother. The high windows, the lack of furnishings, the thick, heavy walls and doors were to keep locked away people who had gone mad. Hemele registered him as a lunatic who was prone to lies and elaborate fantasies. Anything he would say to anyone wouldn't be trusted then. He was even given a woman to attend to him that was mute and wouldn't be able to tell his story even if he somehow managed to convince her.

Galen had to admit it was well played.

Hemele did not doubt that a man as clever as this understood all that had been implied. He nodded and left Galen alone in his cage.

Still, Hemele thought as he closed the door and latched it behind him, there was something that wasn't quite right. He didn't want to admit it, but Galen said some things that rang true to him. How it made him feel aside, he couldn't shake the impending ramifications if this man were right. Perhaps he would talk with Jian about it at the fire tonight.

Though She Be But Little, She Is Fierce!

For who would bear the whips and scorns of time,

The oppressor's wrong, the proud man's contumely,

The pangs of dispraised love, the law's delay,

The insolence of office, and the spurns

That patient merit of the unworthy takes,

When he himself might his quietus make

With a bare bodkin? Who would fardels bear,

To grunt and sweat under a weary life,

But that the dread of something after death,

The undiscovered country, from whose bourn

No traveler returns, puzzles the will,

And makes us rather bear those ills we have

Than fly to others that we know not of?

A steady rain fell heavily drumming both the roof and the puddles made on the ground outside. Once calming sounds with the promise of renewal and growth turned into persistent and ominous battle drums filled with foreboding. The steady downpour had persisted since the early morning; no light would reach the earth this day. The heavens broke forth their sorrows, and there seemed no signs of dwindling or stopping.

Althea registered being awake before she had the heart to open her eyes. She didn't know where she would be now, but unless it was far away from the castle and the cursed Hill, she knew she didn't want to know. After a time, she did find the will to open her eyes even though it was tediously slow. She could tell that she was back in Durai's bedroom and on his bed. The light was a dingy grey and seemed to mirror the weight of her sorrows. The air felt heavy and thick with the moisture of the rain and the heat of the summer air. It was almost hard to breathe, or was that just in her mind?

She awoke lying on her stomach on this bed after she passed out. She wanted to fully survey the room to make sure she was safe and hopefully alone, but she couldn't pick herself up to do so. When she tried to draw in her arms underneath her to push herself up, she realized she could not move them. She tried again with no better luck. Looking down at her outstretched arms, she realized she was bound again. Her arms were held out to either side of her and held in place by silk ropes against the bedposts.

Damn...

What small range of motion she was able to have when she tried to move brought her swift and severe pain searing like molten metal from her shoulder all the way through her blood and stopped the thoughts of her brain. The pain she felt suddenly reminded her of what had all happened only hours before. She could still feel his knee upon her back, hear that dreadful voice that haunted her soul, and vividly recall every bit of what he inflicted upon her. She fought hard against the tears that felt determined to escape her eyes. She didn't want to give him the satisfaction of her breaking even if she couldn't, especially at this moment, fathom how she was going to go on.

She had no choice but to lie there in the greying light. All she could sense was the smell of the rain, the oppressive heaviness of the air, the sound of the fire in the fireplace, and the pounding of her heart as it somehow managed to keep beating despite being broken. But in all that she sensed in that room, she could tell that she was alone. She could not sense him in that room. Even as devious, graceful, and surreptitiously silent as he could be, she always could manage to tell when he was near her. In the beginning, she thought it was because he was so beautiful to her that her love could feel when he was with her. Later, she felt that it was because of how masterfully manipulative he had become that she could tell when her master was close and ready to pull her strings. Now she wasn't sure what the reason was, survival instinct or a foreboding sense of evil, but she felt him whenever he was close.

The longer she was awake, the more even the air started to cause the wound on her back to spread like hot fire. Soon she started to writhe in agony. No matter what she could do, and she could do nothing, she was begging silently for the pain to at least cease its increasing intensity. It moved from stinging to throbbing to warm, red ache to the final blaze of searing misery that kept growing and growing. She thought surely that this amount of pain would start to fall away into numbness, but it kept on without any leniency.

She clenched the satin sheets she lay face down upon into her fists and finally started to let out some small sound in desperation. She tried to draw upon the songs to heal herself, but she couldn't manage the concentration needed for such a task. Tears began to roll down her face. She begged for some mercy. In the end, she even begged for Durai.

Just when she thought she might scream with the pain she felt or pass out from not being able to bear the rising swells anymore, she heard the door open, and she could sense it was him. She didn't care. She even let out something like a grateful sob when she heard him walking toward her. Whatever hoops he'd have her go through, no matter what words he'd force her to say or what tricks he'd have her perform, she'd do them happily for even a small sign of hope that the pain would end.

He sat near her on the bed gracefully and very carefully. He didn't say a word. She could hardly hear him breathe. She couldn't even see his face, or much of him for that matter, as she was still lying on her stomach with limited range of motion with her neck. Without much hesitation, he put his hands near the site of the burn on her shoulder, and at the cold sensation of his hands, she dropped her head down so grateful for the cooling touch. Even if he hadn't touched the branding directly, the skin around it was still incredibly red and irritated. The tears of relief came silently then, and she didn't care if he knew.

She felt his hand stroke her hair once before she heard the sound of a jar being opened. Immediately she recognized the smell of Aloe, the sap-like smell of Calendula, and strong lavender to mask the more unpleasant odor of Comfrey. Surely this was a burn salve that she had made that he either got from her pack or left behind in her old suite of rooms. She didn't care where; she was just utterly grateful that it was here and being used.

However, she noticed the agonizing seconds go by without the soothing sensation of the medication on her shoulder. She turned her head towards him for what little good that did. She was desperate for what she could see he held in his hands. She was so anxious for the relief that she was almost willing to try and grab at the jar with her teeth.

Durai recoiled his hand holding the salve slightly. He bent down and kissed the top of her head. Even doing so, he could feel on his cheek the heat radiating off the skin of her shoulder. He knew very well she had to be in pure agony. With his lips close to her, his deep voice slithered into her ears like a venomous serpent. "Say please," his words might have been the tone of seduction if the situation were different or if he were anyone else.

The thought of being proud, being stalwart, or making a statement occupied her mind for maybe the smallest fraction of a second before the sounds of her broken spirit broke free from her throat as she sobbed a breathless, "Please. Please, Durai."

Though she couldn't see it with her eyes, she knew he had a smug smile on his face as he bent again to kiss her hair. "That's my good girl."

She wanted so much to vomit to hear him refer to her like that.

Then, as promised, she felt the thick, sap-like salve be put incredibly gingerly onto her marred skin. A pitiful sound escaped her lips as the relief of her slave was almost instant. The sensation felt like tiny streams of water brought from the river to the sun-dried fields bringing blessings to the thirsty crops. The cooling sensation on her seared skin was so deeply contrasted she almost thought it would sizzle or steam.

As she started to think clearer with her relief washing over her, she was able to notice more and more the motions of his fingers, the pressure, and the rhythm of his application. He could have been harsh, he could have used this moment to remind her of his dominance, but he did not. At this moment, he was handling her with such care and warm devotion that she couldn't rationally believe that it was him. The same man that forced himself upon her, scarred her permanently, who broke her over and over again was now a tender and caring attendant to her needs.

The jar was closed then, and he got up from the bed and moved away. She turned her head from side to side to find where he had gone. She did not want to remain the day this way and in this debased pose like some imprisoned whore. She refused to continue to be at such a disadvantage. Every small sympathy she ever had, every small appreciation towards him including his applying her salve now, she pushed aside. People were relying on her to bring this sickening game to an end. This marionette would no longer suffer strings.

"Durai, these bonds are unseemly and quite unnecessary. Release me, or I will do whatever it takes to release myself. Even if I have to break my own arms." The determination in her voice even surprised her. But she didn't feel like she had anything to celebrate about. Even if she found some way to fly from this place right this moment, find her Magic to save the world, and never lay eyes on this monster again; she wasn't strong enough to fight him off last night. And she would carry his mark on her for the rest of her life. In the end, she would never truly be free from him. Not ever.

To her surprise, he didn't argue, he didn't taunt, and he didn't demand tricks or favors. The light from his hands extended forth and broke her bonds. She felt the pressure of her arms go slack and she slowly brought them under her chest. Even with the salve, she could feel the pain of her motion. Perhaps he had her in that position to keep her from further injury. Though she strongly doubted that was the only reason. The sickening pose was horribly base and had filled her with shame, and she did not doubt that this was part of his intention

With admittedly admirable determination, she managed her pick herself up slowly to sitting as she held one hand to keep her torn dress covering her chest. Durai then looked at her as she did her best to carry herself with pride even now. She was like a broken doll ragged, torn, and damaged by a careless child. The satisfaction of his actions, claiming her in this way, seemed to dissolve slightly. He had felt her injury with his fingers, and he saw now how it looked now when she bore it. In just this short time, he was seeing the damages surface and her fire diminish somewhat. Though her determination was unabated, the strength she had was already starting to waver. He wasn't sure about himself for a moment.

Althea then raised her head still covering her vulnerabilities with her hands, and she said with steady determination, "If we keep going on this road you are set to travel and drag me down, I will undoubtedly be no use against this plague you've unleashed." She got up then and took one labored step towards him. She did not show fear, though she was horribly afraid. "You have what you want, you have me back here and at your miserable mercy. You have made sure I have nowhere to go even if I somehow find the strength to run." She put out a hand towards him then, her eyes holding a truth begging to be understood. "Please," she said with a change in her voice, no longer proud but strong enough to beg, "let me try my best to help this world before you continue. I won't fight you, I won't run, but please let me have this chance before I lose the strength to try."

Durai felt the muscles of his face furrow in confusion. What was she trying to manipulate? What was her tactic? He attacked her, he hurt her, and he struck and burned her with a brand of his making, and yet she said that she would not run. She had to be lying; he had no doubt of it then. He knew women in his life just as precious as her who would break their word at less than this. He couldn't possibly give her what she asked. He couldn't possibly give her the one thing that would keep her here.

"Please," she pleaded again more desperately, "people are *suffering*. I have to try to bring this to an end. Please." With her final words, she took even another step toward him. And to his surprise, he instinctually took a step back from her.

That step back shocked them both. They stood in silence as if the next move by either one of them would bring their undoing.

The sound of rain kept steadily on as each passing second ticked forward as surely as each drop from the clouds. The heaviness of the air swirled around them like thick liquid adding to the anxiety and tension. Althea felt for the first time that she might have gained some leverage, and she was afraid of what that might mean.

Don't screw this up!

Durai felt for the first time that he may have lost some leverage, and he was afraid of what that might mean. The earth and time pivoted around a single point that was created in the space between them then.

Possessed by an inner impulse that even surprised herself, Althea closed the distance between them in two steps as she pleaded with him one last time for mercy for the world. "Please, Durai," she said more forcefully but with the same compassion.

At that moment that they stood face to face only inches apart, she placed her free hand on his chest. She didn't even notice the golden glow from her hands. She didn't even really consciously register that she was drawing from Magic within herself then. As she thought back on that moment later, she wasn't able to explain how her body did what it did. It was just like the river.

In the instant that her hand made contact with Durai's chest, oddly enough close to his heart, her eyes lost all color and turned a blinding white. Images flashed before her eyes that were vivid but confusing to her. Feelings surged through her that was full of anguish, despair, and tremendous power. She saw a small boy, a woman pass from vitality in life to a bruised and battered remains, a powerful man looming like a mountain, and a hurricane of a boy's transformation through terrible potential.

Though it felt like what she experienced lasted hours, it was over in less than a second. She staggered back slightly dazed from the experience, but she somehow managed to stay standing.

The same could not be said for Durai. The moment he felt her touch, he saw her eyes glow white and registered the warm sensation from her touch. The light from her hand burst forth like an explosion, and the sensation that followed felt like an electrical surge through every vein of his body filled with heat and pity. The same images and the same emotional feelings swirled through him as they did with Althea; only for him, the images were not confusing, the emotions familiar instead of foreign. All of what he saw and felt was pulled from his past, his own life, and his own experiences. He felt as though this touch and this light pulled forth deeply buried feelings from the base of a mountain he had built over them, and the shock of that experience dropped him to the floor.

He looked up at her from the ground. He was filled with fear, disorientation, fury, and even reverence. This demonstration of power, which neither of them understood, made her appear to Durai then that she glowed with an awesome, radiant aura. He didn't know whether to be impressed, infuriated, or terrified.

Althea looked down at her hand which no longer had the light coming from it. She looked at Durai with great apprehension. She could tell that, at least in some way, a few images she saw were of Durai. There was so much that she couldn't quantify, and the parts that eluded her were a mystery both compelling and frightening.

Durai finally picked himself up and took an aggressive step toward her. "What did you do to me?" he demanded. He wasn't shouting, but his tone was no less daunting. All Althea could do was look at him not knowing whether to be more afraid of him or herself.

Overcome with the sight of those haunting, repressed images and embarrassment at his loss of composure, Durai quickly turned around and hurriedly left the room like a wind through a canyon.

Leaving the door open…

Now I'll Set My Teeth and Send to Darkness All That Stop Me

The open door seemed miles away, and Althea looked at its welcoming openness with apprehension. She couldn't help but look at the one thing she wanted so badly and only see a trap. It couldn't possibly be this easy, could it? What if Durai only faked his emotional break to catch her running away? What terrible actions could he justify with that? What pain would he then further inflict? Her muscles were tensed to run, but her fear kept her body frozen in place.

"Don't let the darkness win, Althea..."

She swallowed down the ball of terror she had in her throat and took a deep breath to steel her courage. She began to take slow, timid steps towards the open door. Her footfalls were soft and silent, and her breathing was full, deep, and steady to make as little noise as possible. With every step, she was ready to run in the opposite direction wary of attack. But her ears could hear nothing, and her body reaching out into the air couldn't detect a waiting presence. The rain kept steadily on in heavy falls.

When she reached the door, she reached out her hand first through the threshold. As strange as it might have looked, she leaned her upper body through the door while keeping her lower half safely in the room she was still confident was safe. Well, relatively safe.

But upon inspection, there were no signs of Durai in the main room beyond the bedchamber. No presence of him was left at all as far as she could sense. However, the main doors were closed. He at least then had the presence of mind as he left to seal her in. How securely, she couldn't know. She looked around in the darkened grey light of the room and found only burned down candles and slight signs of the struggle from the night before. She also could see the rod that he used to brand her on the ground amongst the rubble of the turned-over table and dishes. She was hesitant to pick it up, but she had to know more about what had been inflicted on her. She lightly touched the cold metal half expecting it to still hold burning heat. She slowly closed her nimble fingers around the rod and brought the designed end up for inspection.

She saw that this rod and the design had been meticulously crafted. The level of intricacy of even the smallest detail was haunting. The main design was the floral mark she bore upon her ankles; the mark of a Healer. However, the more terrifying part of the design was a slender, malicious serpent that wrapped the Healer's flower in its coils. What she was, what he was. And this would be with her all her life and remind her always that he possessed her. Even if she broke free someday, found freedom somehow, she would always bear this as surely as her skin. What must the person who made his for Durai have been thinking at such a request? Did he commission this right after she left, or only just recently upon learning she would be back? The more she thought of the questions and possible answers, the more she realized that none of it truly mattered. What had been done was done.

She walked over to a large wall mirror and turned her shoulder to inspect the burn. She could see now the design red and angry upon her skin. Though the detail would be sharper with time and healing, it was now blurred and slightly indistinguishable with the blistering and swelling. And no matter what she could try to do, it would be with her forever.

The anger and resentment she felt at this violation grew within her, and she had more determination than ever to leave. She reached the suite's main door that lead to the castle's hallway. She could sense something then. She placed her palms flat against the wood and pressed her ear to it as well. She could hear deep vibrations of men's voices outside. No doubt they were Durai's guards, probably from the same group that brought her here. They would be the only ones that knew she was alive, the only ones he would trust to keep the truth a secret and hidden. There were two sets of voices, at least. In her state, she assessed she could overcome maybe one of them if that one happened to be a small boy. Forceful escape through the front door was out of the question, and she couldn't trust the character of these men.

She turned around then to see the glass doors she had looked out of the night before that stood between her and the outside. It was hard to tell what time of day it was as there was no sun to make that distinction. The rain poured steadily on, but the droplets of rain were smaller now than she had heard before. She approached the glass and saw the rain run down the length of the clear panes like tears. Like her tears.

With less effort than she planned, she opened the door. The cool air and scent of rain hit her as both refreshing and inexplicably sorrowful. Slowly she stepped onto the stones of the patio with her bare feet and felt the cold beneath them. As she went further into the deluge, she found some comfort in the water wetting her body and slowly rolling down her skin as it accumulated. The coolness on her shoulder was so welcomed in its relief it almost felt sinful. The further she ventured out, the more she knew that she could not find an escape this way. At the end of his vast private courtyard was a security wall about the height of her waist. But beyond that wall was the steep and treacherous drop of the hill. And as he was in the farthest room of this wing, the space was jutted and separated from all others. She was on a type of peninsular plateau with no hope of someone spotting her or her signaling out.

Her head dropped at the thought that though he may be gone in this moment, and she may be a little less confined and at least no longer bound, she was still trapped in the last place she ever wanted to be. And she was still no closer to the temple and her chance to end the Mist. Would he even let her still go? Was all of this for nothing? No salvation, only damnation?

She was so wrapped in her doomsday thoughts that she didn't even notice the flapping of settling wings beside her as she leaned on the waist-high wall. Though she continued in stillness as the water continued to roll down her skin and pool at her feet not noticing the bird, it watched and noticed her. Only when it let out a cry did she take notice of it. Even though the sound was near and resounding, she did not flinch or jump at the sudden sound. She simply turned slowly as if the newly realized presence was almost expected. Althea regarded the large, black crow, and the crow regarded her in stillness as well.

Althea said nothing, and the crow made no other noise. She went back to staring ahead at the sprawling land beyond the drop beneath her. She seemed to search the vastness that laid before her for answers, and none came. She searched for clarity through the peaceful blanket of rain, and she found no mindfulness, no revelation.

The crow made another small cry, much quieter and calmer. When she turned to it, she could swear its eyes were upon her shoulder and her wound. She sighed still looking at the bird, and the bird made the smallest hop towards her. "I know," she said softly as to not scare it. She was no Leporem, but speaking to a living presence made her feel better, even if she were to get no intelligible response back. Maybe it was because she felt she was talking to Galen with this bird – maybe she was just losing her mind. "This is so ugly. And, yes, it does hurt a lot. Maybe that might fade in time, but the mark itself will be there forever, I guess. In a way, his mark was always with me. It's just...other people can see it now." She dropped her hands from her chin then, but the bird didn't move. "There's a lot I don't know. I know where I need to be, I know the results I want. But the way to get there, the way to make it all happen - it's hidden from me. How can I do what seems impossible when I couldn't even prevent this?" she said as she gestured to her shoulder with one hand.

She half smiled to herself realizing she was speaking to a bird. She knew it might look ridiculous, and she didn't care. If the bird was willing to listen for whatever good it did either of them, she would keep talking it out.

Her thoughts then went to what she had done and what she saw in Durai as she laid her hand upon him. She could feel a pulling sensation from her hand as if she had drawn out those images. She tried to lock down her exact movements, what she was thinking, and anything else specific enough to at least attempt to understand what any of it meant. She closed her eyes to concentrate harder. In the darkness behind her eyes, all fell away. She no longer felt the fall of rain, smelled the wet earth, or heard the breathing of the large bird next to her.

The more she fought to delve deeper and deeper into the hidden parts of her for answers, the more she felt as though she was wandering through uncharted space within her soul that she didn't even know existed. There was only black to see, but sensations kept brushing past her like scents hanging in the air. She could feel sensations change from moment to moment. She was moving, yet she was standing still.

Suddenly there was light and colors in the black, and images began to emerge. She focused hard and found she was in a memory – a long-forgotten memory that felt blurred and vague at first but grew into sharpness and clarity.

She saw her mother, and she saw her younger self. Her mother was mixing herbs of the earth and creating and crafting in the hut where they both used to live. Her mother stroked Althea's long hair and smiled so warmly. Althea could even feel the touch then. Her mother continued with her work and pointed out every name of every element and explained every step in the process to her student and daughter. Althea remembered often watching her mother's work knowing that she must someday take it up as her own.

"Mamma, I want to learn more about the songs."

"You just want to make the lights, don't you?"

Little Althea blushed a bit at having been so transparent. Then again, there was nothing her mother didn't appear to perceive. "I do want to make the lights."

Her mother smiled. "You know, there's nothing wrong with that. We are the keeper of the light in all things, you know. It's our job to protect it, make it strong, and even give it life from the deep cloak drawn from the darkness in people."

Althea's eyes were wide at everything her mother ever said. She would hang on every note of every syllable as a child, and now in her recalling, she was listening even more intently. Tears in her remembrance of her mother's voice welled in her eyes. She saw her younger self put a hand on her mother and reply, "You mean I can make light after it's lost to darkness?"

Her mother stopped her work and turned to her daughter. "No light is ever truly lost to darkness, little bit. It can be hidden away, buried deep, or locked deep in places not meant to be seen. But it is never fully gone." At that moment she saw her mother close her eyes and extend a hand. After a time of concentrating, the same familiar glow and streams of twisting light emerged from her mother's palm and danced up towards the sky. "A Healer's power comes from the light. The light from the earth and the heart give more life than people give it credit for. But the true gift of healing a person's body comes from deep within a person's soul. Our medicine, our Magic, is all a means of reaching the light and touching the place where healing begins."

The light from her mother's hands abruptly faded and fell out of the air. Her mother seemed to struggle, was slightly out of breath even, from the exertion. Little Althea seemed concerned, so her mother smiled reassuringly. "It isn't easy. Even for your grandmother, it was never really easy. Sometimes the light within a soul is buried and locked away so deep and so tight, that it may seem completely lost. The evil that has managed to find and gain strength in the hearts of the wicked is a powerful adversary. But you remember, you have that power. And I truly believe with all my heart that you will have the skill to draw out the light even stronger and more powerful than mine or your grandmother's."

"Do you really really think so?"

"I know so."

Althea seemed to be shocked back into the world of the present and out of her memories. She again became aware of the rain, of the cold, and the still present bird at her side. She turned to it, "Is that what I did? Did I draw out the light he locked away?" The bird did not respond, but she kept asking the questions to herself. "But the images were so dark, so terrifying. That couldn't be the light. It would be hard for me to believe that there is even light left in him. Maybe my mother was wrong."

The bird flew down into the courtyard then. He hopped into some bushes beyond her sight to see. She just continued to think more about whether or not what she had done was this ability her mother spoke of. If it was, how could she do it again? Would she even want to do it again?

The answer to that came as soon as she thought it. The only way to fight darkness was with the light.

"Don't let the darkness win, Althea…"

The bird then arrived again at the stone wall next to her carrying something in its beak. It was dropped onto the wall as the bird hopped back in nervous apprehension. Althea picked up what was dropped. It was a frail stick covered in thick, dark mud. She wiped away part of the mud and found beneath a bright, yellow flower. She looked at the crow unmoving next to her. "Pulling the light through the dark may bring parts of the darkness with it. Nothing can go through that much muck and come out completely clean. I understand now. You're very clever."

The crow let out a loud cry then. She turned from the crow and looked out at the hillside again. "The only defense against the darkness is the light, and it's the only way that I'll be able to fight him." She stopped and sighed then, turning again to the bird. "He's not going to like it. Whatever he has buried on top of what was once good in him will be devastating to face."

The crow then seemed to regard the wound on her shoulder and made another cry. Maybe it was just her imagination that the bird sounded concerned. Either way, she replied more to herself than the bird, "Oh don't worry about that. I'll find some way to make it through to the other side."

With that, the crow flew off and far away from where her eyes could follow. She reached back with one hand to the swelling, bubbled skin on her shoulder and winced slightly. She looked back at her hand and pulled forth the tiniest sign of warmth and light.

"My turn…"

•••••••

The crow visited the little hospital room for only a moment. Small caws filled the room speaking and telling a tale to the lone man within. It suddenly flew away frightened as a cry of unimaginable guilt and anguish reverberated within the walls.

Every Subject's Duty is the King's, but Every Subject's Soul is His Own

The storm had not diminished and put Hemele in a foul mood as he rode down to the Courtside hospital at sundown. It had been a full day since he left Galen in the madhouse, for all intents and purposes, and he was riding down in the rain still not knowing what he would do with this man. Part of him hoped that Galen would be a stubborn and sentimental idiot pledging loyalty to the truth so the easy decision to lock him in that room for the rest of his days would be made for him. However, he didn't have high expectations for that. This man seemed smart and clever, and he probably would not allow himself to be idealistically condemned.

Hemele hated riding near sundown. He didn't like the empty, quiet streets as everyone was locked away in their barricaded homes. The sounds of emptiness always played tricks on his ears. Like just now as he neared the hospital he could hear anguished screams ring out from his nightmares playing tricks on him. A crow flew from a window in the hospital at the sound. He stopped his horse. Perhaps that scream had not been a trick of his memories after all. Maybe this scream was real.

He entered the hospital and walked the long corridors to the secluded room in which Galen had been left. With each step closer he knew that his time for a decision was running out. He decided to just trust his instincts. He would follow orders always and would depend on his honor. But as he reached for the lock and handle of the door, he paused. He wasn't quite certain of his instincts anymore. What does one do when their instincts go against orders? Where then do honor and duty lie?

He decided to not announce his entrance or stand on ceremony. Hemele opened the door with confidence with no intent to toy with this man. The sight of the room took him aback. The bedside was overturned. The clay pitcher that held his water was shattered against a wall. Hemele saw Galen on the floor with his back against the overturned bed. His fists lay at his side red and swollen. Hemele could see signs of bruising then as well.

The scream he had heard outside came from this man. Something very recently snapped in him.

Hemele stepped into the room and closed the door behind him. Galen didn't even look up at Hemele's entrance. He just continued to sit on the floor and catch his breath. His tirade and outburst had to indeed been only moments ago.

"Did you get it out of your system?" Hemele asked as he looked around the room and then again at Galen.

Galen didn't respond but did get visibly angrier at the words or perhaps the sound of Hemele's voice. His fists clenched tighter. This did not go unnoticed by Hemele; his training had kept his senses always detail-oriented and heightened for danger.

"You know, you didn't need to play the part of a madman just because you were in the room. But if you're trying to convince me to keep you here…"

"I need to see her," Galen interrupted what he considered instigating dribble coming from his captor.

Hemele looked at Galen and noted that his voice was clear and not raving. "Not the answer I wanted to hear," Hemele admitted. He thought long about what he would have to do to this man now. To keep the secret, to follow orders, he would have to essentially take this man's life away. He was risking it all for this woman. "What is it about this woman? Help me understand what is so amazing about her that you would knowingly persist against my warnings to try and get to her? You do know that by not taking my strong hints to forget her that you could be throwing away your life?" Hemele thought that maybe if he made this man think hard enough to put this woman into words, he would realize that it wasn't worth his life.

"You tell me. Maybe instead think what is so horrible about her that you would knowingly condemn her?"

Touché.

Hemele decided then to sit down with this man with his back against the door. "I'm not condemning her. I'm following orders. As far as I know, it's for her own good. As far as I know, her secrecy is necessary for her safety. As far as I know, she has my man under a spell just as much as she has you under one. What makes you so convinced that she is being harmed by my actions? What makes you right and me wrong?"

Galen smirked then and turned his head. Every part of him didn't want to keep up with this conversation. As far as he was concerned, this man was a mindless drone, and nothing he said was going to make it through to his head to change his mind. He was a believer, and he believed that the letter of his orders was correct and true. Galen knew that nothing from a stranger was going to turn this man's face towards the light. But Althea was worth every breath spent to try.

"You haven't seen her recently, have you? Of course, you haven't. You wouldn't be asking me about her being in danger if you'd have seen her."

Hemele thought maybe that this man had truly gone mad. "I'm not sure I understand a word of what you said. Are you saying she's been harmed? And that you know this for a fact from within this locked room? You know that makes it sound like you belong here."

"I'm sure you were going to end up keeping me here anyway," Galen responded resigned.

"Maybe I was."

With the tone he was hearing from his warden, Galen looked up and realized that maybe this man wasn't quite as determined in his path as he had once been. What was changing his mind?

Galen seized his opportunity then to try and reach him, "I have my ways of knowing. Ways you probably won't believe but are no less true. I know for a fact that you are keeping her in Durai's suite of rooms which is in the farthest wing of the palace. It has a courtyard that sits on a plateau-like hill, and even if one tried, they wouldn't be able to see her there. Not even if that person knew what they were looking for."

Hemele perked up at his words. Only those who resided in the palace knew where the individual nobility's Suites were, and even at that, not many knew exactly which belonged to Durai. Certainly, even fewer people knew about Durai's courtyard patio and what it looked like. How was it this man knew these details?

Galen noticed that he was at least being heard, and he continued. "I also happen to know that she has come to harm. She has a burn, a brand, on her right shoulder now. I can only assume it was from 'your man.'"

"That's quite a claim," Hemele said a little indignant.

"A claim I'm willing to stake anything I have left on. That's beside the point. I know she was brought there like a sacrificial lamb, and now she's at the mercy of a sadistic sociopath. And you were the one that delivered her." Galen tried so hard to keep the venom he held in his heart at bay, but this man had clipped the wings of an angel and delivered her helpless into Hell. There was no forgiveness in his heart for that. "How does that fact sit with you?"

Hemele didn't respond for a long time. He couldn't deny that he had felt suspicions about his orders. He even confronted the inconsistencies and discussed his lingering doubts with Jian. He couldn't help but hear his misgivings mirrored in this man's speech. "Let's say I were to believe you. Let's say that this very specific claim of yours is true. What then? What would you do against a 'sadistic sociopath'? One with immense Magical power, I might add."

Galen turned his face from Hemele's mocking tone. He was right. What was his plan? What could he do against a man so powerful? He had to admit he had no plan and was woefully underprepared for the next step, whatever it might be.

The two men then made eye contact with expressions the other had not expected. Hemele had sincerity and genuine concern behind his questioning yet authoritative look. Galen had apprehension and uncertainty behind his indignation. Perhaps the vulnerabilities they saw in the other were enough to trust.

"Maybe," Galen said dropping his aggressive tone, "maybe I wouldn't be against him alone."

Hemele made a small flinch at what those words could mean, but he kept listening anyway.

"Listen, maybe there is something about her, and it casts something like a spell. But it's not a deception, and it doesn't harbor manipulative ill intent. Just as every good leader inspires those around him, she inspires me. The spell she has is being so purely good that I want to be the best of myself. It's not a spell; that's just goodly influence."

"And Durai?" Hemele asked then putting pressure on his proof.

Galen didn't have an easy answer. "Sometimes the shadows seek to overtake the light. I cannot say. But if you were to spend any time with her, you wouldn't be questioning what I clearly see in her. The things she's told me," Galen continued despite the faltering he felt at remembering her stories and the memories of her haunted by her nightmares, "were unthinkable. What she had fought through, what she ran away from, was terrible. No one should go through what she did. And yet she went back willingly to try and save us all. The least I can do is try and save her. She deserves at least that much from me, if not from others."

Hemele found he couldn't speak. The conviction of this man was admirable and full of honor. It seemed idealistic, and it reminded him of himself when he was sure he was right. And he couldn't help but notice that he didn't feel that way now. Maybe what he had been a part of was monstrous. Maybe what he had been a pawn to was the damnation of all of their hopes to a man he barely knew anything about except the fear he invoked in everyone he had ever talked to.

How does one live with the knowledge that they helped destroy someone? How would he live with it?

Was it even true?

Hemele rose to his feet. Galen's expression went into a panic. Maybe he hadn't reached this man after all, and he misread the whole interaction. Maybe he was about to lose his only chance to get out. Would he ever get another shot?

Galen lifted himself from the floor as well. "Please," Galen begged, "I would be willing to be subject to any terms you lay out just to see her and do all I can to help her one last time. I'd do anything if you would let me. You can send me away, lock me up here until I die…I'd even let you kill me on the spot. But I cannot stay here another day while I know she suffers alone. Please!"

Hemele didn't move to leave, but he didn't make a sign that he would consent to any terms. Galen lowered his tone to slight resignation, though he was far from giving up. "Please, if I'm wrong, and she's safe, then me seeing her in secret one last time will not hurt anyone. I'll quietly be silenced in any way you would see fit, and gladly." He then took one step forward to Hemele who did not retreat at it. "But if I'm right…" Galen swallowed hard at the pain in his words. He knew he was right, he had been told so by the visiting crow. He knew what she was suffering through without any help at all. He was in torment within these four walls knowing that she was facing all of her nightmares with no one at her side, and he had promised to be there with her. "She is probably our last hope. I don't doubt that the ills of this world can be made right by a Healer. More than that, I know that it can be made right by her specifically. I've seen what she can do, and I know her heart. If I am right, then our last hope is in danger. She is being tormented and cut down piece by piece. Can you take that chance to simply follow orders if I'm right?"

Hemele heard every word that had been said to him then. More than that, he felt them in the deepest parts of him and reached the idealism that he had once had in his boyhood hearing of heroes fighting dragons and defying all odds. That idealism had been buried deep under the heavy weight of honor and duty. Somewhere along the way, his honor in stories and the honor of the job had been muddied. But for that moment, those words reached through it all and reached him where he thought had been lost.

Hand upon the door, Hemele didn't turn to Galen. He kept his back to this man and his inconvenient truth. He wanted to shut it out, forget what he heard. He wanted to deny his speech and pass it off as ranting falsehoods. But the light that had been given the air to breathe wouldn't be stifled within him again. He knew the possibility existed that this man could be right, and he would be wrong to keep on his path unchanged.

Hemele heard a sigh behind him. Galen's voice sounded more defeated than ever, but he was not resentful. He knew the strength it took to change the course of a heart, and he knew that perhaps he didn't have the persuasion enough to give him that direction. Not even with all of his gifts. "If you won't take me to her," he said, "then at least please talk to her. Given that you drugged her, you owe her at least a minute of your time. See if I'm not right. It's the right shoulder."

The door latched and bolted as Hemele left the room. He didn't see the sharp details of the places he passed as he walked out. He saw only blurred lines and the dancing contrast of light and dark as he rode further away toward the castle.

Galen watched after the door and did not feel despair. Instead, he held onto the smallest flame of hope. He knew that Althea would want him to. And if he read this man right, his soul would speak to his conscience. The way for him was lit, and it was the path a good man must walk. Galen felt confidence that, in the end, and given enough time, the Captain would prove a good man.

Truth is Truth, to the End of Reckoning

What a piece of work is man?

How does one prepare for a battle? What had she to do but don her armor and prepare her battle? However, she had no idea what she could use for armor. In all her dealings with him, especially of late, even her most steeled defenses managed to be cut down rendering her as naked and helpless as a babe. She also knew nothing of where or when she would be ready for her move, so her battleground was equally as unknown.

One thing she knew for certain: standing in the rain wasn't going to make her any more prepared. The rumbling of thunder seemed to grow louder. The storm was coming in for a second wave; this was long from over.

She walked through the rooms like an unwilling trespasser and only lingered in one spot for as long as absolutely necessary. The bath had been drawn for her already, more than likely before he went in to visit her that morning. By then the water was tepid, hardly warm at all, but she washed anyway. The heat would have been unwelcomed on her scorched skin or even the skin around it, so she counted it lucky.

The marble countertops held an array of choices of clothes for her to wear. As much as she hated how revealing her choice was, the open-backed dress was the best choice to give her wound air to breathe. The dress itself was a deep blue, almost black the hue was so deep. The neckline itself was high and hugged her neck. But there were no sleeves and the back was exposed from the cut that plunged to the bottom of her waist almost revealing the swell of her backside. The bottom portion was heavy and flowed quite gracefully. The only other color was floral embroidered designs in white thread along the floor-length hemline.

With the open back and shoulder, she was able to regularly keep up with applications of her burn salve that she found on the table by the bedside. As for her hair, she kept it bound high near the top of her head not only because it kept her hair from brushing her wound, but he liked it best when her hair loosely flowed. Even in the threat of violence, she would do nothing to purposefully please him.

The minutes passed in a flow of time as steady and sure as a river. Instead of agonizing over the change from hours to minutes left in solitude, she simply sat near the fireside and meditated. She reached as deep within herself as she possibly could. She tried to memorize the path between her waking mind and the world of her innermost memories and subconscious instincts. If the path became familiar, she would find it when she needed it. With practice, she could be more confident that she wouldn't be at the mercy of chance.

Meditation became harder and harder as she became more aware of her hunger and thirst. She had no way of telling for sure, but the greying light became darker and darker seemingly signaling the passage into the evening. She had gone all day without food or drink. The storm outside increased its passion, and she was almost prepared to go outside under the darkening skies to drink from the rain.

Just before she made the move to rise, the door handle signaled someone approaching. She got to her feet quickly and put on a strong stance to face him. Would he be coming at her with the same anger and fury as he had left with? Would he be slithering in holding over her the key to things she needed? She wasn't sure if she was present enough to adapt efficiently to his mystery mood.

But it was not Durai who stepped through the open door. Though it took her a moment, she recognized the Captain who was responsible for bringing her here and in the state in which she arrived. This was certainly not what she was expecting, and she tried to hide her inner fumbling to adjust. She hadn't the slightest idea what he could want. He came in with nothing, not even a weapon against her. Not that he needed one. Even at her strongest, she would be no matched for a high-level guard.

He walked in and stood just within the frame of the door. She reached out with her senses and found him different than before. He wasn't as confident this time; his bravado had diminished. He was almost like a scolded pet with a tail between his legs, but not quite. He still held his pride and his honor. But something else was missing. Something he seemed to be searching for.

She wasn't the only one keenly inspecting. With her slight change in appearance and time away from the weathering of the wild, he was surprised at what the polish revealed. His memories of her looks didn't do this sight justice. She seemed so beautiful, so purely stunning that he knew in an instance what drew so many to her. This was surely the face that inspired the stories of dragon-guarded maidens that ignited the bravery and passions of knights and heroes in the old stories of faeries long ago. Something magnetic shone through her eyes. It was so tangible that he almost was compelled to reach out and grab at it.

She very much seemed to him to be an angel.

In the wake of her silence and scrutiny, he decided to speak first. His voice held no arrogance; it hardly held authority at all. He cleared his throat almost as if knowing his voice had shrunken small within him from the shine she emitted. "I, uh…I brought you some food. It's in the main room."

She took a step forward surprising herself with grace and confidence she had not shown in a very long time. If this was her chance, she would take it. "Did you pick the table up first?" she asked with pointed assertion. She notice his confidence drop even more at the words, and she wasn't about to stop there. She had a chance before to come in with stealth and secrecy. She had a chance to be spared all of this. This man took it from her.

"I take it that wasn't from dancing," he said without hiding the guilt in his voice then. She was surprised that he wasn't masking it in the least. Was that a trap? Could she trust that?

"Not any dance that I'd care to repeat. Though, I must say, thank you so much for delivering me to the ball." She noticed as he talked that he seemed to be searching for something. But the more she thought about the suffering she could have been spared, the less she was willing to graciously humor this man.

"I was just –"

"If you say 'following orders,' I will strike at you any way I can with anything I can get my hands on. That excuse is cheap. Sins asked of you from your masters make them no less sins." Althea felt the power she had long since counted as lost within her growing stronger. She thought maybe she had what it took to reach the other side of the story she was thrust into. However, she realized that this man was hardly the evil adversary she would have to face in the end.

Now it was he who took a step closer. He didn't hang his head in shame, his voice held no excuse or pitiful contrition. He looked her dead in the eyes and answered her, "I know."

What had he come for?

"You're seeking something. What is it? What do you need from me?" Her tone dropped its harsh intent somewhat. One cannot deny human nature, and her nature was, at its basest, helpful and hopeful. Even if time and again it put her under the heel of oppression and misery, she couldn't seem to shed the skin she was born with.

Hemele's eyes darted this way and that momentarily almost as though he didn't know the answer himself. Althea closed her eyes for a moment and felt deep within him. She saw two souls fighting for the reign of his heart. They swirled inside of him and all around him like rapids in a violent river. Hemele could feel her inward gaze penetrating where no one else had looked before, and he felt vulnerable. Perhaps for the first time in his life.

"I guess I need to understand. There's a lot of shadows that seem to follow you, and I don't know if they are the bidding of the devil or you." Hemele's question seemed to confuse Althea for a moment. She never for once in her life had given anyone a reason not to trust her. She wasn't used to not being trusted. Even a complete stranger in the woods at the end of the world seemed to instinctually trust her. Now this man poses the possibility that she is the mastermind behind all of the manipulated situations surrounding her.

But then, somehow, the idea was not incomprehensible. His position, his questions, and every action he took made sense if he had walked in the darkness cast by Hell itself for long enough. He didn't know her, he only knew the whispers she left behind and the orders without the context of the most perversely powerful person she had ever known.

Althea spread her arms away from her body in an attempt to appear open and clear. "I don't hold the strings here; I never have. All I want is a chance to stop the suffering that has touched everyone. I'm sure it's touched even you here high on the hill. Instead," she said as she turned towards the fire and looked deep into the dancing flames, "I am held here stifled by the shadows of which you speak. I am not the master of them. At least not yet."

At her final words, she turned back to Hemele and saw his eyes wide with horror and disbelief with her turned head. She knew at that moment that he had found the horrible site on her shoulder. She realized also that, somehow, that was what he had been looking for.

"It's true," he whispered so quietly and unintentionally that he wasn't sure himself if he had said it out loud.

Althea looked at his reaction to his discovery and knew that this moment was important. This was the pivotal moment in the fight for a man's conscience and soul. She was afraid to move and tip the balance wrong.

Then, to her surprise, he seemed to tremble. It was as if something in him broke and crumbled at his feet, something terribly important. And it had. Hemele was standing at the center of the pillars holding high his lofty aspirations and the idealism he aspired to, and it was crumbling around him into dust at his feet. All he had done shamed who he wanted desperately to be. The possibility of his sins was so dauntingly massive that he was drying up inside like the rain gone from summer. At that moment, all sound faded far away and all he could feel was the cold sweat on his hands and tasted the white electric panic in his mouth.

He hadn't even noticed her approach, but he felt the hand through the darkness and the touch drive out the despair. He looked down at his hand as it was held by two very small ones. He looked up and saw her. The light from the fire threw brilliant light from behind her, and she was even more assuredly an angel then.

273

Hemele swallowed hard the dryness in his mouth. "I was sent to bring you food and leave. He instructed guards all night…he will be gone until dawn." He stopped as he realized that the man had left and a boy was left talking.

He turned her slightly, and to his surprise, she let him. He looked closer at the mark on her shoulder and saw that everything Galen had told to him was true in every detail. He looked back at her then. Her expression was frightened and brave at the same time.

He opened his mouth. His voice was small and wavered in his inner crisis. "I want to understand, and I think that I've read this, all of this, all wrong. Do you think you can tell me a story?"

"I will tell you the truth."

There's No Trust, No Faith, No Honesty in Men

"I don't want to believe you," Hemele said. He refused to look at Althea after about half of her story. The lightning and thunder had returned and mirrored the tale he was being told.

"That's your decision. Certainly the easier one." Althea had once again relived her past filled with everything she wished she could forget. It was no easier the second time. "And I can't say I'm much surprised. And now you are no doubt going to ask me to prove it to you. Well, outside of what you have already seen," she gestured to her shoulder then and the upturned room behind them, "I have nothing else to offer other than my truth."

Hemele shook his head at her. "No," he said more to himself than to her. He began to fidget with his fingers in his discomfort. "No, there's no need. Something has stunk throughout this whole castle for as long as I've been assigned to his guard. I guess I've always known - something has always toyed with my instincts. Your words make more sense than I thought they would. Maybe I turned my sights away from it to avoid my own damned complacency in the whole thing."

Disappointment appeared clearly in Althea's face, and Hemele took the pain he felt from it rightly. Althea felt truly despondent over the prospect that he was not the only one to take the easier road and turn from hateful malice because to fight would risk too much. Maybe there was no true courage left. If not completely gone, bravery was at least surely dying out.

"I…" Hemele seemed to break in his attempt at first. He turned his head from her gaze then and found it easier to speak. "I won't ask for your forgiveness. Not until I do what I can to make things right. Though I must admit, I cannot fathom how I can make that much wrong right again."

In a surprising move, Hemele felt Althea's hand on his once again. "Listen, I understand shame, especially in all of this. I turned away from all of this too. I ran from it and left him here free to do the harm he did. I have forgiveness to seek as well."

Hemele pulled his hand away from hers. He knew very well that she was trying to comfort him and put him at some ease. Instead, her words only deepened his shame. In his mind, she had absolutely nothing to seek forgiveness for. The very idea that she felt this way made him angry. If the whole world were to be damned to keep her from facing the worst again, so be it. At least that was his belief. Since the start of the Mist, even before that, he had witnessed so much selfishness and the human capacity to take goodness for granted. The breadth of society's depravity that only seemed to grow in tragedy was grotesque, and she would seek forgiveness from it. Those who cower in the shadows deserved nothing from the light that would lead them to salvation.

The thought that this woman with a bruising eye and angry, welting burn would seek forgiveness from anyone for wanting to protect herself only proved more that she was every bit the inspirational good that Galen spoke of. It also showed just how much guilt she had been trained to take onto herself. Most of all, it made him all the more painfully humbled.

Turning from self-pity, Hemele put his mind to practicality and tactical moves. "What should we do now? Where should we go first?" Hemele found that with these words, this thought into action, he was able to look at her in the eyes once again. She seemed lost, however.

"Thank you," she said relieved that she no longer had to stay on the subject of her past. "Honestly, I have no idea. Just when I think I can handle how bad I can imagine it can be, I am shown just how short my imaginings fall." She shook herself out of any thoughts of her pain. What she could not do, what was out of her control, was not worth the wasted effort. "I mean, I guess I'm so lost as to what's around me to know what direction is right. Okay, what are your men's orders as they stand now?"

He nodded his head in agreement that this was a good place to start. "Our orders were to report that your body was found in the town where we picked you up and to report also that you were killed by Immortuos. It was hinted that this was for your protection. The rest was left to rumor and speculation." Hemele could see that she was confused but pushed it aside to follow all he had said. "We are ordered to never reveal that you are alive until further instructed. Two men are to guard this door at all times letting only Durai or myself pass."

"Do you think you can trust the men posted now to let me leave?"

Silence followed her question. He wasn't entirely sure. His men followed his ideals of duty and orders to the letter, but he had no small manner of influence over them as well. "Let me worry about getting us through the door. I have my assurances. The big question is where do we go first?"

"What do you mean?" Althea only had one goal in mind: get to the temple and stop the Mist. She hadn't even thought of anything outside of that.

Hemele put a hand to the floor to outline some potential routes as he explained. "I know that you want to get as fast to the temple, but there is a lot of ground between here and there, and a lot of ways that you can be stopped. I'm not just talking about running into Durai; I mean we could be stopped by people who knew you before and thought you dead, gossipers that would get word back to Durai, the Queen herself, and whatever her reaction might be…you get what I'm saying?"

"I do." Althea felt the strain of all the possibilities pressing down on her. She was trying to keep up her optimistic determination despite that strain, but she was quickly losing stamina.

"Wait here." Hemele left through the doors and came back incredibly quickly with a handful of cheese and bread from the tray he had left. Althea wondered if she looked as worn as she felt or if perhaps he was just incredible perceptive. Whatever the reason, she took the food happily and ate while he continued to plan out loud.

"Perhaps the best move would be to get more people on our side. If we're stopped or discovered, the more of us there are, the less of a problem it would be."

Althea swallowed what was in her mouth then. "But that would cost time, and the more time we wait, the more chance we have of being discovered. Is there no one you could send for now that we could trust right away?"

Hemele thought for a second.

Suddenly, Althea dropped her food and grabbed at both of his arms. "Galen! Where is he? What did you do with Galen?!" All the color was lost from her face at the remembrance that she didn't know where her friend was. She dropped her head for a moment then, "God, how could I forget…"

Hemele wrapped his hands to hold her arms just as she held his. "It's not like you didn't have more imminent dangers to worry about. He's safe. Though I am ashamed to say that I've kept him isolated in a room of the hospital, at least until …" Hemele was having a hard time finishing his explanation of another wrong, but she nodded her head in understanding.

"At least he's safe. Right?"

Their nods in agreement were more relief than she would have thought. Galen was safe, and that was the most that mattered to her at the moment.

Hemele rose to his feet and offered his hand out to her. "I have one man that will come no questions asked. Let's get started."

Althea looked at the outstretched hand and decided to take it. If she made one more mistake in trusting him, then so be it. She had no other choice. True forgiveness would take some time, but she wasn't about to refuse help.

They walked together quietly up until the main door to the castle's hallway. He turned to her and motioned for her to be directly behind him. "I'll go first, and then you follow. Don't look at them directly; let the focus be on me. They won't question a direct order if you look confident too."

Althea nodded in agreement and took a deep breath in. Hemele did the same.

"Okay," he said to her as he opened the door and simultaneously took a step forward. However, he stopped after that first step, and Althea who was looking at the ground ahead almost ran into him as he stopped instantly in front of her.

She looked up at the delay, and Hemele seemed to bow his head to the figure waiting at the opened door. Althea couldn't help but make a small, frightened noise that she brought her hands to her mouth to stifle. Durai had been waiting for them. How long had he been waiting? Althea felt frozen just as Hemele was before her. The shock of him there, the familiar and terrifying brilliant glow from his green eyes, and all of the blackened aura he exuded held them petrified.

Slowly Althea felt wetness and warmth on her bare feet. She was so terrified at the sight of him that she thought perhaps she had released her bladder in shock. However, when she looked down, she found that what she felt was pooling blood before her feet.

She met Durai's eyes then and felt the cold sweat forming on her face. She shook her head in disbelief while slowly taking steps backward. The knife that Durai had thrust into Hemele's chest as he took his fatal step forward was taken out with a sickening sound as Hemele dropped to the floor in a broken heap. Durai then wiped the blood from his blade with the fabric of his dark green robe. He continued to keep Althea locked with his eye contact the whole while.

"This is quite a body count you are responsible for." Durai's evil voice had returned and reached her ear like a creeping fire.

·······

Jian left the room where the candle had burnt down. He walked sullenly down the darkened hall lit only by the flashes of lightning to the Queen's room. He paused only slightly to take a breath and opened the door unapologetically.

Mireya was sitting on her chair at the fireside reading quietly when the door opened suddenly and made her jump. No one had ever come into her room unplanned to say nothing of unannounced. She rose to her feet indignantly until she saw the determined and concerned look on the man's face. "What is the meaning of this?" she asked more out of apprehensive worry than fury.

"I beg your Majesty's forgiveness for the rude intrusion. I would not be bothering you if I didn't think this was important."

Mireya approached the man who stood at a respectful distance. She never wore the tyrant role well, and she often defaulted to helpful than self-importance. "I'm listening," she told the guard.

"I have instructions from my Captain to come to you if he did not return by an appointed time. Well, that time has passed, and he is still gone."

"And you believe your Captain is in danger?" Mireya said already looking as though she were to jump into action.

"I have no doubt of it. At his request, I ask to pass you this letter and discuss it in privacy." With that, he handed a rolled parchment written, signed, and sealed by Hemele to the Queen. "I think we're all in further danger."

Smiling, Damned Villain

"This is quite a body count you are responsible for." Durai's evil voice had returned and reached her ear like a creeping fire.

However, this time it was different. Perhaps, rather, she was different. Instead of his demonic eyes and terrible voice holding her frozen in fright, she found that she was brought out of her fear instead. Her glazed eyes sharply focused in that instant, and her rigid limbs snapped forward towards Hemele's still bleeding body. She paid no mind to Durai or how close he was. Instead, she focused everything on reaching into herself to pull forth the power to reach Hemele, save him if she could. She had helped a mortally wounded man before. She had to try.

She dropped to her knees hard beside Hemele. The wound in his chest was deep, and the blood that was seeping out past his hand gushed with each beat of his heart. She closed her eyes and searched for a song, light, anything she could bring as fast as possible. Her mouth and throat were so dry, but she had to try. She could feel the warmth and light start to grow in her hands.

A sharp, jerking pain wrenched her back into the present. As her eyes opened she saw Hemele's body as she was being dragged away from it. Durai had walked over Hemele's body and grabbed Althea's hair easily in a gathered bun on top of her head as he passed by. Althea grasped onto a bunch of her hair as he continued to pull; this relieved the tension as she released the pressure on her scalp.

Durai threw her to the ground, "You're being very naughty." He turned then and placed the knife on the mantle of the room's fireplace. His aura seethed then of black, malicious intent.

When he looked back, Althea was already scrambling on her hands and knees trying to make her way back to Hemele. She didn't know how far she would make it before he moved to stop her, but she had to try. Even if there was the slightest chance that she could reach him for even a moment and do some good, it was worth the fight. It was all she could do.

As it turned out, she didn't make it far at all.

Althea felt hands upon hands upon her body pulling her from all directions. She could feel at least five distinct hands upon her, and she looked up then in shock and terror at feeling these impossible feelings. The light was falling away fast and frightened as the shadows grew in the room. Then the shades seemed to move and writhe like living beings residing within the darkness itself. From the twisting black hands outstretched and pulled at her. She could feel enormous strength behind the disembodied hands, and they cared not for the harm and damage they could do to her body that was fragile in comparison.

Thud!

Before she could assess her situation, she was being picked up from the floor. She felt her head and back thrust against the wall beside the fireplace and Durai. She looked down at her body and saw the arms from the darkness, of the darkness, pushing against her and holding her in place. A final hand reached up larger than the rest, reached back, and flew towards her. It landed on her right shoulder and pushed it back against the wall.

Althea screamed in agony feeling the pain shoot from her wound down to through her body. A hand came then and covered her mouth to silence the scream. But it was not a hand of the shadows. The hand across her mouth was Durai's. She could smell the blood still lingering on his sleeve against her mouth. She wanted to gag, but she couldn't breathe enough to do so. She had no idea a body could endure this much pain.

When Durai slowly pulled his hand away, he stroked her hair and met the vengeful burning in her eyes. Her voice deepened then, coming from a place deep within her; a place that he had pushed her to. "Let me go," she said lowly.

Durai had never heard this from her. Althea's voice had always been melodic like a songbird. Even in defeat, even in sadness, even in pain, she always possessed a bird-like lilt. Now the sound from her throat was like the rumblings of the earth. He was admittedly impressed if slightly apprehensive. Mostly, he was excited as to what sport this would lead to.

"Little Dove, where would you fly?"

Althea shook against the hands binding her to the wall. "Let me help him," she pleaded. "Please let me try. He's dying!" Her voice returned to her regular sound then. It was as she was possessed before, and the force moving her had left her behind to fight alone. Durai hoped it would return.

Durai leaned in towards her face then. He grabbed her head with both of his hands and forced her gaze to the man on the floor and the now sizeable pool of blood so dark it was almost black. "Look at him. There's nothing you can do no. The breath has left him. You've led one more to a bloody end. One more you've failed."

Althea couldn't turn her gaze away as much as she desperately wanted to. Hemele's back was to them, curled into his wound. But there was no rise or fall to his body. There was no sign that his body continued to fight. She had never before seen a person die so violently. In fact, she had hardly witnessed death at all in her limited years. Althea started to heave at the sickening thought that she had just watched a human life being struck down, stolen away, but nothing came up. She felt so ill. Even more than that, she felt utterly defeated and alone.

"Aren't you so ashamed?" Durai asked into her ear.

Althea then felt overcome by the vilest, blackest hate she never dreamed she could possess within her. Her face started to be lit by a bright red light. It started at her core and slowly radiated to all of her extremities. She had become fire, she had become vengeance. The light from her body pushed back against the shadows holding her in place, and the forces seemed equally matched.

"You are a monster," Althea's voice spoke out again finding that deepness, that possessed quality. "If it's the last thing I do, I will send you back to the Hell that spat you out."

Durai's expression seemed elated then as he leaned into her closer. He inhaled deeply as if to savor the scent of her. "Sounds like fun. Shall we begin?"

At the close of his words, she felt the force of the shadows seize her once again and fling her across the room. She stretched out her arms to catch her flailing form as best as she could and braced herself for the pain of impact. To her surprise, the light from within her shot out from her arms just before impact.

It seemed like flames burst forth from her and cradled her as she fell. It was far from graceful, and she still hit the floor with a painful force, but the impact was far from as bad as it would have been. The ruby flames spread across the floor as she landed, and they flared up high before disappearing altogether.

It was hard to tell then which face held the most surprise, his or hers. Althea pushed back her reaction, though, and picked herself up to her feet. She brought back her right foot slightly behind her and angled her body in a defensive posture against the attack from him she knew was coming. She noticed her hands still held the red light that danced about her skin like smoke. Half of her mind focused then on her defense. The other half, however, retraced her practiced path to try again to pull from within him the things he resisted. If she could touch him again, replicate what she had done before, and if she could hold onto those images he found so painful a little longer this time, she might have him beat.

The prospect of this fight terrified her. At least Galen was safe.

In the split second that her mind lost focus to think on Galen, she felt the air leave her lungs completely as he closed the distance between them with unnatural speed and strike her directly and forcefully in the abdomen. She bent forth at the impact and looked up into his eyes made of ominously bright green light.

She pushed past the pain with every agonizing ounce of effort she could muster. The ache lingered long after the impact, but she had to focus and make the sensation inconsequential. She closed her eyes and traced the steps she had practiced in her mind as she had meditated all day. When she opened them again, her own eyes were overtaken and glowed in blinding white light.

The scene was a battle of Titans then. They ceased to be two earthly bodies and became the very forces of light and dark, good and evil.

Althea seized her moment and reached out a hand forcefully against Durai's chest and braced herself for the overflow of images she sought to pull from him and hoped would bring him down. The light that exploded from their bodily contact flashed so brightly that details of the room were swallowed in it.

However, this time, something was wrong; she could tell right away. There were no images of a boy, no menacing man, and no sight of a mother at all. This was nothing like before. It was darkness like a hidden room filled with consuming nothingness. She felt lost in it, and she looked around desperately for any sign, any direction she could take against this.

Her hair now around her shoulders blew back with a sudden rush of wind, or something like wind, as lights and colors flew past her, around her, even into her. It was as if her own body had been rushed to a scene within Durai. In pulling from within him, she took herself along.

The sight of the room was all too familiar. She recognized the furnishings, the tapestries, and the little nuances that she knew intimately as Baldrik's room. She was confused as she had recounted all she had done when she placed her hand on Durai. She was sure that she performed just as she had before to pull forth from him the sights of his past. What could he possibly be holding within this room?

Oh no.

Her head suddenly pounded with immense, all-consuming pain. She had felt panic and horror before, but never like this. What she felt now was not the petrified, out-of-body numbness where sight became blurred and sound shrank away. This was apprehension and dread like she had never known before. "Oh, God, no!" she begged into the images of the room. She covered her mouth with both of her hands to try to keep her body from hyperventilating in her desperate wish to be anywhere else in the entirety of time.

As if compelled by a force of the Magic that brought them there, she was turned to see the sight she had prayed every day for a year she would never have to know.

She saw Baldrik in his bed reclined back amongst many pillows. His arms were splayed out on either side of his body with vast pools of thick, horribly red blood beneath them. She looked into Baldrik's eyes still opened and facing her now. His life, his spark, had left them. He was a shell, hollow and empty. Eyes that once danced with laughter, joy, and passion even in pain were now glazed back in a mockery of the life that had possessed them once. Everything that had made him special, everything she had ever loved about him, was gone. In its place, there was this sight right out of Hell.

She began to go to him, but could not move. She felt herself die inside at the sight of what he had done to himself. "Baldrik," she whimpered out between her fingers. "My brother…" But there was no response, no motion at all. He never failed before to light up at the sound of her voice. Now there was nothing. She lingered on the expression on his face. It was of sorrow and remorse. It was as if, just perhaps, he had decided too late to change his mind. Or maybe he was thinking in regret of what he would be leaving behind.

She thought to herself, did he think of her at the end? Did he cry out for her? Was he sad to leave her at all? Did he care at all that he was leaving her behind?

She lost sight of the scene as the tears overtook her sight entirely. She had seen his face in her memories, and now that fond remembrance of light and joy was burned away, replaced with the sight of his empty stare.

Thud!

She was on the floor in Durai's room pulled out of the worst place she could imagine back into the worst position possible. This time she was the one repelled back by the images she pulled forth, and Durai was unphased. He stood above her as she choked on her sobs caught between the incomprehensible sorrow and horror at the scene she just witnessed knowing she had to get up and fight back. She pushed back on her hands and feet, but she slipped and faltered as if her muscles had been drained from the pressure of her adrenal response to what she had been forced to see.

As she tried to crawl backward and away from Durai, he slowly stalked above her with his hands held behind his back. His eyes had stopped glowing and resumed their menacing stare into hers. His smile curved upwards with a sickening delight at towering once again over his helpless victim.

She gave one final push off her right arm, and the pain from her burn shot through her and deadened her whole body to give up. With that, Durai lowered himself on top of her. His legs straddled her abdomen as he put a hand on either side of her body. His long, fair hair showered around his head and around her own as he bent down to her. "I held onto that image, saved it in detail, just so I could show it to you one day, somehow. Now you see what you could have stopped. Now you see what he did because you ran away. You left him with no hope."

She felt his body press against hers harder. Every squirm she made to escape from beneath him only excited him further, and she could feel it as tears continued to roll down her face.

"What shall we do with you so you don't lead more men to their deaths?"

False Face Must Hide What False Heart Doth Know

"I don't know what to say to all this," Mireya sat slumped upon her throne drained completely at the overwhelming story she was just told. She brought a hand to her throat. It was an old habit since she was a child in training to be the next monarch of her people. The feeling of her pulse and the tender skin of her neck always reminded her to keep her composure, remain calm in adversity, and not lose her temper when she felt it rise. Right now, she was in danger of failing all three.

"Your Majesty," Jian said with both confidence and contrition, "I am willing to accept all punishments you see fit when this is all sorted and over. However, it might be best to keep me in action until then. And whatever action you intend to take, I might suggest that we do so soon."

Jian had come before Mireya as instructed by Hemele. Jian remembered with perfect clarity the seriousness on Hemele's face when he had returned from the Madhouse to visit the man they had left there from the abandoned village. Hemele was like a man in great turmoil whose thoughts were far away and caught within a storm.

"Jian," Hemele finally said after thinking for what seemed like an eternity. Jian hadn't pressured him to talk the entire time. He just sat beside his Captain, his friend, the man he trusted most in life, and patiently waited for whatever it was that he would be called upon to do. "I have some questions that I am going to investigate."

"Figured you did, figured you would," Jian responded to Hemele as he downed the last of his warmed wine in preparation for whatever he would need to do.

Hemele went to a trunk in a supply room of the barracks with Jian following him and brought out a medium-sized candle. Jian recognized it as a Three-Hour Candle. These candles were measured out and had two red lines within the white wax. If uninterrupted, the candle would burn down to the red marks to mark the passage of an hour. Three-Hour Candles would mark three hours passed once burned completely.

The candle was set upon a table in Hemele's private room. "Jian, if I'm not back by the time this has burned completely, I need you to go to the Queen."

"What are you talking about?" Jian had noticed clearly that Hemele was solemn the whole evening, but nothing like the tone change he was sensing now. Suddenly, Jian felt like this was no ordinary order, no ordinary investigation. "Is there going to be trouble?"

"I'm not sure. There's just a chance that there could be." He gave a mixture of a chuckle of obviousness and a sigh of desperation. "More than a chance, actually."

"If that's the case," Jian offered, "shouldn't I be going with you, sir?"

"No!" Hemele responded rather suddenly. Jian seemed to puff his chest out slightly in an almost subconscious attempt to appear braver. He never thought Hemele would take him for someone scared of danger or who would shirk away from a fight. And though Jian was older by at least five years, he always looked up to Hemele like a big brother. Hemele's tone wounded Jian's pride. Hemele decided to explain further, something he rarely did. "It's not that I wouldn't welcome some additional muscle, and it's not that I don't think you aren't brave enough. It's just..." and again his mind seemed so far away. He was being swept up like a leaf lost in the flow of the river with all of the possibilities of what the next hours could reveal and bring. "It's just, you're the only one I can trust. I mean truly trust. And if the absolute worst should happen, I need you to get word to the Queen."

At that moment, he began to take out a parchment and some ink. Jian watched on in silence as Hemele wrote out a hasty letter. "Jian, if I do not come back, then that means that certain things were both proven right and then went horribly wrong. If I am not back by three hours, I won't be coming back."

Jian's body went stiff at the thought that he might be watching as his Captain walked willingly into the pit of lions just then. He had to fight the urge to try and stop him. But just as Hemele trusted Jian, Jian trusted Hemele more than he had trusted his father. If Hemele thought that something was worth risking everything for, he would stand by it.

"Jian, this letter will explain everything. It will tell the Queen that the Healer is alive and that our Master Durai is dangerous."

Jian knew Hemele for many years, and never once had he seen his Captain go against orders, and certainly not with the implications this could mean. And to be speaking out against a trusted member of the court…

"What happened down there?" Jian asked referencing Hemele's visit to Galen.

Hemele sighed, handed the sealed letter to Jian, and said, "Please, just trust me on this one. And if I don't come back, remember what we talked about." Jian thought then about their talks at the fire lately. The more he thought about it, the more Jian realized that all of his and Hemele's suspicions had been leading up to this. This was turning into something bigger than a gut feeling, something far greater than doubts that tickled in the darkness.

And now he was here before the Queen after the last flickering of the candle's flame died out. He was standing as a representative of Durai's Guard that lied to their sovereign about the death of the Healer, and he was ready to take the full force of the Queen's wrath. But the Queen's wrath was not what he feared the most now; he feared most what could have happened to Hemele. He wished that whatever fury she was going to rain down would hurry up and get over with so he could go and help his best friend.

When her reaction broke, it was nothing that Jian was expecting. She neither yelled in her anger at betrayal nor had underlying, subtle hostility whatsoever. Instead, she started to cry. The second the first tear started down her cheek, she brought both of her hands to cover her face and started to sob. Jian took a step back not knowing where the tears were coming from or quite what to do about them. All he could do was watch.

"She's alive? Althea…she's actually alive." Mireya couldn't believe the reality of it, but in her heart, she wanted more than anything for it to be true. More than that, in her heart she knew it *had* to be true. Within a matter of a few seconds, she lived through every painful emotion she felt over the past year. The confusion at her disappearance, the sadness of clutching the hairbrush left behind, the anger at her leaving when Baldrik died, and the pieces of her that she could feel die each time the search parties for her came back with no sign. With all of that, she had never had any hope of her return. No real hope, anyway. She told herself to hold onto hope, but deep down in the deepest parts of her heart, she knew the moment she realized that her sister left behind a memento that Althea was lost to her one way or another forever.

But now…now she had hope. Real, warm, and golden hope budded and bloomed within her soul for the first time since she lost Baldrik - since her life turned completely desolate. Now there was a chance for light to flourish within her again.

Jian looked on no longer feeling fear of the repercussions and punishment, but now he was overcome with remorseful guilt at having kept this from her. He didn't know. How could he? He wasn't a confidant; he was a soldier following orders. But somehow Hemele knew. He knew there was a wrong that needed to be set right. His Captain, his friend - he was something special.

"My lady, I ask for forgiveness. Had I known -"

"Let's skip that for now," she said wiping her eyes and bringing herself to the present. "Your Captain writes here with some urgency, and he gave you a short time frame in which to expect him back or act immediately. Something tells me that time is of the essence."

Jian was surprised, but then again, that's why she was such a beloved ruler. She never dwelled on the negative. She always moved fast to what can be done, what should be done, and not on matters not important to the moment or self-indulgent. He respected that immensely. "I agree," he said eager to join her in action. "He didn't mention to me where he was going, but in all our talks, I have a pretty good idea."

Mireya raised her hand, "Wherever he is, I want to pay an immediate visit to the man who had you keep this news from me. I have some things to sort with Durai."

Jian squared his shoulders and stood at attention. "Your Majesty, please permit me to go with you. If Hemele was walking into danger like he thought he might, I cannot let you go alone."

She nodded at the request. She gave a thought or two for a moment as to what exactly she intended to do when she asked, "What exactly made him finally go against Durai's orders? What made him suspect something wasn't right?"

"My lady, there was a man found with Althea in the village. When our orders were given to us, his presence presented a complication. However, we couldn't just leave him or otherwise silence him; the Healer insisted he be kept safe. It was the only condition she asked for herself. We dropped him off in the secluded ward of the Hospital, the one used for madness, and he had visited this man."

This information certainly hit Mireya badly, and she was angry that one of her people had been made to suffer because of an order that should never have been given. She called over to a waiting attendant that stood at the door always at attention. "Go to the Courtside Hospital. See to it that the man brought there and placed in isolation be freed immediately and with apologies."

The attendant bowed and left immediately. The tone he heard in her voice explicitly urged haste and severity; he did not linger for further ceremony.

Jian watched the attendant leave and then looked back at Mireya, "That man may come to the palace. He might be in danger then. Is that really wise?"

She thought about those implications but then replied, "If that is his choice, it is his choice. We have kept him from the actions of his free will long enough. Besides, we might need all the help we can get. And if Althea spoke for this man, then he has my trust."

Mireya heard her own words and realized they sounded ludicrous. However, something about it seemed like the will of fate. Something she couldn't quite explain. It didn't matter.

In haste and impulsiveness, there is a larger chance for mistakes. And in such a dangerous game, mistakes can prove grievous if not fatal. The two figures left the throne room in such haste with no thought as to planning, no orders for additional guards, and no escape route should things go wrong. And in these dangerous games, something always goes wrong.

They arrived breathless at the long hall running the entire way there. As they turned the corner to face the long corridor leading to Durai's room, a blinding flash of white light came from the open door. It was so bright that the two of them fell over as if struck by a physical force. They struggled for sight for long moments shaking their heads in a dazed manner. What could that light be? What the Hell was going on?

Once the flecks in front of their eyes diminished and their sight returned, they looked at each other both in disbelief of what they had just witnessed. Then at the same time, they looked towards the hallway and the open door to Durai's rooms. Jian saw the figure of a body still as death, and his heart dropped so far through the floor that it surely made contact with the center of the earth. His breath completely left him, and he choked at what he prayed he wasn't seeing.

He got up first sparing not a thought for the sovereign he left behind on the floor and ran towards the body. Each footfall he prayed desperately that the body wasn't Hemele, each swing of his arms he bargained with the spirits of the world to be anyone but him, and with each breath he took he pleaded to fate to be merciful.

He arrived at the door. He couldn't hear the battle raging on in the room. He didn't see the dancing glow of Magic. He saw nothing in all of the world except for the face of Hemele blank before him. He fell to his knees before the last sight he ever wished to see. He felt numb, simply numb. He kept thinking all through the night that Hemele would die, kept expecting the worst that couldn't possibly happen so that he could be so relieved when he would be proven wrong. But he wasn't wrong. The worst that couldn't possibly happen lay before him in a pitiful pool of his blood.

Jian didn't even notice when Mireya came up behind him. However, seeing the reaction of this guard, she knew right away that this was Hemele. She didn't have time to react to that as she was seeing all that Jian did not. She saw the fight taking place in the room before her. She couldn't believe her eyes. It was like battles you hear about in fantasy. She never thought she would see Magical clashes like she was beholding now. She couldn't even fully comprehend what she was seeing. Even the air of the room, the power radiating out from it, seemed utterly overwhelming.

But most of all, she saw her sister. She was overcome with the most devastating desire to go to her and hold her so tightly that she would never let go. More than that, she saw that the last person she truly cared about in this world was being attacked. And her attacker was someone she had trusted with everything. The sense of betrayal hit her so completely that she felt her blood heat and boil within her.

"Althea!

By Heaven, My Soul is Purged from Grudging Hate

Althea felt Durai's body press against hers harder. Every squirm she made to escape from beneath him only excited him further, and she could feel it as tears continued to roll down her face.

"What shall we do with you so you don't lead more men to their deaths?"

Althea seemed to lose her strength to fight, if only for a moment. Then from somewhere behind her closed eyes, deep within her mind, and in the truest place in her heart, she heard a familiar voice. "I came here because of how proud I am of you. I don't blame you for a single thing in life. Not now, not then. You are finally free of the hold the past had on you. And I love you, sis, just as much now as I did back then."

In the darkness where she found herself, in the place where one goes when hope begins to die, she saw Baldrik's face. He seemed far away yet close at hand. He was with the same heavenly light as in her dream and held the same loving, forgiving look. If she had ever thought to see an angle in life, she believed she was seeing one now. She remembered all he had said to her in that dream. How far away that dream had seemed. She recalled his words and all the pain that lifted from her. It was the same pain that Durai tried to burden upon her once again.

Her eyes flashed then with realization. That was his power all along. That was the key to his hold over her all this time. He took her greatest fears and made her believe them to be true. He looked into her heart and twisted her intentions into something grotesque. Durai's perceptive nature saw into the treasured parts of her soul, and he used it as a weapon against her spirit.

"I'm proud that you are turning to fight. Just like I always knew you would."

The voice within her heart reached out to Baldrik then, "I won't let you down. I won't give up."

"Never once doubted it."

Though still roughly pinned to the floor by Durai's body, Althea opened her eyes with her newfound strength and will to keep fighting. Her eyes were once again glowing white with the extraordinary power she was drawing from within herself, from those she loved, from the very earth, and the elements of all the heavens. "Your control over me has ended. These deaths were not of my making. Your forked tongue can no longer have me believe your lies and guiling tricks. This ends now!"

Durai saw the conviction in her expressions and believed the truth of her words. Truly now the time of manipulating her into a prison of her own making was ended. The command he once had over her guilt and the nature of her giving heart was gone. Enraged by the realization, he lifted one hand off of her shoulder and struck her unimaginably hard across the face. Despite all the power that Althea was drawing from, Durai was drawing from just as much power but from a darker, more malicious source. The blow to her face seemed to knock her out of her head and her sight began to double in a daze. Before she could shake off the pain, her face received another strike with the back of his hand. She felt blood dripping down from her nose warm and thick.

"Althea!"

The battling pair both heard Mireya's voice coming from the doorway. Durai turned his head in surprise that his Queen had walked in on this scene. He was stunned momentarily realizing he had lost more than his power to control Althea, but his facade before Mireya was lost as well.

At that moment, Althea took a free hand and placed it on the side of his face. Lightning flashed and thunder struck in the same instant. Swirls of light both white and red flowed from not just her outstretched hand, but her entire body. It encircled Durai and bound him motionless to resist her hold. Durai could only turn his head to look at her head-on, but his limbs were bound tight by the energy held within the Magic and lights. And as he looked into her eyes, he saw that they not only glowed with the white light as before, but it flickered with electricity just as the storm was beyond them.

Althea still kept her one hand beside Durai's face as she wiggled herself out from under him. His eyes were alight with rage that she held him powerless.

"I have made peace with the shadows in my past," Althea said with that same deep, elemental voice. "Can you say the same?"

With that, she placed her other hand on the other side of his face. A wind blew fiercely into the room, and as the air passed them both the lights and images rushed into both of them. Althea saw the room where Baldrik died just as she knew Durai would conjure it. This time, however, she pushed past it. She could feel him resisting, but she didn't care. She had this one chance, and she knew she was not assured another one. She could feel small beads of sweat forming on her forehead as she fought against his defenses.

"I am the keeper and defender of light. And I will light the darkened places you do not wish to see!" One final push and she was able to barrel through the walls of his mind and moved through them as easily as water.

The images terrified her. They were violent, manipulative, and sickening. She forced him to see his father as he beat his mother on countless occasions. Each occurrence was more heinous than the last. She listened and watched as Durai used his cunning, scheming speech that brought his mother to her doom. Durai's mother had managed to escape, come back for her son, and then was guilted into staying. Then the images of the last beating, the images of her broken body, and the sight of his once-vibrant mother full of life and love laid hollow before the alter of the burial within an empty church.

Durai began to shake and tremble at the images played back for him with calculated clarity. The images were not in a sudden flash like the last time; instead, they were played back for him in agonizing slowness. In the end, he heard Althea's powerful voice disembodied within his mind, "You twisted her mind. You learned your terrible power of control then, and you liked it. You shamed her into staying, and it cost your mother her very life. I see your heart – you didn't even feel sadness."

Durai struggled against her words. The truth that she spoke was almost more painful than the images alone. Within his mind, he tried to put his hands to his ears to keep from hearing her voice, but the voice was within his soul.

"Aren't you ashamed?"

Finally, Durai's resistance overpowered Althea's diminishing strength from holding him in place. The light flashed through the room once again as their connection and contact broke. Everyone present flew backward as if struck down by a mighty wind. Althea was the first to come out of the daze, and she quickly scrambled to her feet and prepared to defend herself.

But no attack came.

She saw Durai on the floor curled into himself trembling. She carefully walked over and saw him clutching at himself as his eyes looked distantly to the horrors she brought forth into his mind. Slowly drool started to escape the corner of his mouth. He had been stunned and incapacitated by his horrors.

"Althea!" Mireya yelled from the door. She was far too terrified to cross the threshold of the room. Althea turned at the sound of her sister's voice and ran to her with all the strength she had. Their embrace was like the singing of the earth emerging from frozen winter. They were two parts once again joined feeling whole.

But Althea knew the moment could not linger. Who knew how long Durai would be like that. She looked down at Hemele on the ground and the soldier she had remotely recognized from the village. "Quick," she said at Jian, "Which way is it to the temple? The one where Durai works his Magic?"

The urgent sound in her voice brought both Mireya and Jian out of their joy and grief respectively. They looked at her and saw that she was convinced this was not a safe place to stay.

"I'll escort you there," Jian said as he lifted himself from the floor.

"Please hurry. I may only get this one chance. If he gets up…"

At that they all three looked at the pathetic heap on the floor. But none of them felt relieved. They all knew that at any moment the spell could be broken, and what might emerge could be even more terrible than before. At any moment, he could emerge from his ashes and bring forth such fire in his vengeance.

O, While You Live, Tell Truth...

The rain from the storm outside flew by the wind into the room and upon Galen's feet. He watched the storm with impatience hoping that any moment Hemele would see the truth and come to set him free. He felt in that instant he would fly like a bird from a cage and not stop until he reached Althea again.

In between the flashes of lightning, a different flash of light lit up his room that came from the outside. He knew lightning, and this was not lightning; this was stronger, brighter, and more purely white. Somehow, he could feel in his heart that it was from Althea. He dropped to his knees and prayed that she was safe.

Even through the loud raging of the tempest outside, he could still hear distinctly the faint sound of the latch lifting and the door being opened. The boy that came forth barely had time to say, "Her Majesty wishes –" before Galen was gone from the room in a mad dash.

He just prayed he could arrive in time to be of any help. He prayed he'd arrive on time and find her alive.

·······

Althea, Mireya, and Jian ran like those pursued by Hell itself through the corridors of the palace towards the Temple of the Court Enchanter. It was a place of study and practice for the highest skilled of Enchanter Magic. Since the conjuring of the Mist, it was only used by Durai himself and no other Enchanter of Nobility as he supposedly worked tirelessly to find a way to end it. Mireya couldn't help but feel anger at Durai as well as herself for believing in him, trusting in him that he would keep his word. Everything she had ever known to be true when it came to Durai was now completely demolished and burned to ash in the fires of truth. The jagged fragments felt as if they broke her skin as they lie in pieces on the ground.

How fragile then is the perception of truth? How easily it can be shattered a the coming of true light.

Mireya took them through secret, mostly unknown corridors through the castle towards the private areas of the garden that saved them time and aided in concealment. Once they left the palace walls, they followed the garden paths towards the concealed temple. The ground was incredibly slick and thick with mud with so much rain from the ceaseless storm. Their way was inconsistently lit with the flashes of lightning making the going treacherous. As much as the trio wanted to hurry, they were forced into slow caution.

When the small but elaborate temple was in sight, Mireya turned to Althea to inform her that they were close. She could see Althea's face lit by lightning in front of her, and she could see the blood still coming from Althea's nose as it became a thin, red river down her face with the rain. How long had Durai been this way towards her? Mireya suddenly realized that this had to be why Althea felt she had to go and not say goodbye. If Durai was that dangerous, Mireya would have moved to stop him. In so doing, she would be pitting herself against a might too dangerous to take down.

Mireya felt shame then; shame for her feelings of resentment towards Althea when she left, and even more shame that she didn't perceive the signs of her abuse until this moment.

All the pain and anguish in Mireya's heart was worn clearly on her face; she was never good at hiding her true feelings. She was always as transparent as glass, and perhaps that is why people trusted her so completely. There was never deception.

Althea looked upon the pain now and knew exactly what her cherished sister must be feeling and thinking. She reached out and took her hand, "But you're here with me now."

Despite the pressure of speed and time, Mireya couldn't help but pull Althea in and embrace her even more tightly than before. Althea didn't pressure the release; she seemed to need it just as much as Mireya did.

Seeing the temple just ahead of them, Jian changed position from the rear of the group now to the front to check for any traps or treachery. He wouldn't underestimate anything about Durai after realizing all he must have done. Jian suspected the possibility of dangerous pitfalls within the temple.

The three approached the white tiled steps that were exceedingly slick in the rain. The two women held onto one another as Jian took out his sword and braved the way ahead. He opened the door with golden inlays thinking how pretentious this small building was. All three bodies stiffened with complete unease to see that the inside of the temple was black as a starless night. There were no windows, no access to the elements whatsoever. The building smelled old and full of books and parchment. There were holders for torches and candles, but none of them had anything with which to light it.

They could see the outline of shadows within the temple from the slightly brighter black of the storm outside, so they left the door open. Althea pushed her way to go first. With each step, she reached out with her hands first to keep from bumping the unseen in front of her. She had only ever been to the temple once with Durai in what seemed like a lifetime ago. She could remember very little of it except that the alter was at the farthest end from the door. Mireya and Jian stayed behind to give her space and guard the door.

Althea finally came upon a large, waist-high object with a cold, smooth surface. She correctly assumed that it was the alter. She didn't know what to do. Though she had thought all these days about what she would do once she reached the temple, she found that she only had one vague thought that may be a long shot. Just as she sought to draw the light into Durai, she would try to draw the light into this place where this evil sprouted. Failing that, she was lost.

She placed her hands on the top of the altar and began to close her eyes and concentrate. She walked the path in her mind every step she had taken with Durai, and to her surprise, it started to work. Light grew from her hands and the contact they made with the alter. The cold surface began to spread with warmth at her touch. The light and warmth spread so much with her practiced, confident motions that the candles suddenly lit on their own and glowed with a brilliant, unnatural flame. Jian and Mireya looked on in astonishment at what they were seeing. Mireya was so overwhelmed at the familiar light from Althea that she felt overcome with passionate remembering and the fond thoughts of her tending Baldrik with it.

The images coming to Althea from the alter were faint at first as only blurred colors and shadows. She was swimming in a torrent of feelings, mismatched directions, and what seemed like instructions she couldn't interpret. Then the lines became sharper and the images played before her as if she were there. She saw Durai, and she saw the devious aura about him almost tangible in its ill-intent. Though he had the intended spell before him on parchment, he didn't look at it at all. He proceeded through the motions as if he had intended to fulfill this curse for a long time.

Very subtly Durai seemed to birth a grey smoke emerging from his body that quickly moved to and enveloped the whole of the alter. The color changed with Durai's words and became the familiar purple. It rose from the top surface of the alter almost resembling a human body as it looked towards Durai. The Enchanter's eyes glowed with the terrible green as Althea had become familiar with as he spoke in a language she did not know. The figure made of the Mist seemed to acknowledge the words in a bow, and it soon dissipated into a living, formless mass of sparkling color and sweet smell. It made its way out of the temple then to complete the story the whole world knew.

Althea snapped back into the present to see the temple lit with candles which she guessed was her doing. With her more relaxed posture, Mireya moved from the door towards Althea. She grasped Althea's warm hands within her cold ones and asked, "Did it work? Is it done?"

Althea's eyes were far away, but at Mireya's words, she came back and bowed her head in resignation. "No. No, I don't think so. I have to heal the Mist from its source. I thought it was here at this altar in this temple. But the source of the Mist was Durai. It was a creation borne from his malice; it's purely his manipulative and insidious will. That's the true source of this Mist."

Mireya's spirit dropped. "Then how does it end? Does that mean you have to kill him?"

Althea was so lost about what to do. She leaned against the alter suddenly so drained and exhausted as she was overwhelmed by so much she did not know. She concentrated hard again on the impression she was getting through her contact and the feelings, the impressions she couldn't interpret. She thought about them and Jian standing guard at the door became anxious at the time sitting there helpless. Then his anxiousness melted into sympathy; all the world's high hopes rested on this woman who began to show her body covered in bruises and signs of abuse. He even noticed her burn and the markings upon it that clearly showed a vicious act.

Althea touched the alter again in hopes of gaining further insight into the parts she couldn't quantify. She searched through so much confusion to the point where she was clearly overwhelmed. She felt as though she were drowning. She frantically pushed through this image, that shade, and all the jumbled thoughts and pictures - until she could feel her heart pounding too hard. Her lungs burned with needing more and more air as she began to hyperventilate.

"Althea? Althea?" Mireya called out to her seeing the increase in Althea's distress. But Althea couldn't hear her. She was too entrapped in the whirlwind of information; she was being consumed by it.

"Althea..." suddenly a voice did reach her, but it wasn't Mireya's. She recognized it immediately as Baldrik's. He had become her guide and guardian, the rational, inner calm when she reached despair. "Althea."

"I'm trying. I'm trying so hard, but I can't figure out what to do. I can't make sense of anything this is trying to tell me."

She felt warmed then as his presence became more pronounced within her mind. He pushed away all of the confusion until it became just him and her in the space of her thoughts. The image of herself in that space collapsed to her knees while Baldrik kneeled beside her and held her. She could feel the calming effect of his presence and felt bitterness as she knew it would not last. She was so tired of fighting for so long; she wanted to stay in the warmth she knew she could not stay within.

"You're lost. You're looking for the path out of the woods."

"Don't tease," Althea chuckled at her response, and she felt Baldrik smile. She sighed at her failed attempt at levity. "Baldrik, I'm scared. There is no path that I can see. There's nothing but the woods. And time is running out; the light is leaving."

She felt him reach for her shoulder enthusiastically. "That's just it! You're looking for the light. So, do what you've learned to do best. You have to kill the darkness with the light."

"But I've tried that already! I've tried to bring the light to his darkness. Was that all it was? Is the curse broken?"

Baldrik looked at her with such reassuring patience. "No, and I'm so sorry. You only made him look upon the darkness. What's needed to extinguish the source of the Mist and dispel the curse is to make him truly feel the light."

Althea felt her body fall and caught herself with her hands against the ground. "But...last time...brother, I could barely hold on that long. What if he won't see?"

He then began to glow with a radiant light so bright that his form disappeared within it. The light even surrounded her form, and she could feel him within it. "Make him *feel* it then!"

Mireya saw Althea finally open her eyes as she stood beside the altar. Her eyes had the glow of revelation, and she felt incredibly hopeful that Althea was shown something to help.

While Mireya's hair clung to the side of her face and down her back, Althea's had fully dried with the warmth that had come from within her. She looked at Mireya's anxious face and smiled a half-smile. "I know what I must do."

Mireya's hopeful expression turned downward hearing the solemn tone behind the hopeful expression. "Is it bad?"

Althea sighed a heavy sigh, "It isn't great."

With that, the three began a slow walk through the rain back towards the castle. Neither Jian nor Mireya pressed Althea for further explanations. They could tell in her demeanor that a heavy cloud had set upon her heart. They watched as a soldier marched to danger with her head held high. She was afraid, she was uneasy, but she gathered courage from the heavens and the strength of the earth to power herself to do further battle with the beast she had just angered.

...And Shame the Devil

I have seen tempests when the scolding winds
Have rived the knotted oaks, and I have seen
Th' ambitious ocean swell and rage and foam
to be exalted with the threatening clouds,
But never 'till tonight, never 'till now,
Did I go through a tempest dropping fire.
Either there is a civil strife in heaven,
Or else the world, too saucy with the gods,
Incenses the to send destruction

Althea's soul and spirit seemed to watch the motions of her body from high above within the storm itself. She moved by a will she could not name, a force she could not see, and a faith she could not understand. She seemed so far from herself, she did not know what would become of her if a stronger wind should blow this night. Indeed, how hard must the heavens shake before she broke upon the earth ready to take her back? Or how little? Would merely the slightest rise be enough to destroy the already breaking body as it bore too much?

She walked as though she knew any moment would bring the attack she knew was coming, any second the spark of their final battle would ignite, and any flash of the torrential heavens could mark the beginning of the end – one way or another. In her march back to meet with fate, she thought for the first time how truly real her death might be. When she had decided to come back, she never feared that her life would be brought to a violent end. Durai may be a monster, but she knew he would keep her; he had needed her in some way. Now she was certain of nothing. She accepted now that her transgressions against him may have tipped him into further violence, perhaps even insanity. She wasn't sure if Durai would not want to end her violently or conquer her completely to a life of broken spirits. In that thought, she wasn't sure which she feared more.

Jian held out a hand and stopped the small company just before the threshold of the stone castle. He crouched and held tighter to his sword as he heard the tiny sounds outside the makings of the storms. Mireya put her body before Althea. Mireya may not be able to fight in the battle of good and evil's champions and their inconceivable level of Magic and power, but she would be damned if she wouldn't try to protect her sister, her last love on earth, for as long as she could.

A cold hand reached out from the shadows and pulled Althea around with desperate force. Before Althea could brace herself against the pull, she found herself wrapped and pressed against the wet body and heaving motions of gasping breaths.

"You're safe! You're alive. Thank God, thank God, thank God."

"Galen?!" Althea pushed back in disbelief from the chest she was held to and found the sight she didn't think she would again see in life. As soon as she was certain of the figure before her in the dark, she pulled herself back into his arms and he into hers.

"I ran here the second that door opened. Permission or not, I was leaving. I saw this light…I didn't know what it meant. But I was done waiting around to hear the worst." He held her tightly as he spoke. But then he suddenly recoiled with passionate contrition and looked upon her with the most apologetic face. "I'm sorry! Did I hurt you?" He looked toward her shoulder filled with worry, sorrow, and furious anger.

At first, she didn't know what he meant. She was so happy to see him she forgot about the pain she carried. Then she was so shocked that he would know. Surely he hadn't seen her wound in the darkness. "The crow…" she said to him, and he nodded.

"He told me the things he saw, the sorrow in your face. I wasn't about to stay any longer to see what more Durai would do." A tear mixed with the rain upon his face, and she moved a hand to wipe away both.

Mireya looked at Jian then; her eyes silently asking if this was the man they spoke of. Jian nodded. His expression was equal parts shame at his part in the man's imprisonment and astonishment that he made it to the castle so fast. He must have run the entire way without stopping. It wasn't that far from the castle, but it was still an impressive feat. What had given him such fire? Examining the look in Galen's eyes, the way he looked at Althea even as broken and bruised as she was, he could see what made him fly so fast.

"You must be the man they found with Althea in the village," Mireya offered quietly. "Please accept my deepest apologies for what was done to you, as well as my thanks for being there with her."

As Galen nodded in acceptance, Althea took his arm and introduced the two of them. Galen could feel how weak Althea's body had become. In all their travels she had never leaned on him quite the way she had now. He could feel the exhaustion in her shuddering muscles. Certainly, she would sleep for days once they survived this. And he was determined that she should.

Galen put a hand upon Althea's as he asked, "What do you need?"

Althea smiled warmly if not weakly. "We need to make it back to Durai. I left him on the ground... long story. He is the source. I have to end the Mist within him."

Galen's face dropped as he could hear the fear she was trying to hide. He squeezed her with just the right combination of tight reassurance and considerate gentleness. "You lead the way. I'll follow."

Mireya stepped in and placed a hand on Althea's good shoulder and smiled reassuringly. "We all will follow. You won't be going in alone."

Althea appreciated the comfort and the solidarity, and it helped somewhat. But the truth was that she would be fighting this very much alone. And the success or failure was solely her burden. As she looked into the faces depending on her, she donned a mask of confident bravery. In so doing, she half believed it herself.

The four entered the castle and knew at once that Durai had recovered. Every light that was once lit in the corridors was extinguished. The smell of lingering candle and torch smoke still hung heavy in the air. Althea could feel the hands of Mireya and Galen tighten their grip on her, so she tried her best not to show her paralyzing dread. Jian took a step to head for Durai's room, but Althea stopped him.

She reached out with all of her senses to see if she could determine something, anything, about their surroundings and where he could be. The very air seemed to be thick with a foreboding sense of treachery. Althea felt very keenly that they had walked into a very primal predator/prey situation, and in the darkness, they were at a disadvantage. She was not used to hunting, yet she couldn't afford to be prey. She did not want to be there walking towards risk and peril, yet she could not run this time.

Mireya put both arms around one of Althea's. Althea could feel her start to tense and tremble; she was certainly afraid. "This is my castle," Althea could hear Mireya whisper to herself.

Jian had heard also. He turned to his Queen and responded, "But this is HIS darkness."

Althea felt all three pairs of eyes on her. As much as they all knew that she was burdened by so much, they had nowhere else to lay their hopes. Althea closed her eyes. She didn't know where to turn herself. She was so scared, she just wanted to be warm and safe far from this night. With that strong desire, Galen's face appeared in her mind as he cared for her on their hill. She pictured Mireya and her brushing their hair together. She saw Baldrik's smile. And she imagined a future far from now surrounded by all of their love.

As the warm feelings flooded into her mind and soul faster and faster, her whole body began to glow with the light of love, friendship, and trust. The sight was so beautiful, the three that accompanied her looked on breathless in astonished amazement. Althea opened her eyes, and the glowing remained. She held onto the feelings that she had brought to her heart, and the light followed. She reached out one of her hands and conjured elemental fire with bright red flames that flickered and danced from her palm. Althea extended her hand, and the flame flew in different directions towards the extinguished torches and candles and lit them brightly.

With the corridors lit, Althea turned to Mireya, "This IS your castle. We are not helpless against the dark. Not anymore." Mireya smiled and straightened her body with pride, both for herself and her dearest sister.

The group walked the long hallways in utter silence. Even their footfalls were careful and as quiet as possible. Though their way was lit, they felt uneasy and vulnerable. The walls seemed to watch them and gave them the feeling of a deep breathing and sleeping dragon tracking their every step. The air slowly grew dense and humid adding to their discomfort. Galen, Mireya, and Jian began to subconsciously slow their pace, but not Althea. She knew that if she were to hesitate for even a second, she would not find the courage to keep going. So, she kept her steady pace and walked towards the last place she had left him.

When they arrived at Durai's rooms, they weren't really surprised to find that he was not there. He wouldn't be waiting for them in the spot where he had fallen; rather his nature would suggest he would seek out another spot and meet with Althea on his terms.

"What do we do now?" Galen asked Althea. Althea tried to reach out throughout the palace to try and sense where he was. She spread out her warming sense of light through every part of the castle that she could reach. Finally, she came upon a place so cold that it burned, so dark that it swallowed all light.

"The throne room," Althea said to herself, and she began in that direction with the others following her. She was the very image of the lamb walking up to the lion.

Sooner than any of them would have liked, they reached the door to the massive, grand throne room. It felt like the mouth of an ominous cave that reeked of chilling dread. Althea put her hands against the door to open them, and they felt like ice. She knew then that he had been building up Magic within that room; she would be walking onto the battleground of his making and on his terms.

But she had no other choice.

The door opened with great resistance. The wood snapped and cracked against the movement, and the air seemed to creep out in a visible wintery chill. Althea stepped through the door into the room and felt her entire body freeze.

Before the others had a chance to react, the door slammed violently shut seemingly on its own. Althea could hear pounding on the door by multiple fists and Galen's voice calling out for her in vain. She blocked out the sounds from behind her as she was enveloped in the darkness of the room, and she was searching out her surroundings for her adversary lying in wait. She took a step forward carefully, and then two – the further into the vast room she treaded, the darker and colder it became.

Just as she had expected, a pair of glowing, green eyes eventually appeared before her; they were elevated and seemed to come from the throne. The light from his eyes seemed to radiate outward like smoke. Instead of awaiting his attack from the darkness, Althea brought light to her hands just as she had done in the hallway. But the light could only penetrate the black so far and brightened a mere few feet in front of her. The darkness he had created was unnatural and powerful. But a few feet of light was enough to show his reclined outline upon the throne. One couldn't even tell that moments ago he was a quivering mess. His resilience was frustratingly remarkable.

Durai slowly leaned forward towards her on the throne, and though his eyes were mere slits of glowing green, she knew he was looking at her. He began to make a "Tsk" sound as he shook his head. It made her skin crawl. It was infuriating.

She took a step confidently towards him hiding well how much she was shaking inside. Her shoulders were back, and her head was held high. "The site was you all along. The temple had nothing to do with any of it. It's you who must be cleansed with light. And…you knew it this whole time, didn't you?"

He started to stand and said, "Well, it was my spell." He also was hiding something, but her keen eyes from so much experience in the perilous wilds could pick up the slight shudder of his muscles and the hand he left against the throne carrying more of his weight and support than he was letting on. He was weakened. And that made him even more dangerous.

She fought back an urge to take a step back as he descended one step from the elevated throne towards her. Before he seemed to slither gracefully like a snake, but now he seemed like a prowling bear or lion whose clambering steps were full of power if not grace. The darkness in his aura seemed to drip off of him like thick poison. "Whatever shall we do with you?" his deep voice asked. "What punishment is worth what you've done to me?"

The green glow seemed to extend from his eyes in long streams of dancing light. It slithered like a serpent towards Althea before it wrapped itself around her. She took a step away from it to find that it held no substance and could create no bindings against her.

"Oh, Durai," Althea said as her breath blew visibly before her. "I plan to do far more. That before? That was just a taste of my intent. I am far from fully paying you for all you've done."

Truly the Souls of Men are Full of Dread

"Your game is over. You've been beaten," Althea said with a splendid show of borrowed bravery. She was still shaking in her skin, but she had come too far to succumb to her fear and trepidation. "Now," she said as she extended her hand stiffly in an outstretched arm, "let me help you."

Durai looked at her outstretched hand like a wounded dog looks at a passing Samaritan with food and good intent. He didn't trust it, and he was confused by it. What was her angle now?

"Help me?" he chuckled to himself amused. "You help me?" His eyes searched hers for a sign that she was teasing him or toying with him. However, her eyes were completely honest and innocent in their earnestness. Her arm remained outstretched, and he felt overcome with resentment. "I don't need your help! I don't need any helping!" he shouted at her in a terrible tone and volume that shook her bones and blew a fearsome, abnormal wind towards her as if emanating from his rage.

Althea couldn't help but recoil her extended hand and brought her arms around her body to shield herself from his assault. She stifled the rising tremors in her muscles. Her blood was chilled so deeply that she felt she'd never feel warmth again. She looked down at her hands to see even her fingers began to turn blue. They began to tingle and then sting with the pain of the cold, and the frozen blood started to reach her whole body and seize her heart.

At that moment Durai's eyes lit as he saw her vulnerable again. She was cowering, shielding herself, body weak from this cold he had brought, he could see her begin to tremble slightly, and he felt his power over her begin to return. He began to speak to her again; his melodic tone returned with an undertone of sinister, ominous intent. "Little Dove, my precious little thing. I think it's you who need the help."

He began advancing towards her stronger and stronger with each calculated step. Althea's muscles seemed to act on their own as she cowered slightly more and took a step back. Her heart ran like a frightened rabbit into a hole, and she felt as if she were right back where she was so long ago.

"No, Dove. That's what it is. Let me help *you*. I will forgive you, I will forgive all the terrible things you've done if you let me help you. I'll take care of you, just like before. We can go back to where we began, and this time will be better. We can be happy again."

Althea could hear the seductive sweetness in his words. For a moment, it truly did seem as though he wanted to start again to find a way to be together. She could hear love beneath the distorted filter he experienced it with. She could hear the little boy needing his mother's love. He could hear the beautiful man she left her whole world for. He seemed truly genuine.

But then again, he always had. She no longer trusted it.

In movements that seemed lightning fast, he was before her again with his arms wrapped around her body. He could feel her body stiffen and shudder within his entwining arms. He pressed her head to his chest despite her resistance. He began to stroke her hair despite her protests and said, "In time, I can even love you again despite what you've become."

Althea pushed against him and tried desperately to pry herself from his tight embrace. Durai grabbed a large fistful of her thick hair in his hand and pulled it sharply down forcing her to look up at him. He pulled so hard that tears of pain sprung to her eyes, but she didn't cry out. He reached up with his other hand then and placed it upon her face.

The blacks of her pupils then grew larger and larger taking over the whites of her eyes until all of her eyes were completely black. It was like the darkness filled her at his touch. The darkness found its way inter her from the inside, and the black could be seen all around her.

A sharp sensation hit her then very similar to what she had done to Durai. Images flew past her like a sudden wind. There was a haze about the scenes playing out in her mind; they were not of the same, sharp clarity as to the images of past recollections she had forced Durai to see had been. These seemed like shades, suggestions, or fantasies. If her Magic brought forth forms and likeness in truth, what he was doing was shaping lies and dressing them with false shape and substance.

Althea could see herself in these visions. She was beside Durai as he had a hand around her waist. Her arms were folded carrying a swaddled bundle while two other small boys played at her feet. Durai was forcing fantasized images of a family, a family he forced her to bear, and Althea could feel her face whiten with fear. Through the images projected into her mind, she could hear his voice speaking to her as it came through with enticingly tempting tones. "This is what I can give you. This life, these children, our children. I can forgive you, and we can be happy again."

The pure eyes of the child seemed to warm her at first. They held her in love and an innocent dependence. They were innocent.

Then the light of the scene started to darken into shades of red and black. The children's eyes no longer seemed innocent. They turned into his eyes. She noticed her image in this scene had chains slither up her body like snakes. Her figure became completely incapacitated by the bindings as Durai came and took the swaddled baby from her arms. The scene became darker and more terrifying. The three children looked at Althea, not her figure bound in the vision, but into her very soul that was looking on. They looked at her with Durai's glowing green eyes.

"And I will make my sons like me, strong, cunning, and powerful. And we will keep you safe with us. Forever."

It was like she was falling off a cliff. She could feel the sensation of falling, though she was standing still. Her fear of what he projected into her mind, the terrifying horror of what she witnessed, shocked her so violently that she was jerked back into her body as if she had been dropped. Her eyes returned to her normal color and saw herself still in Durai's grasp. His eyes were eager and lustful, and the corners of his mouth curled into a sinister grin.

How had she been so in love with someone she now felt such overwhelming hate for? How can this man be so beautiful despite how hideous he was in his heart? He was like the angel Lucifer, and she was the fool who had revered and idolized him.

At that moment, she would have happily died to pay for the sin of loving him.

Durai began to press his body against hers, and she could feel the heat of him against her frigid skin. She couldn't take his touch a second longer. The amount she was disgusted with him was suffocating - the mere thought of creating a family with him to have children corrupted into his perverted image and power scheme - made her insides build with so much pressure she felt she would explode. The more she tried to fight him off, the harder he pressed against her. He was almost feeding off her misery, and he found it delicious.

Suddenly her body began to glow with a faint light before exploding from her body violently in the same brilliant red flames that caught her in her fall before. The force of the burst of fire from her body sent Durai flying back a few feet. While the flames were warmer than his cold darkness, the flames did not burn. Althea relished the feelings of heat returning to her body and smiled slightly to herself as she realized she wasn't as helpless as she had thought. Certainly not as helpless as he was hoping.

She stepped towards Durai as he tried to get to his feet gracefully but failed. Instead, he looked like a small boy only able to flail his limbs in a clumsy mess. She held out her hands to the side of her body palms up while flames appeared from them and grew tall. She was truly in command of this warmth and this light, this was not an accidental conjuring as before. Durai looked at her with actual dread in his eyes for the first time. The light she held, the light that covered her and radiated out from her, grew brighter and brighter with each passing moment until Durai raised a hand to shield his eyes.

"No, Durai," Althea said with that voice full of power. "Do not shy from the light. Let it help you. Let me help you tend to the good parts of yourself that you have let become warped and corrupted by the seduction of your power. Let me help the light in you that's worth saving."

Hearing her words made Durai angrier and more venomous. Shadows began to grow from his feet and creep towards Althea. "Bow to you, you mean! After all I've done, you would show me compassion? I think not. I will not be at your mercy. I've had you once, all of you, and I will never be satisfied until I possess you - body and soul - again. You are mine. The light you're looking for isn't there!"

As he finished his words Althea made the fire flair even higher and spread along the ground. The shadows that had reached for her hissed and screeched as they were devoured by the light of the flames. Althea's eyes began to glow all white again as she took another step forward. "If you refuse to see it if you refuse to embrace the light calling to you to end this, then I will make you *feel* it!"

It is Not in the Stars to Hold Our Destiny, but in Ourselves

At the sound of her threat, Durai's eyes narrowed to furious slits. The mere thought that the tables could be turned on him, and to this extent, was the most unacceptable possibility.

He stood there and looked at her impressive stature up and down. Before this moment he had wanted to break her spirit so completely that she would barely have the will to live much less fight him on anything. He had hopes of her being the ultimate trophy, a beauteous gem who depended upon him so completely that she would be his to do with as he pleased. The most gorgeous woman, the most powerful Healer, and then the strongest fighter against him to become an ornament on his arm had given him such erotic excitement that he could barely contain himself. Now, however, he looked upon just how strong and resilient she stood before him. Now the option of toying with her was too risky; he stood a good chance now to lose it all.

No, he thought with regret and apprehension, he would have to destroy her.

Althea seemed to sense the change in his resolve, but she didn't let it concern her. She let all worry and trepidation wash through her as if it were the wind dancing off her skin. The cold could not touch her; she would no longer allow it. The darkness would not fill her; she forbade it. She became the warrior embodiment of the righteous good.

And she would not stop.

Durai bent down and put his hands against the floor. The room darkened even more completely. The only light in the room was the light around Althea, and even she couldn't see Durai's figure though he stood only a few meters from her. She increased the flames around her, and still, she could not see. Shadows began to creep into her light in the forms of the familiar hands reaching out to her. She was able to deter and destroy some of them as they grabbed at her, but still, others persisted and pulled at her dress and hair.

She did not panic; she did not distress or cry out. She methodically went after the most aggressive force and blasted it with fire one right after the other with an almost eerie calm. They gave pathetic screeches in their death thralls. Though Durai remained hidden in the darkness, he was beginning to note that the fire which had merely been warm before was becoming more intense; he could feel the heat even from his position. He could tell then that his shadow creatures wouldn't work. He had to change tactics.

Althea blasted one last shade reaching for her before she noticed all movement in the darkness cease suddenly. She stood alert and poised for the next tactic of attack that she knew was coming. The darkness was so black and dense that it was enough to drive one mad. From the black, she began to sense a presence. Indiscernible whispers began to swirl about the air giving the atmosphere an ominously portentous feeling. The sounds became louder; specific words could be distinguished. Then the whispers became familiar voices calling out to her.

She could hear Baldrik's voice full of accusation and enmity. "You left me. You left me alone to suffer and die. This is your fault."

She could hear Mireya's voice in the dark. "You left me like I was nothing. You don't love me. You never did. You played me."

She heard the nameless voices of countless others, "This is your fault. You did this. We suffer because of you!"

The voices began to blend together in such an overwhelming heaviness and the animosity became so strong that Althea could almost touch it. She closed her eyes at the barrage of painful accusations, and the light within her dimmed. The flames died down, and the light faded into the darkness before there was nothing left of her to see. It had swallowed her completely.

Durai lowered his hand as he saw his ploy work at shrinking her away and wearing her down to nothing. He smiled to himself feeling victorious and clever. He took a step towards where he last saw her. He was ready to scoop her up from the floor expecting to see her in a pile as she had made him earlier.

But he could not find her.

Now he was in the darkness at a disadvantage. He tried to seek her out, feel her within the darkness in some way, but he couldn't feel anything in the darkness. He felt trapped in a void, and he had made it so. He tried not to let the panic he felt rising to overtake him, but for the first time since he was a small child, he felt vulnerable. He was even admittedly afraid.

Before he could fully register the warm breath on his neck, he became surrounded by red flames. Durai felt her presence behind him, and the aura she emitted was overwhelming and full of strength. She wrapped her arms tight around him from behind and held him tight. The flames billowed high around the both of them and at that moment locked them together.

He turned to her then. He was only able to see her face and the flames. He felt angry, but mostly he felt afraid. In his fear, he locked onto her eyes. Her eyes were unwavering amid his anger and the warmth of the flames. She was not backing down, she had come so far, and she was taking him with her. She would not settle for less than the end of this.

He tried so hard to keep up his hatred and anger towards her, but she would not be swayed from her persistent looks of kindness and gentle helpfulness. He sneered at her in order to push her into her previous passions, but she refused to reflect the monster facing her. She was the guardian of light, and if he was going to accept that light within himself, she would do so her way.

Seeing her unmoved and completely in control began to affect Durai. But to his surprise, the effect was not what he was expecting. He thought that her continued defiance would infuriate him to become more physically violent. Instead, the blood that boiled up inside of him began to cool. The pressure he was building up in his fervor started to release and diminish. The negative turmoil behind his eyes began to fade and soften, and he saw her clearly then – maybe for the first time in a very long time. She was no longer a decorative prize for his inflated pride and ego. He saw a woman pure and beautiful – not just in a physical sense, but in every sense – that stood before him.

He thought then that she looked like such an angel. How had he not seen this before?

Althea raised one hand and laid it on the side of his face. He felt her touch; it was soft, it was tender. "Durai," she said in her normal voice, her bird-song voice, "it's time to turn away from the shadows. It's time to turn from what you became."

Durai placed a hand upon her hand that caressed the side of his face. This tenderness was once his, and he cut it up mercilessly and carved it to his will. He had rendered the most exquisite flower to a wilted death husk with his selfish manipulation and cruelty. Not even a saint could forgive what he had done.

And that thought then turned him away from the salvation of the light.

Durai took the hand within his own and squeezed it hard with his anger rising once again. "You mean it's time to go and be punished. Do you think you can fool me? No one can forgive what you promise to resolve. Nothing will be back to serenity and peace after this. I've gone too far. Now I must go the rest of the way."

"No, Durai. You're so close!"

"Little witch, you can't trap me! No one can go back after what I've done. No one! No light forgives that much dark!"

In his rage, he raised his hand and reeled it back to strike her with the most force that he had ever used on her. But she didn't flinch at his actions. She saw his motions as if he were moving in half-time, or maybe she had just known deep down that it would come to this.

She moved with the grace of a smooth river, of a breeze in spring, of the gentle brilliance of a rising sun; she had become an elemental force of the earth, and she laid both of her hands against his face. As she closed her eyes, the light from her body spilled into every corner of the room. Durai fought against the light, and the harder he fought against it, the harder he tried to keep it out, the fiercer the light became. He fought against it so hard that the brilliance of the light began to sting and singe.

Fire emerged from her hands then, and the warmth of flames came with it. While her hands were unfeeling with accepting the light, creating it, Durai's body that was resisting it felt the heat of the blaze was all too real. He began to steel himself against the pain, but he would not let the light that shone from her into his heart. The heat surged and began to singe his skin. He cried out in pain, but she wouldn't let go. His eyes were held shut so tightly that it seemed his eyebrows would meet his cheeks.

"Don't fight it, Durai. The light is a part of you. Let it!" Althea screamed at him as the intensity of the flames seemed to drown out all sound.

"Althea! There's smoke! Althea! Please! Are you alright?!" Althea then heard the voices on the other side of the door calling out for her in terrified concern. They banged hard against the wood terrified of the smoke coming from beneath the door. That's when she started to feel the anxiety rise within herself. She struggled to keep control and the command of the light. She was so close!

"Durai, please!" she shouted with one final push of everything she had within herself. She felt as if she had pushed her insides to the outside. An explosion went off at her core, and the flames blasted with her effort. The light from the surging flames seemed to cascade down in radiant, twinkling orbs from the ceiling.

The light from her final, exhaustive push pierced through Durai's heart like a flying arrow. His eyes flew open then, and they were filled with the same white light that Althea had held within hers. His body went rigid. She had given everything she had to get the goodness and truth into him, and it now began to take hold. They shared each other's joys and pains, a lifetime's worth. The complexities of their intertwining destinies coursed through them both. The sensation was so intense that it began to hurt them. It filled every cell within their bodies, the agony of giving and receiving. And for a moment, the whole world's orbit spun around them.

Slam!

With Durai's body held trapped within Althea's hold, the hold of the light, the Magic he used to keep the room sealed and dark fell away. Galen finally forced the door open with Jian's help, and with the room breached, the torches and night candles of the room lit themselves. The three ran up the carpeted walk just in time to see the last seconds of the red flames that encompassed two figures locked within them. Both were a vision of purely powerful Magic with their hair blowing in a wind only around them and their eyes alight purely white. The three stood and stared. The sight was breathtaking. The sight was terrifying.

The moment faded almost as soon as the trio came upon it, and both Durai and Althea collapsed upon the ground. They were unmoving; they did not even show the motion of breath. Galen ran to Althea's body almost choking on his fear. He didn't know what he had just witnessed, but he prayed that whatever it was didn't take her life with it. He dropped to his knees beside her and cradled her within his arms. Jian and Mireya watched on holding their breaths praying along with him that life was still within her.

"Althea?" Galen brushed back her hair. Her body was cold and unmoving against his warm, gentle touch. Her limbs were stiff and unreceptive. "Althea? Please?"

With his angel fallen and lying within his arms on the ground, tears escaped his eyes as he rocked back and forth still holding tight to the woman he had loved so much.

I Feel Within Me a Peace Above All Earthly Dignities, a Still and Quiet Conscience

"Galen, you really should eat something. It won't do you good to pass out from hunger." Mireya stood above Galen's slouched form. He had grown pale and gaunt, and she was worried about him.

"Your Majesty, I don't feel much like eating."

"Do you think that is what she would want you to do? Waste away to nothing?" Mireya put a comforting arm around the figure stoic in his silence.

After a moment in the hushed atmosphere between them, he looked up from his vigil to face her. "What if she wakes up, and I'm not here? What if she needs something, and she's all alone?"

Mireya crouched onto her knees beside Galen who was still at his post beside the bed where Althea lay very deeply asleep.

It had been three days since that night in the throne room. As Galen rocked her back and forth on the floor in his arms, he could feel the cold on her skin. He couldn't feel her breathing, the blood in her body had seemed still. He held his breath to try and will the air into her lungs. He never in his entire life had been more petrified and mortally scared as he had been at that moment.

After what seemed like an eternity, he felt her body take in a sudden gasp of air. It was as if the fire of life had suddenly sparked within her. He looked eagerly at her face, but she was still far away. Her eyes remained closed, and she would not stir. She simply remained alive but reposed like a princess in a faerie story. Galen just clutched her more tightly then, thankful to all of heaven that she was alive. If she survived that, she would make it through to the other side. Holding her in his arms, he bent his head and laid his lips on her forehead. Her cheek was whetted with a single tear.

The three days and night's vigil at her bedside wore heavily on Galen. He hardly ate or slept. There were a few instances of a fevered sweat that put her body into twitching fits, and Galen was beside her every second of it tending to her. He would wipe her brow and even rubbed her body with scented oils and massaged her muscles.

"Galen," Mireya said as she had stooped down to him, "I'm going to have to insist. You need to keep up your strength to take care of her more when she wakes. But if you waste what you have now, you'll be no good to any of us later. Please. I promise that she won't be alone. I'll be right here while you get some food, a good bath, and a night's sleep." Her tone was incredibly compassionate and trustworthy, but it was not to be mistaken for a suggestion.

Galen bowed his head in concession. He got up from his chair and offered it to Mireya. "Thank you, Your Majesty."

Mireya stepped to the chair but first turned to Galen's tired face. She brushed a wisp of his hair back from his face. He looked so disheveled - it made her want to take care of him too. She could see his innocent nature each more as the days progressed. And the devoted looks he gave Althea as she slept were so precious that she felt he was family already.

Galen walked out of the door giving Althea one final look before he closed the door behind him. He saw the two women together, and he saw what they must have been many times and what they must mean to each other. When he closed the door on the scene, he looked down the long hallway towards Durai's rooms. It had the same bustle of people in and out as there had been nonstop since it happened. He shrugged it off. He was too tired to try and evaluate how that whole affair made him feel.

He went towards another room a small way from Althea's that was vacant before and now belonged to him. The room had all the necessities it needed, but no additional, personal touches. He barely had been in it since it was assigned to him. A warm meal waited for him in the main room under a dome, and he was very grateful that it was brought to him there. He was in no condition to go to the main hall to be fed and put up a show and deal with the questions.

After a filling, wholesome meal and a long, warm bath, he put on a pair of clothes that had been provided for him. He went to the bed and collapsed into a deep sleep on top of it. He hadn't even the strength to get under the blankets.

Meanwhile, Mireya took out a familiar bush and began long, loving strokes through Althea's hair. With the repetitive motions, she felt more and more at peace. A peace that had eluded her for far too long. She looked upon Althea's face and was happy to see that it was still full of color. Mireya knew she was in a Healer's Sleep; Althea had spoken of it before. The fever spells and the twitching had frightened her just as it had frightened Galen, but she knew that Althea was too strong to succumb at this point.

With each loving stroke, Mireya started to think back to her memories and felt warmed by them. She began to hum a song she often hummed to Baldrik when they were younger and he would be sick. In a way, it felt like he was there in the room with her, and the three of them were united once again. She knew that it wasn't so, her feelings couldn't possibly be real, but she immersed herself in the thought just as happily nonetheless.

Mireya looked from the hair she had just finished brushing to Althea's face, and Althea's warm, brown eyes looked hazily back at her. Mireya thought for a second it was because of her wishing it would be so that she was seeing what she saw. She willed the sight of Althea's waking that her fantasy looked so real.

But then Althea smiled to see her soul sister, and Mireya knew then that it was real.

Tears immediately flowed freely from Mireya's eyes as she let a few giddy breaths escape. She was so happy and so relieved, yet she began to cry and sob. What was wrong with her?

Mireya grabbed one of Althea's hands and held it fast in both of hers. Althea didn't break her loving look at Mireya as she said, "Baldrik says he loves you."

·······

For the next few hours, young girl attendants came to help Mireya feed and bathe Althea. The Healer's movements were very slow and stiff. Mireya's heart broke over and over to see her so weak; she couldn't even imagine the full extent of the tole this had taken on her physically. And she didn't want to know the spiritual exertion what she had done must have taken.

As they bathed Althea in a warm and pampering bath, Mireya could see Althea's body covered in bruises ranging in size, color, and severity. Some seemed older, some seemed recent, and must have been from the fight three days ago. But the other ones...how long had she been locked in the room down the hall? What had she endured there?

One of the more tenured attendants suddenly stopped her cleansing motions of Althea's back as she came upon the right shoulder. She couldn't believe what she was seeing. Mireya noticed the attendant's movements stop, and she looked over at the expression of appalled shock. Mireya then dismissed everyone from the room and took over helping Althea herself. She looked at the brand upon Althea's back. The skin was still angry, red, and blistered. Parts of her skin were starting to flake off. Mireya couldn't believe what she was seeing. She put a finger against the skin – she still couldn't believe it was real – and recoiled suddenly when Althea flinched. Mireya covered her mouth with both of her hands to keep from crying. Even through the Healer's Sleep and the regenerating effects, this brand remained.

Althea's voice broke Mireya's stunned silence, "It's okay. I've accepted it." Her voice seemed so wise now. It was as if she had lived a lifetime through the battle and her sleep. Her voice, while still being sweet and demure, now held a quality to it that commanded reverence. It was as if Althea had elevated to a plane beyond the rest of them.

After she was fully washed, Mireya assisted her with her clothes. Althea had walked her through how to carefully bandage and wrap the still healing wound, and they put on clothing very loose around the top. Mireya was far from a Healer, but Althea benefited greatly from her naturally tender and graceful touches.

Mireya put Althea back into bed propped up on pillows. Althea gave her soul sister a look, and Mireya crawled into the bed next to her. After a few moments of comfortable silence, Althea turned to Mireya. "What happened?" she finally asked her.

Mireya grew a little more serious then. "I'm not sure what you did, but you won. We came up to you, and there was fire everywhere. I was so scared you'd be burned and killed, but the flames didn't seem to touch you. Your eyes...your eyes were pure white. And so were Durai's. It was like you filled him with it. And then you both collapsed."

Althea barely remembered that part. "What happened after that? Did it work?"

Mireya smiled at her, "Yes, yes it did. Yesterday our men reported from outlying villages that were abandoned that the bodies of Immortuos were lying in the streets. They were inanimate, unmoving, and seemed to go back to their rest leaving only the bodies behind." She turned to Althea then full of awe and gratitude, "You saved us all, Althea. You did it. You really did it!"

Every muscle in Althea's body seemed to relax then. So, it was all over. Her long fight, all of the fear, all of the violence...it was over. The dead loved in life had once again returned to where they belonged. One silent, alleviated tear rolled down the side of her face as she let out a deep sigh.

"What about Durai?" Althea asked.

Mireya looked at Althea as if she disapproved of the question. As far as Mireya was concerned, that monster didn't deserve a thought from her. "He's alive. We had to have what few people adept to medicine we have left in the kingdom come to do what they could, but he's not in good shape." Mireya noticed Althea's brow knit with worry as she looked blankly ahead. "He is very badly burnt on one side of his face. His body seemed like it was damaged inside. I don't know how to describe it. His body was bruised all over, like yours is, only much worse. It was almost like something bigger put itself inside of his skin and burst from the inside.

"He was unresponsive for the first day and a half, then he went into fits. He tore at his bandages and screamed gibberish. Althea, it was horrible."

Every word painted a picture for Althea, and she could see the scene play out in her mind. "He had to face the light, but he fought it. He fought it so much that the light had to force itself to make him see. And he did see it, he was washed over with what he had to accept, or else the Immortuos and the Mist would still be around. But he fought it every step. Maybe he's still fighting it."

Mireya nodded. It made as much sense as anything else she had seen so far. "Well," she continued, "he's not fighting much of anything anymore. He's become...I don't know. It's like he's empty inside. He has to be fed, given water, bathed, and bandages changed. But he doesn't do anything for himself anymore. At least not now. He just...exists."

Althea cast her eyes down feeling somewhat responsible. Mireya noticed as Althea took on that burden willingly, and she grabbed her hands. "Nuh-uh! You're not doing that to yourself. When he gets stable enough, we're sending him to a small hut that's been prepared near the base of the hill. He'll be cared for, but no longer is he going to be a burden on you. You've borne enough by him. He'll live out the rest of his life where he won't harm again. Better than he deserves."

Althea tried to smile a weak smile, but she just accepted Mireya's judgement. It was probably for the best. No, it was for the best. Althea would continue to harm herself more and more as if she deserved punishment if it weren't for Mireya reaching in to save her.

They spoke long into the night. They spoke of joys and deep sorrows. They had reunited again; they were family again. They talked until the both of them fell asleep still propped up on the bed with their hands together and fingers intertwined.

As the sun came up on Althea's face as it spilled like gold through the windows, she opened her eyes. The first thing she saw was Galen.

When their eyes met, they both smiled a deep and knowing smile.

Hope is a Lover's Staff; Walk Hence with That

The hut was modestly sized with a heavily fortified exterior on the outskirts of Base Village. All of the windows were small and held high. They were a welcomed source of light to the rooms within. They also kept the air fresh and moving within the walls keeping out a sense of staleness.

Althea walked into the main room and stared at the only other two doors within the hut. A small woman slightly younger than her stood at the door to her own set of rooms and gestured to the latched room adjacent. She didn't say much, and she kept her eyes down with her head bet forward. Her lighter gold hair covered her face when she did so. Althea couldn't tell if this woman was afraid of her, revered her, or both. The young woman was one of the few people who had volunteered to be taught the art of medicine. Through the exhaustive searches of the Queen's many teams of scouts since the end of the Mist, they still could not find another Healer alive. It truly seemed as if Althea were the last.

Jian moved past Althea then and unlatched the bolted door across from the silent woman. When he opened it, he peered inside before standing still beside it. His eyes still questioned Althea and her decision, but she was certain that this was one last thing she had to do. She passed through the door and gestured for Jian to close it behind her. He agreed to close it but kept the bolt from locking.

In a cushioned rocking chair along the wall in front of one of the high windows, Althea saw the figure of Durai sitting motionless. She had received reports that he still had not spoken a word or barely even uttered a sound for the three months since being moved here after being as healed as he could be. And since being moved to this house, he automatically complied with the motions of being fed and bathed and other necessities, but only with assistance.

Althea walked gracefully and confidently to face him. She stood before him as he showed no signs of registering her presence. He simply continued to look forward, and when she put herself in his line of sight, he simply looked past her as if she weren't there. She kneeled before him and inspected his physical state.

His face remained heavily bandaged across the left side where the burns were worst. The right side of his face still looked the same as it ever had. He was still as handsome as he ever was, but the spark behind his eyes was completely gone.

When she was convinced that he had been well cared for by the young woman outside, she rose from her knees and sat at the end of the bed still facing Durai. Still, he looked through her. Wherever he was, it didn't seem to be there.

Althea finally opened her mouth to speak. "Durai, do you remember who I am?" Her question was met with a nothing stare. "Do you remember who you are? What you've done?" There was still nothing from the man in the chair. Althea simply had the smallest flash of a smile grace her lips. It was not the smile of smug superiority, just the smile one has when expectations were met without surprise. The reports of his nearly comatose behavior were not exaggerated. Probably for the best.

After a moment, she leaned forward towards him. The light from the high window seemed to light her from behind. If Durai were any more present, he would have mistaken her for an angel. "Durai, this is the last time you will ever see me. I'm telling you now that I will never again visit you here. The things you've done may be in the past, and we all may have lived to tell about a happily ever after, but -"

Althea struggled then to find the right words. She wondered if it even mattered, he wasn't hearing her. Or so it seemed. "What you've done, as much as I would love to be able to, I can never forgive. I certainly will never forget. You've made it so, no matter what the outcome may have been that night, that you would always be a part of me. Forever. You've left your mark on me, both physically and mentally. Though I may spend my whole life trying, I may never succeed in being fully at peace again. I may fight every day to keep my body, my mind, and my spirit from responding out of the fear you've put within me or remembering the pain you've instilled in me, but I will fight. In the end, you did not win."

The air between them was both heavy and empty. There was so much that Althea would say, but the empty vessel that sat before her offered no closure. Althea felt frustrated. She even felt a bit angry. She wanted him to own just how monstrous he had been to her. She wanted to see in his eyes the realization of all he had done and hear the words of remorse and regret. In a way, she even wanted to see him in pain. It was no less than he deserved.

And she would never get that. She would live her whole life carrying that emptiness and need alone.

The more she thought about that, however, the more she realized she didn't need it. She had become something out of myth to conquer this embodiment of evil and malice. She had risen so high from what he had her believing she was for so long. She began to see that whatever she was seeking from this man, whatever she surely would not get, was nothing she truly needed.

She took one final look at his pathetic figure and rose to her feet. "I'm leaving you now with everything you've done. And I will go on. I will live out my life in the love I've found and the people I care for and the light I hold. Where you find yourself, the state you're in now, you will bear it alone."

With a small tap at the door, Jian opened it immediately and hastily. He saw that the scene was unchanged, and he sighed deeply in relief. As soon as Althea exited the door, he closed it and bolted it securely shut. Althea and Jian exchanged a glance. He nodded and stood at attention. "I will make routine checks on him myself. I promise." Jian took the order on himself. It was his way of honoring his friend. Hemele would have done no less than keep this man from causing harm until he lay cold in the ground. And that's what Jian would do.

She smiled at him and put a hand on his arm. "Thank you."

As she exited the hut, she saw Galen on a horse as he held the reins of her horse as well. He looked at her apprehensively, but seeing the peace in her face made him smile. She mounted the horse and looked at Galen. "It's over," she said to him with her melodic voice.

Galen spurred his horse, and the two mounts began their trek back up the hill towards the castle. "No, it's not. And it is okay that it's not." Galen said comfortingly. "You'll be dealing with all of this for a long time, and it's ok not to be comfortable with that. It's normal to still feel incomplete by it."

She smiled sweetly at him. "I know. I know this won't be fixed easily. But my final say has been said. I don't ever have to look at his face again. And that is what is over."

Galen nodded happily that she had done the final act she had wrestled with for so long. They kept their pace all the way to the castle where they were happy to settle together. Galen added to his rooms and claimed them happily as they were next to Althea's. Their bond had grown even stronger and stronger during the last three months of healing together. Through every rough day and night terror, he had been there for her. And in his loneliness and fumbling with his new surroundings, she was there for him.

That night they sat on a small hill within the garden watching the stars. They held tightly to each other as the air began to get cooler. Even with Durai, even on the best days, she had never felt this safe and comfortable. With Durai, she had always had a thrilling sense of newness as if each moment pushed a boundary to further intimacy. But in that lies the danger that she didn't know when the flutters in her stomach were from arousal and excitement or the warnings when things became worse. Now, however, though she still felt the exhilaration of warm, loving affection, it never felt like it did before. And that was a good thing.

Galen turned to her before they decided to go in for the night. He looked longingly into the eyes of his angel. "When I first saw you, you were like a figure I had dreamed up. But even so, I never intended to fall in love with you. I never assumed..."

Althea leaned in and placed her lips upon his cheek. "I know. I know. I never intended to fall in love again period. And maybe, since it happened when we weren't looking for it, it's what was meant to be. Maybe since our desire for it didn't manipulate and force the feelings to happen, that's how we know it is real."

They held each other more tightly then and let the stars shine upon them in the darkness. The dark of night was never the same, each night was never like the last and never like the next. But in every dark night, there's the light of some kind. Even if the moon and stars were hidden from sight, the light would always be there. No matter what may come to mask the stars, and there would be storms surely, the light is never truly gone. And even if happily ever after was a dream chased by children, sometimes it lives in a moment, if only just a moment, and it's worth the pain to reach it.

CPSIA information can be obtained
at www.ICGtesting.com
Printed in the USA
LVHW041334290422
717072LV00002B/80